VAN RICHTEN'S GUIDE TO
RAVENLOFT®

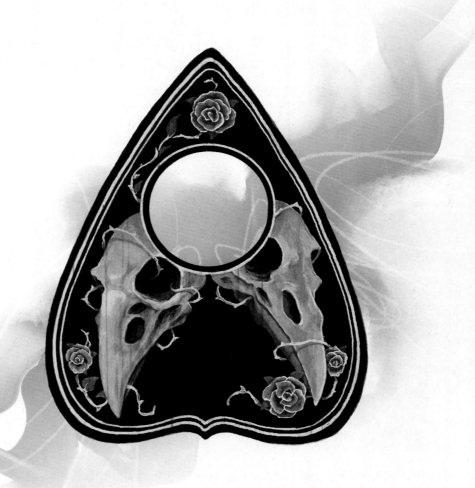

CREDITS

Project Lead: F. Wesley Schneider

Art Director: Kate Irwin

Writing: Whitney Beltrán, Bill Benham, K. Tempest Bradford, Banana Chan, Jeremy Crawford, Dan Dillon, Crystal Frasier, Ajit George, Amanda Hamon, Cassandra Khaw, Renee Knipe, Kira Magrann, Molly Ostertag, Ben Petrisor, Jessica Price, Taymoor Rehman, Jessica Ross, John Stavropoulos, Jabari Weathers, James Wyatt

Rules Development: Ben Petrisor, Jeremy Crawford, Christopher Perkins, Taymoor Rehman

Editing: Judy Bauer, Michele Carter, Scott Fitzgerald Gray

Cultural Consultancy: Adam Lee, Tim Stone, Ivan Wong

Graphic Design: Trystan Falcone, Emi Tanji, Trish Yochum

Cover Illustrators: Scott M. Fischer, Anna Podedworna

Interior Illustrators: Helder Almeida, Mark Behm, Eric Belisle, Zoltan Boros, Christopher Burdett, Dawn Carlos, Paul Scott Canavan, Kai Carpenter, Sidharth Chaturvedi, David René Christensen, CoupleOfKooks, Nikki Dawes, Olga Drebas, Wayne England, Caroline Gariba, Lake Hurwitz, Sam Keiser, Julian Kok, Katerina Ladon, Olly Lawson, Titus Lunter, Andrew Mar, Scott Murphy, Irina Nordsol, Stephen Oakley, Robin Olausson, Livia Prima, April Prime, David Sladek, Anna Steinbauer, Shawn Wood, Zuzanna Wuzyk

Cartographers: Francesca Baerald, Jared Blando, Dyson Logos, Mike Schley

Concept Illustrators: Shawn Wood, Titus Lunter, Kieran Yanner, Richard Whitters

Project Engineer: Cynda Callaway

Imaging Technicians: Kevin Yee

Prepress Specialist: Jefferson Dunlap

Special Thanks: Heather Cenis, Laurie Marquess, Stephanie Nudelman, Stas R., Morrigan Robbins, T. Alexander Stangroom, and the hundreds of playtesters who made this book more terrifying!

D&D TABLETOP TEAM

Executive Producer: Ray Winninger

Principal Designers: Jeremy Crawford, Christopher Perkins

Design Manager: Steve Scott

Design Department: Sydney Adams, Judy Bauer, Makenzie De Armas, Dan Dillon, Amanda Hamon, Adam Lee, Ari Levitch, Ben Petrisor, Taymoor Rehman, F. Wesley Schneider, James Wyatt

Art Team Manager: Richard Whitters

Art Department: Trystan Falcone, Kate Irwin, Emi Tanji, Shawn Wood, Trish Yochum

Senior Producer: Dan Tovar

Producers: Bill Benham, Robert Hawkey, Lea Heleotis

Director of Product Management: Liz Schuh

Product Managers: Natalie Egan, Chris Lindsay, Hilary Ross, Chris Tulach

MARKETING

Director of Global Brand Marketing: Brian Perry

Global Brand Manager: Shelly Mazzanoble

Senior Marketing Communications Manager: Greg Tito

Community Manager: Brandy Camel

The following D&D books provided material and inspiration:

Connors, William W. and Steve Miller. *Domains of Dread*. 1997.

Golden, Christie. *Vampire of the Mists*. 1991.

Hickman, Tracy and Laura. *Ravenloft*. 1983.

Hickman, Tracy and Laura. *Ravenloft II: The House on Gryphon Hill*. 1986.

Mangrum, John W. and Steve Miller. *Carnival*. 1999.

McComb, Colin and Scott Bennie. *Islands of Terror*. 1992.

Nesmith, Bruce and Andria Hayday. *Ravenloft: Realm of Terror*. 1990.

Perkins, Christopher. *Curse of Strahd*. 2016.

ON THE COVER

In the shadow of Castle Ravenloft, Doctor Rudolph van Richten and Ez d'Avenir confront the vampire Strahd von Zarovich, in this painting by Anna Podedworna.

620C9280000001 EN

ISBN: 9-780786-96725-4

First Printing: May 2021

9 8 7 6 5 4 3 2 1

ON THE ALT-COVER

Monster hunter Ez d'Avenir stands against the assembled nightmares of the Demiplanes of Dread, a phantasmagoria revealed by Scott M. Fischer.

Disclaimer: By the sole act of opening this book, you acknowledge your complicity in the domains-spanning conspiracy that denied me, Azalin Rex, Wizard-King of Darkon, my rightful place as both author of and cover model for what could have been so much more than this doubtful collection of lies and slanders. Fortunately, as I've recently found my immortality unburdened by the trivialities of rule, I have endless opportunity to pursue thorough vengeances for even the pettiest affronts. Please prepare for my coming. I expect to be quartered in the utmost comfort while we personalize your redefinition of the word "horror."

CONTENTS

Introduction 4

Ch. 1: Character Creation 12
Haunted Heroes 13
Lineages 15
   Creating Your Character 15
   Dhampir 16
   Hexblood 18
   Reborn 20
Dark Gifts 22
   Dark Bargains 22
   Dark Gift Descriptions 22
Subclass Options 28
   Bard: College of Spirits 28
   Warlock: The Undead 30
Backgrounds 31
   General Background Features 31
   Horror Characteristics 32
   Haunted One 34
   Investigator 35
Horror Trinkets 36

Ch. 2: Creating Domains of Dread ... 38
Creating a Darklord 39
Creating a Domain 42
Genres of Horror 45
   Body Horror 46
   Cosmic Horror 48
   Dark Fantasy 50
   Folk Horror 52
   Ghost Story 54
   Gothic Horror 56
   Other Horror Genres 57

Ch. 3: Domains of Ravenloft 60
Nature of Ravenloft 61
   The Mists 61
   Magic and Metaphysics 62
   Life in the Domains of Dread 63
Featured Domains 65
Facing Darklords 65
Characters from Domains 65
Barovia 66
   Strahd von Zarovich 67
   Adventures in Barovia 69
Bluetspur 72
   The God-Brain 73
   Adventures in Bluetspur 74
Borca 76
   Ivana Boritsi 78
   Ivan Dilisnya 80
   Adventures in Borca 81
The Carnival 84
   Isolde and Nepenthe 86
   Adventures in the Carnival 87
Darkon 88
   Inheritors of Darkon 90
   Adventures in Darkon 91
Dementlieu 94
   Saidra d'Honaire 96
   Adventures in Dementlieu 97
Falkovnia 100
   Vladeska Drakov 102
   Adventures in Falkovnia 103

Har'Akir 106
   Ankhtepot 108
   Adventures in Har'Akir 110
Hazlan 112
   Hazlik 114
   Adventures in Hazlan 115
I'Cath 118
   Tsien Chiang 120
   Adventures in I'Cath 121
Kalakeri 124
   Ramya Vasavadan 126
   Adventures in Kalakeri 128
Kartakass 132
   Harkon Lukas 134
   Adventures in Kartakass 135
Lamordia 138
   Viktra Mordenheim 140
   Adventures in Lamordia 141
Mordent 144
   Wilfred Godefroy 146
   Adventures in Mordent 147
Richemulot 150
   Jacqueline Renier 151
   Adventures in Richemulot 153
Tepest 156
   Mother Lorinda 157
   Adventures in Tepest 159
Valachan 162
   Chakuna 164
   Adventures in Valachan 164
Other Domains of Dread 168
   Cyre 1313, The Mourning Rail 168
   Forlorn 168
   Ghastria 169
   G'henna 169
   Invidia 169
   Keening 170
   Klorr 170
   Markovia 170
   The Nightmare Lands 170
   Niranjan 170
   Nova Vaasa 170
   Odaire 171
   The Rider's Bridge 171
   Risibilos 171
   Scaena 172
   Sea of Sorrows 172
   The Shadowlands 173
   Souragne 173
   Staunton Bluffs 173
   Tovag 173
   Vhage Agency 173
   Zherisia 173
Travelers in the Mists 174
   Keepers of the Feather 174
   Vistani 176
   Other Groups 178
Mist Wanderers 178
   Alanik Ray and Arthur Sedgwick ... 178
   The Caller 179
   Erasmus van Richten 180

Ez d'Avenir 180
Firan Zal'honan 181
Jander Sunstar 182
Larissa Snowmane 182
Rudolph van Richten 182
The Weathermay-Foxgrove Twins ... 183

Ch. 4: Horror Adventures 184
Preparing for Horror 185
Running Horror Games 187
After the Horror 190
Tarokka Deck and Spirit Board 191
Horror Toolkit 192
   Curses 192
   Fear and Stress 195
   Haunted Traps 196
   Survivors 198
The House of Lament 202

Ch. 5: Monsters of Ravenloft 222
Horror Monsters 223
Bestiary 226
   Bodytaker Plant 226
      Bodytaker Plant 227
      Podling 227
   Boneless 228
   Brain in a Jar 229
   Carrion Stalker 230
   Carrionette 231
   Death's Head 232
   Dullahan 233
   Gallows Speaker 234
   Gremishka 235
      Gremishka 235
      Swarm of Gremishkas 235
   Jiangshi 236
   Loup Garou 237
   Necrichor 238
   Nosferatu 239
   Priests of Osybus 240
   Relentless Killer 242
      Relentless Slasher 242
      Relentless Juggernaut 243
   Star Spawn Emissary 244
      Lesser Star Spawn Emissary ... 245
      Greater Star Spawn Emissary ... 245
   Strigoi 246
   Swarms 247
      Swarm of Maggots 247
      Swarm of Scarabs 247
   Ulmist Inquisitors 248
      Inquisitor of the Mind Fire ... 248
      Inquisitor of the Sword 249
      Inquisitor of the Tome 249
   Unspeakable Horrors 250
   Vampiric Mind Flayer 252
   Wereraven 253
   Zombies 254
      Swarm of Zombie Limbs 254
      Zombie Clot 255
      Zombie Plague Spreader 255

Appendix: Spirit Board 256

WELCOME TO
RAVENLOFT

A SCREAM SHATTERS THE STILL GLOOM. Inhuman shapes slip between crumbling tombs. The shadows reach forth. Do instincts and imagination conspire against you? Or have otherworldly evils claimed you, drawing you into the mists of Ravenloft?

In hidden corners of the Shadowfell are nightmare domains that hunger for the brave and the innocent, the ambitious and the wicked. Some call this collection of eerie realms the Land of the Mists, but monster hunters know it as Ravenloft. Terror, magic, mystery, and suspense fill these fractured domains, an infinite gallery of unfolding evils, age-old plots, cursed bloodlines, legendary monsters, and immortal villains. Evildoers from countless worlds regard Ravenloft as their prison—infamous figures such as the lich-king Azalin Rex, the unscrupulous scientist Viktra Mordenheim, and the diabolical first vampire Strahd von Zarovich. These Darklords wield incredible power within their isolated domains, yet they're held captive in eternal torment as victims of malign forces known as the Dark Powers.

Ravenloft is a fundamentally magical realm, one that takes its name from its most infamous haunted location, the dreaded Castle Ravenloft in Barovia—home of the notorious Strahd von Zarovich. In this mysterious setting, the land, the passage of time, the tides, and every other reliable truth can shift unpredictably. Rather than being bound by proximity or politics, the lands of Ravenloft—also known as the Domains of Dread—are mist-bound islands drifting through the boundless gloom of the Shadowfell. Innumerable domains lie hidden within these supernatural mists, and of these secret realms, the most terrifying are those born of your nightmares and given grim life through your adventures.

Although Ravenloft is a setting of storied evils, the domains aren't without heroes. Brave souls such as the investigator Ez d'Avenir, the monster-hunting Weathermay-Foxgrove sisters, and the scholar Rudolph van Richten explore the domains' secrets. Though few in number, such adventurers represent defiant lights that shine like beacons through the darkness, and characters from all lands and worlds may be eager—or compelled—to challenge the sinister forces lurking in the shadows.

The Mists of Ravenloft are rising. What mysteries will you discover among the Domains of Dread? What nightmares will you shape? And once you enter the Mists, will you ever escape?

EZ D'AVENIR BRAVES THE MISTS, HER PATH HAUNTED BY PAST AND FUTURE TERRORS.

USING THIS BOOK

This book explores the Domains of Dread, the mysterious expanses of the Shadowfell that serve as backdrops for excitement and terror. It guides players and Dungeon Masters through the process of creating characters, domains, and stories ripe for chilling D&D adventures.

Chapter 1 details how players can create characters primed for fright-filled adventures. It presents options for lineages and backgrounds that provide ominous pasts for any character as well as Dark Gifts and subclasses to shape their fates.

Chapter 2 explores how Dungeon Masters can create their own new Darklords and domains, custom-made foundations for fear highlighting the creator's and players' favorite types of terror.

Chapter 3 provides an overview of dozens of Ravenloft's domains, along with details on the characters and adventures found in these haunted lands.

Chapter 4 offers tools for Dungeon Masters running frightening adventures, from rules for creating curses and running out-of-body experiences to advice for building safe, suspenseful campaigns. It also includes an atmospheric adventure to draw characters into Ravenloft's fearful grip.

Chapter 5 details how to make any foe into a notorious terror, as well as a collection of monsters that roam the Domains of Dread and other D&D worlds.

HORROR IN YOUR GAME

Ominous shadows rise beyond the campfire's light. Steps echo through the halls of a supposedly empty house. Something whispers from under the stairs. Such details fill horror tales, but what place do they have in your D&D game? As a DM, you determine what place horror has in your adventures. Consider the following topics and how this book can aid you in determining the role of suspense in your game.

Foundations for Fears. Facing frightening creatures and venturing into the unknown are staples of both D&D adventures and horror stories. This book explores how to interweave suspense and mystery with familiar features of D&D, creating gloom so your heroes' light shines all the brighter.

Genres of Horror. Horror comes in broad varieties. You and your players decide what types of horror stories are right for your group. Do your prefer gothic moodiness, mind-bending mysteries, or something else entirely? Use this book to discover your group's perfect horror experience and how to bring it to life through your adventures.

Creating Atmosphere. Threatening traps and monsters alone don't create exciting D&D adventures. This book provides techniques to help you build atmosphere, a pervading mood for your game that encourages immersion and suspense.

Doctor van Richten,

I'm writing this from Rivalis, a town where I'm surprised to find your name on the villagers' lips. You're more than merely a well-remembered citizen, Doctor. The folk here talk of disappearances and hungry shadows and the evil of an abandoned estate: Richten House.

This place. The crimes and tragedies that transpired here. I know we'd both rather forget them—this whole accursed land—but the Mists drew me back. Now that I'm here, I know. The past we both hoped to bury is not done with us yet. Something terrible festers here in Darkon, sir, lurking in your own family home.

My investigations begin with the sealing of this letter. This time, I hope our families can stand together against whatever haunts us both.

Yours,
Ez d'Avenir

Thrills You Control. Like a roller-coaster, exploring frightening themes in a safe environment creates thrills without threat. Use this book to help you and your players communicate about a game's rules, plots, and other content, assuring it includes only the elements you all enjoy.

Focus on Fun. Suspenseful stories don't need to be somber or shocking. Action, mystery, and comedy can feature in your adventures to any degree. Heroes can be bold monster-hunters or bumbling mystery-solvers. Choose what elements of this book are right for your game and promise the most fun for all players.

Uncle Rudolph,

We continue our pursuit of that were-wretch, Natalia Vhorishkova. Before she fled our last confrontation, she shed a cord threaded through a wolf's tooth. Laurie used the talisman as you and Uncle George taught us, and it guided us through the Mists to Skald, a quaint, music-loving place in a land called Kartakass. The folk here are hospitable. Fawning actually. They hang on our every word. I've escaped their attentions by sequestering myself in our room at a local taverna while Laurie overindulges in attention for both of us. We've found no trace of Vhorishkova since arriving, but I feel her watching. It's like she's everywhere.

It's bad here, Uncle. Not snake-headed hogs bad. Like, full Delmunster plant-peasants bad. I've enclosed the tooth we followed here. If this message finds you free and well, your presence and perspective would be an enormous comfort.

Your devoted students,

Gennifer and Laurie Weathermay-Foxgrove

SEVEN SECRETS OF RAVENLOFT

Countless mysteries pervade the Domains of Dread, but these strange truths underpin the setting:

1. **Ravenloft Is Not a World.** The lands and characters of Ravenloft don't share a planet. Rather, the Domains of Dread consist of innumerable demiplanes hidden amid the Plane of Shadow. Mysterious Mists surround each of these island-realms. The bravest souls might creep from one domain to another, but doing so involves considerable danger, and many who enter the Mists are never seen again.

2. **The Dark Powers Control All.** Sinister entities known as the Dark Powers manipulate the Domains of Dread and all who dwell within. Immortal, unknowable, and omnipotent, the Dark Powers revel in sowing terror and subtly manipulating their captives over the course of generations.

3. **Domains Imprison Darklords.** Ravenloft's demiplanes range in size from solitary structures to vast regions. These domains serve as the prisons of Darklords, villainous beings trapped and tormented by the Dark Powers. The specifics of each domain exist to ironically twist its Darklord's desires, capturing them and their lands' residents in cycles of dread and despair.

4. **The Mists Encompass All.** Supernatural haze suffuses the Domains of Dread. These are the Mists of Ravenloft, ominous fogs that gird each domain, rising and falling as the Dark Powers desire. Tales attribute ominous powers to the Mists, from cloaking monsters to causing entire villages to vanish. The Mists are not bound to Ravenloft and slip across the planes, potentially dragging anyone into the Domains of Dread.

5. **Nowhere Is Safe.** The Mists of Ravenloft are notorious for kidnapping innocent souls and trapping them within the Domains of Dread, but they also collect characters to participate in specific terrifying adventures. Ravenloft can claim a soul for one night of terror or for an inescapable nightmare, whichever suits the needs of your adventures.

6. **Heroes Confront Horrors.** Ravenloft is not a land of heroes. Few seek out danger in the Mists or challenge Darklords. Fear and forces within characters themselves—potentially in the form of rare lineages or Dark Gifts—threaten personal dooms. Yet those who face these terrors shine as lights amid the Mists, beacons to attract other heroes but also greater threats.

7. **Only Fear Is Certain.** The Domains of Dread provide malleable settings for any kind of horror adventure. As domains are unmoored from conventional reality, anything can happen within their borders. Normal people undergo terrifying transformations, whole villages disappear unnoticed, and the Mists bar every method of escaping a threat. Any surreal development you desire is also the will of the Dark Powers, assuring that the most terrifying possibilities come to pass. As a result, even the most familiar races, magic items, and monsters in the *Player's Handbook*, *Dungeon Master's Guide*, and *Monster Manual* have places in Ravenloft, but with twists that make them creepy or mysterious.

The Land of the Mists

Although the Domains of Dread are dramatically different, certain realities underpin their terrors. The nature of domains, the influence of Darklords, the mysteries of the Mists, and the machinations of the Dark Powers present a wealth of ominous possibilities. All these elements share a shadowy uncertainty and the potential for terror to take on unpredictable forms.

The following sections are written for you, the DM, to consider and incorporate into your adventures as you see fit. If you wish to reveal the core mysteries of Ravenloft to your players and explore the Land of the Mists with shared knowledge, by all means do so. Alternatively, you can cultivate dread by leaving the fundamental truths of the world vague or defined by your group's theories. Deep shadows immerse the Domains of Dread. Whether you cast light on them or leave them an inky mystery, their potential for terror remains endless.

This section provides an overview of the dreadful forces at work in Ravenloft, elements the following chapters explore as tools for crafting horror adventures. For details on specific Domains of Dread and interactions between these realms, see chapter 3.

Nightmare Logic

By the standards of what other worlds' inhabitants consider true and sane, the Domains of Dread don't make sense. The setting's domains don't neatly flow into one another, histories don't record a collectively remembered past, fictions spawn terrible facts, and sheltered villagers remain stubbornly ignorant about the world beyond. Ravenloft is a setting designed to cultivate uncertainty, mystery, paranoia, and dread in defiance of logic or common sense.

The characters in your Ravenloft adventures might be the first to inquire after obvious inconsistencies or to notice plain impossibilities. But why has no one before them sought answers to such unignorable questions? The Dark Powers, the Mists, and the nature of domains and Darklords all claim part of the answer, but ultimately they reflect aspects of the same cause: nightmare logic.

Ravenloft is inherently a vast nightmare. Most of those who experience its terrors never suspect its surreal nature; only a few gradually realize that things don't add up. Whether they do or don't, the setting's supernatural features and malicious masterminds exist to foster terror. The details described in this section are true, but truth is malleable in Ravenloft. The exact limits of the Dark Powers' influence, the Mists' reach, and the Darklords' control over their domains are purposefully vague.

As with any nightmare, the Domains of Dread aren't shackled to the laws of reality. Domains exist

> ## This Book Gives Characters Nightmares
>
> Ravenloft is a setting designed to bring nightmares to life—for characters, not for players. While the Land of the Mists is rife with sinister plots and terrifying tales, they're meant to stay within the world of your game, not to prey upon the fears of players. Chapter 4 details ways to make sure you're crafting adventures that are spooky in ways your players will enjoy. Chapter 1 also provides guidance for players so they can work together to create horror experiences that are safe and fun for the entire group. Revisit these considerations and safety tools often, until they're just as much a part of your game as character sheets and dice.
>
> ***Content Warning.*** With this in mind, be aware that this book contains suggestions for adventures meant to be horrifying. While these plots are no more explicit than those you might find in any other Dungeons & Dragons product, the horror genre in all its myriad forms is explored—from moody gothic horror and ghost stories to visceral body horror and mind-bending cosmic horror. Chapter 2 explores how to choose the horror themes that are right for your game, but read on at your discretion.

not to simulate a believable world, but to terrify. This flexibility provides a powerful tool to upend assumptions of safety and tailor your characters' struggles. It also encourages layers of mysteries about the nature of the setting. Is each domain unique or just one in a series of recurring nightmares? How many forms of Castle Ravenloft exist, have existed, and will yet reveal themselves in the Mists? What is truth among the Domains of Dread, and how long will that remain certain? The answers are for you to decide.

In Ravenloft, tales like the treasure-haunting Bagman come to terrifying life.

THE DARK POWERS

Unfathomable, hidden forces manipulate life, death, and reality within Ravenloft. These mysterious, deathless beings are the architects of the Domains of Dread, and have secreted these pockets of terror deep within the Plane of Shadow. The Dark Powers watch and influence events within their dominion. When their gaze drifts, they reach into other planes to collect heroes and villains to add to their terrifying menagerie. To what end, no one knows.

The Dark Powers don't move in the shadows of Ravenloft; they are the shadows. They're the Mists and the darkness. They're the reason water manifests as rivers and stars appear in skies divorced from universes. They are the wardens that hold the Darklords prisoner. Ever-present and inscrutable, the Dark Powers are akin to gods in Ravenloft, but they are unknown to mortals and desire no worship.

Despite the control the Dark Powers exert, these beings remain distant from the domains they manipulate. Although some of their names whisper through sinister lore—names like Osybus, Shami-Amourae, and Tenebrous—domain inhabitants know almost nothing of the Dark Powers. While some Darklords realize they're imprisoned by antagonistic entities, discourse regarding the Dark Powers remains the province of soothsayers, obsessed scholars, and otherworldly beings. Anyone who spreads tales of sinister forces manipulating reality is ignored or worse. For residents of Ravenloft, ignorance provides a well-defended shelter against unfathomable truths.

THE SECRET OF THE DARK POWERS

The true nature of the Dark Powers is for you to decide. How you perceive these forces can influence your view of their actions and agendas, who they abduct into Ravenloft and why. Through your adventures, you might reveal these mysteries and use them to hint at ways to escape the Domains of Dread. Consider the following possibilities when developing your perspective on the Dark Powers:

Amoral Guardians. The Dark Powers are a group of powerful beings who believe they're beyond morality. They identify dangerous individuals and imprison them within the Domains of Dread, where they ostensibly do less harm than they would if they were free. Those trapped along with the Darklords are acceptable sacrifices.

Evil Architects. The Dark Powers are embodiments of evil, mysterious entities of the Plane of Shadow, or a conspiracy of wicked gods. They treat the denizens of the Domains of Dread as their playthings, sowing fears and fomenting despair. This pleases or sustains them, or perhaps they're searching for individuals worthy of joining their ranks.

Rudolph,

I write you in the throes of a most perplexing case. Here in Port-a-Lucine, we pride ourselves on our rationality. Good detectives are best served by clear-headed reason and keen observation (and a clean flintlock, my dear Arthur would add). You know I'm not prone to superstition or mystical flights of fancy. Yet that's exactly what my recent experiences have led me to.

When these Keepers of the Feather first hired me, I took them for a social club of eccentric dilettantes. When they claimed someone was trying to murder them, I tried not to dismiss it as imaginative paranoia. Now, though, I know something wants these spiritualists dead—and that this murderer might be dead themselves. Have you heard of the Mill Road hags, doctor?

Arthur and I invite you to fair Dementlieu, dear Rudolph. And please, when you come, bring any notes you didn't publish in Van Richten's Guide to Witches.

Yours in reason,
Alanik Ray & Dr. Arthur Sedgwick

Undying Remnants. The Dark Powers are all that remain of a multitude of vanquished evil deities and demigods. Traces of their power linger in amber sarcophagi scattered throughout the Domains of Dread. These diminished vestiges manipulate their realm to create negative forces that sustain their essence and build toward renewed apotheosis.

THE MISTS

Known throughout Ravenloft, the Mists are manifestations of the Dark Powers' will. They divide, surround, and isolate every domain, creating fog-shrouded borders that imprison Darklords within their territories. The Mists slip through the

Domains of Dread, rising to claim unwitting travelers or releasing terrors upon unsuspecting villagers. Most infamously, the Mists slither into other worlds to claim innocents, villains, or whole lands, dragging them back to become the newest prisoners of Ravenloft.

Inhabitants of the Domains of Dread know of the Mists and ascribe sinister stories to them, but they accept the Mists as a natural part of their homeland. Many who travel between domains even refer to their world as the Land of the Mists. Any supernatural happening, inexplicable disappearance, or malicious force can be blamed on the Mists, and those who interact with the Mists or who come from beyond them are met with suspicion. The Mists confound travel between domains, whether one wishes to leave a place to reach another land or to escape the realm they're in.

Beyond these truths, the Mists are your tool to establish the boundaries of your horror stories. See the "Nature of Ravenloft" section in chapter 3 for details on employing the Mists to focus your horror adventures, leading characters to engage with certain elements while cloaking others in mystery.

DOMAINS

Sinister demiplanes known as domains constitute the realms of Ravenloft. These domains vary widely, but they share a number of common features:

Domains Are Finite. The domains vary in size from countries or geographic regions to a single city, structure, mobile conveyance, or specific location.

Domains Are Isolated. Each domain is surrounded by the Mists, its boundaries fading away into haze. Domains share neither borders nor common geography, and you can't peer from one domain into another. The environments, cultures, and residents of one domain don't influence those of other domains.

Domains Hold Darklords. Domains exist to contain and torment a villain. Though Darklords exert control over their domains, they are each tormented by a personal terror playing out in their realm.

Domains Are Cages. Those who run afoul of a Darklord might find that the Mists prevent them from leaving the villain's domain. Like a haunted house that conveniently seals its doors or summons a deadly storm, so do domains create inescapable spaces where horror adventures unfold.

Domains Are Themed. Each domain reflects its Darklord and facilitates horror tales related to that villain. Just as creepy manors suit ghostly inhabitants, so does each domain inspire and encourage a distinct type of terror.

In Ravenloft, the Dark Powers control reality, the Mists foil escape attempts, and terrifying Darklords can appear at any moment. What hope do heroes have against such overwhelming evils?

The nature of Ravenloft provides powerful tools to craft tales of terror. Shifting reality, inescapable danger, and foes with shocking powers are useful for creating horror adventures (a topic further discussed in chapter 4). As a balancing factor, use these tools judiciously and occasionally, in the characters' favor. The Dark Powers delight in tormenting villains as much as they do innocents, the Mists equally confound both predators and prey, and Darklords frequently exhibit hubris or other exploitable flaws. Use Ravenloft's nature to sow dread but also to inspire hope. Relentless despair gradually beats characters down and takes the fun out of adventures. Punctuate your horror tales with moments of relief, comedy, and fortuitous coincidences. These moments of hope help characters push through the dark to the thrill of dawn.

Details on how to create your own domains appear in chapter 2, while chapter 3 describes some of the most notorious Domains of Dread.

DARKLORDS

Central to each domain is a Darklord, the seed from which a thorny thicket blooms. The villain might be a nation's leader, a prominent citizen, a notorious monster, a mysterious recluse, or a seemingly innocuous character. Regardless of the Darklord's current role, their wickedness led to the creation of their domain and their imprisonment in Ravenloft.

Though these individuals vary widely and exceptions occur, Darklords share a number of qualities:

Darklords Are Evil. Each Darklord is the ultimate villain of a domain and the root of the suffering and terror that unfold there.

RUDOLPH VAN RICHTEN PREPARES FOR HIS NEXT EXPEDITION,
WATCHED OVER BY THE SPIRIT OF HIS SON, ERASMUS.

Darklords Are Prisoners. Darklords cannot leave their domains. If a Darklord enters the Mists or uses another method to attempt an escape, the Dark Powers return them to their domain. Even death rarely allows a Darklord to escape their prison for long.

Darklords Are Tormented. Every domain torments its Darklord in a poignant way tied ironically to their past crimes, failures, or unattainable ambitions.

Darklords Influence Domains. Although Darklords hate their domains, they exert considerable control over them. This might be the influence of a governmental leader, the magic of a supernatural overlord, or a more fundamental connection. Most possess the ability to prevent others from leaving their domains (further explored in "The Nature of Ravenloft" in chapter 3).

Darklords Vary in Threat. Darklords range from monstrous tyrants to depraved individuals who otherwise appear as ordinary people. A Darklord's position and powers stem from their deeds, not their game statistics. While some Darklords are deadly or possess foul gifts from the Dark Powers, many pose little threat in battle. Their menace is the result of capabilities beyond physical prowess.

Darklords Are Active. Darklords might brood over their failures, but nevertheless they relentlessly strive to achieve their ambitions. Their desperate struggles fuel their conflicts with characters. Liberally use Darklords in your adventures rather than saving them for distant climactic plots.

Darklords Don't Realize They're Darklords. With a few exceptions, Darklords don't realize they occupy a special place in the world. Their agendas, obsessions, and egotism distract them from focusing on the strangeness of the world and petty concerns such as eerie fog.

Darklords Are Immortal. Darklords are casually immortal, many having no concept of how long they've lived, how many times they've died, or why they returned to life. Should a Darklord fall, the temporary defeat lasts until they're restored by the Dark Powers. In their absence, those who sought to escape or supplant them seize their chance.

ZUZANNA WUZYK

ADVENTURERS

The Domains of Dread don't typically breed heroes. For the inhabitants of most domains, simply surviving the night is an act of courage. Those willing to confront the terrors of the Mists are rare, but when they do, they have one of the following origins:

Mist Wanderers. The Mists reached into these characters' worlds and dragged them into the Domains of Dread. Whether these adventurers are trapped in Ravenloft for a night or an eternity, their spirits mark them as outsiders but also as rare beacons in the endless darkness.

Roused Locals. Some shock jarred these unusual individuals from the apathy pervasive to the Land of the Mists. Witnesses to evil, these characters will never know the solace of ignorance again. Chapter 3 explores details on creating characters unique to various domains.

Adventurers find few peers in the Land of the Mists. While there are exceptions—many of whom are illustrated throughout this book and detailed in chapter 3—such individuals are few and their lives are often short. Guilds of adventurers and shops catering to their needs generally don't exist. As a result, the challenge of confronting evil rests squarely with a few rare souls. Read on to chapter 1 for details on creating your own haunted heroes.

My Friends,

I send this ahead of me with capable souls I'm paying enough to trust. I received your last letter pre-opened. Whatever eyes are fixed on you might be keener than you fear.

Tomorrow I depart on an expedition, one that can't be delayed—perhaps the most important of my life. Thus, I won't be joining you in as timely a manner as I'd like. In my stead, I've sent enough coin to ensure these messengers' assistance and silence for even the most daunting work.

I'm also sending an apology, one this might be my last chance to make. There are a thousand times I wish I'd been better, when I should have spoken not from the past but from my heart. I'm sorry I wasn't more patient and that I never told you how often your bravery and wit dazzled me—and still do. Ez, Laurie, Gennifer, Alanik, Arthur, you're all I have left of family. I haven't said it enough, but I love you all like my own. For what it's worth, I consider you all van Richtens now. My name is yours to use as you please—I pray it brings you more joy than it's brought me. But whatever name you use, I know you'll carry it as a candle to ward off the shadows.

Always,

Doctor Rudolph van Richten

Monster hunters Gennifer and Laurie Weathermay-Foxgrove corner the werewolf Natalia Vhorishkova.

CHAPTER 1
CHARACTER CREATION

THE MISTS OF RAVENLOFT DRIFT ACROSS WORLDS, sowing fear and abducting unsuspecting souls. These forces don't claim individuals at random, though. The fear of innocents, the turmoil of the corruptible, the resolve of the truly heroic—the Dark Powers savor these traits. Whether for a night or an eternity, Ravenloft seeks heroes of all sorts and pits them against their greatest nightmares.

This chapter explores how to create a character prepared to face the horrors of Ravenloft, while also forging ties to the haunted pedigrees and grim fates common to the Domains of Dread. This chapter offers you, the player, the following tools and choices:

Haunted Heroes. Explore your role in creating a tale of terror and how you might design a character that contributes to frightful adventures.

Lineages. Consider an origin that ties you to a grim progenitor or inexplicable experience. Lineages can serve as your character's race or overshadow your previous race.

Dark Gifts. Determine whether the Dark Powers of Ravenloft have exerted their influence upon you, granting you a double-edged supernatural gift.

Subclass Options. Consider choosing the College of Spirits bard or the Undead patron warlock subclasses to give voice to ageless forces.

Backgrounds. Choose a fateful cast to your origins with optional features for any background. The haunted one and investigator backgrounds also explore how mystery might drive your character.

Horror Trinkets. Learn what creepy curio inspires or haunts your adventures.

HAUNTED HEROES

Ravenloft encourages you and your group to safely explore the thrill of all manner of ghost stories, mysteries, and other tales of terror. While chapter 4 guides DMs in how to craft atmospheric adventures, the spookiest scenarios will fall flat if you and the other players aren't prepared to engage with some degree of suspense. By the same token, the DM can't craft an enjoyably spooky experience if they're not aware of your interests in and thresholds for participating in fear-focused adventures. This section highlights elements common to frightening D&D games, features that you should be mindful of as a player and that will help you create a character prepared to participate in suspenseful adventures.

But it all begins with one question: Are you sure?

INVITATION TO NIGHTMARE

You've been invited to play a scary game. What does a horror adventure or campaign mean? Who's it supposed to be scary for, you the player or your character? Is it scary like a mystery cartoon or a slasher movie? What content makes it scary? What do you not want to see in a horror story?

These are all legitimate questions and ones you should have answers to before participating in a fear-focused D&D adventure. Horror, as a genre, covers broad swaths of material. What you shrug off other players might find personally unsettling—everyone's experiences and tolerances are distinct and real, even if they differ from your own. Before creating a character, ask your DM and the rest of the group the aforementioned questions, along with any others that come to mind. Chapter 4 encourages DMs to facilitate pregame discussions to make sure the entire group agrees on content, boundaries, and tools to keep the terror fun. Think of this as establishing a film-like rating and content warning for the story you'll all be creating. If you're uncertain about aspects of the game, ask about them—before the game, during play, or whenever a concern arises. Everyone's comfort and enjoyment of spooky adventures are what matter most!

PREPARE TO BE SCARED

When planning to play a scary adventure, create a character prepared to be scared. Consider how your character reacts to being frightened and how that affects the creepy atmosphere of the adventure. Don't consider fear a tactical disadvantage or something to be avoided. As part of playing a frightening game, you're a participant in building and reinforcing a sense of dread for everyone at the table. If your character laughs in the face of every danger, they undermine the adventure's threats and its broader atmosphere.

When creating and playing your character, consider courage not as the absence of fear but as the process of overcoming it. How might your character react in surprise before they rally to overcome the terror they face? Do they scream, flee, or freeze? Or might they throw themself into battle, perhaps recklessly or for too long? Record a default reaction on your character sheet so you can respond consistently when shocking events occur.

Not everyone exploring the Domains of Dread comes from those grim lands. Work with the DM to determine your character's origins. Has your character lived their entire life among the Mists? Or do they hail from another D&D setting, a place of your own design, or a more mysterious homeland?

 If you decide your character calls some corner of Ravenloft home, ask your DM which domains they could originate from. The DM can provide details from chapter 3 to help inform your decision. Although humans predominate many of the Domains of Dread, adventurers in Ravenloft can belong to any race in the *Player's Handbook* or other sources. The domains of Darkon, Dementlieu, and Hazlik, for example, all feature particularly varied populations.

 If you decide your character is from some other world, collaborate with the DM to determine how you came to the Land of the Mists. As they're familiar with true terrors, inhabitants of the Domains of Dread rarely mistake characters from even the most outlandish worlds for actual monsters.

Beyond this, discuss with your group how much fear ties into the game's rules. Would you prefer to keep frightful reactions narrative, or would you like to use game rules that present additional challenges and benefits? Ask your DM about the possibility of using the rules for inspiration to motivate fearful character reactions, as detailed in the "Fear and Stress" section of chapter 4. Using this system, a character who possesses particular fears and uses them to guide their responses to horrific scenes might earn inspiration for reinforcing the adventure's frightful atmosphere. The DM might not employ these rules every time something frightening occurs, but your group might use them as a way to highlight individual fears and build an adventure's overarching sense of dread.

KNOW YOUR FEARS

Knowing what frightens your character provides insight into their past and can motivate their behavior. A character's fear of cats might stem from a terrible sight they witnessed at their grandmother's home, while a fear of earthquakes might hearken back to the experience of being trapped after a tremor. Consider two or three things that unsettle your character, what they tell you about their past, and if those fears shape who they are now.

EVIL INSIDE

This book assumes you're playing a character who pits themself against fearful foes. That said, if you're eager to play a character with a shadowy past or sinister origins, the lineages and Dark Gifts presented

DESPITE A VAMPIRE'S BITE, AN ORC HERO FACES HIS FEARS.

later in this chapter provide such opportunities. How a character engages with the evil inside themself can make for exciting conflicts. Be sure that your choices allow your character to remain a reliable part of your adventuring group, though, and not a near-villain the other heroes only tolerate.

HABITS OF HORROR HEROES

Playing horror adventures is similar to telling ghost stories around a fire. You and the game's other players are allies in creating a fun, safe, moody atmosphere for your game. Contribute to this by keeping the following elements in mind:

Focus on the Game. Atmosphere requires attention. You're not embracing or contributing to the adventure's moody atmosphere when you're focused on something else.

Limit Comedy. Be aware that comedy breaks tension. Nothing dispels an ominous atmosphere like jokes, be they in character or otherwise.

Player Fears Versus Character Fears. Understand the difference between scaring characters and scaring players. If you know a player has a fear of spiders, never employ that knowledge when contributing to a creepy scene.

Consent Is a Priority. If a plot leads you to consider a path involving another player's character, always ask that player's permission before acting. Their enjoyment is more important than shock value.

Know What's Too Far. If a game gets too intense or goes a direction you don't want to explore, make sure you and the other players have a method for raising concerns mid-game and support one another in doing so. Techniques for facilitating this are further explored in chapter 4.

Add to Your Own Terror. Feel free to make horrific circumstance worse for your character. If your character has a fear of goats and the DM describes some eldritch horror, don't hesitate to ask if the creature has hooves or hourglass eyes.

Enjoy the Struggle. Not everyone can expect to escape a horror story unscathed. While your character should do everything they can to survive and triumph over challenges, any scars they gain along the way are part of what makes the horror meaningful and memorable.

LINEAGES

In the Land of the Mists, power and dread lie in the simple question "What happened to me?" The following lineages are races that characters might gain through remarkable events. These overshadow their original race, if any, becoming their new race. A character might choose a lineage during character creation, their transformation having occurred before play begins. Or, events might unfold during adventures that lead your character to replacing their race with this new lineage. Work with your DM to establish if you're amenable to such a development and how such stories unfold.

CREATING YOUR CHARACTER

At 1st level, you choose whether your character is a member of the human race or of one of the game's fantastical races. Alternatively, you can choose one of the following lineages. If you choose a lineage, you might have once been a member of another race, but you aren't any longer. You now possess only your lineage's racial traits.

When you create a character using a lineage option here, follow these additional rules during character creation.

ABILITY SCORE INCREASES

When determining your ability scores, you increase one of those scores by 2 and increase a different score by 1, or you increase three different scores by 1. You follow this rule regardless of the method you use to determine the scores, such as rolling or point buy.

> ## WHAT HAPPENED TO ME?
> The lineages provided in this section represent a physical and magical transformation that alters you in fundamental ways. You can still appear as you once were, but you've changed in significant ways that might overwrite your once physical or magical capabilities. A dragonborn who becomes a dhampir, for instance, loses their connection to their draconic ancestry as the deathless power of vampirism surges through them. Once able to exhale destructive energy, the dragonborn now feels a powerful hunger inside, and their bite is now able to drain life. Some racial traits might remain after you gain a lineage, a possibility captured in the Ancestral Legacy trait. Keep this in mind when you explore the details of how you change after gaining a lineage subsequent to character creation.

Your class's "Quick Build" section offers suggestions on which scores to increase. You're free to follow those suggestions or to ignore them. Whichever scores you decide to increase, none of the scores can be raised above 20.

If you are replacing your race with a lineage, replace any Ability Score Increase you previously had with these.

LANGUAGES

Your character can speak, read, and write Common and one other language that you and your DM agree is appropriate for the character. The *Player's Handbook* offers a list of widespread languages to choose from. The DM is free to add or remove languages from that list for a particular campaign.

If you are replacing your race with a lineage, you retain any languages you had and gain no new languages.

CREATURE TYPE

Every creature in D&D, including every player character, has a special tag in the rules that identifies the type of creature they are. Most player characters are of the Humanoid type. A race option presented here tells you what your character's creature type is.

Here's a list of the game's creature types in alphabetical order: Aberration, Beast, Celestial, Construct, Dragon, Elemental, Fey, Fiend, Giant, Humanoid, Monstrosity, Ooze, Plant, Undead. These types don't have rules themselves, but some rules in the game affect creatures of certain types in different ways. For example, the text of the *cure wounds* spell specifies that the spell doesn't work on a creature of the Construct type.

DHAMPIR

Poised between the worlds of the living and the dead, dhampirs retain their grip on life yet are endlessly tested by vicious hungers. Their ties to the undead grant dhampirs a taste of a vampire's deathless prowess in the form of increased speed, darkvision, and a life-draining bite.

With unique insights into the nature of the undead, many dhampirs become adventurers and monster hunters. Their reasons are often deeply personal. Some seek danger, imagining monsters as personifications of their own hungers. Others pursue revenge against whatever turned them into a dhampir. And still others embrace the solitude of the hunt, striving to distance themselves from those who'd tempt their hunger.

DHAMPIR HUNGERS

Every dhampir knows a thirst slaked only by the living. Those who overindulge their thirst risk losing control and forever viewing others as prey. Those who resist might find exceptional ways of controlling their urges or suppress them through constant, molar-grinding restraint. In any case, temptation haunts dhampirs, and circumstances conspire to give them endless reasons to indulge.

While many dhampirs thirst for blood, your character might otherwise gain sustenance from the living. Roll on or choose an option from the Dhampir Hungers table to determine what tempts your character to feed.

DHAMPIR HUNGERS

d6	Hunger
1	Blood
2	Flesh or raw meat
3	Cerebral spinal fluid
4	Psychic energy
5	Dreams
6	Life energy

DHAMPIR ORIGINS

Dhampirs often arise from encounters with vampires, but all manner of macabre bargains, necromantic influences, and encounters with mysterious immortals might have transformed your character. The Dhampir Origins table provides suggestions for how your character gained their lineage.

DHAMPIR ORIGINS

d8	Origin
1	You are the reincarnation of an ancestor who was a vampiric tyrant.
2	Your pact with a predatory deity, fiend, fey, or spirit causes you to share their hunger.

DHAMPIR ROGUE

d8	Origin
3	You survived being attacked by a vampire but were forever changed.
4	A parasite lives inside you. You indulge its hunger.
5	Tragedy interrupted your transformation into an immortal.
6	You are a diminished form of an otherworldly being. Slaking your hunger hastens your renewal.
7	One of your parents was a vampire.
8	A radical experiment changed your body, making you reliant on others for vital fluids.

DHAMPIRS IN THE DOMAINS OF DREAD

When creating a dhampir, ask your DM if it makes sense for your character to have ties to one of the following Domains of Dread (detailed in chapter 3):

Barovia. In the shadow of Castle Ravenloft, tales flourish of those who love or descend from vampires. You might have such a connection, but dread what would happen if others in your insular community found out.

Darkon. The Kargat, this shattered domain's secret police, supposedly know the secret of immortality. Perhaps you joined and advanced through their lesser ranks, known as the Kargatane, and were rewarded by being transformed into a dhampir.

KATERINA LADON

I'Cath. At night, the starving city of I'Cath is over-run by vampiric jiangshi (described in chapter 5). You were left with a cold hunger after an encounter with one of these unquiet ancestors.

Dhampir Traits

You have the following racial traits.

Creature Type. You are a Humanoid.

Size. You are Medium or Small. You choose the size when you gain this lineage.

Speed. Your walking speed is 35 feet.

Ancestral Legacy. If you replace a race with this lineage, you can keep the following elements of that race: any skill proficiencies you gained from it and any climbing, flying, or swimming speed you gained from it.

If you don't keep any of those elements or you choose this lineage at character creation, you gain proficiency in two skills of your choice.

Darkvision. You can see in dim light within 60 feet of you as if it were bright light and in darkness as if it were dim light. You discern colors in that darkness as shades of gray.

Deathless Nature. You don't need to breathe.

Spider Climb. You have a climbing speed equal to your walking speed. In addition, at 3rd level, you can move up, down, and across vertical surfaces and upside down along ceilings, while leaving your hands free.

Vampiric Bite. Your fanged bite is a natural weapon, which counts as a simple melee weapon with which you are proficient. You add your Constitution modifier, instead of your Strength modifier, to the attack and damage rolls when you attack with this bite. It deals 1d4 piercing damage on a hit. While you are missing half or more of your hit points, you have advantage on attack rolls you make with this bite.

When you attack with this bite and hit a creature that isn't a Construct or an Undead, you can empower yourself in one of the following ways of your choice:

- You regain hit points equal to the piercing damage dealt by the bite.
- You gain a bonus to the next ability check or attack roll you make; the bonus equals the piercing damage dealt by the bite

You can empower yourself with this bite a number of times equal to your proficiency bonus, and you regain all expended uses when you finish a long rest.

HEXBLOOD

Where wishing fails, ancient magic can offer a heart's desire—at least, for a time. Hexbloods are individuals infused with eldritch magic, fey energy, or mysterious witchcraft. Some who enter into bargains with hags gain their deepest wishes but eventually find themselves transformed. These changes evidence a hag's influence: ears that split in forked points, skin in lurid shades, long hair that regrows if cut, and an irremovable living crown. Along with these marks, hexbloods manifest hag-like traits, such as darkvision and a variety of magical methods to beguile the senses and avoid the same.

While many hexbloods gain their lineage after making a deal with a hag, others reveal their nature as they age—particularly if a hag influenced them early in life or even before their birth. Many hexbloods turn to lives of adventure, seeking to discover the mysteries of their magic, to forge a connection with their fey natures, or to avoid a hag that obsesses over them.

A HEXBLOOD CREATED
BY A NIGHT HAG

HEIR OF HAGS

One way hags create more of their kind is through the creation of hexbloods. Every hexblood exhibits features suggestive of the hag whose magic inspires their powers. This includes an unusual crown, often called an eldercross or a witch's turn. This living, garland-like part of a hexblood's body extends from their temples and wraps behind the head, serving as a visible mark of the bargain between hag and hexblood, a debt owed, or a change to come.

HEXBLOOD ORIGINS

A bargain with a hag or other eerie forces transformed your character into a magical being. Roll on or choose an option from the Hexblood Origins table to determine how your character gained their lineage.

HEXBLOOD ORIGINS

d6	Origin
1	Seeking a child, your parent made a bargain with a hag. You are the result of that arrangement.
2	Fey kidnappers swapped you and your parents' child.
3	A coven of hags lost one of its members. You were created to replace the lost hag.
4	You were cursed as a child. A deal with the spirits of the forest transformed you into a hexblood, now free of the curse.
5	You began life as a fey creature, but an accident changed you and forced you from your home.
6	A slighted druid transformed you and bound you to live only so long as a sacred tree bears fruit.

HEXBLOODS IN THE DOMAINS OF DREAD

When creating a hexblood, consult with your DM to see if it's appropriate to tie your origins to one of the following Domains of Dread (detailed in chapter 3):

Hazlan. The bizarre magic of this crumbling domain exposes the populace to supernatural forces, occasionally giving rise to hexbloods.

Kartakass. Whimsical witches make their homes in the forests of Kartakass. They eagerly grant the wishes of locals seeking grand fortunes for their children.

Tepest. Many of the children in the town of Viktal are hexbloods who exhibit their supernatural natures from a young age. Each youngster is considered a gift from the town's patron deity, who is known as Mother.

HEXBLOOD TRAITS

You have the following racial traits.

Creature Type. You are a Fey.

Size. You are Medium or Small. You choose the size when you gain this lineage.

HEXBLOODS INFUSED WITH THE MAGIC OF SEA, GREEN, AND
ANNIS HAGS SHARE A MOMENT AROUND THE CAULDRON.

Speed. Your walking speed is 30 feet.

Ancestral Legacy. If you replace a race with this lineage, you can keep the following elements of that race: any skill proficiencies you gained from it and any climbing, flying, or swimming speed you gained from it.

If you don't keep any of those elements or you choose this lineage at character creation, you gain proficiency in two skills of your choice.

Darkvision. You can see in dim light within 60 feet of you as if it were bright light and in darkness as if it were dim light. You discern colors in that darkness as shades of gray.

Eerie Token. As a bonus action, you can harmlessly remove a lock of your hair, one of your nails, or one of your teeth. This token is imbued with magic until you finish a long rest. While the token is imbued in this way, you can take these actions:

Telepathic Message. As an action, you can send a telepathic message to the creature holding or carrying the token, as long as you are within 10 miles of it. The message can contain up to twenty-five words.

Remote Viewing. If you are within 10 miles of the token, you can enter a trance as an action. The trance lasts for 1 minute, but it ends early if you dismiss it (no action required) or are incapacitated. During this trance, you can see and hear from the token as if you were located where it is. While you are using your senses at the token's location, you are blinded and deafened in regard to your own surroundings. When the trance ends, the token is harmlessly destroyed.

Once you create a token using this feature, you can't do so again until you finish a long rest, at which point your missing part regrows.

Hex Magic. You can cast the *disguise self* and *hex* spells with this trait. Once you cast either of these spells with this trait, you can't cast that spell with it again until you finish a long rest. You can also cast these spells using any spell slots you have.

Intelligence, Wisdom, or Charisma is your spellcasting ability for these spells (choose the ability when you gain this lineage).

> ### BECOMING A HAG
> Hags can undertake a ritual to irreversibly transform a hexblood they created into a new hag, either one of their own kind or that embodies the hexblood's nature. This requires that both the hag and hexblood be in the same place and consent to the lengthy ritual—circumstances most hexbloods shun but might come to accept over the course of centuries. Once a hexblood undergoes this irreversible ritual, they emerge as a hag NPC no longer under the control of the hexblood's player, unless the DM rules otherwise.

KAI CARPENTER

Reborn

Death isn't always the end. The reborn exemplify this, being individuals who have died yet, somehow, still live. Some reborn exhibit the scars of fatal ends, their ashen flesh or bloodless veins making it clear that they've been touched by death. Other reborn are marvels of magic or science, being stitched together from disparate beings or bearing mysterious minds in manufactured bodies. Whatever their origins, reborn know a new life and seek experiences and answers all their own.

Faded Memories

Reborn suffer from some manner of discontinuity, an interruption of their lives or physical state that their minds are ill equipped to deal with. Their memories of events before this interruption are often vague or absent. Occasionally, the most unexpected experiences might cause sensations or visions of the past to come rushing back.

Rather than sleeping, reborn regularly sit and dwell on the past, hoping for some revelation of what came before. Most of the time, these are dark, silent stretches. Occasionally, though, in a moment of peace, stress, or excitement, a reborn gains a glimpse of what came before. When you desire to have such a dreamlike vision, roll on the Lost Memories table to inspire its details.

Lost Memories

d6	Memory
1	You recall a physically painful moment. What mark or scar on your body does it relate to?
2	A memory brings tears to your eyes. Is it a bitter or cheerful memory? Does recalling it make you feel the same way?
3	You recall a childhood memory. What about that event or who you were still influences you?
4	A memory brings with it the voice of someone once close to you. How do they advise you?
5	You recall enjoying something that you can't stand doing now. What is it? Why don't you like it now?
6	A memory carries a vivid smell or sensation. What are you going to do to recreate that experience?

Reborn Origins

Reborn might originate from circumstances similar to those of various undead or constructs. The Reborn Origins table provides suggestions for how your character became reborn.

Reborn Origins

d8	Origins
1	You were magically resurrected, but something went wrong.
2	Stitches bind your body's mismatched pieces, and your memories come from multiple different lives.
3	After clawing free from your grave, you realized you have no memories except for a single name.
4	You were a necromancer's undead servant for years. One day, your consciousness returned.
5	You awoke in an abandoned laboratory alongside complex designs for clockwork organs.
6	You were released after being petrified for generations. Your memories have faded, though, and your body isn't what it once was.
7	Your body hosts a possessing spirit that shares its memories and replaces your missing appendages with phantasmal limbs.
8	In public, you pass as an unremarkable individual, but you can feel the itchy straw stuffing inside you.

A reborn with a phantom limb takes aim.

NIKKI DAWES

WARY AND CONFUSED, A REBORN EMERGES AFTER THE INFAMOUS APPARATUS OF MORDENT MALFUNCTIONS.

REBORN IN THE DOMAINS OF DREAD

When creating a reborn, consult with your DM to see if it's appropriate to tie your origins to one of the following Domains of Dread (detailed in chapter 3):

Har'Akir. You died and endured the burial rites of this desert realm, yet somehow a soul—yours or another's—has taken refuge in your perfectly preserved remains.

Lamordia. You awoke amid the bizarre experiments of an amoral scientist. They consider you their finest creation or have a task for you to fulfill.

Mordent. You emerged from the mysterious device known as the Apparatus, your body a lifeless shell and your past a mystery.

REBORN TRAITS

You have the following racial traits.

Creature Type. You are a Humanoid.

Size. You are Medium or Small. You choose the size when you gain this lineage.

Speed. Your walking speed is 30 feet.

Ancestral Legacy. If you replace a race with this lineage, you can keep the following elements of that race: any skill proficiencies you gained from it and any climbing, flying, or swimming speed you gained from it.

If you don't keep any of those elements or you choose this lineage at character creation, you gain proficiency in two skills of your choice.

Deathless Nature. You have escaped death, a fact represented by the following benefits:

- You have advantage on saving throws against disease and being poisoned, and you have resistance to poison damage.
- You have advantage on death saving throws.
- You don't need to eat, drink, or breathe.
- You don't need to sleep, and magic can't put you to sleep. You can finish a long rest in 4 hours if you spend those hours in an inactive, motionless state, during which you retain consciousness.

Knowledge from a Past Life. You temporarily remember glimpses of the past, perhaps faded memories from ages ago or a previous life. When you make an ability check that uses a skill, you can roll a d6 immediately after seeing the number on the d20 and add the number on the d6 to the check. You can use this feature a number of times equal to your proficiency bonus, and you regain all expended uses when you finish a long rest.

DARK GIFTS

The Dark Powers influence many who struggle within their clutches, tempting both the innocent and ambitious with whispered promises. These sinister bargains are rarely spoken, coming in dreams or mysterious visions, but their terms are always clear and their prices terrible.

A character can select a Dark Gift from the "Dark Gifts Descriptions" section. This supernatural gift expresses both a mysterious power and insidious influence. Work with your DM to determine how your character gained this Dark Gift. Is it the manifestation of a family curse? Is it a reward for a sacrifice you made at a forgotten shrine? Did you bargain with a voice whispering from a mirror, the sea, or the Mists? Does the Dark Gift compound with your other character choices to reinforce your unique origin? Each Dark Gift can be expressed in various ways, with the following options exploring various manifestations to spark your imagination.

Dark Gifts are intended for starting characters, but characters who don't choose one might be presented with opportunities to gain a Dark Gift as their stories—and desperate circumstances—unfold.

DARK BARGAINS

Characters who don't have a Dark Gift might gain one in the course of their adventures. At the DM's discretion, sinister forces might contact a character and offer them a Dark Gift in return for some service or future favor. If a character already has a Dark Gift, accepting such a bargain causes them to lose their current Dark Gift and gain a new one. A Dark Gift gained as a result of such a bargain reflects the agenda of the being or beings offering the bargain, be it the Dark Powers, a Darklord, or a more mysterious force. The particulars of the Dark Gift and how it will affect a character must be clear to a player before they choose whether or not to accept.

The offer of a Dark Gift might manifest in a dream, in a moment of frozen time, or when the character is alone. Typically, only one character is aware of a bargain, its terms, and whether or not it was accepted.

The DM might have a mysterious force intervene and offer a Dark Gift whenever a desperate or thematic instance presents itself, such as in any of the following cases:

- A Darklord will negotiate with a party only if a character seals the deal by accepting their Dark Gift.
- Time stops while a character is on the brink of death. A mysterious voice offers to save the character's life, but only if they accept its Dark Gift.

- An experiment or magical accident goes wrong. The DM allows a character to accept a Dark Gift or some other peril as a result.
- A character breaks a vow or suffers a curse (see chapter 4), gaining a Dark Gift as a result.
- A character touches a mysterious amber sarcophagus, and a force within entreats them to accept its influence in the form of a Dark Gift.

DARK GIFT DESCRIPTIONS

This section presents a selection of Dark Gifts in alphabetical order.

ECHOING SOUL

Your soul isn't your own or, at least, it wasn't always yours. Whether you've lived past lives, your soul was swapped into a different body, or you have a link connecting you to another being, you experience echoes from another life. These echoes grant you knowledge, talents, or even languages you can't always explain, but they also intrude on your perceptions and beliefs unexpectedly.

Roll on or choose an option from the Soul Echoes table to determine the nature of this Dark Gift. Additionally, you gain the traits that follow.

SOUL ECHOES

d6	Echo
1	My soul is linked with that of a person elsewhere, perhaps another domain, world, or plane.
2	I have lived many times before, my soul reincarnating each time I die rather than passing on.
3	My consciousness was removed from my original body and implanted in this one.
4	I was physically and spiritually merged with another being.
5	I share my body with an intangible, otherworldly force.
6	Time fractures around me, and I sometimes collide with my own past or future.

Channeled Prowess. You gain proficiency in two skills of your choice.

Inherent Tongue. You can speak, read, and write one additional language of your choice.

Intrusive Echoes. Immediately after you make an attack roll, an ability check, or a saving throw and roll a 1 on the d20, your soul's memories emerge and overtake your perceptions and experiences. You might see people around you as someone other than who they are, or you become disoriented by a double-experience of the world around you. Roll on the Intrusive Echoes table to determine the effect of these vivid memories and perceptions. Once one of effects occur, these intrusive echoes can't manifest again until you finish a short or long rest.

SINISTER FORCES LURK IN THE SHADOWS, ENTICING THE UNWARY WITH DARK GIFTS.

INTRUSIVE ECHOES

d6	Effect
1	You are charmed by a creature you can see (of the DM's choice) for 1 minute or until the creature damages you.
2	You are frightened by a creature you can see (of the DM's choice) for 1 minute, or until the creature damages you.
3	You perceive another time or place around you until the end of your next turn. During this time, you are blinded to your actual surroundings.
4	You perceive a different time or place overlapping your surroundings. Your speed is halved until the end of your next turn.
5	Memories and sensations overwhelm you. You are incapacitated until the start of your next turn.
6	Your memory is one of triumph. You can reroll the ability check, attack roll, or saving throw that you just made. You must use the new roll.

GATHERED WHISPERS

You are haunted by spiritual beings, whether the souls of the departed or entities from another plane. Their voices endlessly whisper, taunt, or cajole, sometimes rising to unearthly howls. Only you can perceive the spirits, unless you allow them to speak through you. The spirits are intangible and invisible; anyone who can see invisible creatures sees only fleeting glimpses of these spirits as they haunt you.

Roll on or choose an option from the Whispering Spirits table to determine what haunts you. Additionally, you gain the traits that follow.

WHISPERING SPIRITS

d6	Spirits
1	A council of my dead ancestors watches over me.
2	Fiendish presences vie for my soul.
3	Unquiet souls are drawn to me and beg for peace.
4	The spirits of those I killed linger around me.
5	An alien intelligence intrudes upon my thoughts.
6	A sibling I don't have shares my body.

Spirit Whispers. You learn the *message* cantrip if you don't already know it, and require no components to cast it. When you cast the spell, the messages are delivered by one of your whispering spirits rather than you or the target's voice. Your spellcasting ability for this spell is Intelligence, Wisdom, or Charisma (your choice when you gain this Dark Gift).

Sudden Cacophony. When you are hit by an attack roll, you can use your reaction to channel your haunting spirits, letting their voices howl through you. If the attacker isn't deafened, add your proficiency bonus to your AC against that attack, potentially causing it to miss. Once this trait causes an attack to miss, you can't use the trait again until you finish a long rest.

Voices from Beyond. Immediately after you make an attack roll, an ability check, or a saving throw and roll a 1 on the d20, the haunting voices grow too loud to ignore. Roll on the Voices from Beyond table to determine the effect of these voices. Once one of these effects occurs, none of these haunting voices manifest again until you finish a short or long rest.

VOICES FROM BEYOND

d4	Effect
1	You have disadvantage on the next attack roll, ability check, or saving throw you make.
2	You are deafened by the voices for 1 minute.
3	You are frightened of the creature closest to you, other than yourself, until the end of your next turn. If multiple creatures are closest, the DM chooses which creature you are frightened of.
4	Within the next 10 minutes, you can ask your spirits about the results of a specific course of action that you plan to take within the next 30 minutes. You can receive an omen as if you had cast the *augury* spell. The omen manifests as whisperings from your spirits perceptible only to you.

LIVING SHADOW

The shadow you cast is animate and ever-present, even when lighting conditions would otherwise prevent it. Your shadow occasionally moves out of sync with you. Sometimes it appears to be undertaking random but mundane tasks, while at other times it acts out your darker impulses, threatening or even attacking other shadows. With effort, you can bend this shadow puppetry to your will.

Roll on or choose an option from the Shadow Quirk table to determine how your living shadow behaves. Additionally, you gain the traits that follow.

SHADOW QUIRK

d6	Quirk
1	My shadow often holds weapons or bears wounds that don't exist.
2	When I'm distracted, my shadow panics and tries to get other people's attention, as if it's desperate to escape me.
3	When it's not being watched, my shadow makes threatening gestures or creeps toward people.
4	My shadow's movements mirror mine incorrectly—when I raise my left hand, my shadow moves its right.
5	My shadow fiddles with or occasionally breaks Tiny, nonmagical objects.
6	There's a slight but noticeable delay between my movements and those of my shadow.

Grasping Shadow. You learn the *mage hand* cantrip if you don't already know it, and require no components to cast it. The hand created by the spell is shadowy but is not bound to your actual shadow. Your spellcasting ability for this spell is Intelligence, Wisdom, or Charisma (your choice when you gain this Dark Gift).

Shadow Strike. When you make a melee attack roll, you can increase your reach for that attack by 10 feet. Your shadow stretches and delivers the attack as if it were you. You can use this feature a number of times equal to your proficiency bonus, and you regain all expended uses when you finish a long rest.

Ominous Will. Immediately after you make an attack roll, an ability check, or a saving throw and roll a 1 on the d20, your shadow exerts a will of its own and might assist or hinder you or those around you. The next time you or a creature within 30 feet of you that you can see makes an attack roll, an ability check, or a saving throw, roll a d4. If the number is odd, reduce the total by the number rolled. If the number is even, increase the total by the number rolled. Once this effect occurs, it can't happen again until you finish a short or long rest.

MIST WALKER

The Mists grip all who tread the Domains of Dread, but you know how to slip through their grasp. You can navigate the Mists successfully given enough time and a little luck, but this freedom comes with a price; if you remain in one area for too long, the Mists find you and drain your life force.

Roll on or choose an option from the Misty Travels table to determine how you developed this Dark Gift. Additionally, you gain the traits that follow.

MISTY TRAVELS

d4	Origin
1	You learned a secret about the nature of the Mists. Ever since, you can manipulate them, but the lands you walk have turned against you.
2	You fled into the Mists to escape someone or something that's hunting you. You can never rest for long, knowing you're still being pursued.
3	You're part of an organization, a family, or an itinerant community with experience traveling the Mists. They taught you how to do the same.
4	The Mists stole you from your home and fractured your memories of where you're from. You've been on a quest to find your way back ever since.

Misty Step. You can cast the *misty step* spell, requiring no spell slot, and you must finish a long rest before you can cast it this way again. Your spell-casting ability for this spell is Intelligence, Wisdom, or Charisma (your choice when you gain this Dark Gift). If you have spell slots of 2nd level or higher, you can cast this spell with them.

Mist Traveler. When you enter the Mists intent on reaching a specific domain, you are treated as if you possess a Mist talisman keyed to that domain. To use this trait, you must know the name of the domain you have chosen as your destination, but you don't need to have previously visited that land. This trait doesn't allow you to bypass domain borders closed by a Darklord's will.

Poisoned Roots. When you finish a long rest, the world around you in a 10-mile radius becomes a siphon that will eventually leech away your vitality. You can remain in the area safely for a number of weeks equal to your Constitution modifier (minimum of 1 week). Thereafter, each time you finish a long rest in the area, you must succeed on a DC 15 Constitution saving throw or gain 1 level of exhaustion that can't be removed while you remain in the area.

SECOND SKIN

There is another side of you that most people never see. When you show this side of yourself, you might become another person entirely, a celestial-like avenger, or a walking nightmare. Whatever the specifics of this form, it exaggerates some drive or hidden nature within you.

Roll on or choose an option from the Second Form table to determine this other side of yourself. Additionally, you gain the traits that follow.

SECOND FORM

d6	Form
1	An exaggerated version of your own form
2	Hybrid form of humanoid and beast
3	An angelic, a demonic, or an aberrant form
4	A vaguely human-shaped creature made of slime
5	A fey-like shape, either brooding or passionate
6	A body constructed of metal, stone, or machinery

Transformation. You can cast the *alter self* spell to appear in your second form. When you do so, you gain the effects of that spell's Change Appearance option and cannot end it to gain the benefits of a different option. Casting *alter self* in this way requires no spell slot, and you must finish a long rest before you can cast it this way again. Your spellcasting ability for this spell is Intelligence, Wisdom, or Charisma (your choice when you gain this Dark Gift). If you have spell slots of 2nd level or higher, you can cast this spell with them.

When you cast *alter self* using this feature, some cosmetic aspect of your second form remains after the spell ends. This visibly marks you unless you actively hide or disguise it. The mark is a perceptible change such as scaly skin, stunted wings, eyes without pupils, or horns. The mark fades after you finish a long rest.

Involuntary Change. Certain circumstances can activate your Dark Gift. After you experience this catalyst, at the start of your next turn you must succeed on a DC 15 Charisma saving throw or use your action to cast *alter self* as described in the Transformation trait, even if you have already used it.

Roll on or choose an option from the Change Catalyst table to determine what triggers your involuntary change.

CHANGE CATALYST

d6	Catalyst
1	Seeing a particular phase of the moon
2	The smell of a certain type of flower
3	The sound of ringing temple bells
4	Hearing a particular melody
5	Touching pure silver with your bare skin
6	Seeing someone resembling a specific individual

SYMBIOTIC BEING

A second being resides within your body along with you. It manifests physically somewhere on you and relies on you for its survival. At the same time, it offers you knowledge and other assistance, either of its own volition or because of your intertwined nature. The symbiote has its own personality and agenda, which might be at odds with yours. If you ignore the symbiote's desires, it might strive to interfere with you. There is no way to be rid of the symbiote while you have this Dark Gift. Even if you go to drastic lengths, such as severing the part of your body where the symbiote resides, it reappears on your body in another location at the next midnight.

Roll on or choose an option from the Symbiotic Nature table to determine what sort of symbiotic being shares your body. Additionally, you gain the traits that follow.

SYMBIOTIC NATURE

d6	Symbiote
1	Tiny humanoid facial features protruding from your torso, palm, or the back of your head
2	An alien appendage inside an unhealing wound
3	A burrowing, worm-like being
4	An intrusive thought that inhabits your mind
5	A living tattoo
6	Crystal growths that replace a portion of your body

Entwined Existence. Your symbiote is a separate entity with its own physical form bound to yours. It isn't a separate creature and relies on you to survive. It has Intelligence, Wisdom, and Charisma scores. The DM sets the symbiote's abilities or determines them randomly (roll 4d6 for each score, ignoring the lowest roll and totaling the rest). The symbiote can see and hear using your senses.

The symbiote speaks, reads, and understands two languages; one that you speak, as well as one appropriate to its nature. Choose one of the following skills: Arcana, Deception, History, Intimidation, Insight, Investigation, Nature, Religion, Perception, or Persuasion. You gain proficiency in that skill if you don't already have it, representing the symbiote's counsel and guidance.

If you die, so does your symbiote. If you are subsequently returned to life, your symbiote revives as well.

Sustained Symbiosis. Your symbiote has a vested interest in your survival and takes steps to ensure it. When you fail a saving throw, you can choose to have your symbiote expend one of your Hit Dice to roll it and add the number rolled to the saving throw, potentially turning the failure into a success. If it uses this feature on a death saving throw, you

succeed on the save and regain 1 hit point regardless of the number rolled on the d20.

Once you succeed on a saving throw due to this trait, the symbiote can't use it again until you finish a long rest.

Symbiotic Agenda. Your symbiote has an agenda that drives it, and it expects you to assist it in achieving those goals. How permissive or patient it is in resolving its agenda depends on its personality (work with your DM to determine these details). If you have an opportunity to advance its agenda and don't act on it, the symbiote can try to force your hand. You must succeed on a Charisma saving throw (DC 12 + the symbiote's Charisma modifier) or be charmed by the symbiote for 1d12 hours. While charmed, you must try to follow the symbiote's commands. If you take damage that is not self-inflicted, you can repeat the saving throw, ending the effect on a success.

Roll or choose from the Symbiotic Agenda table to determine the symbiote's goal, working with your DM to detail the specifics or create another agenda.

SYMBIOTIC AGENDA

d6	Agenda
1	The symbiote seeks to destroy a specific type of being, such as fiends, trolls, or paladins.
2	The symbiote craves knowledge and is determined to solve a mystery or learn a secret.
3	The symbiote wants to bring a prophecy to fruition or to thwart one.
4	The symbiote seeks to defend the servants and interests of a powerful being or organization.
5	The symbiote wants to keep you from harm at all costs and believes it knows what's best for you.
6	The symbiote seeks to experience new sensations, the more bizarre the better.

TOUCH OF DEATH

Your touch is pain, harming whoever you come in contact with. The deathly power within you is beyond your control, afflicting any who touch your bare skin. By the same token, you can deliver death to your enemies with your touch.

Roll on or choose an option from the Deadly Touch table to determine how this Dark Gift presents itself. Additionally, you gain the traits that follow.

DEADLY TOUCH

d6	Manifestation
1	Your body is alchemically or biologically altered, infusing you with deadly chemicals.
2	The magic of a slighted druid or fey makes small plants wither and insects die in your presence.

d6	Manifestation
3	You're the harbinger of a grim prophecy. Any creature your touch damages is marked with a temporary scar of a group, fiend, deity, or other force that takes an interest in you.
4	You survived a near-death experience—but shouldn't have. Ever since, death and ill omens follow you.
5	You are out of sync with time or reality. Anything you touch is warped by the distortion.
6	Every time you touch a creature, you hear the laughter of someone you once harmed.

Death Touch. You can focus your deadly touch against your foes. As an action, make one unarmed strike. On a hit, the target takes an additional 1d10 necrotic damage. This damage increases by 1d10 when you reach 5th level (2d10), 11th level (3d10), and 17th level (4d10).

Inescapable Death. When you hit a target with an attack roll and deal necrotic damage, you ignore the target's resistance to that damage.

Withering Contact. When you start your turn grappling a creature or grappled by it, the creature takes 1d10 necrotic damage.

WATCHERS

Something is always watching you and draws ethereal spirits that take the form of creatures made of shadowstuff, usually in the shape of Tiny beasts, that follow you and gather in your general vicinity. These creatures act like normal examples of their kind, but their behavior suggests a hint of malice. No matter what precautions you take, you can't permanently drive these spirits away. They always return, wait just beyond the reach of deterrents, or later crawl out of your clothes and equipment.

Roll on or choose an option from the Watchers table to determine what sorts of forms the spirits typically take when they follow you.

WATCHERS

d8	Watchers
1	**Carrion Eaters.** Jackals, ravens, vultures
2	**Inescapable Judgments.** Animate tools of punishment, drifting eyeballs, religious iconography
3	**Night Wings.** Bats, moths, owls
4	**Plague Carriers.** Fleas, rats, squirrels
5	**Unnatural Observers.** Animate objects, clockwork devices, otherworldly voyeurs
6	**Sea Skulkers.** Crabs, eels, jellyfish
7	**Stray Souls.** Ghost orbs, shadows, ectoplasmic wisps
8	**Venomous Vermin.** Scorpions, serpents, spiders

A DWARF OCCULTIST FINDS HERSELF WATCHED BY THE STARING CATS OF ULDUN-DAR.

Borrowed Eyes. As an action, you can influence the presence guiding the watchers for 1 hour. For the duration, you gain advantage on Intelligence (Investigation) and Wisdom (Perception) checks, and you can't be blinded. Once you use this feature, you can't use it again until you finish a long rest.

Dread Presence. You have disadvantage on Charisma (Deception), Charisma (Performance), and Charisma (Persuasion) checks made against creatures that can see the watchers, and you have disadvantage on saving throws made against the *scrying* spell.

You can temporarily disperse or hide the watchers with some effort. With 1 minute of work and a successful DC 15 Charisma (Animal Handling) check, you can suppress your Borrowed Eyes and Dread Presence for 1 hour. Once you successfully suppress these features, you can't do so again until you finish a long rest.

Subclass Options

At 3rd level, a bard chooses a Bard College. At 1st level, a warlock chooses an Otherworldly Patron. This section offers the College of Spirits for the bard and the Undead Otherworldly Patron for the warlock, expanding their options for those choices.

Bard: College of Spirits

Bards of the College of Spirits seek tales with inherent power—be they legends, histories, or fictions—and bring their subjects to life. Using occult trappings, these bards conjure spiritual embodiments of powerful forces to change the world once more. Such spirits are capricious, though, and what a bard summons isn't always entirely under their control.

Guiding Whispers

3rd-level College of Spirits feature

You can reach out to spirits to guide you and others. You learn the *guidance* cantrip, which doesn't count against the number of bard cantrips you know. For you, it has a range of 60 feet when you cast it.

Spiritual Focus

3rd-level College of Spirits feature

You employ tools that aid you in channeling spirits, be they historical figures or fictional archetypes. You can use the following objects as a spellcasting focus for your bard spells: a candle, crystal ball, skull, spirit board, or tarokka deck.

Starting at 6th level, when you cast a bard spell that deals damage or restores hit points through the Spiritual Focus, roll a d6, and you gain a bonus to one damage or healing roll of the spell equal to the number rolled.

Tales from Beyond

3rd-level College of Spirits feature

You reach out to spirits who tell their tales through you. While you are holding your Spiritual Focus, you can use a bonus action to expend one use of your Bardic Inspiration and roll on the Spirit Tales table using your Bardic Inspiration die to determine the tale the spirits direct you to tell. You retain the tale in mind until you bestow the tale's effect or you finish a short or long rest.

You can use an action to choose one creature you can see within 30 feet of you (this can be you) to be the target of the tale's effect. Once you do so, you can't bestow the tale's effect again until you roll it again.

You can retain only one of these tales in mind at a time, and rolling on the Spirit Tales table immediately ends the effect of the previous tale.

If the tale requires a saving throw, the DC equals your spell save DC.

Spirit Tales

Bardic Insp. Die	Tale Told Through You
1	**Tale of the Clever Animal.** For the next 10 minutes, whenever the target makes an Intelligence, a Wisdom, or a Charisma check, the target can roll an extra die immediately after rolling the d20 and add the extra die's number to the check. The extra die is the same type as your Bardic Inspiration die.
2	**Tale of the Renowned Duelist.** You make a melee spell attack against the target. On a hit, the target takes force damage equal to two rolls of your Bardic Inspiration die + your Charisma modifier.
3	**Tale of the Beloved Friends.** The target and another creature of its choice it can see within 5 feet of it gains temporary hit points equal to a roll of your Bardic Inspiration die + your Charisma modifier.
4	**Tale of the Runaway.** The target can immediately use its reaction to teleport up to 30 feet to an unoccupied space it can see. When the target teleports, it can choose a number of creatures it can see within 30 feet of it up to your Charisma modifier (minimum of 0) to immediately use the same reaction.
5	**Tale of the Avenger.** For 1 minute, any creature that hits the target with a melee attack takes force damage equal to a roll of your Bardic Inspiration die.
6	**Tale of the Traveler.** The target gains temporary hit points equal to a roll of your Bardic Inspiration die + your bard level. While it has these temporary hit points, the target's walking speed increases by 10 feet and it gains a +1 bonus to its AC.
7	**Tale of the Beguiler.** The target must succeed on a Wisdom saving throw or take psychic damage equal to two rolls of your Bardic Inspiration die, and the target is incapacitated until the end of its next turn.
8	**Tale of the Phantom.** The target becomes invisible until the end of its next turn or until it hits a creature with an attack. If the target hits a creature with an attack during this invisibility, the creature it hits takes necrotic damage equal to a roll of your Bardic Inspiration die and is frightened of the target until the end of the frightened creature's next turn.

Bardic Insp. Die	Tale Told Through You
9	**Tale of the Brute.** Each creature of the target's choice it can see within 30 feet of it must make a Strength saving throw. On a failed save, a creature takes thunder damage equal to three rolls of your Bardic Inspiration die and is knocked prone. A creature that succeeds on its saving throw takes half as much damage and isn't knocked prone.
10	**Tale of the Dragon.** The target spews fire from the mouth in a 30-foot cone. Each creature in that area must make a Dexterity saving throw, taking fire damage equal to four rolls of your Bardic Inspiration die on a failed save, or half as much damage on a successful one.
11	**Tale of the Angel.** The target regains hit points equal to two rolls of your Bardic Inspiration die + your Charisma modifier, and you end one condition from the following list affecting the target: blinded, deafened, paralyzed, petrified, or poisoned.
12	**Tale of the Mind-Bender.** You evoke an incomprehensible fable from an otherworldly being. The target must succeed on an Intelligence saving throw or take psychic damage equal to three rolls of your Bardic Inspiration die and be stunned until the end of its next turn.

SPIRIT SESSION
6th-level College of Spirits feature

Spirits provide you with supernatural insights. You can conduct an hour-long ritual channeling spirits (which can be done during a short or long rest) using your Spiritual Focus. You can conduct the ritual with a number of willing creatures equal to your proficiency bonus (including yourself). At the end of the ritual, you temporarily learn one spell of your choice from any class.

The spell you choose must be of a level equal to the number of creatures that conducted the ritual or less, the spell must be of a level you can cast, and it must be in the school of divination or necromancy. The chosen spell counts as a bard spell for you but doesn't count against the number of bard spells you know.

Once you perform the ritual, you can't do so again until you start a long rest, and you know the chosen spell until you start a long rest.

MYSTICAL CONNECTION
14th-level College of Spirits feature

You now have the ability to nudge the spirits of Tales from Beyond toward certain tales. Whenever you

A HUMAN BARD OF SPIRITS EVOKES A TALE INSPIRED BY THE AVENGER TAROKKA CARD.

roll on the Spirit Tales table, you can roll the die twice and choose which of the two effects to bestow. If you roll the same number on both dice, you can ignore the number and choose any effect on the table.

> ### SPIRIT TALES
> Storytellers, like bards of the College of Spirits, often give voice to tales inspired by some greater theme or body of work. When determining what stories you tell, consider what unites them. Do they all feature characters from a specific group, like archetypes from the tarokka deck, figures from constellations, childhood imaginary friends, or characters in a particular storybook? Or are your inspirations more general, incorporating historic champions, mythological heroes, or urban legends? Use the tales you tell to define your niche as a storytelling adventurer.

IRINA NORDSOL

Warlock: The Undead

You've made a pact with a deathless being, a creature that defies the cycle and life and death, forsaking its mortal shell so it might eternally pursue its unfathomable ambitions. For such beings, time and morality are fleeting things, the concerns of those for whom grains of sand still rush through life's hourglass. Having once been mortal themselves, these ancient undead know firsthand the paths of ambition and the routes past the doors of death. They eagerly share this profane knowledge, along with other secrets, with those who work their will among the living.

Beings of this type include the demilich Acererak, the vampire tyrant Kas the Bloody-Handed, the githyanki lich-queen Vlaakith, the dracolich Dragotha, the undead pharaoh Ankhtepot, and the elusive Darklord, Azalin Rex.

WOOD ELF WARLOCK
OF THE UNDEAD

Expanded Spell List
1st-level Undead feature

The Undead lets you choose from an expanded list of spells when you learn a warlock spell. The following spells are added to the warlock spell list for you.

Undead Expanded Spells

Spell Level	Spells
1st	bane, false life
2nd	blindness/deafness, phantasmal force
3rd	phantom steed, speak with dead
4th	death ward, greater invisibility
5th	antilife shell, cloudkill

Form of Dread
1st-level Undead feature

You manifest an aspect of your patron's dreadful power. As a bonus action, you transform for 1 minute. You gain the following benefits while transformed:

- You gain temporary hit points equal to 1d10 + your warlock level.
- Once during each of your turns, when you hit a creature with an attack roll, you can force it to make a Wisdom saving throw, and if the saving throw fails, the target is frightened of you until the end of your next turn.
- You are immune to the frightened condition.

You can transform a number of times equal to your proficiency bonus, and you regain all expended uses when you finish a long rest.

The appearance of your Form of Dread reflects some aspect of your patron. For example, your form could be a shroud of shadows forming the crown and robes of your lich patron, or your body might glow with glyphs from ancient funerary rites and be surrounded by desert winds, suggesting your mummy patron.

Grave Touched
6th-level Undead feature

Your patron's powers have a profound effect on your body and magic. You don't need to eat, drink, or breathe.

In addition, once during each of your turns, when you hit a creature with an attack roll and roll damage against the creature, you can replace the damage type with necrotic damage. While you are using your Form of Dread, you can roll one additional damage die when determining the necrotic damage the target takes.

DAWN CARLOS

Necrotic Husk
10th-level Undead feature

Your connection to undeath and necrotic energy now saturates your body. You have resistance to necrotic damage. If you are transformed using your Form of Dread, you instead become immune to necrotic damage.

In addition, when you would be reduced to 0 hit points, you can use your reaction to drop to 1 hit point instead and cause your body to erupt with deathly energy. Each creature of your choice that is within 30 feet of you takes necrotic damage equal to 2d10 + your warlock level. You then gain 1 level of exhaustion. Once you use this reaction, you can't do so again until you finish 1d4 long rests.

Spirit Projection
14th-level Undead feature

Your spirit can become untethered from your physical form. As an action, you can project your spirit from your body. The body you leave behind is unconscious and in a state of suspended animation.

Your spirit resembles your mortal form in almost every way, replicating your game statistics but not your possessions. Any damage or other effects that apply to your spirit or physical body affects the other. Your spirit can remain outside your body for up to 1 hour or until your concentration is broken (as if concentrating on a spell). When your projection ends, your spirit returns to your body or your body magically teleports to your spirit's space (your choice).

While projecting your spirit, you gain the following benefits:

- Your spirit and body gain resistance to bludgeoning, piercing, and slashing damage.
- When you cast a spell of the conjuration or necromancy school, the spell doesn't require verbal or somatic components or material components that lack a gold cost.
- You have a flying speed equal to your walking speed and can hover. You can move through creatures and objects as if they were difficult terrain, but you take 1d10 force damage if you end your turn inside a creature or an object.
- While you are using your Form of Dread, once during each of your turns when you deal necrotic damage to a creature, you regain hit points equal to half the amount of necrotic damage dealt.

Once you use this feature, you can't do so again until you finish a long rest.

Backgrounds

The following background features explore origins suited to characters in horror adventures. Optional features and characteristics for characters of any background suggest how portentous forces might influence anyone's life. Additionally, the haunted one and investigator backgrounds provide options for characters shaped by or determined to reveal the mysteries surrounding them. Finally, a selection of horror trinkets provide characters options to carry their own personal terrors.

General Background Features

This section presents optional features for any background. You may replace the standard feature of your background with any one of the options presented here.

Inheritor

An ancestor or mentor's deeds earned them a place in legend. Now it's your turn. You are the clear inheritor of a famed legacy. You've inherited a token from your predecessor, something that marks you as their inheritor, such as a signet ring, signature piece of clothing, or notable weapon.

Additionally, any time you reveal your legacy, you swiftly learn the local opinion of your predecessor. If locals have never heard of your predecessor, nothing changes. If they have, rumors of your connection spread swiftly, and many locals consider you either a hero or a threat. Heroes are welcomed and might easily gain an audience with local leaders. Threats are encouraged to leave before they invite danger.

Mist Wanderer

The Mists whisper to you and guide you through their mysterious eddies. You immediately know if an object you're touching is a Mist talisman (detailed in chapter 3). You recognize where the talisman originates from if you have been to its domain of origin.

Spirit Medium

After a fateful experience, you believe you're aligned with spirits and can serve as a conduit for their insights and goals. You have advantage on any Arcana or Religion check you make to remember or research information about spirits and the afterlife. Additionally, you begin your adventuring career with a custom-made device for communing with otherworldly forces, perhaps a spirit board, a tarokka deck, an automatic writing planchette, dowsing rods, a cup for tea leaves, or a device of your own design. Add your proficiency bonus to any ability check you make using this type of divining tool.

GENERATIONAL BACKGROUND FEATURES

You can use background features to connect characters between campaigns. Characters who have previously adventured in Ravenloft, such as those from a previous *Curse of Strahd* campaign, make good candidates for being your new character's mentor or relative. Alternatively, the deed of your characters in past adventures might have impacted your new character, throwing them into action or danger. Whatever details you and your DM decide upon, such connections can forge the continuing legend of a whole family of heroes.

If you're interested in exploring this, the Inheritor background feature provides a token that might be passed on from a previous character. Perhaps it's a signature tool, a journal, or a dormant (or misplaced) magic item. Work with your DM to detail this inheritance and how it can factor into future adventures.

TRAUMA SURVIVOR

You survived. Whatever it was, you made it through, and you can help others do the same. People view you as an expert on the traumatic situation you faced—be it a specific sort of violence, illness, or otherwise. You are aware of nonmagical recovery techniques, common resources, and misinformation. You know how to speak to sympathetic doctors, clergy, and local leaders and can convince them to shelter one person (other than yourself) at a modest lifestyle for up to one month.

TRAVELER

You come from somewhere else, a place others couldn't begin to understand. Perhaps your home is a unique corner of the Land of the Mists or another world entirely. In any case, you and other travelers have shared experiences. You can find a place to hide, rest, or recuperate among sympathetic trading caravans, itinerant families, or displaced groups, so long as you don't present yourself as a danger. Such groups will hide you from the law or anyone searching for you, though they won't risk their lives for you. Additionally, you can tell whether an object you can see and touch is from your homeland with near perfect accuracy.

HORROR CHARACTERISTICS

Characters in a horror-focused campaign might have distinct motivations and characteristics. Use the following tables to supplement your background's suggested characteristics or to inspire those of your own design.

HORROR CHARACTER PERSONALITY TRAITS

d12	Personality Trait
1	I had an encounter that I believe gives me a special affinity with a supernatural creature or event.
2	A signature piece of clothing or distinct weapon serves as an emblem of who I am.
3	I never accept that I'm out of my depth.
4	I must know the answer to every secret. No door remains unopened in my presence.
5	I let people underestimate me, revealing my full competency only to those close to me.
6	I compulsively seek to collect trophies of my travels and victories.
7	It doesn't matter if the whole world's against me. I'll always do what I think is right.
8	I have morbid interests and a macabre aesthetic.
9	I have a personal ritual, mantra, or relaxation method I use to deal with stress.
10	Nothing is more important than life, and I never leave anyone in danger.
11	I'm quick to jump to extreme solutions. Why risk a lesser option not working?
12	I'm easily startled, but I'm not a coward.

HORROR CHARACTER IDEALS

d12	Ideal
1	**Adrenaline**. I've experienced such strangeness that now I feel alive only in extreme situations.
2	**Balance**. I strive to counter the deeds of someone for whom I feel responsible.
3	**Bound**. I've wronged someone and must work their will to avoid their curse.
4	**Escape**. I believe there is something beyond the world I know, and I need to find it.
5	**Legacy**. I must do something great so that I'm remembered, and my time is running out.
6	**Misdirection**. I work vigorously to keep others from realizing my flaws or misdeeds.
7	**Obsession**. I've lived this way for so long that I can't imagine another way.
8	**Obligation**. I owe it to my people, faith, family, or teacher to continue a vaunted legacy.
9	**Promise**. My life is no longer my own. I must fulfill the dream of someone who's gone.
10	**Revelation**. I need to know what lies beyond the mysteries of death, the world, or the Mists.
11	**Sanctuary**. I know the forces at work in the world and strive to create islands apart from them.
12	**Truth**. I care about the truth above all else, even if it doesn't benefit anyone.

A KNIGHT OF THE CIRCLE TAKES UP HER ANCESTORS' SACRED CHARGE TO CHALLENGE THE DARK.

HORROR CHARACTER BONDS

d12	Bond
1	I desperately need to get back to someone or someplace, but I lost them in the Mists.
2	Everything I do is in the service of a powerful master, one I must keep a secret from everyone.
3	I owe much to my vanished mentor. I seek to continue their work even as I search to find them.
4	I've seen great darkness, and I'm committed to being a light against it—the light of all lights.
5	Someone I love has become a monster, murderer, or other threat. It's up to me to redeem them.
6	The world has been convinced of a terrible lie. It's up to me to reveal the truth.
7	I deeply miss someone and am quick to adopt people who remind me of them.
8	A great evil dwells within me. I will fight against it and the world's other evils for as long as I can.
9	I'm desperately seeking a cure to an affliction or a curse, either for someone close to me for myself.
10	Spirits are drawn to me. I do all I can to help them find peace.
11	I use my cunning mind to solve mysteries and find justice for those who've been wronged.
12	I lost someone I care about, but I still see them in guilty visions, recurring dreams, or as a spirit.

HORROR CHARACTER FLAWS

d12	Flaw
1	I believe doom follows me and that anyone who gets close to me will face a tragic end.
2	I'm convinced something is after me, appearing in mirrors, dreams, and places where no one could.
3	I'm especially superstitious and live life seeking to avoid bad luck, wicked spirits, or the Mists.
4	I've done unspeakable evil and will do anything to prevent others from finding out.
5	I am exceptionally credulous and believe any story or legend immediately.
6	I'm a skeptic and don't believe in the power of rituals, religion, superstition, or spirits.
7	I know my future is written and that anything I do will lead to a prophesied end.
8	I need to find the best in everyone and everything, even when that means denying obvious malice.
9	I've seen the evil of a type of place—like forests, cities, or graveyards—and resist going there.
10	I'm exceptionally cautious, planning laboriously and devising countless contingencies.
11	I have a reputation for defeating a great evil, but that's a lie and the wicked force knows.
12	I know the ends always justify the means and am quick to make sacrifices to attain my goals.

Haunted One

You are haunted by something so terrible that you dare not speak of it. You've tried to bury it and run away from it, to no avail. Whatever this thing is that haunts you can't be slain with a sword or banished with a spell. It might come to you as a shadow on the wall, a bloodcurdling nightmare, a memory that refuses to die, or a demonic whisper in the dark. The burden has taken its toll, isolating you from most people and making you question your sanity. You must find a way to overcome it before it destroys you.

Skill Proficiencies: Choose two from among Arcana, Investigation, Religion, or Survival

Languages: Choose two, one of which must be Abyssal, Celestial, Deep Speech, Draconic, Infernal, Primordial, Sylvan, or Undercommon

Equipment: A monster hunter's pack (containing a chest, a crowbar, a hammer, three wooden stakes, a holy symbol, a flask of holy water, a set of manacles, a steel mirror, a flask of oil, a tinderbox, and 3 torches), one trinket of special significance (choose one or roll on the Horror Trinkets table later in this chapter), a set of common clothes, and 1 sp

Harrowing Event

Prior to becoming an adventurer, your path in life was defined by one dark moment, one fateful decision, or one tragedy. Now you feel a darkness threatening to consume you, and you fear there may be no hope of escape. Choose a harrowing event that haunts you, or roll one on the Harrowing Events table.

Harrowing Event

d10	Event
1	A monster that slaughtered dozens of innocent people spared your life, and you don't know why.
2	You were born under a dark star. You can feel it watching you, coldly and distantly. Sometimes it beckons you in the dead of night.
3	An apparition that has haunted your family for generations now haunts you. You don't know what it wants, and it won't leave you alone.
4	Your family has a history of practicing the dark arts. You dabbled once and felt something horrible clutch at your soul, whereupon you fled in terror.
5	An oni took your sibling one cold, dark night, and you were unable to stop it.
6	You were cursed with lycanthropy and later cured. You are now haunted by the innocents you slaughtered.
7	A hag kidnapped and raised you. You escaped, but the hag still has a magical hold over you and fills your mind with evil thoughts.
8	You opened an eldritch tome and saw things unfit for a sane mind. You burned the book, but its words and images are burned into your psyche.
9	A fiend possessed you as a child. You were locked away but escaped. The fiend is still inside you, but now you try to keep it bottled up.
10	You did terrible things to avenge the murder of someone you loved. You became a monster, and it haunts your waking dreams.

Feature: Heart of Darkness

Those who look into your eyes can see that you have faced unimaginable horror and that you are no stranger to darkness. Though they might fear you, commoners will extend you every courtesy and do their utmost to help you. Unless you have shown yourself to be a danger to them, they will even take up arms to fight alongside you, should you find yourself facing an enemy alone.

INVESTIGATOR

You relentlessly seek the truth. Perhaps you're motivated by belief in the law and a sense of universal justice, or maybe that very law has failed you and you seek to make things right. You could have witnessed something remarkable or terrible, and now you must know more about this hidden truth. Or maybe you're a detective for hire, uncovering secrets for well-paying clients. Whether the mysteries you're embroiled in are local crimes or realm-spanning conspiracies, you're driven by a personal need to hunt down even the most elusive clues and reveal what others would keep hidden in the shadows.

Skill Proficiencies: Choose two from among Insight, Investigation, or Perception
Tool Proficiencies: Disguise kit, thieves' tools
Equipment: A magnifying glass, evidence from a past case (choose one or roll for a trinket from the Horror Trinkets table later in this chapter), a set of common clothes, and 10 gp

PATH TO MYSTERY

Your first case influenced the types of mysteries you're interested in. Why was this case so impactful, personal, or traumatic? Whom did it affect besides you? Why and how did you get involved? Was it solved? How did it set you on the path to investigating other mysteries? Roll on or choose details from the First Case table to develop the mystery that started your career as an investigator.

FIRST CASE

d8	Case
1	A friend was wrongfully accused of murder. You tracked down the actual killer, proving your friend's innocence and starting your career as a detective.
2	You're told you went missing for weeks. When you were found, you had no memory of being gone. Now you search to discover what happened to you.
3	You helped a spirit find peace by finding its missing corpse. Ever since, other spectral clients have sought you out to help them find rest.
4	You revealed that the monsters terrorizing your home were illusions created by a cruel mage. The magic-user escaped, but you've continued to uncover magical hoaxes.
5	You were wrongfully accused and convicted of a crime. You managed to escape and seek to help others avoid the experience you suffered, even while still being pursued by the law.
6	You survived the destructive use of a magic device that wiped out your home. Members of a secret organization found you. You now work with them, tracking down dangerous supernatural phenomena and preventing them from doing harm.
7	You found evidence of a conspiracy underpinning society. You tried to expose this mysterious cabal, but no one believed you. You're still trying to prove what you know is true.
8	You got a job with an agency that investigates crimes that local law enforcement can't solve. You often wonder which you value more, the truth or your pay.

FEATURE: OFFICIAL INQUIRY

You're experienced at gaining access to people and places to get the information you need. Through a combination of fast-talking, determination, and official-looking documentation, you can gain access to a place or an individual related to a crime you're investigating. Those who aren't involved in your investigation avoid impeding you or pass along your requests. Additionally, local law enforcement has firm opinions about you, viewing you as either a nuisance or one of their own.

AN INVESTIGATOR CONSIDERS
EVEN THE STRANGEST EVIDENCE.

ZUZANNA WUZYK

HORROR TRINKETS

Sinister deeds and festering evils take many forms, sometimes as stories and sometimes as physical scars. All manner of talismans, mementos, criminal evidence, mysterious devices, cursed relics, and physical impossibilities might embody just such scars—summaries of terrors in material form.

Before you finish making a character, roll once on the Horror Trinkets table for a unique object your character has with them at the start of their adventuring career. These trinkets hint toward various horrific tales and might lead to dreadful revelations or be nothing more than grim keepsakes. At the DM's discretion any of these trinkets might also be a Mist talisman (detailed in chapter 3), a focal item that can lead the bearer through the Mists to a particular Domain of Dread.

HORROR TRINKETS

d100	Trinket
01	A picture you drew as a child of your imaginary friend
02	A lock that opens when blood is dripped in its keyhole
03	Clothes stolen from a scarecrow
04	A spinning top carved with four faces: happy, sad, wrathful, and dead
05	The necklace of a sibling who died on the day you were born
06	A wig from someone executed by beheading
07	The unopened letter to you from your dying father
08	A pocket watch that runs backward for an hour every midnight
09	A winter coat stolen from a dying soldier
10	A bottle of invisible ink that can only be read at sunset
11	A wineskin that refills when interred with a dead person for a night
12	A set of silverware used by a king for his last meal
13	A spyglass that always shows the world suffering a terrible storm
14	A cameo with the profile's face scratched away
15	A lantern with a black candle that never runs out and that burns with green flame
16	A teacup from a child's tea set, stained with blood
17	A little black book that records your dreams, and yours alone, when you sleep
18	A necklace formed of the interlinked holy symbols of a dozen deities

d100	Trinket
19	A noose that feels heavier than it should
20	A birdcage into which small birds fly but once inside never eat or leave
21	A lepidopterist's box filled with dead moths with skull-like patterns on their wings
22	A jar of pickled ghouls' tongues
23	The wooden hand of a notorious pirate
24	A urn with the ashes of a dead relative
25	A hand mirror backed with a bronze depiction of a medusa
26	Pallid leather gloves crafted with ivory fingernails
27	Dice made from the knuckles of a notorious charlatan
28	A ring of keys for forgotten locks
29	Nails from the coffin of a murderer
30	A key to the family crypt
31	A bouquet of funerary flowers that always looks and smells fresh
32	A switch used to discipline you as a child
33	A music box that plays by itself whenever someone holding it dances
34	A walking cane with an iron ferrule that strikes sparks on stone
35	A flag from a ship lost at sea
36	A porcelain doll's head that always seems to be looking at you
37	A wolf's head wrought in silver that is also a whistle
38	A small mirror that shows a much older version of the viewer
39	A small, worn book of children's nursery rhymes
40	A mummified raven claw
41	A broken pendant of a silver dragon that's always cold to the touch
42	A small locked box that quietly hums a lovely melody at night, but you always forget it in the morning
43	An inkwell that makes one a little nauseous when staring at it
44	An old doll made from a dark, dense wood and missing a hand and a foot
45	A black executioner's hood
46	A pouch made of flesh, with a sinew drawstring
47	A tiny spool of black thread that never runs out
48	A tiny clockwork figurine of a dancer that's missing a gear and doesn't work

d100	Trinket
49	A black wooden pipe that creates puffs of smoke that look like skulls
50	A vial of perfume, the scent of which only certain creatures can detect
51	A stone that emits a single endless sigh
52	A rag doll with two red dots on its neck
53	A spring-loaded toy with a missing crank
54	A mason jar containing a harmless but agitated, animate ooze
55	A black wooden die with 1's on all the faces
56	A child's portrait with "born" written on the back, along with next year's date
57	A dagger-sized shark tooth
58	A finger that's taken root in a small pot
59	A toolbox containing the remains of a dangerous but broken clockwork arachnid
60	A pitcher-sized, opalescent snail shell that occasionally, inexplicably shudders or tips over
61	The logbook of an ice-breaking ship called *The Haifisch*
62	A small portrait of you as a child, alongside your identically dressed twin
63	A silver pocket watch with thirteen hours marked on the face
64	A woodcut of a wolf devouring its own hind leg
65	A planchette etched with raven skulls
66	A moist coral figurine of a lamprey with arms, legs, and a bipedal stance
67	A bronze fingertrap sculpted with roaring tigers
68	A pearl necklace that turns red under the full moon
69	A fossil of a fish with humanoid features
70	A plague doctor's mask
71	A paper talisman with smudged ink
72	A locket containing the smeared image of an eyeless figure
73	A canopic jar with a lid sculpted like a goat
74	A jack-o'-lantern made from a small, pale gourd
75	A single high-heeled, iron shoe
76	A candle made from a severed hand
77	A clockwork device that beats like a heart
78	A blank masquerade mask
79	A glass eye with a live worm inside
80	A sheet with two eyeholes cut in it
81	The deed to someplace called Tergeron Manor
82	An ornate, wax-sealed crimson envelope that resists all attempts to open it

d100	Trinket
83	A mourning veil trimmed in black lace
84	A straitjacket covered in charcoal runes
85	A tattered, burlap mask with a crooked smile painted on it
86	A green ribbon designed to be worn as a choker
87	Dentures with mismatched, sharpened teeth
88	A warm, fist-sized egg case
89	A copper ring with "mine" engraved on the inside
90	A glass ampoule containing a neon green fluid
91	An eye patch embroidered with a holy symbol
92	A severed big toe with a nail that continues to grow
93	A journal that has been heavily redacted
94	A glove with a mouth-like design stitched on the palm
95	An ornate but empty reliquary made of silver and fractured glass
96	A ceramic figure of a cat with too many eyes
97	A crumpled paper ticket bearing the words "admit none"
98	An electrum coin with your face on one side
99	A shrunken gremishka head that twitches when anyone casts magic nearby
100	A sunburst amulet with a red stone at the center

THE RIVALRY BETWEEN DARKLORDS STRAHD VON ZAROVICH AND AZALIN REX SPILLS THROUGH ENDLESS AGES AND COUNTLESS DOMAINS.

CHAPTER 2
CREATING DOMAINS OF DREAD

RAVENLOFT IS A PLACE WHERE YOUR nightmares can run wild, where anything you can imagine in moments of dread or despair can come to frightful life among the Mists. The setting as a whole is made up of countless isolated domains, each one a perfect expression of a particular flavor of the macabre. Creating your own domain allows you to blend legendary evils, unexpected monstrosities, and grim settings into a tailor-made whole, bound together by mysterious mists and buried alive inside your favorite horror genres.

This chapter explores how to create such domains, a process that starts by defining a Darklord—the villain at the heart of each sinister realm. Descriptions of various genres of horror also provide details to guide and inspire your creations.

CREATING A DARKLORD

Domains are mocking reflections of the evils they confine. Each has a purpose, being a prison designed to torture a deliberately chosen villain. To devise a Domain of Dread, you must first conceive its central antagonist and prisoner: its Darklord. The following sections detail how to develop a Darklord that contrasts your characters and can serve as a central rival in your horror adventures.

SINISTER REFLECTIONS

A Darklord's memories, desires, mistakes, and evil deeds shape the domain's twisted lands, inhabitants, and features. You need not create these in a vacuum, though. When creating your own Darklord, consider the relationship that will define their evil in your adventures: their conflict with your players' characters. Just as a Darklord is the inspiration for a domain, players' characters can be a source of inspiration for a Darklord. Consider a Darklord a sinister reflections of those characters. If you explore this connection, have your players create characters then involve them in the process of creating a Darklord in the following ways:

What to Reflect. Ask your players which of their characters' personality traits, ideals, bonds, and flaws are their favorites. Request at least two favorites from each player. Write them down. If players have been playing characters for a while, ask them to rewrite these personal characteristics to reflect who their characters are now.

Exaggerated Reflections. For each favored personal characteristic, imagine and write down a version twisted to its extreme. For example, transform "I idolize a particular hero of my faith, and constantly refer to that person's deeds and example" into "I'm obsessed with a hero of my faith, and I must become exactly like them so I can take their place." The more unreasonable, the better.

Opposite Reflections. For each favored personal characteristic, imagine and write down its opposite—specifically, a version that compels characters into conflict. For example, transform "I idolize a particular hero of my faith, and constantly refer to that person's deeds and example" into "I loathe a particular hero and their followers, and I will prove the hypocrisy of that person's deeds and example." The harsher, the better.

Use these exaggerated and opposite reflections as inspirations for creating your Darklord. By basing your Darklord on intimate details drawn from the players' characters, you create a feeling that the characters are trapped inside a collective nightmare. Through their interactions with a Darklord who mirrors them, characters discover how easily they could become the villains they face.

PAST LIFE

Darklords aren't mindless killing machines; they are full but monstrous individuals. In a few sentences, describe who the Darklord was before they chose to become irredeemable. For inspiration, consider how the Darklord is a reflection of the players' characters. You might also look ahead to the "Genres of Horror" section to see if any of these types of horror seem right for your Darklord. Then consider the following questions.

- Where was the Darklord before the Mists took them?
- Who was the Darklord's family?
- How was the Darklord's family oppressed, oppressive, or both?
- What was the Darklord's childhood like?
- Whom did the Darklord care about?
- Who cared about the Darklord?
- Who hurt the Darklord?
- Whose respect or love did the Darklord crave?
- What did the Darklord value?

Consult the *Dungeon Master's Guide* or the "This Is Your Life" section of *Xanathar's Guide to Everything* for additional inspirations for your Darklord's motivations.

WICKED PERSONALITY

Detailing the Darklord's personality gives them a unique identity that will help motivate them in your adventures. To do this, give them ideals, bonds, and flaws similar to those you might give any NPC, as detailed in the section on creating nonplayer characters in the *Dungeon Master's Guide*:

Ideal. In one sentence, describe an ideal that the Darklord holds dear and that governs their greater actions.

Bond. In one sentence, describe a person, place, or object that the Darklord desires. Avoid a bond that is simply about power; power isn't an end in itself—power is a means to obtain a bond.

Flaws. In one sentence, describe how the Darklord's personality causes them to act against their own best interests, especially in their quest to win their bonds and desires. Flaws are often a negative emotion or destructive behavior—such as fear, hatred, insecurity, jealousy, mayhem, obsession, selfishness, shame—that drives an irrational habit causing the Darklord or others harm. Alternatively, you can choose or randomly determine a flaw from the Fatal Flaws table.

FATAL FLAWS

d10	Flaw
1	Once someone questions me, I won't stop until I befriend them and then betray them.
2	Others' concerns bore me, and I would rather have my lessers handle everything possible.
3	I am always right, and anyone who doesn't agree with me is cut out of my life.
4	When someone loves me, I will do anything for them, no matter whom they hurt.
5	I've given up resisting my habits and indulge myself whenever possible.
6	I would rather be righteously angry at problems than solve them.
7	I assume everyone is lying to me, even my most trusted allies, and constantly test their loyalty.
8	I don't know love, only domineering obsession, and I chain objects of my affection to pedestals.
9	When I see something priceless or rare, I sacrifice all of my beliefs and loyalties to possess it.
10	I'm distrustful of anyone who seems pure of heart and will prove to all their admirers how secretly ugly they are.

CORRUPT BEYOND REDEMPTION

Darklords aren't misunderstood souls condemned through no fault of their own. If a person's potential for evil is particularly great, the Dark Powers might indirectly nurture further transgression, but they don't force individuals to undertake actions against their will. When an evildoer's wickedness ripens, the Dark Powers engulf them forever.

When creating your Darklord, consider the depth of their greatest evil and what made it more significant, abominable, or poetic than more common forms of villainy. The following elements all might be aspects of this corruption:

Evil Acts. The Dark Powers consider an act to be evil if it is intentional, unnecessary, and successful, and most importantly, if it causes significant harm. Accidents, self-defense, deeds necessary for survival, and forced or coerced actions do not qualify. Early in the character's creation, consider what evils your Darklord performed, and revisit these crimes as you develop the villain's other details.

Those Harmed. The people the Darklord harmed need to feel real. Give them names. Imbue them with agency, and don't define them as victims or props. The people who survived the Darklord's evil might be part of a Darklord's history or allies who join the players' characters, or might hold the key to righting the Darklord's wrongs. For each character, consider whether they were important to the Darklord and how that relationship changed.

Irredeemable. Once the Dark Powers take an evil person, that individual's fate is sealed. Before the final corruption, a person can atone—but only if they take genuine responsibility, heal the harm caused, and reform to prevent future harm. Once an evildoer becomes a Darklord, it is far too late. Consider whether your Darklord had a chance to redeem themselves and the decision that led to their current fate.

DEVELOPING A DARKLORD

Darklords are villains because of what they choose to do, not because of who they were. As you refine your idea for a Darklord, determine what deeds a Darklord committed, who was harmed, how the Dark Powers encouraged them, and the price the Darklord paid. Describe why they chose to commit these evil acts, including their ideals, flaws, and bonds.

Consider these questions when creating your Darklord's backstory:

- What was the first depraved act the Darklord chose to commit, and how did their ideal encourage them down this path?
- Was the Darklord rewarded or celebrated for their evil? Did that reaction encourage greater crimes? Were these rewards earned or justified?
- Did the Darklord repeat or escalate their wickedness to obtain something they selfishly desired?
- Did the future Darklord realize that they were losing any hope of redemption, yet choose to commit other heinous acts in keeping with their flaw?
- What evil act was so atrocious that the future Darklord's friends and family rejected them? Did the Darklord think this was warranted or an unreasonable judgment? How did they react?
- When and how did these acts attract the attention of the Dark Powers?
- How did the Dark Powers use these acts to craft the perfect prison domain for the Darklord?

MONSTROUS TRANSFORMATION

Some Darklords have features that make them similar to familiar monsters. The Darklord might have been a supernatural creature to begin with, or perhaps they gained their form and related powers through their deeds or a curse. Maybe they even gained supernatural abilities via a pact with the Dark Powers or upon arriving in their domain.

Consider whether or not your Darklord has a monstrous form. If so, in a few sentences, describe how the Darklord gained this form. You might also roll or choose an option from the Monstrous Transformations table to provide a twist on a Darklord's monstrousness. The Dark Gifts in chapter 1 serve as examples of the sorts of forms and powers a Darklord might possess. In any case, consider how this transformation embodies the Darklord's evil.

MONSTROUS TRANSFORMATIONS

d10	Transformation
1	The Darklord loses their voice; their words now carve themselves on their skin as lingering scars.
2	Something the Darklord stole or used in a terrible crime becomes part of their body—perhaps a sizable jewel, emblem of rulership, or suit of armor.
3	The Darklord's eyes distend from their sockets like a slug's tentacles, in the mouths of serpents, or on metallic cables.
4	The Darklord's most painful memories visually repeat in reflections around them or amid illusory projections.
5	The Darklord gains an idealized form, though it's made of an inorganic material or others react as if it were terrifying.
6	The Darklord's body disintegrates, leaving only an animate heart, hand, gory ooze, or nervous system that must attach to new, temporary bodies.
7	Clouds of incense, insects, poison gas, or smoke leak from the Darklord's mouth, fingers, or pores.
8	The Darklord appears as someone they wronged, and their true appearance is revealed at particular hours, in reflections, or under certain lights.
9	The Darklord splits into multiple creatures, each representing them at a different time in their life.
10	The Darklord retains their memories and intellect but is otherwise any monster from chapter 5 or the *Monster Manual*.

BIRTH OF A DARKLORD

Upon the completion of the Darklord's greatest irredeemable act, the Mists drag them—and perhaps the lands around them—into the Domains of Dread. At this point, you should have an idea of who your Darklord is, what they did, what form their evil takes, and how they came to the attention of the Dark Powers. Flesh out these details, referring back to how the Darklord reflects your players' characters and the section on creating nonplayer characters in the *Dungeon Master's Guide* as you desire.

Now, everything the Darklord knew changes and they find themself a prisoner within a domain of their own.

Creating a Domain

The guidelines in this section help you create your own unique Domain of Dread. This setting's details should reflect the Darklord of the domain, being a reflection of that villain's evil and torment. Use the "Genres of Horror" section later in this chapter or your own grim imaginings to inspire the details of your nightmare domain.

Darklord's Shadows

A Darklord lurks at the heart of every Domain of Dread. Everything in their realm is inspired by or personalized to them in some way. Some domains might be dismal ruins reflective of past glories, others might be cheery realms where the Darklord is forever an outsider, and still others might embody everything a Darklord once strove for and be awful nonetheless.

A Darklord's domain often includes sights, sounds, and smells that serve as constant painful reminders of the Darklord's wicked past. To start creating your domain, choose three of the evil acts your Darklord committed. Consider selecting those that best complement the players' characters and that don't conflict with any boundaries discussed in your group's session zero (see "Preparing for Horror" in chapter 4). For each evil act, imagine the scene where it took place, and then answer the following questions:

- What does the act sound like from a distance or to someone in the next room?
- How does the act, or its consequences, smell?
- What colors demand attention from the surroundings, decor, or aftermath?
- What shapes, symbols, or decorations stand out?
- What does the light or darkness hide or reveal?
- Are there any sudden or subtle movements one's eyes are drawn to?
- Who is there?
- How are they breathing?
- What are they feeling or thinking? Is it about this scene or something else entirely?
- Are words spoken? Are they relevant to the scene or unrelated?
- Where does this take place?
- When the scene is over, what evidence remains?
- Before this unfortunate scene happens, what warnings were missed or foreshadowed?

Once you've considered these questions, write down your answers and review them. Mark or highlight the words that resonate or feel creepily evocative. As you proceed through domain creation, refer back to these details for inspiration.

Endless Torment

In every domain, instruments of suffering from the Darklord's past ensure their greatest desire remains in view but ever out of reach. Even though a Darklord is effectively immortal, their psychology never changes and their wounds never heal. Consider the following reasons why a Darklord's torment remains unignorable and central to a domain's story:

Deathless Returns. Those who die in a domain return reincarnated, fated to repeat a version of their former lives.

Endless Cycles. The Darklord shepherds another individual down a path of corruption in hopes of crafting a successor or recreating someone they lost. Despite the Darklord's perceived care and tutelage, the object of their attention never satisfies their expectations.

Last Gasp. An impending threat is on the cusp of overwhelming the Darklord and their domain. They can never look away as they are endlessly assaulted by cascading catastrophes, ever stemming from past choices.

Obstinate Ignorance. The Darklord is cursed to be unable to learn from past mistakes or perceive their own failings, though they're convinced that this time will be different.

Shocking Reminders. The domain is drowning in symbolic reminders of the Darklord's inadequacies. When symbolism is too subtle, the literal specters from the Darklord's past return to haunt them.

Unpleasant Hope. The Darklord's desire—commonly their bond—is present and obvious, but still unattainable. This instills hope in the Darklord that they are unable to deny, resist, or ignore. Furthermore, they are overcome by their desire's presence, spurring them to act irrationally.

Domain Overview

The domain's buildings, natural elements, and landmarks all represent the Darklord's vile past. When developing these features, follow these steps:

Specify Locations. Choose locations similar to settings that appear in your Darklord's past, or take inspiration from the Settings tables in the "Genres of Horror" section later in this chapter.

Combine Locations and Visceral Details. In a few sentences, describe how the domain's most prominent locations are twisted with suggestions that arose from answering the questions in the "Darklord's Shadows" section. Pair opposites together, something creepy with something cute, dead with alive, threatening with welcoming. Mix details together in unexpected ways, the more unnatural or off-putting the better.

ABOARD HER SHIP, *RIVER DANCER*, LARISSA SNOWMANE TRAVELS
THE ENDLESS DOMAINS, GUIDED BY FATE AND SONG.

Rationalize and Normalize. Outline the justifications inhabitants use to pretend nothing is wrong. What could reasonably explain their surreal experiences? They claim rivers of blood are crimson due to natural clay deposits, the devilish lights in the swamp are nothing but swamp gas, and the current reclusive count is the descendant of the region's original reclusive count. Many of the domain's inhabitants are likely creations of the Dark Powers and the domain is the only reality they know, but what logical and psychological leaps might an outsider need to make to sleep at night?

CULTURAL SPECIFICS

As you develop your domain, consider the culture and how it emerges from this tragic setting. What might be most unsettling for the Darklord: if the culture is one with familiar strictures, one they opposed or were an outsider in, or something completely unknown or alien to them? While a domain's culture might take inspirations from fantastical or historical examples, remember that a domain isn't a functional or even logical construction. Domains are glimpses into the Darklord's static and often exaggerated or flawed perception of a time, place, or situation. A domain's inhabitants never develop, and they never reach their goals. A domain's oppressive

inquisition is no closer to rooting out evil today than it was a thousand years ago. This isn't remarkable; it merely is as it has always been, and forces within a domain contort to maintain this status quo.

For inspiration into your domain's culture, consider the following questions:

- What does the culture fear?
- What does the culture consider taboo?
- What is scarce, and how do inhabitants compensate for this scarcity?
- Who or what does the culture inflict harm upon?
- How does the culture treat outsiders?
- What values does the culture hold that not everyone abides by?
- How is the culture exaggerated, a parody, or otherwise unrealistic?
- How does the culture prevent change?
- What is the general attitude toward the Darklord?

Don't get bogged down with the particulars of a working society. It doesn't matter how a village in a domain of endless night grows crops, but it does matter that the supplies are about to run out. These details can fade into the background as your adventures focus on more exciting threats, or you can highlight the cosmic dread that declares, yes, this place doesn't make sense at all, yet it persists.

For a specific example, consider the domain of Barovia in chapter 3. Not one villager in Barovia thinks it's wise to live in the shadow of Castle Ravenloft, and yet the villagers don't relocate, nor can they imagine living anywhere else. Life is as it's always been and could never be better, but it's constantly threatened with becoming worse.

MONSTERS

Ghosts, mind flayers, werewolves—every monster is a story. Consider which monsters complement or contrast a Darklord's story. In a few sentences, describe which monsters best represent the Darklord's evil and which might work against the Darklord's schemes. For example, a wicked scientist Darklord might be aided by flesh golems and crawling claws, but they are opposed by dryads and ghosts who suffer from the Darklord's experiments. For inspiration, refer to the "Darklord's Shadows" section and your answers to the questions there, as well as the Monsters tables in the "Genres of Horror" section later in this chapter.

MISTY BORDERS

In a few sentences, describe how the Mists of Ravenloft operate in your domain. This might largely be the same as detailed at the beginning of chapter 3, or they too might reflect the Darklord's nature. Consider the following questions:

- What shapes, sounds, and smells appear within the Mists?
- Do the Mists behave in some predictable way?
- What stories do the domain's people ascribe to the Mists? Do they ascribe a personality to them?
- Where do the Mists appear besides the domain's borders?
- How does a Darklord use the Mists to close their domain's borders (detailed in chapter 3)?

ADVENTURES

The story of a Darklord and their domain is one and the same. Once you know your Darklord and the general shape of their domain, consider the types of encounters and adventures that play out in this land. For inspiration, refer to the Plots tables in the "Genres of Horror" section later in this chapter, and consider the following story elements.

Captive Audience. Determine some aspect of the domain or Darklord that captures the characters' attention. How is this matter urgent and time-sensitive? What can the heroes learn that points them to larger threats or the Darklord's past? How does this threat connect to the Darklord seeking their desires? Consider who might need the characters' aid and might guide them to deeper mysteries.

Detail Key Locations. Briefly describe distinct locations suitable for adventure, where the heroes confront the Darklord's threats. For inspiration, refer to the Setting and Adventure Sites tables in the "Genres of Horror" section later in this chapter or the "Supernatural Regions" section of *Tasha's Cauldron of Everything*.

Supporting Cast. Consider what types of characters support the Darklord, exacerbate their threat, or oppose them. How do characters take the Darklord's situation from bad to worse, whether as fanatical supporters or tragic victims? Write down three types of characters who are aligned with the Darklord and three who aren't. Sketch out these characters broadly, perhaps noting only their professions or roles in adventures. You can expand on their details as your adventures take shape.

Entangling the Heroes. The Darklord might instantly sense visitors entering their domain, while the heroes have no reliable means of identifying the Darklord. Describe why the Darklord is interested in the characters. The Darklord Connections table provides examples of such connections.

Interactions with the Darklord. Imagine situations that allow the players' characters and the Darklord to socialize without the encounter immediately spiraling into violence. For inspiration, consider the circumstances on the Darklord Interactions table.

DARKLORD CONNECTIONS

d8	Connection
1	An adventurer reminds the Darklord of their bond, desire, or loved one.
2	An adventurer shares a Darklord's flaw.
3	The Darklord and an adventurer share camaraderie over a mutual ideal.
4	The Darklord believes they can teach an adventurer, making them their apprentice or inheritor.
5	An adventurer is a reincarnated version of the Darklord's beloved or their murderer.
6	The Darklord is convinced that an adventurer is the key to finally attaining their desire.
7	The Darklord immediately looks up to an adventurer and seeks to emulate them to grim extremes.
8	An adventurer is a reincarnated younger version of the Darklord before they became irredeemable.

Darklord Interactions

d8	Encounter
1	The Darklord promises to give the adventurers what they want if they join the Darklord for dinner.
2	The Darklord contacts the adventurers via letters or dreams.
3	The Darklord meets the adventurers disguised as a nonthreatening inhabitant or animal.
4	The Darklord meets the adventurers at a ceremony, funeral, or wedding where violence is discouraged.
5	The Darklord meets the adventurers at a public market, festival, temple, or library, surrounded by a crowd of innocents.
6	The Darklord possesses the body of someone the adventurers care about.
7	The Darklord possesses the body of one of the adventurers.
8	The Darklord invites the adventurers to a negotiation, promising nonviolent solutions to a conflict.

The Domain's Downfall

Once you know what your domain and Darklord are, think ahead to the climax of your adventures.

A Darklord likely can't be defeated by combat alone, so what is their weakness? In one or two sentences, describe this weakness, where it is in the domain, how the Darklord attempts to conceal this Achilles' heel, and how adventures might exploit it to bring the Darklord down.

Then, assuming the Darklord is defeated, consider what happens next and how that's relevant to the player characters, addressing the following questions:

- Can the Darklord die permanently?
- Under what circumstances might they return?
- What happens to their domain?
- Does a new Darklord rise?
- Does the domain permanently dissolve?
- Can the adventurers escape the domain?
- Do the adventurers return home or travel to another domain?

Unleash Your Horror

At this point, you should have a wealth of information about your Darklord, domain, the types of adventures you might run involving both, and a general idea of how the Darklord might be defeated. As you review your notes, consider where you can make connections between elements, establish recurring themes, and potentially foreshadow circumstances your adventures will focus on. Don't feel like you need to have answers for every question your Darklord or domain raises; many of these details can be defined as your adventures play out or by focusing on elements your players gravitate toward.

Now that you have a framework for your Darklord and domain, review the following "Genres of Horror" section. The details in that section can help you add exciting and shocking specifics to your creations as you prepare to unleash them on unsuspecting characters.

Genres of Horror

This section describes several horror subgenres, elements common to certain types of horror stories you can use to inspire your own Darklords and Domains of Dread. These sections provide suggestions for creating monsters; villains; torments for Darklords; settings; adventure sites; and plots evocative of horror stories, films, and games rooted in these genres, along with tables of inspiration for each. Don't hesitate to mix and match pieces from different genres to create your own uniquely terrifying adventures.

The monster lists presented throughout this section reference creatures found in chapter 5 of this book (*VGR*) and the *Monster Manual* (*MM*). Also, for examples of fully detailed Darklords and domains employing these genres, look ahead to chapter 3.

BODY HORROR

Body horror as a genre examines a universal fear: our own failing anatomies. We rarely think about what goes on beneath our skin. We understand that the organs operate in harmony: the heart beats, the lungs pump air, and the gastrointestinal system labors to supply us with nutrients. But we don't ponder the minutiae. Like whether embryonic parasites encyst in our brains, or what stage of cirrhosis we might be facing, or if tumors bloom deep in parts of ourselves we hope never to see.

When creating adventures involving body horror, use this lack of awareness. Focus on the unpredictability of flesh. Pull from the knowledge that even seeming robust health might be an illusion, that we're not sacred beasts, that we might be incubating fecund, hungry, or malicious parasites right now.

In addition, consider the following genre tropes when creating your body horror domain:

- Physical transformations are common and might affect more than bodies. Objects, architecture, and the natural world might be anthropomorphized in terrifying ways.
- Characters suffer aberrant or excessive growth, whether of organs, discordant appendages, or unnatural materials.
- Though gore often takes center stage in body horror stories, it's often a side effect of stories about fear of change, difference, mortality, physical harm, disease, or other fears.
- Body horror doesn't need to be messy. Swapping bodies, turning to stone, or even gaining one's ideal form might all feature in this genre.
- The genre has a history of portraying disability as monstrous. Be aware of those tropes and avoid them.

BODY HORROR MONSTERS

Any monster might be the focus of body horror plots. Know what your players are anticipating so you can distort those expectations. A poised elf revealed to be a husk puppeted by sapient worms can be as frightening as any eldritch horror.

A variety of monsters can be used without modification. This includes all manner of parasitic Beasts, Aberrations, Undead, and other creatures with unusual digestive systems or weird reproductive cycles.

BODY HORROR MONSTERS

Challenge	Creature	Source
1	Carrionette	VGR
2	Gibbering mouther	MM
3	Carrion stalker	VGR
3	Doppelganger	MM
4	Black pudding	MM
4	Strigoi	VGR
5	Flesh golem	MM
5	Red slaad	MM
6	Medusa	MM
6	Zombie clot	VGR
8	Chain devil	MM
10	Aboleth	MM

BODY HORROR VILLAINS

Villains of this genre present as tragic figures, whether they're hereditary cannibals, captives enduring some forced metamorphosis, scientists looking to reverse death, or academics who went too far in the pursuit of knowledge.

BODY HORROR VILLAINS

d10	Villain
1	An abandoned homunculus made in the image of its creator's child, now left to fester alone
2	A scientist who, hoping to keep their spouse alive, grafted the spouse onto their body
3	A seething mass of fungi that grows more intelligent with every sapient life it engulfs
4	A guardian angel possessed by the vile blood of the demons it has slain
5	An aging king obsessed with creating a new body so he can continue his reign indefinitely
6	A cancer possessed by the mind of a dead necromancer that seeks to regrow his body
7	A monarch who feeds their cannibal children, no matter the cost
8	The priests of a forgotten god who attempt to raise their deity from the flesh of the faithful
9	A house that remembers having tenants and will do anything to regain them
10	A grieving mortician who sculpts every face she encounters into the countenance of her lost love

BODY HORROR TORMENTS

Darklords in this genre draw their power from their biological changes or gain abilities that assist them in fulfilling their appetites. Their torment is rooted in the physiological and, frequently, in fecund and uncontrollable growth.

BODY HORROR TORMENTS

d8	Torment
1	The Darklord is pockmarked with eyes that never close and never allow for sleep.
2	The Darklord suffers ever-growing, tumorous organs, the mass expanding beyond them to choke their dwelling.
3	The Darklord possesses a second starving mouth in their torso, one that howls unless fed.
4	The Darklord can't control their transformation into a beast and back.
5	The voices of those the Darklord have wronged scream endlessly from inside them.
6	The Darklord aches daily with a monstrous, unceasing hunger.
7	The Darklord is perpetually gravid with monstrous egg sacs that hatch waves of insects.
8	The Darklord has extraneous limbs that tear the Darklord apart then re-stitch the pieces.

BODY HORROR SETTINGS

Body horror can occur anywhere, from mundane backdrops to garishly unsettling locations.

BODY HORROR SETTINGS

d8	Setting
1	A country of red muscle, with bleeding eyes embedded in the hair-strangled trees
2	A world of monuments and houses, all made of flesh
3	A domain ordinary save for the abundance of black hair, the strands always moving even when there is no breeze
4	A neighborhood of derelict houses, each one composed of numerous mimics
5	An ocean of undead leviathans, still moving despite the entrails bubbling from their burst torsos
6	A forest of black pines draped in bodies
7	A slaughterhouse larger than it appears on the outside, full of victims mutely awaiting slaughter
8	A system of subterranean tunnels, their walls spackled with fossils or mummified organs

BODY HORROR ADVENTURE SITES

Body horror is exceptionally unnerving in juxtaposition with mundane settings, particularly in places where the characters are isolated from help, treatment, or confirmation that their torment is real.

BODY HORROR ADVENTURE SITES

d8	Adventure Site
1	A derelict ship, buried for mysterious reasons
2	A vine-covered, ostensibly abandoned prison
3	The cavernous gut of a dead, multi-eyed behemoth
4	An inn in the valley, its insides dark and smoke-drowned
5	An asylum, abandoned save for vermin
6	A cave system, slick and comprised of gleaming black rock
7	An old church sitting astride a warren of ancient tunnels
8	A sprawling university, older than the town surrounding it, and older still than the memories of its inhabitants

BODY HORROR PLOTS

Adventures in body horror realms are often tests of endurance, whether players are attempting to hold out until rescue arrives, endeavoring to mount a rescue themselves, or trying to escape somewhere on their own. Alternatively, they may be investigative in nature, requiring the heroes to uncover what dark secret lies behind the mundane.

BODY HORROR PLOTS

d8	Plot
1	Learn who's organizing the local dinner parties before more epicureans die of autophagia.
2	Stop whatever is stealing the livers from the town's guard.
3	Find out what is causing the children of the city to transform into misshapen statues.
4	Stop whatever is killing the sea life and transforming them into monsters.
5	End the curse that is leaving the beasts of forests dead, mutated, and halfway human.
6	Stop the infestation before it can use more townsfolk as incubators for giant insects.
7	Solve the mystery of whatever is causing a town's inhabitants to melt into giant blobs.
8	Cast out the fiends that have infiltrated a community by wearing the corpses of the recently dead.

COSMIC HORROR

Cosmic horror revolves around the fear of personal insignificance. The genre is predicated on the idea of entities so vast and so genuinely beyond our comprehension that we cannot fathom their simplest motivations. To see them is to become lost in their magnitude and the evidence that we have never, will never, and could never matter to the cosmos at large.

The genre deals with how alien forces might alter us, perverting our expectations and understanding of autonomy, debasing our minds, and separating us from what makes us human. Sometimes it is the result of a process we invite. Other times it simply happens, an accident of circumstance we can only hope to survive.

However you spin it, this genre involves a loss of control, an absence of autonomy, and the sense of insignificance within an indifferent universe.

In addition, consider the following genre tropes when creating your cosmic horror domain:

- There is no good or evil, no law or chaos.
- Be vague. Cosmic horror emerges through imagination and the indescribable, not details.
- At its best, cosmic horror makes characters feel gradually unmoored from their familiar reality.
- Cosmic horror is about ineffable forces driven by motivations humans can't understand.
- Cults, forbidden books, and strange symbols form the cornerstones of cosmic horror.
- The genre has a history of framing marginalized demographics as monstrous and stigmatizing mental illness. Be aware and avoid those tropes.

COSMIC HORROR MONSTERS

Monsters that work well in cosmic horror adventures enact change on their unwilling victims. Cosmic horror focuses on unknowable entities and creatures that see into the minds of their enemies and use what they find against them. Any monster can easily be modified to suit adventures in this genre, perhaps being controlled by a hidden intelligence or vast cosmic force.

COSMIC HORROR MONSTERS

Challenge	Creature	Source
1/4	Kuo-toa	MM
2	Intellect devourer	MM
2	Pentadrone	MM
3	Brain in a jar	VGR
3	Githyanki warrior	MM
3	Grell	MM
5	Vampiric mind flayer	VGR
7	Bodytaker plant	VGR
7	Mind flayer	MM
7	Yuan-ti abomination	MM
8	Unspeakable horror	VGR
10	Aboleth	MM
13	Beholder	MM
19	Lesser star spawn emissary	VGR
21	Greater star spawn emissary	VGR
23	Kraken	MM

COSMIC HORROR VILLAINS

When the cosmic horror villains are mortal, they're wretched creatures, perpetrating unimaginable horrors in the hope of an outcome they can't properly articulate. Beyond them are monstrous beings, the spawn of horrors or those who've come to think of themselves as such. Past these harbingers are true cosmic horrors, inscrutable beings, godlike terrors, and the embodiments of forces unlikely to be interacted with and whose very beings are likely anathema to characters.

COSMIC HORROR VILLAINS

d8	Villain
1	A smiling minstrel with yellow eyes and music that drives listeners to murder
2	A priest obsessed with creating a shelter that will preserve her through the coming apocalypse
3	The mayor of a town who will do anything to make sure the citizens finish their sacred transformation
4	An astronomer broken and enraptured by what they saw in the stars
5	An old scientist convinced he must make his body the perfect host for an ageless being's emissary
6	A coroner who believes a message is being relayed to him through the bodies he autopsies
7	The head librarian of an ancient sect, who seeks secrets hidden within her peers
8	A spoiled noble who intends to raise a cult to feed to the realm they want access to

Cosmic Horror Torments

Darklords in this genre are endowed with powers stemming from their studies or ancestry, or granted by ancient numinosities. Darklords in cosmic horror realms commonly suffer psychological torments.

Cosmic Horror Torments

d8	Torment
1	The Darklord is obsessed with music, their body warping to embody whatever song they hear.
2	The Darklord is transforming into a long-extinct being or something from the far-flung future.
3	The Darklord sees multiple dimensions at once and is going blind from their incandescence.
4	The Darklord is haunted by otherworldly masters that whisper from reflective surfaces.
5	The Darklord incubates something within them, an entity that slowly eats through their skin.
6	The Darklord is emptying of their own thoughts and filling with the voices of their scrolls.
7	The Darklord randomly screams their masters' words, messages that etch upon stone and flesh.
8	Any object the Darklord sees is drained of all but one portentous color.

Cosmic Horror Settings

Cosmic horror frequently takes place in academic or maritime settings, both of which imply access to hidden knowledge, whether literal or metaphorical. When not in mortal realms, cosmic horror dimensions trend toward being unnatural, logic-defying places.

Cosmic Horror Settings

d8	Setting
1	A wind-blasted dimension of indigo sand and eyeless statues
2	A world with slowly vanishing land masses being consumed by an obsidian sea
3	A kingdom of rusting spires ruled by oblivious academics
4	A land possessed by fear of the colossi that move only during dawn and dusk
5	A red ocean that manifested without warning
6	An ambulatory forest riddled with glowing eyes
7	A kingdom of undying monarchs who outnumber their frightened subjects
8	A dimension of featureless white, broken up only by the eyes that blink across the landscape

Cosmic Horror Adventure Sites

Cosmic horror is rarely overt save at critical moments, relying on creating subtle but growing unease and leaving details to the imagination.

Cosmic Horror Adventure Sites

d8	Adventure Site
1	A hidden floor of the royal library
2	The ninth basement beneath a family home that seems normal from the outside
3	A decrepit manor, empty save for staff who swear the lord is merely preoccupied
4	A small inn in the mountains that smells perpetually of brine
5	The place in the forest where all the animals come to die
6	A fortress manned by paladins, all of whom removed their own tongues
7	A sewage system that predates the city above
8	A thin chapel in the woods, whose bells rings without ceasing

Cosmic Horror Plots

Adventures in cosmic horror realms are bleak, desperate affairs where the best one can hope for is to survive relatively intact. There is no stopping the ultimate evil, but players may aspire to temporarily seal it away.

Cosmic Horror Plots

d8	Plot
1	Help a parent recover a child who's gone missing in the impossibly vast space underneath their bed.
2	Stop a sapient, unholy tome from reaching a group of cultists.
3	Save the inheritors of an ancient sect before they transform into horrors.
4	Stop the sacrifice of a young noble by those who believe the noble's grandchild will end the world.
5	Find and stop the musician whose music has robbed entire cities of sleep.
6	Survive an evening in the sinking, ancestral home of a hydrophobic family.
7	Discover what is dragging the people of a hamlet out of their homes, garbing them in silver, and leading them into the surf to drown.
8	Learn why the bakers of a small town have started making pastries filled with a popular, delicious, and faintly glowing blue goo.

DARK FANTASY

Dark fantasy is as much a genre of fantasy as it is a genre of horror. Generally, any tale featuring both supernatural elements and horror themes might be considered dark fantasy, whether it's a fantasy story steeped in horror elements or an otherwise realistic world that features a supernatural terror. Dark fantasy refers to fantasy worlds where grim themes, nihilistic plots, or horrifying elements inform a fantasy tale. Evil dominates a dark fantasy setting, with depravity being commonplace and life holding little value.

How dark you want to make your fantasy is up to you, but keep in mind the role of heroes and ensure places for light in your dark fantasy domain. If a domain holds no place for hope, there's also little call for resistance and meaningful plots.

In addition, consider the following genre tropes when creating your dark fantasy domain:

- Good does not always win. Evil individuals with great power and unopposed schemes might be the norm.
- The lines between good and evil are blurred. Choices involve deciding which outcome is least bad.
- Corruption and suspicion flourish among organizations and individuals.
- Magic and magic items might be rarer or require a bargain or sacrifice to use.
- Antiheroes are common—characters tainted by the world's evil or those who refuse to be considered heroes.

DARK FANTASY MONSTERS

Any monster can find a place in a dark fantasy plot. D&D's most iconic threats—such as dragons and beholders—are well suited to horror-tinged tales, as are any other supernatural foes. Chapter 5 details how to make even the most familiar monsters into fear-worthy threats.

DARK FANTASY MONSTERS

Challenge	Creature	Source
1/8	Gremishka	VGR
1/4	Goblin	MM
1/4	Sprite	MM
3	Displacer beast	MM
4	Shadow demon	MM
5	Umber hulk	MM
6	Drider	MM
7	Necrichor	VGR
8	Fomorian	MM
8	Inquisitor of the Mind Fire	VGR
10	Yochlol	MM
13	Beholder	MM
15	Purple worm	MM
17	Death knight	MM
17	Adult blue dracolich	MM
21	Lich	MM

DARK FANTASY VILLAINS

Villains occupy places of prominence or control in dark fantasy domains. This manifests as political control, military authority, or physical or magical might that allows them to directly dominate others.

DARK FANTASY VILLAINS

d10	Villain
1	A machine that believes it's a resurrected tyrant and seeks to rebuild its empire in iron
2	The leader of a subterranean people who plots to manipulate the moon to blot out the sun's searing light
3	A high priest intent on shifting an entire nation into their god's otherworldly realm
4	A desperate general who unleashes otherworldly armies or war machines that they can't control
5	A massive treant who has allied with exploitative raiders and seeks to fell every forest
6	A sage who, heedless of the consequences, solves an endless war by preventing anyone from dying
7	A member of a cabal of eternal royals who support a war against Mount Celestia, as their immortality relies on the blood of angels
8	The commander of a legion of soul-addicted templars who punish crimes by burning criminals into psychoactive spirit dust
9	An ancient dragon whose godlike magic drains the domain of life
10	A god who killed all their peers and now rules the mortal realm

Dark Fantasy Torments

For Darklords in dark fantasy settings, power is at the root of their suffering. Perhaps their rise to dominance led them to sacrifice what mattered to them most, or they secretly seek to be rid of their might but fear being without it.

Dark Fantasy Torments

d8	Torment
1	The Darklord's regime is fraught with spies and saboteurs, increasing the Darklord's paranoia.
2	Worthless sycophants surround the Darklord, their incessant praise making every success hollow.
3	The Darklord's incredible power uncontrollably damages everything the Darklord cares for.
4	Others excessively revere or fear the Darklord, leaving the Darklord isolated.
5	Imagined or remembered rivals endlessly critique the Darklord, causing them doubt.
6	Society preemptively celebrates an achievement the Darklord will never be able to provide.
7	The Darklord seeks the pleasure of lost glories, engaging in hollow contests against unworthy foes.
8	The Darklord manufactures catastrophes to distract from their inability to fulfill their role.

Dark Fantasy Settings

Sinister individuals leave their marks upon dark fantasy domains, whether as oppressive architecture, unavoidable propaganda, or scars upon an exploited environment. Alternatively, the setting might exhibit the effects of a disaster—perhaps an event that gave rise to brutal powers. Such scars appear both upon the setting and upon its inhabitants.

Dark Fantasy Settings

d8	Setting
1	A land where towering stents pierce magical ley-lines, allowing their power to be drained
2	A country devastated by magical pollution or the fallout of weapons used in an age-old war
3	An empire covered in the watchful symbols of an all-seeing religion
4	A city adrift on a sea full of primeval predators
5	A land dotted with the floating and fallen ruins of magical megastructures
6	A world where an unstoppable ooze, infection, or hive encroaches on civilization
7	A demiplane created by unknowable beings and populated with their test subjects
8	A place of punishment or endless boredom that a Darklord believes is part of the afterlife

Dark Fantasy Adventure Sites

Evil is entrenched and effective in dark fantasy domains, truths reflected by grandiose adventure locations. Their size and grandeur seem out of proportion with the common structures of the domain and the magic that helped create them is clearly beyond the reach of mere mortals to create or destroy.

Dark Fantasy Adventure Sites

d8	Adventure Site
1	An expanding labyrinth that grows to protect the evil imprisoned at its heart
2	A forest where every tree grows from the body of a mummified hero
3	A magical factory that distills living beings into the reagents of a wish-granting elixir
4	A criminal consortium's lavish sewer-academy, where recruits are transformed to be perfectly suited to enacting one near-impossible heist
5	The fractured mind-scape of a powerful but dormant sentient weapon
6	A massive construct-cathedral built to exact the ultimate expression of faith and sacrifice
7	A palace where the nonhumanoid inhabitants purposefully petrified themselves
8	A fortress with seven locked gates that seal off the underworld

Dark Fantasy Plots

Adventures in dark fantasy domains involve unlikely or reluctant heroes (or rival villains) striking back against the evil at work in the land. This might involve taking on a world-ruining conspiracy or the street-level depravity affecting a single slum.

Dark Fantasy Plots

d8	Plot
1	Track down a beholder-shaped flesh golem and learn why it's targeting specific individuals.
2	Seal a portal to a demonic realm that opens within the mouth of an innocent acolyte.
3	Cure a virus turning people into shadows.
4	Mount a defense against the swarm of giant spiders that's declared war on bipeds.
5	Prevent a mighty spell that a coven of witches is casting using a volcanic caldera as a cauldron.
6	Keep a nation from tearing itself apart when it's revealed the beloved ruler is a lich.
7	Banish a spirit haunting the moon.
8	Uncover the identity of an otherworldly coward who's hiding among mortals, avoiding the destructive search of the immortals they fled.

FOLK HORROR

Folk horror adventures involve traditions, beliefs, and perceptions that are passed down through generations and take terrifying twists. For those who ascribe to hidden traditions, sacrifices to strange gods or placations to lurking monsters are everyday events. For outsiders, though, these practices reveal the subjectivity of normalcy, societal truth, and taboos.

Folk horror explores fears of isolation, superstition, paranoia, and lost truths. Seemingly idyllic communities, rural reclusiveness, forgotten traditions, and naturalistic cults all frequently feature in folk horror adventures, particularly as they contrast with what majorities consider the status quo.

In folk horror tales, characters often discover that their beliefs aren't as universally held as they assumed, and those beliefs provide no defense against those who reject them. In such stories, characters discover their perception of the way the world works is in the minority as those around them practice traditions beyond their understanding. Alternatively, characters might realize their own beliefs are lies as others reveal unsettling truths.

Communities that ascribe to the traditions of folk horror stories are rarely tolerant of nonbelievers. Outsiders might be given a chance to adopt the community's ways, but otherwise are considered heretics or corrupting elements. Assuredly, their ancient traditions have ways of excising blasphemers.

Consider the following genre tropes when creating your folk horror domain:

- Strange and potentially dangerous traditions flourish in isolated or otherwise private communities. This might mean a rural village, a lost civilization, or cabal within a larger community.
- A community's surroundings often influence its beliefs. Their traditions might be naturalistic or relate to some sort of ancient lore.
- Art, symbols, tools, celebrations, and other trappings of belief help make a community's traditions more specific and eerie.

- Community members typically hide their beliefs, whether physically obscuring them or by manipulating others in power.
- Communities in folk horror stories often serve as a grim mirror of some aspect of accepted society.
- Beliefs highlighted in folk horror stories might or might not be true.
- Folk horror communities often have dramatic ways of using outsiders or purging nonbelievers.

FOLK HORROR MONSTERS

Eerie traditions and unnatural alliances with monsters fill folk horror tales. When something's been normalized over generations, even the strangest practices and most dangerous beings might be accepted as part of society. Does the community in your folk horror domain live alongside deadly monsters? Does a regional faith consider an obvious abomination their god? Does a group make offerings to placate imaginary spirits of the fields?

Any monster might feature in your folk horror domains. It's acceptance of such creatures and the trappings of willing servitude that provide sources of dread. The Folk Horror Monsters table suggests just a few creatures suited to this genre.

FOLK HORROR MONSTERS

Challenge	Creature	Source
1/2	Myconid adult	MM
2	Awakened tree	MM
2	Cult fanatic	MM
2	Will-o'-wisp	MM
3	Green hag	MM
3	Werewolf	MM
5	Shambling mound	MM
7	Bodytaker plant	VGR
9	Jiangshi	VGR

FOLK HORROR VILLAINS

Folk horror villains are manipulative, leading others to follow traditions they might not even entirely understand. They zealously defend their faith and community, and might eagerly seek new initiates or dangerous blasphemers.

FOLK HORROR VILLAINS

d8	Villain
1	A secluded temple's high priest who needs to find the perfect sacrifice before the annual festival
2	An erinyes that appears when youngsters speak a rhyme into a darkened mirror

d8	Villain
3	A night hag that dwells in the dreams of those who drink a special lavender and ergot tea
4	A shape-shifter that takes on the appearance of the last person it fed upon
5	A wicker giant that animates during the new moon, collecting sacrifices and punishing the unwary
6	A village of people who behave in archaic ways so they don't enrage an ancient, lingering ghost
7	A treant who demands living limbs to replace the branches of trees cleared by a town's construction
8	A protective giant made from the corpses of deceased villagers

FOLK HORROR TORMENTS

A folk horror domain's Darklord has been consumed by the traditions, land, or rituals they embody. They might not fully understand their own beliefs, though, causing them to fail in their duties or cause rites to spin out of control. Such Darklords remain devoted, though, desperately trying to prove themselves or satisfy the object of their belief.

FOLK HORROR TORMENTS

d6	Torment
1	The Darklord can't commune with the spirit they worship. They offer ever greater sacrifices in hopes of proving their worthiness.
2	The Darklord constantly, uncontrollably speaks prophecies.
3	The Darklord is haunted by the judgmental spirits of their predecessors.
4	The Darklord is the only one who adheres to an ancient faith and desperately works to convert nonbelievers.
5	The Darklord seeks to transform their body into a vessel or gate for the subject of their belief.
6	The Darklord knows the community's beliefs are false but keeps up the facade to maintain power.

FOLK HORROR SETTINGS

Folk horror stories often take place in isolated or rural areas, but they could be set anywhere insular communities thrive or traditions stagnate.

FOLK HORROR SETTINGS

d6	Setting
1	A countryside with stretches of hayfields, colorful barns, and perpetually smiling residents
2	An island floating in the air where ground-worshipers dream of the lands below

d6	Setting
3	A telepathic collective that townsfolk join by ingesting a rare fungus
4	Tunnels where sewer dwellers assure that the "blood of the city" ever flows
5	A glacier that residents never leave, lest the icy spirits haunting their community escape
6	Rival villages engaged in a private, age-old war

FOLK HORROR ADVENTURE SITES

The sites of folk horror adventures embody a community's traditions or what shelters it from society at large.

FOLK HORROR ADVENTURE SITES

d6	Adventure Site
1	A seemingly deserted chapel that has been burnt down and rebuilt a thousand times
2	A hag's hut that stands atop a growing hill of rotten sweets
3	A whispering pit once plugged by a monolith covered in prayer scrolls
4	A field where paths grow in corridor-like patterns leading to a ruin at the center
5	A mansion built incorporating a stone circle
6	A cavern where the glowing bones of an otherworldly being jut from the walls

FOLK HORROR PLOTS

Folk horror stories often involve outsiders or an unwitting new member of the community discovering a unsettling practices.

FOLK HORROR PLOTS

d8	Plot
1	Recover a missing villager who ran away to escape the local cult.
2	Hunt down the monster blamed for causing a blight: a unicorn meant to serve as a sacrifice.
3	Discover why anyone entering the city on horseback is imprisoned and sentenced to death.
4	Help a cult summon a fiend to combat an impending greater evil.
5	Defeat a violent hag who's protected by everyone in town and called "grandmother."
6	Escape an estate after the residents adopt the party and refuse to let them leave.
7	Learn why the characters bear uncanny resemblances to the founders of an underground village.
8	Slay a dragon and, in so doing, prove a character is the prophesied chosen one.

GHOST STORIES

Ghost stories number among the more psychologically elaborate genres of horror. Only through revealing tales of tragedy and past wrongs can heroes truly bring peace to forces that share their suffering with the living.

Ghost stories touch on fundamental issues of human existence: the nature of the soul, the weighty fact of mortality, and the burden of ancestry and history. Spirits represent heavy-handed instruments of supernatural justice, plunging those responsible for their deaths into a living hell where they suffer for their sins. They also represent grief and the need for closure, lingering in a place until they bring about the completion of the work they hoped to accomplish in life.

In addition, consider the following genre tropes when creating your haunted domain:

- All hauntings have a deep story, and the smallest details tell it. A simple locket or portrait might contain clues that explain a haunting.
- Personal ties give ghost stories weight. Consider tying the heroes to spirits in ways they won't predict, such as revealing that a phantasmal villain was a hero's ancestor.
- Heroes are pure-hearted or unsuspecting individuals whose resolve is shaken by the story's events. Look for ways to test heroes' psychology with your hauntings.
- Heroes need agency—a way to put spirits to rest. Once the story is revealed, ensure the way to combat the haunting is clear.
- Spirits are often evil, but they need not be. A spirit might appear to warn heroes of impending doom.

GHOST STORY MONSTERS

Any creature that embodies or serves as a response to past injustices or tragedies makes a strong addition to a ghost story. Don't limit yourself to incorporeal undead when creating your own hauntings. The "Haunted Traps" section of chapter 4 also explores options for creating threatening hauntings.

GHOST STORY MONSTERS

Challenge	Creature	Source
1/2	Death's head	VGR
1	Animated armor	MM
1	Death dog	MM
1	Scarecrow	MM
2	Specter (poltergeist)	MM
4	Banshee	MM
4	Ghost	MM
5	Revenant	MM
6	Gallow speaker	VGR
9	Treant	MM
10	Dullahan	VGR

GHOST STORY VILLAINS

While the villains in ghost stories are often spirits or haunted places, they might also be the individuals who provoked a haunting to begin with.

GHOST STORY VILLAINS

d10	Villain
1	A medium who feeds victims to spirits in exchange for power over them
2	The spirit of a long-dead murderer who stalks the same types of victims in death as in life
3	The haunted home of a cruel patriarch, who refuses to relinquish control of his descendants
4	A priest who marks the unworthy for death at the hands of the cathedral's hungry spirits
5	A phantom rider who sweeps through the village, stealing victims who disbelieve her legend
6	An unbound spirit that repeatedly manifests in victims' nightmares
7	The capricious phantasm of an amoral accident victim who torments victims for fun
8	The spirit of a former tyrant who demands sacrifices from the village she once ruled
9	A ghost hunter who inflicts hauntings on unwitting clients—and then charges to remove the undead
10	The spirit of an evil captain who lurks near their shipwreck, harassing vessels and crews that pass

GHOST STORY TORMENTS

Whether they're living monsters or ghosts, Darklords in ghost story settings are the architects of their own tragedies.

GHOST STORY TORMENTS

d8	Torment
1	The Darklord tames the spirits in his haunted mansion, but only when he sacrifices a memory.
2	The Darklord's skin is haunted, but she can temporarily release spirits from her elaborate scars.
3	A dozen phantoms cater to the Darklord; each spirit is an emotion he can no longer feel.
4	Vampiric spirits keep the Darklord forever young, but physical sensation fled them long ago.
5	Despite being alive, the Darklord is cursed with the inability to convince anyone they're not a spirit.
6	All spirits obey a Darklord who can't touch anyone without stealing their soul.
7	The Darklord fully controls the veil between this world and the spirit world, but if he steps outside his mansion, he'll be permanently destroyed.
8	Any animal the Darklord sees dies and comes to haunt the morbid zoo her home has become.

GHOST STORY SETTINGS

Suffering, tragic death, or a villain's monstrous evil manifest subtly in the places ghost stories are set. Typically, a setting's hauntings are revealed slowly, until the full nature of the horror is on display.

GHOST STORY SETTINGS

d8	Setting
1	A realm where speaking to spirits is just like speaking with the living
2	A graveyard city-state where all living residents are grave keepers
3	A nation where the residents observe grueling rituals to keep the angry dead appeased
4	A city where the victims of violence can't cross into the afterlife until their murders are solved
5	A ship with the same name and lines as a vessel lost at sea a hundred years earlier
6	A realm in which a common ritual allows a living individual to trade places with a dead one
7	An expansive forest in which a cruel noble once hunted the poor for sport
8	A land in which mediums are revered because they maintain the veil between the living and dead

GHOST STORY ADVENTURE SITES

Ghost stories are intensely personal, and adventures within the genre take place in a setting dripping with tragic history.

GHOST STORY ADVENTURE SITES

d6	Adventure Site
1	A decrepit conservatory whose inhabitants are prone to terrible accidents
2	A village graveyard that holds the victims of a terrible mass crime
3	A decrepit barn where dozens of remarkable animals lost their lives in a fire
4	An attic in which a hateful spirit has been sealed for decades
5	A theater in which, decades ago, an actor systematically poisoned their rivals
6	A swanky inn where, for years, nobles killed the staff to prevent word of their affairs getting out
7	A picturesque cliff that's a popular destination for lovers, despite the fact that couples frequently fall to their deaths
8	A lighthouse where a lone guard is the only living individual keeping an army of spirits at bay

GHOST STORY PLOTS

Ghost story adventures deal with learning the story behind a haunting and ultimately resolving it. They benefit from preserving the mystery behind a spirit's motivations until the heroes discover a hidden truth.

GHOST STORY PLOTS

d8	Plot
1	Investigate the bloody graffiti being left on the village's ancient walls and stop the vandal.
2	A dying hero is convinced they're going to return as a spirit. Prevent this from happening.
3	Discover why members of a prominent family never allow anyone to enter their guest house.
4	Solve the murder of a phantom who can say only the words "blood," "onions," and "wine."
5	Solve the murder of the countess, who drowned in the same well as her mother and grandmother.
6	Convince a stubborn miser to visit his haunted family home and put his deathless family to rest.
7	Discreetly follow a phantom vagabond to find out where she disappears to and with whom.
8	Learn why a mob of spirits besieges the local temple on the winter solstice each year.

GOTHIC HORROR

Gothic horror is about the terror within, not without. It shatters the illusion of humanity in a poignant way by holding a mirror up to us and saying: look at what we truly are, and look at what we pretend to be. Under that mask of civility, there is depravity. Under that thin veneer of society, there is wickedness. Under all the trappings of sophistication, are we not all predators or prey? Gothic horror shatters the lies we trick ourselves into believing and shows that we, not some distant entity, are and ever shall be the architects of our doom. The quest for perfection leads us to discover our own imperfection. Our quest for the divine leads us to believe we, ourselves, are gods. These are the themes that haunt stories of Gothic horror.

Consider the following genre tropes when creating your gothic horror domain:

- Gothic stories include intense, even exaggerated, emotions. Romances, rivalries, and life-changing events are common in these adventures.
- Atmosphere and a sense of dread are key to achieving a gothic feel. Set your story in an decrepit mansion, ruined cathedral, or other foreboding location.
- Gothic heroes are often virtuous, deeply passionate, or courageous. Find ways for adventures to test characters' beliefs and morality.
- Gothic villains are unrepentantly evil, but this shouldn't be immediately obvious. Drop hints about your villain's awful secrets before revealing them fully.
- Sacrifices feature prominently in gothic stories. Give characters heart-wrenching choices to make.

GOTHIC HORROR MONSTERS

Creatures imbued with tragedy or abominable origins work well in gothic horror adventures. Often, lower-level monsters embody aspects of a more powerful villain's evil, powers, or background. For example, swarms of bats suggest a vampire's connection to the creatures of the night, while werewolves speak toward a vampire's bloodthirsty nature.

GOTHIC HORROR MONSTERS

Challenge	Creature	Source
1/4	Zombie	MM
1	Ghoul	MM
2	Gargoyle	MM
2	Wereraven	VGR
3	Green hag	MM
3	Werewolf	MM
4	Succubus/incubus	MM
8	Nosferatu	VGR
11	Efreeti	MM
13	Loup garou	VGR
13	Vampire	MM

GOTHIC HORROR VILLAINS

Villains in gothic horror tales are subtle or unassuming until they reveal their true nature. Any intriguing figure with a dark secret can serve as a gothic horror villain, and gothic villains are most effective when they are slowly revealed as shockingly cruel, immoral, or the antithesis of goodness.

GOTHIC HORROR VILLAINS

d10	Villain
1	A reclusive noble who isn't a vampire, but uses his reputation as one to terrorize his vassals
2	An indulgent socialite who made a terrible bargain with a fell power to retain her youth
3	A scientist obsessed with creating the perfect poison, machine, or lifeform
4	A beloved magnate who abducts commoners to steal their blood for his beauty rituals
5	A celebrity who openly murders innocents but uses their charm to avoid repercussions
6	Someone who loves a monstrous creature and does anything to keep it fed and safe
7	A wealthy heir who manipulates the ambitious into committing terrible deeds
8	A poisoner who seeks to manipulate history through targeted killings
9	An artist who manufactures terrible accidents to provide inspiration and reference for her art
10	A monster hunter who accuses those they consider sinful of being monsters

GOTHIC HORROR TORMENTS

Self-debasement and self-loathing lurk at the heart of gothic villains' evil, whether they indulge in vices or are consumed with misanthropy. This results in villains who torment themselves viciously.

GOTHIC HORROR TORMENTS

d8	Torment
1	The Darklord's soul is so consumed by shadows that it extinguishes all light that shines on them.
2	The Darklord inherited unlimited wealth, but finery she wears turns to rags and food tastes like ash.
3	The Darklord is incomparably beautiful, but locals perceive him as a terrible beast.
4	Tattoos detailing the Darklord's sins cover their body.
5	Every night, the Darklord is the focus of a lavish ball, but during the day he turns into a lead statue.
6	A choir of spirits follows the Darklord, endlessly singing her sins.
7	The Darklord endlessly cries tears of blood, ink, poison, or molten iron.
8	The Darklord knows how he's going to die and sees evidence of impending doom everywhere.

GOTHIC HORROR SETTINGS

Ominous history, supernatural forces, and an underlying sinister air are staples of gothic horror settings.

GOTHIC HORROR SETTINGS

d8	Setting
1	A city-state where the rulers are secretly warring lycanthropes, hags, and vampires
2	A countryside littered with gigantic pieces of armor
3	A nation where fog hides packs of deadly beasts
4	An island where the inhabitants make sacrifices to avoid eerie transformations
5	A mountain-sized cathedral devoted to transforming a prophesied being into a deity
6	A forest of eternal night where bloodthirsty creatures live in monstrous peace
7	A city where all who die are cast in plaster and used to adorn tableau-covered avenues
8	An artist's paradise where cruelties are elevated to terrible and beautiful art forms

GOTHIC HORROR ADVENTURE SITES

Gothic horror stories often center on a forlorn structure in which depravity finds a welcome home.

GOTHIC HORROR ADVENTURE SITES

d8	Adventure Site
1	A mansion's forbidden east wing, where terrible noises sound from every night
2	A castle where all visitors are transformed into rats, bats, spiders, and other beasts
3	A science lab where preserved body parts carry the consciousnesses of their former owners
4	A hidden fighting arena where rivals and lovers battle to prove the strength of their emotions
5	A beautiful garden where the past keepers find immortality as statues and in ancient trees
6	A tower where honorable heroes are sworn to protect a monstrous ruler
7	A lavish inn where a random guest chokes on their own blood each night
8	A rectory where the stained glass windows hold the trapped souls of the pious

GOTHIC HORROR PLOTS

Poetic tragedy, the dichotomy between goodness and wickedness, and reckonings for wicked deeds are strong fodder for gothic horror plots.

GOTHIC HORROR PLOTS

d8	Plot
1	Discover why anyone who utters the prince's true name immediately turns to dust.
2	Investigate the disappearance of a scientist known only through their correspondence.
3	Help a repentant immortal lose centuries of painful memories.
4	Track down a serial killer who impales her victims on the same monument.
5	End an affliction that turns a noble into a living doll every night.
6	Settle a dispute between mortals and devils who both claim the same child is their next ruler.
7	Put to rest a pair of spirits that bring tragedy to any couple who tries to get married.
8	Find a way to end a land's generational curse that doesn't involve a group of innocents willingly sacrificing themselves.

OTHER HORROR GENRES

In addition to the aforementioned terrors, consider exploring any of the following horror genres when creating adventures in the Domains of Dread. Beyond these, there are dozens of other types of horror tales you can explore. Consider investigating the hallmarks of any of those frightful categories, or look into the genres of your own favorite scary films and stories. Understanding what makes a type of horror story frightening and how you can mimic or subvert genre tropes in your storytelling can provide endless inspiration for your terrifying adventures.

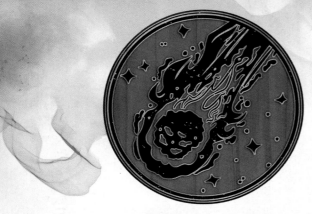

DISASTER HORROR

In disaster horror adventures, the world has fallen to ruin—or it's getting there fast. The unthinkable has happened and, as a result, society is collapsing. In these tales, a monster or villain might be replaced by cascading catastrophes like those brought about by a meteor strike or volcanic eruption. Regardless of a hero's power, the best-timed critical hit or the most powerful spell might not fix a city ruined by an earthquake or a world ravaged by plagues.

The disasters in your horror adventures need not be natural. Magical disruptions, temporal shifts, and violent interplanar rifts might sow all manner of supernatural chaos. Wars and relentless monster hordes—like legions of zombies or fiends—can also cause region- or world-changing ruin.

In all these cases, society breaks down. There are no inns to sleep in, healers are few or overtaxed, and anarchy rises as governments crumble. Environmental hazards, such as those in the *Dungeon Master's Guide*, might be extreme and lead to scarcity of food or other resources. Scared innocents, opportunistic scavengers, and leaderless military forces all seek to survive. The hopeless acts of others might even prove more horrifying than the provoking disaster.

When creating adventures inspired by disaster horror, ask yourself the following questions:

- What is the disaster? Is it natural, a supernatural event, or the effect of a terrifying weapon? Is it war or endless throngs of monsters?
- Was the disaster somehow manufactured? Is there a cause behind it?
- Is there a place that was somehow spared from the disaster?
- What parts of society have collapsed? Are most common people trying to ride out the disaster, or are they fleeing in search of safety?
- Who is taking advantage of the disaster? Are they normal people, monsters, or another threat?
- Does everyone believe in the danger of the disaster?
- Has the disaster given rise to extreme behaviors, such as paranoia, cultic beliefs, or cannibalism?
- Will the world ever be the same again?

OCCULT DETECTIVE STORIES

Adventures rooted in the occult detective genre straddle the line between fantasy, mystery, and horror. For the occult detective, solving paranormal mysteries is all part of the job. In these adventures, villains employ supernatural powers toward nefarious ends while characters act as detectives, interpreting events, learning patterns, deducing goals, and ultimately putting an end to the threat. Investigation and cleverness take center stage in these adventures, though as in the noir stories that inspire the genre, there's plenty of room for action.

Occult detective adventures can be just as terrifying as any other horror adventures, but also might be lighter in tone. Adventurers might experience terrors only after they've happened and face a foe only once they're prepared to end its threat. Of course, there are ways to create threats distinct to this genre, such as when villains view detectives as rivals or targets.

When creating an occult detective adventure, consider what monster, magic, or other supernatural force might lend a thrilling twist to some criminal enterprise. How will the characters catch an invisible assassin or a thief that pilfers extradimensional spaces? Once you know the villain's mode of operation, consider how it might give itself away. Even if you're not sure, listen to the characters' plans and give them opportunities to feel brilliant in the course of running your adventures.

When creating adventures inspired by occult detective stories, ask yourself the following questions:

- What criminal or supernatural force is at large? What crime is it committing, or how is it a problem?
- Who wants the villain stopped? Do they have a personal reason for this?
- What evidence has the villain left behind? How is the evidence initially misleading?
- What clarifying evidence will the characters discover in the course of their investigation?
- How are the villain's deeds terrifying or suggestive of a larger plot? Are the characters threatened?
- How might the characters trap the villain, draw them out, or predict their next move?

PSYCHOLOGICAL HORROR

Psychological horror stories create suspense by heightening or calling into question characters' states of mind, emotions, and perceptions. They often highlight the difference between what characters think and how they behave.

When creating adventures rooted in psychological horror, consider common fears and anxieties. These readily become metaphors for villains and monsters. Fear of being judged by one's peers might manifest as a jury of nothics, while fear of change could be represented by a medusa that petrifies those who threaten her community's status quo.

Uncertainty, paranoia, and blurred lines between reality and fiction also shape psychological horror stories. In your adventures, this might take the form of unreliable information. Characters might experience a deadly encounter only to wake up at the end, not having previously realized they were asleep. Before undermining characters' senses, though, make sure you know what's driving these skewed perceptions and how characters might overcome them. The "Fear and Stress" section of chapter 4 provides options for dealing with the stress of adventuring. If some force is actively trying to cause stress for characters, this might lead to its own psychological horror adventure.

Be aware that some classic psychological horror tales stigmatize mental illness. Work to avoid such tropes in your adventures as you consider the following questions:

- What are characters afraid of? Is a wizard afraid of losing their memory? Is a fighter afraid of growing old? Does a cleric fear their god is a lie?
- If every monster is a stand-in for something people fear, what do your favorite monsters embody? Can your adventures accentuate that?
- Why might a character think everyone around them is lying to them? Might this be paranoia, an actual conspiracy, or both? Who or what could pull the strings of such a plot?
- How can the environment change to undermine characters' sense of reality? The Mists already play into this, as could structures with no doors or stairs with no end, but what else might?

SLASHER HORROR

Every monster is a story, and many of those stories are horror stories. This brand of horror contends with relentless killers, which might be people or monsters. These adventures revel in grisly details, the suspense of an impending showdown with a powerful foe, and the fear that death waits right around the corner.

Adventures of this genre typically include one major antagonist that threatens a group. This might be a particularly large or cunning beast, a murderer who terrorizes a neighborhood, a monster stalking a town, or a supernatural menace who spreads a signature sort of death. When creating your own monster or slasher horror adventures, choose a creature with a challenge rating high enough that your party won't defeat it with a few lucky hits. Also consider foes with details you're eager to explore in various terrifying scenes. A medusa, for example, becomes all the more terrifying when it murders with petrified body parts or forces victims into unsettling poses before petrifying them. Also, consider who the villain's targets are and why the villain has chosen to prey upon that group. Is it out of hunger or for revenge, or does the creature have a more deep seated need to kill?

The relentless killers presented in chapter 5 provide perfect foes for adventures embracing this type of horror. Also, when creating adventures inspired by monster or slasher horror, ask yourself the following questions:

- Who is the monster or slasher? How do they kill? What has made them infamous?
- Why is a community defenseless against the killer?
- In what shocking ways does the killer use its powers?
- How does the killer avoid capture? Where does it hide from its pursuers?
- Does the killer think it's justified? Has the community wronged it in some way?
- What characters in your story exist only to be victims?
- What climactic event is sure to tempt the killer into the open?

Dr. Viktra Mordenheim, Darklord of Lamordia, crafts the perfect body for her newest band of golem-hunting mercenaries.

DOMAINS OF RAVENLOFT

IN A FAR-FLUNG CORNER OF THE PLANE OF Shadow drifts a hidden expanse of roiling mist and vague semi-reality. At this eerie edge of the multiverse, the Dark Powers collect the most wicked beings from across ages and worlds within inescapable, mist-shrouded domains. These are the Domains of Dread, the nightmare demiplanes that form the D&D setting of Ravenloft. Untold terrors lurk within these lands, yet the collection of the Dark Powers is far from complete.

This chapter provides information for the DM and explores the misty truths of the Domains of Dread, along with a sampling of the terrifying domains, dreaded Darklords, and daring wanderers trapped in the Dark Powers' clutches.

NATURE OF RAVENLOFT

Nothing one might assume about any world on the Material Plane is necessarily true in the Domains of Dread. The following sections detail how the Dark Powers manipulate the Land of the Mists, and what domain inhabitants accept as the ways of their world (or desperately avoid pondering).

THE MISTS

The Mists can always be found at a domain's borders but can also appear in dense banks that rise wherever adventures demand. Such banks might veil strangers or hidden foes, or they can transport those who enter them to distant lands, other domains, or even beyond the Domains of Dread. The Mists are inscrutable, but they ever serve the schemes of the Dark Powers, delivering creatures wherever these wicked forces desire.

The Dark Powers also grant Darklords limited ability to manipulate the Mists surrounding their domains, allowing most to open or close their domains' borders to others on a whim. If a domain's borders are closed, supernatural agitation is obvious to any who approach the Mists. This takes the form of roiling disturbances within the haze, menacing silhouettes, threatening sounds, or other activity themed to the Darklord or domain. Creatures that enter the Mists at this time, including flying creatures, are subject to the following effects:

- A creature that starts its turn in the Mists must succeed on a DC 20 Constitution saving throw or gain 1 level of exhaustion. This exhaustion can't be removed while the creature is in the Mists.

- No matter how far a creature travels in the Mists, or which direction it goes, it gets turned around so that it eventually ends up back in the domain it left.
- The area within the Mists is heavily obscured (see the *Player's Handbook* for details).

Most Darklords can keep their domains' borders closed indefinitely and can reopen them at will. For some Darklords, slightly varied effects manifest when they close their domains. Others are limited in their ability to affect their borders. For each domain, specifics appear in the "Closing the Borders" portion of the section on that domain's Darklord.

If a domain's borders are open, the domain is still not easy to escape from. The area within the Mists remains heavily obscured, but the Mists don't cause creatures to gain levels of exhaustion. Characters intent on passing through the Mists travel for 1d6 hours, then roll on the Wandering the Mists table to determine what happens.

WANDERING THE MISTS

d100	Effect
01–20	Characters emerge in a domain of your choosing.
21–40	Characters wander the Mists for another 1d6 hours, then roll on this table again.
41–65	Characters emerge from the Mists on stable ground 1d100 feet away from where they entered.
66–75	Characters emerge on stable ground a mile from where they entered the Mists at midnight of the night after they entered the Mists.
76–85	Characters emerge from the Mists inside a structure somewhere within the domain they tried to leave, perhaps a cave, crypt, shed, or closet.
86–95	Other creatures appear within the Mists. Roll any die. If you roll an even number, a lost and terrified **commoner** appears. If you roll an odd number, 2d6 **skeletons** or 1 **unspeakable horror** (see chapter 5) appears. After the encounter, another 1d6 hours pass, then roll on this table again.
96–99	Characters emerge from the Mists where they entered to find the domain changed. Perhaps someone the characters knew is gone, and no one has any knowledge of them ever existing.
100	Characters emerge from the Mists on a world on the Material Plane. After 1d6 hours, the Mists rise around them once more. Roll again on this table.

MIST TALISMANS

A Mist talisman is a nonmagical object, akin to a dowsing rod or a lodestone, that resonates with the unique nature of the domain where it originates, allowing the creature holding it to find a path through the Mists to that domain. By holding the talisman and focusing on its domain of origin, a creature in the Mists can reach that domain after 2d6 hours of travel. Any creatures that willingly follow the creature with the Mist talisman also reach the same destination. A Mist talisman is no help to a creature imprisoned within a domain's closed borders. If the borders of the destination domain are closed, roll on the Wandering the Mists table to determine what happens.

Mist talismans take ominous forms, and no two are alike. A family's burned holy book, a battered stuffed toy, a papyrus scroll, or any of the items on the Horror Trinkets table in chapter 1 might serve as Mist talismans. Few who dwell in the Domains of Dread know how to use Mist talismans or have interest in traveling to other domains. Those who do, though, might share a Mist talisman with adventurers or could know where such an item is located. You can use Mist talismans to guide characters from one domain to another as your adventures require.

The domains detailed in this chapter suggest Mist talismans that can be used to reach them, but these aren't exhaustive lists. Use them as inspiration for Mist talismans of your own design.

MAGIC AND METAPHYSICS

The Dark Powers manipulate the domains and creatures within their grasp in the most fundamental ways, controlling magic, the nature of life and death, and the means of escaping from their nightmare realms.

MYSTERIOUS MAGIC

In some domains, magic is an everyday part of life, while in others, insular communities fear it as the province of monsters. Few domains deny magic entirely or outlaw its use, but magic might be rare beyond the spellcasting of local healers or the power of the occasional family heirloom. It's up to you to decide how pervasive magic is in a domain, choosing whether a dearth or an excess of magic is more terrifying.

Rarity of Magic. In domains where inhabitants regard simple magic as remarkable, those inhabitants' lack of engagement with the supernatural doesn't mean you should limit magic for adventurers. Rather, use this as an opportunity to feature magic-using characters as figures of awe or terror, or to assign storied origins to common magic items.

Corrupted Magic. The Dark Powers influence magical effects, imparting them with sinister qualities. How these changes manifest are for you to decide and can shift from domain to domain. Do summoned creatures appear undead in one domain or violently mutated in another? Do divination spells rasp in the voices of otherworldly ancients? Do the effects of drinking a *potion of healing* feel like grubs weaving wounds shut from within? Magic looks menacing in the Domains of Dread, but descriptive embellishments shouldn't change the actual effects of spells or magic items.

PRISON OF SOULS

Everyone among the Domains of Dread is a prisoner. The Darklords number among the most prominent captives, but every creature claimed by the Mists dwells outside the natural order of the multiverse. Even death doesn't afford an escape from the Dark Powers, which hoard every soul that falls into their clutches. In the Land of the Mists, death isn't an escape, but the beginning of a new terror.

Soulless Shells. Not every being among the Domains of Dread has a soul. Many inhabitants of each domain are creations of the Dark Powers, whose bodies have been formed from the land and the Mists. For all intents and purposes, and even under magical detection, these beings are what they appear to be. The Dark Powers fashion them as living puppets—individuals who live unremarkable lives that reinforce the status quo, culture, and frustration that torment a domain's Darklord.

Bright Souls. Individuals born in the Land of the Mists who have souls tend to be vibrant, imaginative, and ambitious. But they find these virtues stifled by the dour, soulless individuals who outnumber them, leading many to seek better lives and answers to the mysteries of their home domain. Every player's character who was born in a domain is one of these vibrant souls.

Death in Ravenloft. When a creature with a soul dies among the Domains of Dread, its spirit becomes caught in the Mists and can't travel to the afterlife. If a creature who has been dead for at least 24 hours returns to life by way of a spell or other supernatural means, it realizes that its spirit is trapped within the Mists, likely forever. Using the rules for "Fear and Stress" from chapter 4, the creature gains a new Seed of Fear.

If a being with a soul dies and is not returned to life, that soul remains trapped within the Domains of Dread until it is reincarnated, a process that can take decades. Individuals who inherit the same soul over generations often look alike and might recall memories of their past lives.

Metaphysical Mysteries. The state of souls in the Domains of Dread provides a dose of existential terror to those hoping to manipulate life and death to escape these realms. Beyond that, who does and doesn't have a soul among the domains rarely matters unless an adventure explores themes of life, death, and reincarnation. Players might create ties with long-dead individuals using the Dark Gifts and backgrounds presented in chapter 1. But overall, spiritual stagnation in the Land of the Mists is meant to provide the opportunity for grim revelations, not existential bookkeeping.

PLANAR CONNECTIONS

Each domain is its own demiplane, isolated from all other planes including the Material Plane. No spell—not even *wish*—allows escape from the Domains of Dread. Spells such *astral projection*, *plane shift*, *teleport*, and similar magic cast for the purpose of escaping a domain simply fail, as do effects that banish a creature to another plane. These restrictions apply to all other effects, including magic items and artifacts that transport or banish creatures to other planes. Magic that allows transit to the Border Ethereal, such as the *etherealness* spell and the Etherealness feature of ghosts, is the exception to this rule. A creature that enters the Border Ethereal from a domain is pulled back into the domain it left upon leaving the Ethereal.

For the purpose of spells whose effects change across or are blocked by planar boundaries (such as *sending*), each domain is considered its own plane. Magic that summons creatures or objects from other planes functions normally, as does magic that involves an extradimensional space. Spells cast within an extradimensional space (such as that created by *Mordenkainen's magnificent mansion*) are subject to the same restrictions as magic cast within a domain.

While in the Domains of Dread, characters who receive spells from deities or otherworldly patrons continue to do so. In addition, spells that allow contact with beings from other planes function normally, with one proviso: the domain's Darklord senses when someone in their domain casts such a spell and can choose to make themself the spell's target, so that they become the one who is contacted.

LIFE IN THE DOMAINS OF DREAD

The realities of the Domains of Dread seem strange or impossible to individuals from other worlds, but for those who live among the Mists, they're facts of life. With no basis for comparison, domain inhabitants call those who speak of other worlds liars. For them, the following topics are standard aspects of life in their home domain or in a broader collection of domains they call the Land of the Mists.

EERIE VENDORS SUCH AS THOSE AT THE CARNIVAL'S LITWICK MARKET DEAL IN UNIQUE MIST TALISMANS.

ANDREW MAR

CULTURE AND TECHNOLOGY

Each domain boasts its own culture, either drawn from the Material Plane or a parody manufactured to torment a Darklord. As such, a domain might exhibit traditions and technologies unheard of in other domains. The specifics of each domain's technological advancements are left to you. If you wish domains to feature cutting-edge weird science or inventions such as firearms (see the *Dungeon Master's Guide*), feel free to do so. Regardless of a domain's culture and innovations, the Mists prevent knowledge of them from spreading. Even if an innovation is taken from one domain to another, the suspicion of the new domain's inhabitants prevents it from gaining acceptance. Such is the subtle control of the Dark Powers, ensuring their nightmare realms remain just so.

CURRENCY

Many domains mint their own gold, silver, and copper coins. Though these currencies bear different markings, merchants aren't particular about the designs stamped on coinage. A gold piece from Barovia spends as well in Borca as it does in Har'Akir, as long as it weighs true. Platinum and electrum coins rarely circulate through the domains, but they appear often enough—originating from hidden troves or ancient vaults—that no trader questions their value.

LANGUAGES

By impossible coincidence, all domains share a language despite their profoundly different origins: Common, which functions as a shared tongue throughout the Land of the Mists. Beyond this, all the other languages noted in the *Player's Handbook* and *Monster Manual* are spoken among the Domains of Dread, some more pervasively than others. The same language spoken in multiple domains might bear subtle differences or unique words. Speakers from different domains might also have distinct accents, but their words are understandable.

DM Option: Domain Languages. If you want to highlight the differences between domains, you can do away with Common and decide that the inhabitants of each domain speak their own unique language, which either take the name of their domain or a culturally specific name. For example, the language of Barovia could be Barovian or Balok. The languages of specific races, such as Elvish or Dwarvish, remain the same in every domain. Those who wish to learn a domain's language can do so using the training downtime activity (see the *Player's Handbook*). Although it takes 250 days to gain mastery of a language, consider allowing characters

> ### EZRA, GOD OF THE MISTS
>
> The denizens of several domains worship an aloof god known as Ezra. Depicted as a vague, vaporous figure, the god is known for her dark, billowing hair and for her ability to manipulate the Mists. Her holy symbol is a sprig of belladonna atop a silver kite shield. Beyond that, her disparate sects of worshipers view her differently—and contradictorily. For some, Ezra is a goodly guardian, while others perceive her as a soul-stealing embodiment of the Mists. Ultimately, though, her true nature is a mystery. Whether she's a manifestation of the Dark Powers, an aspect of the Plane of Shadow's mysterious Raven Queen, or something else entirely is for you to decide. Whatever the case, Ezra's followers, traditions, alignment, and the domains she grants her clerics vary widely. Collaborate with players who want to create characters devoted to Ezra to define the god's role in their domain of origin.

to navigate basic social interactions—such as asking for directions or conveying peaceful intentions—after 7 days of training.

RELIGION

In many domains, locals maintain chilly relationships with aloof deities, knowing "the gods" only through hollow rituals and clergy with scant supernatural powers. Conversely, some people privately worship ancestral gods—deities of their family's tradition with whom they form deep, personal connections. Divergent faiths abound, and some that begin as charlatanry inexplicably gain the power of true faith. Ultimately, any deity from the *Player's Handbook* or any other setting might find followers among the Domains of Dread. By the same token, the Dark Powers breathe life into the beliefs of cruel practices and the faiths of false zealots.

One noteworthy exception to this is the worship of the god Ezra, which has its origins in the Mists (see the "Ezra, God of the Mists" sidebar). For your adventures, you define what deities are worshiped in a domain and whether those deities are actual gods, manifestations of the Dark Powers, or one masquerading as the other.

TIME AND DATES

The Domains of Dread don't share a unified calendar. However, in most domains, locals measure time by "moons" rather than months. As a measurement of time, each moon begins on the first night of a full moon and lasts a full lunar cycle. A year consists of twelve moons, or twelve lunar cycles. While domains don't ascribe to a shared history, the populace of all domains inexplicably accept the current year as 735. Some local histories cleave to anomalous dates and methods of tracking years, but these are considered obsolete. No such irregularities exist in Barovia, though, where year 1 corresponds with the founding of Barovia by the von Zarovich family.

Travel and Correspondence

In some domains, the residents are aware that realms exist beyond the Mists, but most have little interest in lands beyond their own. The Darklords' obsessions distract them from concerns about the nature of their domains or what lies beyond the Mists. This preoccupation, along with the lack of shared borders or reliable travel, means that mercantile ventures and military conquests between domains are essentially impossible.

Rare individuals do travel between the domains, such as adventurers or roving Vistani families (detailed at the end of this chapter). Others who wish to travel from one domain to another might wander into the Mists hoping to be carried elsewhere, or they can employ Mist talismans to guide them.

Due to the danger and unreliability of traveling the Mists, those few with interests beyond their home domains make letter writing their preferred method of communication. A group called the Keepers of the Feather (detailed in the "Travelers in the Mists" section later in this chapter) oversees a private network of carrier ravens that possesses the uncanny ability to navigate the Mists. These ravens deliver envelopes and tiny parcels between private rookeries maintained by the Keepers. Individuals and businesses friendly with the Keepers—such as a village notary or inn—might surreptitiously contract their services, allowing customers to send a letter for 1 gp. These letters must include a destination where another Keeper can receive them, then either hold or deliver the correspondence—with delivery costs an additional 1 gp. Letters take at least one day to deliver. The Keepers of the Feather make no assurances about the safe delivery of letters in their charge, but their services prove relatively reliable. Rumors speak of more expensive services the Keepers provide to select clients, such as delivery to individuals whose whereabouts are unknown or verbal messages relayed by talking ravens.

FEATURED DOMAINS

The following sections explore some of the most notorious Domains of Dread. Each of these realms is a setting unto itself and might host adventures of your design. These featured domains share the following format:

Overview. Each domain has a brief overview with its Darklord's name, the horror genres that inspire it (explored in chapter 2), distinctive hallmarks, and related Mist talismans.
Noteworthy Features. Details about the domain known by the domain's residents and those who have traveled there appear in this section.

Settlements and Sites. This section provides an overview of the domain's most infamous locations. In many cases, these locations are represented on a map of the domain. Each map also notes additional sites waiting to be detailed in your adventures.
Darklord. A description of the domain's Darklord appears here, along with details revealing the roots of their evil.
Adventures. This section describes the kinds of adventures that naturally fit within the domain.
Domain Focus. For most domains, this final section highlights specific story elements and provides domain-specific tools to aid you in creating adventures around the domain's Darklord and the horror of their realm.

Facing Darklords

Each Darklord in this chapter has a stat block from the *Monster Manual* or chapter 5 that you can use or customize to suit your adventures. Though you might be tempted to make a Darklord an overwhelming threat, doing so risks distancing a rich, versatile villain from the characters. A Darklord is often far from the most physically daunting creature in their domain, but their nature as a Darklord makes permanently defeating them challenging. To defeat a Darklord, the characters should focus on undermining the Darklord's plots and striking at the core of the Darklord's torments to make them vulnerable (topics explored in "The Domain's Downfall" in chapter 2). A climatic encounter with a Darklord should happen when and how it's right for your adventures. After all, dread isn't a factor of challenge rating or character level, but of the suspense your adventures create.

Characters from Domains

This chapter includes sidebars designed to help create player characters who hail from particular Domains of Dread. These sidebars describe the people of a particular domain, the horrors they routinely face, and their naming conventions. Share these sidebars freely with your players if they create characters from these domains. The naming conventions they reference note the names of peoples featured in the "Character Names" section of *Xanathar's Guide to Everything*, they do not describe a domain's broader culture. Use the questions included in each sidebar to inspire players with ideas for their characters. Players don't need to answer every question or concern themselves with accurately representing a domain. Rather, it's more important they create details that forge a strong sense of connection with their homeland.

Barovia

Domain of the First Vampire

Darklord: Strahd von Zarovich
Genre: Gothic horror
Hallmarks: Undead despot, notorious haunted stronghold, tragic resurrection
Mist Talismans: Barovian wine bottle, von Zarovich family crest, Mark of the Raven talisman

In Barovia, the night is a curse. With the dying of the light, wicked souls slip from the darkened spires of Castle Ravenloft to work the will of an immortal overlord. This is the realm of the vampire Count Strahd von Zarovich, whose depravities have doomed him and countless generations to endlessly repeating cycles of obsession and despair.

The howls of wolves and shrieks of raven swarms echo through the dismal valleys and oppressive forests of Barovia. In isolated communities, superstitious villagers find the brightness in their lives smothered by dread of their aloof overlord, his baleful servants, and ancient evils that fester unopposed. All the domain's residents know to fear the Mists and the long Barovian nights, as through them the Devil Strahd watches and reaches to claim whatever he desires. Yet none realize their torments have played out over and over again, all part of Strahd's plot to claim one victim who has eluded him for generations.

Noteworthy Features

Those familiar with Barovia know the following facts:

- Barovia is a gloomy realm of valleys isolated by wolf-prowled forests and treacherous mountains. Dense clouds cast the land in perpetual gloom.
- The land's somber, superstitious people live in small, scattered villages. These communities are each led by a burgomaster who seeks to avoid the ire of the land's aloof lord, Count Strahd von Zarovich. Strangers are widely viewed with suspicion.
- Many locals believe Count von Zarovich is a vampire. He dwells in Castle Ravenloft, a citadel from which few return.
- Vistani bands passing through Barovia are under the protection of the count. This protection stems from a past kindness the Vistani showed the count and from his long association with the fortune-teller Madam Eva. (See "Travelers in the Mists" at the end of this chapter for details on the Vistani.)
- The stories of Barovia's people are full of hidden evils: treacherous witches, secretive cults, portentous ravens, vicious werewolves, and worse.

Barovian Characters

A diverse populace dwells in Barovia, their ancestors drawn from lands long ago conquered by Count von Zarovich. The people favor dressing in muted but functional clothes, have a wide range of skin and hair colors, and often have names inspired by Slavic peoples. When players create characters from Barovia, ask them the following questions.

What was your life like in Barovia? Were you the child of a shepherd, vintner, or burgomaster? Was your life humble, or were you spared scarcity of coin and food? Did someone in your life vanish, or did you suffer some brush with the creatures of the night?

What superstitions do you cleave to? Is there something you do or say every morning or at night? Do animals—particularly bats, ravens, or wolves—feature in your superstitions? What superstitions do you have regarding coins, doorways, meals, or wounds?

Do you have recurring dreams or visions of unfamiliar experiences or past lives? Who were you in these dreams? What do they tell you about Barovia? Do you believe they hold any truth? Does Count Strahd von Zarovich feature in any of these visions?

Settlements and Sites

Barovia's people are slow to trust strangers, but they eagerly share tales of the past tragedies and grim rumors that haunt every corner of their land. Ancient mysteries pervade the domain, and those who leave the relative safety of Barovia's settlements enter perilous lands where mortals aren't welcome.

Castle Ravenloft

Castle Ravenloft is Count Strahd von Zarovich's accursed sanctuary. Here Strahd committed his bloodiest crimes and began the cycle of despair in which all Barovia remains locked. Lurking Undead, tormented spirits, and Strahd's other servants haunt the vast castle, each serving the count's schemes; reflecting some aspect of his depraved past; or protecting his coffin, which lies hidden within the castle's vast catacombs. Mementos of lost times and fallen heroes lie scattered throughout the count's home. Strahd keeps these relics close, but that might hold the key to his undoing. Castle Ravenloft is detailed in the adventure *Curse of Strahd*.

Krezk

Nestled on the edge of Barovia, Krezk is a hardy and self-sustaining village. Burgomaster Dmitri Krezkov scours the land for wine and other small luxuries, hoping to infuse some happiness into the villagers' lives. Krezk's most prominent landmark, the Abbey of Saint Markovia, looms high on a nearby cliff. This abbey is the home of a group of strange, afflicted creatures who work for a young and striking abbot. Some believe the abbot to be Strahd in disguise, although in truth he is a celestial being who has been corrupted by the Dark Powers.

MAP 3.1: BAROVIA

VALLAKI

Isolated from the rest of Barovia, Vallaki appears at first as an oddly mirthful place, but this seeming joy is an illusion. The burgomaster, Baron Vargas Vallakovich, is convinced happiness holds the key to Vallaki's salvation, and so he convenes festival after bizarre festival with titles such as the Festival of the Blazing Sun, the Promenade of Coffins, and the Wolf's Head Jamboree. Additionally, numerous factions are active within the town, including the Keepers of the Feather and the priests of Osybus (see "Travelers in the Mists" and "Other Groups," respectively, later in this chapter).

VILLAGE OF BAROVIA

Lying in the shadow of Castle Ravenloft, the village of Barovia is oppressed by fear. The villagers rarely venture from their homes, suspecting their neighbors of wickedness and fearing evils are taking root in the shadows. Their fears are largely justified, as ghosts and vampire spawn haunt the town, and many locals have been consumed by their own callousness or wicked temptations. A rare exception to the village's cold desperation can be found at the local tavern called the Blood of the Vine. Those few who would oppose Strahd's evil congregate here—and are in turn spied upon by the count's agents.

THE AMBER TEMPLE

Once a haven of virtuous wizards, the Amber Temple was long ago corrupted by evil. It was here that Strahd made his pact with the Dark Powers to become a vampire, with the blessing of the lich Exethanter. While the lich remains, albeit as a mere shadow of its former self, the true evil within the Amber Temple lies within its collection of amber sarcophagi. These monoliths hold vestiges of dead, hateful gods—beings that aspire to re-create past depravities and manipulate mortals to fulfill unspeakable agendas. Various evil forces set their intentions upon the Amber Temple, viewing it as a nexus of secrets underpinning the nature of the Domains of Dread. The priests of Osybus (detailed in the "Other Groups" section later in this chapter) have particular interest in this site.

STRAHD VON ZAROVICH

In life, Count Strahd von Zarovich was a ruthlessly effective conqueror. Over decades of brutal military campaigning, he defeated his rivals and forged a nation. Retiring from war, Strahd settled in the beautiful valley where he'd won his greatest victory. There, in the way of his ancestors, he spilled his blood into the earth, sealing a pact between himself and the land. In honor of his parents, King Barov and Queen

Ravenovia, he named the valley Barovia and constructed his fortress-home, Castle Ravenloft.

Strahd had spent his youth at war fighting alongside Ulmed, the founder of the Ulmist Inquisition, but as he reached his middle years he sought the comforts of family. He invited his kin to live with him at Castle Ravenloft, and was eventually joined by his younger brother, Sergei.

Sergei was everything Strahd wasn't—youthful, empathic, and warm. Soon after he arrived in Barovia, the younger von Zarovich and a local villager named Tatyana fell in love. Strahd resented his brother, even more so after meeting Tatyana and experiencing her pure kindness. Obsessing over her, Strahd sought to woo Tatyana but was soundly rebuffed. Unwilling to accept her wishes or Sergei as his better, Strahd delved into the sinister secrets of his land and came to learn of the Amber Temple. There, amid hidden lore and the imprisoned vestiges of ancient evil, Strahd first encountered the Dark Powers—and made a bargain with them to regain his vitality and ensnare Tatyana's heart.

The day of Sergei and Tatyana's wedding, Strahd murdered Sergei and, to seal his pact with the Dark Powers, drank his brother's blood. He revealed his new might to Tatyana, expecting to enthrall her. Instead, horrified by Sergei's murder, Tatyana fled Strahd, ultimately leaping from the height of Castle Ravenloft to escape him and vanishing into the Mists. At the same time, traitors from among the castle's guards and wedding's guests rose up to assassinate Strahd. Despite suffering countless wounds, Strahd did not die. The nature of his bargain with the Dark Powers was revealed, and Strahd became the multiverse's first vampire. A night of bloody rage followed, and when dawn touched the parapets of Castle Ravenloft, no living soul survived within. But Strahd remained.

Little is known of the origins of the Domains of Dread, but what's certain is that they began here. Strahd's villainy, his connection to his land, and his entanglement with the sinister priests of Osybus (detailed in chapter 5) drew all of Barovia into the Shadowfell. This began a succession of torments that haunt the Count still and spill forth to drag others into the Land of the Mists.

Strahd's Powers and Dominion

Strahd is a patient and dramatic mastermind. His statistics are similar to those of a **vampire** and his spellcasting prowess is formidable, enabling him to face most threats directly. Strahd ever seeks to escape his boredom and draws challenges out for as long as it entertains him. However, if insulted, the Darklord can turn all of Barovia against his foes.

The Ancient, the Land. Strahd is bound to Barovia and it to him in a way few rulers or Darklords understand. As part of this relationship, Strahd knows when any creature enters or dies violently within Barovia—and takes personal offense when his agents or the domain's wolves are slain. Strahd can also manifest a variety of dramatic effects, such as causing his voice to be heard on the wind, making his visage appear in the clouds, changing the weather, and so forth. He can't use these effects to aid him in combat, but they can make his presence known throughout the land.

Master Vampire. Strahd eagerly plays the parts of nobleman and gracious host, but drops these pretenses when they no longer serve him, revealing his megalomania and monstrous nature. Strahd believes he has no peers and eagerly cultivates servants, particularly vampire spawn. He hasn't survived for ages by being reckless, though, and he retreats or sacrifices even his favorite agents when necessary.

Vistani Sanctuary. The ancient Vistani fortune-teller Madame Eva makes her home in Barovia. She knows much of Strahd and has occasionally served as an intermediary between him and various Vistani bands when it serves her own mysterious goals. As part of this arrangement, Strahd avoids harming Vistani who travel within his land.

Closing the Borders. Strahd closes Barovia's borders whenever something that interests him threatens to escape, surrounding the domain with poisonous mist. Those who enter the Mists choke and are affected as detailed in "The Mists" section at the start of this chapter.

Strahd's Torment

Eternity is a cruel consort. The following are just a few of the torments Strahd endures:

- Through endless generations, Tatyana has been reincarnated again and again. Each time Strahd believes he can undo his past failures, win Tatyana's heart, and in so doing free himself from his ages-long curse. Each time, though, Tatyana renounces him once more.
- Strahd chafes within the borders of his domain. His desire for novelty, passion, and conquest matches his thirst for blood.
- Strahd considers Barovia's people dull inferiors, even as he resents them for the simple pleasures of hope and companionship they possess.

Roleplaying Strahd

Strahd von Zarovich is infinitely egotistical, cruel, and manipulative—a charming monster who wears the trappings of power and class. The vampire victimizes his subjects whenever the urge strikes, reveling in the fear he causes.

Personality Trait. "I am Barovia's lord. All within this land are mine."

Ideal. "I sacrificed my life to forge this land. None deserve respect and love more than me."

Bond. "My subjects exist to serve and sustain me. The blood of the defiant tastes the sweetest."

Flaw. "I crave the company of equals—if only such individuals existed."

ADVENTURES IN BAROVIA

Count Strahd von Zarovich casts a shadow no matter where heroes tread in Barovia, and sooner or later, they'll face an inevitable showdown with the land's vampiric overlord. The domain's innumerable evils all ultimately tie back to Strahd. Any corrupt individual, sinister cult, or rampaging monster might have been inspired by the Darklord, their evil ultimately furthering the count's plots and infamy.

Strahd's depravity takes physical form in the vampire's lair, Castle Ravenloft. The castle is itself a notorious legend intrinsic to the count's terror. The Mists often deposit strangers to Barovia within sight of the fortress, daring the unwary to approach. Ultimately, only the bravest lay siege to the castle or accept the count's invitations to visit him there. But Castle Ravenloft needn't be challenged in a single assault, and defeating Strahd might not be the only goal of those who enter. The library, chapel, and catacombs of Castle Ravenloft all hold tempting secrets that might be vital to countering the count's plots or undoing other evils. Or Strahd might make good on an invitation to grant guests shelter and safety within the Castle Ravenloft—for a time. Ultimately, don't hesitate to employ the setting's most infamous castle even if you don't plan to run a lengthy siege.

The adventure *Curse of Strahd* explores Barovia and Castle Ravenloft in detail, but you can also use the ideas on the Barovia Adventures table to create your own plots.

BAROVIA ADVENTURES

d8	Adventure
1	The Mists draw the characters into Barovia, where the fortune-teller Madam Eva sets them on a dark course that leads them to Castle Ravenloft.
2	**Priests of Osybus** (see chapter 5) have gained a following in Vallaki. They consider Strahd a demigod of their faith and drain the blood of nonbelievers in his name.
3	A merchant working for a mysterious patron hires the party to recover the bones of Tatsaul Eris, a noble buried in the catacombs of Castle Ravenloft.
4	The Martikovs, owners of the Wizard of Wines winery, seek aid recovering a shipment of cursed wine that turns drinkers into **vine blights**.

IN THE HALLS OF CASTLE RAVENLOFT, COUNT STRAHD VON ZAROVICH CLINGS TO ANCIENT OBSESSIONS.

d8	Adventure
5	A dying **wereraven** (see chapter 5) gives the characters a scroll and an amulet bearing the Mark of the Raven. It begs the characters to deliver the message to the Keepers of the Feather.
6	A megalith erected by Barovia's original inhabitants topples near Vallaki. Beneath lies the tomb of an ancient **nosferatu** (see chapter 5) who calls himself Duke Gundar; he immediately takes a disliking to Count Strahd von Zarovich.
7	From the ruined mansion of Argynvostholt, the **revenant** knight Vladimir Horngaard dragoons innocents into the Order of the Silver Dragon and pits them against Strahd's servants.
8	The characters are accused of a crime. Surprising everyone, word arrives that Count Strahd von Zarovich will serve as their judge.

INCARNATIONS OF TATYANA

The curse that engulfs Barovia means that the soul of Tatyana, the subject of Strahd's obsession, perpetually reincarnates into new physical forms. No matter what form she takes, Strahd unceasingly seeks her, determined to possess her and soothe his rejected ego. The following section explores creating stories with Tatyana's latest incarnation at their center. This incarnation—whether an unwitting innocent, a determined vampire, a villain, or something else entirely—influences both Strahd's and the characters' relationship with her. Consider how changing Tatyana's incarnation allows you to give your own distinct spin to Ravenloft's classic tale.

Characters and groups marked with an asterisk on the following tables are further detailed in the "Travelers in the Mist" section at the end of in this chapter.

WHO IS TATYANA?

When building your version of Tatyana, use the Tatyana's Incarnation table to determine the character's basic description. Once you're satisfied, consult the following "Connection to Strahd" section to determine the incarnation's relationship to Barovia's Darklord. Alternatively, if you wish Tatyana's incarnation to appear outside Barovia and potentially lead adventurers to Strahd's domain, consider the plots in the "Beyond Barovia" section.

TATYANA'S INCARNATION

d8	Who Is Tatyana's Newest Incarnation?
1	Ireena Kolyana, the adopted daughter of burgomaster Kolyan Indirovich of the village of Barovia
2	Ez d'Avenir,* vampire slayer and protégé of Rudolph van Richten
3	Vasilka, a **flesh golem** or reborn (see chapter 1) who lives in the abbey near the village of Krezk
4	The identical twins Yasmine and Nasseri, who are devout servants of the god Ezra
5	Renoir Laurent, the teenage son of Chantal Laurent, a woman Strahd abducted years ago
6	Petra Rilenovich, a young prodigy who has gained local renown for her remarkable paintings of what she calls her "dream lives"
7	Vanasia, the leader of a far-ranging Vistani band
8	Quentin L'Argent, the dragonborn son of human goat herders living near the ruined manor Argynvostholt.

CONNECTION TO STRAHD

Once you know what form Tatyana's current incarnation takes, consider how the character feels toward Barovia's Darklord. If your version of Tatyana wants to stay away from Strahd, whether or not the incarnation knows they possess Tatyana's soul, roll on the Avoiding Strahd table. Alternatively, if they're compelled to destroy Strahd, roll on the Hunting Strahd table.

AVOIDING STRAHD

d8	Concealment
1	The incarnation pretends to be a religious zealot who took a vow of silence.
2	The incarnation (or their guardians) made a bargain with Madam Eva or the Keepers of the Feather to hide the incarnation from Strahd.
3	The incarnation is the ward of a famous monster hunter, who might not know the soul's identity.
4	The incarnation was adopted by a group of Vistani travelers and rarely visits Barovia.
5	The incarnation hides from Strahd by taking a magic potion that causes them to sleep for all but one hour a day.
6	The incarnation uses magic to appear as an old person, a child, or a white raven.
7	Some evil, such as the Abbot of the Abbey of Saint Markovia or an inhabitant of the Amber Temple, cloaks the incarnation's existence from Strahd.
8	The incarnation lives a charmed life and is heedless of the count, not realizing Strahd is cultivating them until a particular time.

HUNTING STRAHD

d10	Hunting Method
1	The incarnation seeks to become the greatest monster hunter ever, training constantly so they're prepared when Strahd eventually appears.
2	The incarnation misguidedly plans to redeem Strahd through their exceptional kindness or faith.
3	The incarnation knows their true nature and has weaponized their blood with poison that will put Strahd to sleep for a generation.
4	The incarnation seeks to resurrect a historic figure to battle Strahd, perhaps Sergei von Zarovich, the first Tatyana, or another enemy of the count.
5	The incarnation has located a relic that can weaken Strahd. However, they need the heroes to recover the item while they distract the count.
6	The incarnation used powerful magic to lead the heroes to Barovia so they can destroy Strahd.
7	The incarnation has joined the Keepers of the Feather* and seeks to organize a siege of Castle Ravenloft.
8	The incarnation feels the weight of their past lives and seeks a way to end their cycle of rebirth by freeing Barovia from the Mists—or destroying it.
9	The incarnation falls in with a sinister group such as the priests of Osybus* and seeks to manipulate Strahd to further their organization's schemes.
10	The incarnation has drawn an enemy of Strahd's to Barovia, such as Firan Zal'honen* or Jander Sunstar,* hoping the rivals will slay one another.

BEYOND BAROVIA

It's not necessary to have Tatyana's incarnation appear within Barovia. Rather, Tatyana's spirit might arise in another land or under strange circumstances. The Lost Tatyana table provides suggestions for such characters and their objectives.

LOST TATYANA

d6	Resurrection Circumstances
1	Tatyana's incorporeal spirit assembles and haunts heroes whom she believes have the best chance of defeating Strahd.
2	A character's friend or loved one is the incarnation of Tatyana. When the Mists claim that individual, the character is drawn into Barovia as well.
3	A character's own reincarnation allows Tatyana's soul to enter their body, bringing with it memories in the form of vivid dreams.
4	Tatyana's soul was captured by an effect similar to the *magic jar* spell. Strahd or another entity hires the characters to seek out the container holding the soul, not revealing its true nature.
5	Tatyana's soul reincarnated as someone another Darklord covets, such as the bearer of Ankhtepot's *ka* in Har'Akir or Elise in Lamordia (both detailed later in this chapter).
6	Tatyana's soul found its way into a distant relative of Strahd, Lyssa von Zarovich. Lyssa seeks to grow more powerful and claim Castle Ravenloft for herself. Her first step to deposing Strahd was to become a vampire. Now she needs allies.

TATYANA MIGHT BE REBORN IN ANY NUMBER OF GUISES, SUCH AS IREENA KOLYANA OR LYSSA VON ZAROVICH.

BLUETSPUR

Domain of Alien Memories

Darklord: The God-Brain of Bluetspur
Genre: Cosmic horror
Hallmarks: Alien abductions, otherworldly landscapes, untrustworthy memories, monstrous experimentation
Mist Talismans: Dream journal, metallic implant, scrap of bizarre technology

Protean apocalypses scar the impossible vistas of Bluetspur, and none who witness them remember. This alien domain etches itself not upon the waking mind, but rather upon the body as inexplicable scars and on the psyche through nightmares.

Not all the Domains of Dread are drawn from worlds hospitable to life. Bluetspur's scale and impossible geometry induce instinctual anxiety. Gaseous tempests whirl upon the hooked peaks of gravity-defying mountains, oily spires twist in semi-organic contortions, caustic fumaroles yawn and snap shut hungrily, and above it all hangs a dying red orb. Little can survive this wasteland, which is why Bluetspur's masters dwell underground.

Beneath the alien surface, the mind flayers of Bluetspur drift through the howling darkness of their ancient metropolis-laboratory. Within this sprawling installation, the illithids' numbers are few and their tentacles twitch with undisguised urgency. They toil to prevent the unthinkable: their primordial leader, the God-Brain of Bluetspur, is dying. Through these end times, the mind flayers work desperately to reconcile their god's demented whims even as they struggle to delay its demise. To those ends, their tentacles slip through the Mists to drag unwitting souls back to Bluetspur for all manner of experiments. Many abductees are returned with only psychic scars, while others are never seen again. An unlucky few find themselves set upon strange routes leading back to the alien realm, arriving only to realize they've visited Bluetspur before.

NOTEWORTHY FEATURES

Those few people who glimpse Bluetspur know it only as a nameless realm from their impossible dreams. These visions share the following facts:

- The land's surface is a lethal, alien place, scattered with the ruins of long-extinct civilizations.
- A mountain—massive beyond all words—looms as a constant presence and thrums with a soundless pulse that nonetheless demands attention. Misshapen shadows crawl among its fissures.
- Those who dream of events in this land often bear inexplicable scars, marks lending impossible evidence to their visions.

Settlements and Sites

The surface of Bluetspur is vast, spanning a continent-sized region that is hostile to all but the most tenacious forms of life. Due to the endless assault of supernatural weather and earthquakes, civilization—as defined by the illithids—exists entirely below the ground. The Mists encroach even here, filling shadowed chasms and abandoned corridors. While the mind flayers have their own ways of describing the realm's features, the half-lucid ramblings of those who dream of the domain stretch to name and relate several prominent sites.

Mount Makab

Calling Makab a mountain is a wild misnomer; it is a malignant deformation on a planetary scale, a spire with no apparent summit. Its contorted slopes stretch into the toxic heavens, and its form occupies the periphery of viewers' attention no matter which direction they look.

Mount Makab is not a natural feature, but rather part of a colossal, illithid-designed device. Its purposes remain largely mysterious to outsiders, but one thing is certain: it amplifies psionic energy, allowing Bluetspur's mind flayers to project their thoughts into other Domains of Dread.

Citadel Subterrene

Below Mount Makab stretches the hive-like lair of the illithids. This mind flayer metropolis comprises innumerable interconnected compounds—laboratory vaults, custom prison-habitats, intellect devourer preserves, incubation domes, brain-filled synapse libraries, testing hippodromes, surgical theaters, and facilities that beggar rational description. Non-illithids find travel within the citadel maddening, like trying to find a specific point within a writhing knot of worms. Locations are inaccessible to creatures reliant upon basic terrestrial mobility or without the ability to access psionically controlled mechanisms. Entering Citadel Subterrene is simple, though, as fissures across Bluetspur, particularly upon Mount Makab, lead within.

The Chamber of the God-Brain

The Chamber of the God-Brain rests miles below Citadel Subterrene. The cathedral-like chamber is roughly ovoid in shape, with walls of gleaming, organic metal. The massive God-Brain trembles in a pool of medicinal brine and experimental chemicals capable of dissolving most other creatures. The massive, alien brain's affliction is clear from the leaking holes pocking its deep-wrinkled lobes. Illithid attendants in eerie protective garb endlessly attend to their dying overlord and indulge even its most blasphemous schemes, such as the creation of vampiric mind flayers (see chapter 5).

Mount Grysl

Mount Grysl's polypous spires once served as a secondary installation of the domain's resident mind flayers, but the residents rebelled against the God-Brain's self-serving obsessions. As one might amputate an infected limb, the God-Brain cut off Mount Grysl from its psychic network. The abandoned residents largely succumbed to infighting and each other's amoral experiments. The spirits of these tormented mind flayers remain within Mount Grysl, as does the rebellion's leader: a bloated deviant that calls itself the High Master and seeks to undermine the God-Brain.

The God-Brain

The scope of what mind flayers call history exists on a cosmic scale. Through ages of empire and conflict, the illithid elder brains indulged experiments without comparison or reference for lesser beings, explorations beyond the boundaries of time, reality, immortality, and the multiverse. Many failed—at least one catastrophically so.

To summarize an eon of atrocities, one elder brain's reality-bending research had an unexpected result, revealing to it a malignant truth for which existence was unprepared. Guided by this burgeoning revelation, the elder brain turned and preyed upon its peers, consuming their discoveries and their physical forms to fuel an impossible apotheosis. Ultimately, though, the weight of the elder brain's deeds caused its own physicality to rebel, giving rise to an alien disease that began devouring its fleshy form. Horrified by an affliction that infected only them, the other elder brains united and psionically expelled the diseased brain from existence.

Or so they thought.

From a place without time or reality, the Dark Powers plucked the dying elder brain and planted it upon a tormented world. Ever since, the God-Brain of Bluetspur has dreamed and desperately indulged ever more demented schemes as it seeks to save its own life and give action to a thought alien even to it.

The God-Brain's Powers and Dominion

The God-Brain is more akin to a physical location or massive object than a creature. Its droves of servants are more direct threats than the inscrutable Darklord itself.

Overmind. The God-Brain commands untold numbers of **mind flayers**, **intellect devourers**, and other creatures. Within Bluetspur, it is constantly telepathically linked with all its servants and knows anything that they know. The God-Brain delegates broad goals to its most effective servants, encouraging them to indulge all manner of radical experiments.

Mist Vibrations. Through the awesome psychic resonances of Mount Makab, the God-Brain can guide any of its servants or other psychically aligned minds through the Mists to Bluetspur. In effect, it provides a vision or dream of the domain that itself functions as a Mist talisman.

Life Support. The illithids of Bluetspur toil to save their elder brain through all manner of outlandish scientific and medical means. Among the most bizarre of these schemes is the God-Brain's own: the creation of degenerate servants that hunt for balms for its affliction. These **vampiric mind flayers** (see chapter 5) slip from Bluetspur to prey upon Humanoids. They then return to the God-Brain, bloated with cerebrospinal fluid to momentarily dull its suffering.

Closing the Borders. When the God-Brain closes Bluetspur's borders, the surface of the domain is wracked by extreme electrical storms, and alien vapors rise at the domain's distant edges and within its hidden tunnels. Rather than barring creatures' escape, these Mists repress memories. Any non-Aberration who leaves Bluetspur is transported to a familiar place where they soon wake up, even if they weren't previously asleep. Their time in Bluetspur is repressed, altered as if by the *modify memory* spell. See "Recovering Memories" below for more details.

The God-Brain's Torment

The God-Brain of Bluetspur is an entirely unreliable cosmic entity, an immortal inflicted with mortality. Although its death is likely still millennia away, this inevitability leads it to hastily indulge all manner of amoral extremes.

Roleplaying the God-Brain

The God-Brain's influence drives the mind flayers beyond their domain to purse all manner of subtle observations, bizarre experiments, repeat abductions, and visceral mutilations.

Adventures in Bluetspur

While Bluetspur's otherworldly hazards and the mind flayers' defenses can challenge even the highest-level heroes, the domain's menace proves most pernicious when it intrudes on other domains. Taking inspiration from sci-fi horror and tales of alien abduction, adventures involving Bluetspur's mind flayers might begin anywhere with bad dreams or a stranger's impossible rantings. Over time, disappearances, inexplicable scars, subdermal implants, and unlocked memories might reveal the mind flayers' tentacles enwrap more than anyone thought possible. See "Return to Bluetspur" for details on running adventures featuring lost memories, or consider developing other plots using the Bluetspur Adventures table.

Bluetspur Adventures

d8	Adventure
1	Characters awake within the shattered remains of a fluid-filled tube deep in Citadel Subterrene. They have no idea how they arrived there.
2	A cavern the characters were exploring seamlessly abuts with Bluetspur, trapping them in caves overrun with **vampiric mind flayers** (see chapter 5).
3	A strange message leads characters to a silvery vessel full of alien mysteries wrecked on Bluetspur's surface. The only surviving creature in the wreck is a cunning **displacer beast**.
4	The characters find a strange but adorable creature trapped within an abandoned alien installation. The being is a lovable companion, until it reveals itself to be a **star spawn emissary** (see chapter 5).
5	An acquaintance of the characters complains of reoccurring nightmares. The complaints stop when the dreamer is taken over by an **intellect devourer**.
6	An inventor requests the characters' insight into a pill-sized device she extracted from her own body. As the characters examine it, the device projects a map into their minds and emits a telepathic call for help. The map leads to a **mind flayer** who wants to put the God-Brain out of its misery.
7	A farmer hires the characters to protect his family, whom he believes—without evidence—are being abducted and returned every night.
8	The High Master mind flayer of Mount Grysl seeks to claim all the God-Brain knows. To do this, it creates a copy of the Apparatus (see "Mordent" later in this chapter). All it needs is a relic called the Rod of Rastinon, which it wants the characters to retrieve for it.

Return to Bluetspur

Bluetspur can be more chilling as a memory than as a new discovery. Use this section to create adventures that reveal impossible knowledge, hint at unremembered experiences, or take place as recollected adventures out of continuity with a campaign.

Recovering Memories

Knowing that secrets lurk within one's own mind holds unique terror. When running adventurers featuring hidden memories, consider how those memories might be revealed.

Magical Recovery. Both the mind flayers of Bluetspur and the Mists surrounding the domain employ methods similar to the *modify memory* spell to obscure victims' memories of their abduction, replacing them with hazy events or gaps of missing time. A character's true memories can be restored by a *remove curse* or *greater restoration* spell. A victim of the mind flayers might have endured dozens of memory modifications, each requiring its own magical removal, resulting in the recovery of a few traumatic memories at a time.

Alienism. Scientifically curious lands in your campaign might feature burgeoning practitioners of alienism or psychiatry. Inexperienced practitioners of these disciplines merge scientific treatments, spiritualism, magic, and hokum, yet still obtain results. A session or series of sessions with a committed alienist might allow a character to remember a forgotten event. By the same token, though, time spent with a duplicitous alienist might leave a character vulnerable to suggestion and false memories. Such revelations can play out in your adventures narratively at any pace you desire.

Gradual Recovery. Lost memories might gradually reveal themselves in response to events in adventures. As the characters encounter evidence of Bluetspur's mind flayers, consider giving individuals access to information they shouldn't logically possess or granting them advantage on rolls related to their hidden memories, doled out as you deem appropriate. This might take the form of allowing the character to navigate an alien installation, operate an inscrutable device, or read an otherworldly language. Don't explain why the character gains these benefits, though, and let them make their own explanations to other characters. Lost memories might also take the form of Dark Gifts (see chapter 1).

ALIEN ARTIFACTS

The mind flayers of Bluetspur might leave evidence of their bizarre plots behind in other domains. Use the artifacts on the Aberrant Evidence table to provoke investigations, trigger lost memories, or even serve as Mist talismans.

ABERRANT EVIDENCE

d6	Evidence
1	A needle-like device buried under someone's skin
2	An inexplicable crater or circle of scorched crops
3	A stable full of exploded livestock
4	An antimatter rifle (detailed in the *Dungeon Master's Guide*)
5	A missing person or otherworldly being transformed into a **brain in a jar** (see chapter 5)
6	The damaged corpse of a **vampiric mind flayer** (see chapter 5)

LOST MEMORIES

When revealing lost memories, cultivate the disquiet that comes with vivid recollections out of sync with a character's history. The scenes on the Suppressed Memories table include deliberately disjointed specifics that you can adjust or leave incoherent as you please. Many can also be used as the first moments of a longer memory. If you'd like the memory to continue, ask the player of the character remembering the event what happens next.

SUPPRESSED MEMORIES

d6	Memory
1	You're paralyzed on a cold table. Clicking sounds surround you. Pallid tentacles slither toward your face, each ending in gleaming surgical instruments. What are they trying to do?
2	Some unfamiliar reflex moves your arm. Looking, you catch a glimpse of a bruise slithering beneath your skin. What do you do?
3	A many-legged, ferret-like creature floats into your cell. You feel multitudes of unseen eyes upon you. What do your captors expect you to do with this? What do you do?
4	Rainbow storms assail the heights of a mountain so tall it seems to curve over you. You're floating over a red wasteland, just one in a line of hovering beings. What do you see ahead?
5	You knew a stranger. You were each other's comfort against fear and pain. Then they were taken away. What were their final words to you?
6	The figure hovering before you is deemed acceptable. They're lowered into a pool, where pale, slug-like beings set upon them. You float forward. Why are you deemed unacceptable?

ADVENTURES OUT OF TIME

The most effective way to reveal characters' missing memories is to revisit them as an adventure. Players might run lower-level versions of their characters or use the survivors from chapter 4 to represent their past selves. Or characters might play forgotten versions of themselves—perhaps very different from who they are now—or individuals in the memories of another character. Run this adventure as an experience detached from your campaign's timeline, a flashback that relates the terrors of being a victim of the mind flayers' plots. Death likely doesn't mean much in these adventures, as characters somehow survived to remember their traumas—perhaps through miraculous mind flayer surgeries. However, developments in the past can provide all manner of revelations, potentially unveiling terrifying truths hidden within characters' own minds and bodies.

BORCA

Domain of Desire and Deceit

Darklords: Ivana Boritsi and Ivan Dilisnya
Genres: Gothic horror and psychological horror
Hallmarks: Political intrigue, poison, revenge
Mist Talismans: Dram of sweet-smelling poison, singed love letter, tarnished signet ring

Borca's nobles entangle the domain in a web of intrigues. While the common folk scrape for survival, the domain's callous aristocrats distract themselves with cruel diversions. They pay what they consider pittances in gold, land, and lives in pursuit of power, thrills, and the rarest pleasure: untarnished emotion. The common folk are merely tools to be exploited and discarded. Silver-tongued schemers use dreams and ambition to tempt innocents into debt, blackmail, and ruin, while furthering their rivalries or searching for decadent thrills. Guile and apathy are virtues in Borca, and none embody them more than the domain's two Darklords: the genius poisoner Ivana Boritsi and the childishly cruel stalker Ivan Dilisnya.

Outside the bejeweled playgrounds of the land's elite, Borca's common folk struggle against crime, poverty, and starvation. In scattered villages and tenement-filled cities, locals view nobles as celebrities, and their idealized vision of noble life leads them to mimic the aristocrats' callousness and appetite for empty fads. These starry-eyed innocents provide ready pawns for corruption. And those who don't bend to the whims of Borca's rulers face humiliation before they're inevitably crushed.

NOTEWORTHY FEATURES

Those familiar with Borca know the following facts:

- Powerful families control the government, commerce, and entertainment in Borca. The Boritsi family holds the greatest influence.
- Borcan noble families include a dominant main family and lesser branch lineages. Branch noble families (sometimes with different surnames) are subservient to the main family.
- Each noble family maintains an estate with village-sized holdings nearby. These estates are testaments to the family's prestige, fortune, and hidden secrets.
- The common folk live in rural villages that serve noble interests or in crowded cities. Most either avoid entanglements with powerful but fickle nobles or desperately court their favor.
- Culture and prestige in Borca reach their height in the fabulous city of Levkarest. At its heart rises the Great Cathedral of the god Ezra.

SETTLEMENTS AND SITES

Most of Borca's people live in small agricultural communities under the rule of noble landlords, or in poverty in the larger settlements of Lechberg, Levkarest, or Sturben. Nobles keep country homes among the nation's forests or rolling hills, well apart from the common rabble. Mobility between country and town is a luxury of the wealthy, making horses and coaches symbols of prestige.

LEVKAREST

Borca's capital stands at the pinnacle of culture and power. Unpopular members of the noble families squabble in the halls of the People's Parliament, the land's ineffective seat of government. The true rulers of the nation conduct business in the offices of faceless mercantile ventures and the back rooms of avant-garde clubs. The commoners of Levkarest glimpse this world of toxic glamor only from afar, or when nobles exploit street-level fads.

Beyond the nobles' elaborate rivalries, another force moves in Levkarest. At the Great Cathedral, pious commoners and aristocrats alike beg for the favor of the deity Ezra, but in the catacombs beneath the cathedral, a hidden cell of the Ulmist Inquisition meets. This society cultivates psionic prowess to undermine the evil in people's souls before it comes to fruition. Yet despite its ties to heroes and vast lore, the society finds its numbers dwindling. (See "Other Groups" later in this chapter for details.)

NEW ILVIN

Remarkably, when the town of Ilvin burned, no lives were lost. Rather than rebuilding, the seven hundred survivors moved their homes a few miles east and founded New Ilvin. This sleepy community seems ordinary in every way, but residents avoid speaking of Old Ilvin and never return, going so far as to pave a new road to avoid the burned-out ruins.

MAP 3.2: BORCA

STURBEN

Long considered Levkarest's unfashionable shadow, the city of Sturben has become a haven for those seeking distance from the domain's elite. To counter the half-hearted justice doled out by local nobles, the city council of Sturben reinstituted a severe court system from Borca's past, where anyone can bring and argue cases before five masked judges. The judges who hear cases at the Faceless Court change, but their masks remain the same: grimly ornate visages inspired by Borca's mysterious first inhabitants. The court sends iron-masked circuit judges into the surrounding lands to execute justice. For especially contentious cases, judges imprison all involved and drag them to Sturben to face trial.

MISERICORDIA AND OTHER NOBLE ESTATES

Each of the domain's prominent families maintains an opulent and extravagantly named manor, as noted on the Noble Families and Estates table. Following the custom of Borcan high society, each family is expected to host at least two formal balls, banquets, or other extravagances annually. These events provide the setting for intrigues, politics, business arrangements, seductions, embarrassments, and social warfare. (See the "Nobles of Borca" section for more on these families.)

Among the most decadent noble holdings is Misericordia, the Boritsi estate. Situated amid miles of fields, greenhouses, and alchemy labs used to create exceptional Boritsi-branded perfumes and tinctures, the manor features multiple widow's walks and more than three hundred rooms. An awe-inspiring array of unique plants grows within the estate's private conservatory wings. The distillates from these plants furnish the lady of the house, Ivana Boritsi, with a room-sized perfume organ—along with a hidden, parallel collection of remarkable poisons.

NOBLE FAMILIES AND ESTATES

Noble Family	Estate Name
Boritsi	Misericordia
Dilisnya	Degravo
Eris	Coairdeiador
Ivliskova	Abreptoro
Nobriskov	Cubratdis
Nuikin	Esecklae
Ocrotire	Sanctesalat
Olzanik	Kinisaradia
Piechota	Alieselti
Pretorius	Mundorhova
Ritter	Vetistiqua
Tatenna	Fulchighora

IVANA BORITSI

The firstborn of the fantastically wealthy Boritsi aristocrats, Ivana was clever, poised, and—in her father Klaus's eyes—utterly unfit to lead their family. Unwilling to accept her father's view, Ivana spent her youth eschewing the dalliances of her kin, instead learning every aspect of her family's business in perfumes and medicinal herbs. Her mother, Camille, encouraged her daughter and tried to ensure that Ivana would one day lead the family.

Ivana's focus on her goals faltered when she met Pieter, a skilled chemist in the family's service. From him, Ivana learned alchemy and the perfumer's art, and the two grew close. Camille recognized Ivana's budding romance and saw the lowborn Pieter as a threat to Ivana's prospects. Camille thus seduced the young man and arranged for Ivana to discover them, intent on convincing her daughter to forsake this and all future romances.

Ivana took a different lesson from the experience. Realizing the depths of her family's corruption, she poisoned her mother and her callous brothers, with the goal of forcing Klaus to name her his heir. Creating and employing a series of aromatic toxins, she watched her siblings and treacherous mother sicken and die. None suspected her involvement.

On Ivana's eighteenth birthday, the aged and ailing Klaus summoned her to his office to share a momentous decision. Having lost his sons, Klaus named Ivana's cousin, Ivan Dilisnya, his heir. He had already announced his decision to the estate staff and sent a messenger to inform the Dilisnyas.

Ivana only laughed as a toxic mist poured across the Boritsi estate. Having expected her father's pettiness, she had manufactured a disaster that turned all the estate's perfume into poison. Drinking the antidote, Ivana watched as Klaus and all the manor's workers and inhabitants died choking amid a violet fog. By the time the poison cleared, the land of Borca had become surrounded by the Mists.

IVANA'S POWERS AND DOMINION

Ivana appears to be a young human woman with statistics similar to a **spy**. Since her arrival in the Land of the Mists, her blood has been tainted with poison, and angry red-and-black veins visibly show through her pale skin. While this discoloration is unignorable, the toxins grant her immunity to poison damage and being poisoned. Her genius and ambition define her manipulations.

Alchemical Innovator. By spending one uninterrupted hour within her laboratory at the Boritsi Estate, Ivana can create ten doses of any poison or re-create the effect of one wizard spell of 7th level or lower. She keeps a variety of poisons on hand at all times. See "Intrigue in Borca" later in this section for details on how Ivana uses alchemy in her manipulations.

Callous Genius. Ivana's genius and cynicism, in combination with the Dark Powers' aid, grant her insight into the nature of Borca's people that borders on precognition. She's always one step ahead of her rivals and has prepared the perfect situation, stand-in, or poison accordingly. However, Ivana has a facile understanding of true love and companionship, so those who behave in an unexpectedly selfless manner might undermine her elaborate contingencies.

Gardens of Evil. Ivana delights in her gardens, both the exotic conservatories within the Boritsi Estate and the flower fields surrounding her manor. She has created innumerable unique plants, as well as plant creatures with strange abilities and unflagging loyalty to her.

WAYNE ENGLAND

Tyrant Maker. Ivana's ambition drives her to take on any challenge. She reflexively seeks political and financial control over all Borca, and casually manipulates the domain's noble families into destroying one another.

Closing the Borders. Ivana can close or open Borca's borders once per day. She rarely closes the borders, as her manipulations typically prevent her victims from leaving. She might open or close the borders to confound the whims of her co-Darklord, Ivan, though. When she does close Borca's borders, the Mists rise as a wall of acrid chemicals that affect creatures as detailed in "The Mists" section at the start of this chapter.

IVANA'S TORMENT

Ivana conquered her rivals, yet still suffers. The following circumstances endlessly torment the Darklord:

- Ivana has not aged since the Mists claimed Borca, and her youthful appearance leads many to underestimate her.
- Ivana rules her family's business and political empire brilliantly. Despite this, she is endlessly doubted and second guessed. Many believe she is a typical, vacant noble youth or the puppet of her elder cousin, Ivan Dilisnya.
- Ivana's genius and refinement lead her to grow swiftly bored of most potential allies and rivals. She ever seeks her equal in intellect and ambition, and she is ever disappointed. Maintaining her family's vast array of social expectations is especially tedious.
- Ivana never found her father's will and knows that should it fall into the wrong hands, her depraved cousin Ivan could claim all she's earned. She'll do anything to prevent this.

ROLEPLAYING IVANA

Ivana Boritsi's exceptional mind and remarkable senses of hearing, taste, and smell inform her elevated fancies and expansive knowledge of art, food, fashion, social protocols, alchemy, and perfume. Few people can hold her attention, and none can redeem themselves in her eyes from even a moment's boorishness.

Personality Trait. "I'm perfect, and no one else understands the strain and expectation that comes with being the best at everything."

Ideal. "One day I'll find someone worth my time. Everyone else is boring at best."

Bond. "Only my plants and formulas never disappoint me."

Flaw. "It's insulting to think I haven't anticipated every possible outcome."

IVANA BORITSI WELCOMES GUESTS TO THE POISONOUS CONSERVATORIES OF MISERICORDIA.

IVAN DILISNYA

The Dilisnya family maintains a tradition of treachery. The land of Borca originates from the same world as Barovia's conquerors, the von Zaroviches, and Dilisnyas were present at Castle Ravenloft the night of Strahd von Zarovich's transformation.

Ages later, the siblings Boris and Camille Dilisnya each plotted to steal the prestige of their cousins, the Boritsis. Camille manipulated her way into the Boritsi family while Boris prepared his son Ivan to be the new head of a united Boritsi–Dilisnya line. Despite abundant opportunities to excel, Ivan grew to embody childish vice and impulsiveness, with his family's wealth and doting servants exacerbating these whims. Frequent "accidents" transpired around Ivan, forcing his family to cover up the maimings and deaths of numerous pets and servants. Only Ivan's sister, Kristina, was exempt from his bullying and wicked tricks.

Over time, Kristina proved precocious and eager to learn. Ivan, however, became stubbornly obsessed with childish toys and behaviors. He encouraged his sister to indulge his idealized visions of their childhood, going so far as to affect childlike behaviors and ways of speaking. Although his family members grew increasingly unsettled, they sheltered the future head of their house, reshaping their estate and investing in whimsical diversions for him.

On the night Ivana Boritsi poisoned her family, Ivan learned of his parents' intention to send Kristina to a prestigious boarding school. Screams, cruel cackling, and clockwork screeching filled the Dilisnya estate that night. When it ended, Ivan was the last living member of the Dilisnya family, and the Mists closed in around Borca.

IVAN'S POWERS AND DOMINION

Ivan isn't a physically or magically powerful Darklord. He's an extremely old man, but supernaturally he remains as physically fit as he was in the prime of life and has the statistics of a human **noble**. His menace manifests in the form of psychological manipulation, making others doubt reality, and causing victims to overestimate his control.

Cursed Correspondence. Ivan loathes leaving his estate, but the Dark Powers have granted him the ability to have his letters delivered anywhere he pleases. See "Intrigue in Borca" later in this section for details on Ivan's letters.

Manipulative Actor. One of Ivan's favorite manipulations is using his letters and his high-pitched voice to pretend to be a lonely youngster. Ivan keeps out of sight from those he targets for deception so they don't realize the discordance between his childlike affectations and his appearance. If forced to reveal his aged form, he pretends to be confused and employs elaborate clockwork toys, disguises, and conveyances that further mask his true ability.

Toy Maker. The Dark Powers provide Ivan with any toy he desires. Creatures of many sorts serve Ivan, and any of them, from maids to monstrous guardians, could be clockwork devices or stuffed toys. This doesn't change the creatures' statistics and is revealed only in dramatic moments. Individuals the characters have known for years might eventually be revealed as Ivan's toys.

IVAN DILISNYA IN HIS FAVORITE
CLOCKWORK PRAM

SHAWN WOOD

Wicked Wonderland. The Dilisnya estate, Degravo, is a confusing tangle of topiary gardens, hedge mazes, and neglected petting zoos that abut sheer cliffs. The mansion lies at the heart of the estate, and is divided into multiple structures, including the Laughing House, a playhouse where life-sized toys enact brutal operas, and Ivan's Playroom, a wing dedicated to the master of the estate's clockwork tinkering and private decadences. Ivan tempts victims to his home, where they gradually realize they're trapped in a fun house of childish grotesqueries. Those unable to escape are eventually forced to don the ludicrous livery of the Dilisnya household staff and become Ivan's new servants.

Closing the Borders. Ivan can close or open Borca's borders once per day. He closes them to prevent those he's obsessing over from escaping. When he closes Borca's borders, the Mists rise as detailed in "The Mists" section at the start of this chapter. Additionally, the fog is filled with Ivan's taunting voice and patrolled by grim clockwork toys.

IVAN'S TORMENT

Since the night the Mists took Borca, Ivan rarely leaves the Dilisnya estate. The following circumstances endlessly torment him:

- Ivan is alone, and the solitude terrifies him. He was given everything, destroyed it all, and doesn't know how to live. He endlessly creates fawning, fake family from clockwork creations to distract him from his solitude.
- Ivan resents Ivana Boritsi, his closest relative, for having the power he was groomed for, but he also views her as his only peer and as a potential replacement for his sister. Ivana, however, avoids him at all costs.
- Ivan looks like a fantastically unkempt old man, a state he believes he has no control over and that grows more pronounced daily. He thinks Ivana keeps the secret of her eternal youth from him.

ROLEPLAYING IVAN

Ivan demands to be the center of attention while remaining deeply suspicious of the world beyond Degravo. With his family gone, he coaxes guests to his home to indulge in a perverse mixture of fabulous decadence and his off-putting, childish whims. Ivan delights in his guests' discomfort and in forcing them to entertain him.

Personality Trait. "The world exists only to bring me pleasure."

Ideal. "I never want to be bored or alone again."

Bond. "My possessions are mine to do with as I please. I decide their fate."

Flaw. "I break whatever bores me. At least a broken toy is unique."

ADVENTURES IN BORCA

Borca provides opportunities for political intrigues, family power struggles, and callous betrayals set amid a backdrop of ludicrous wealth and perverse visions of refinement. Adventures set in Borca often involve characters participating in the machinations of the domain's nobles, whether as involuntary pawns or as part of schemes to see them indebted to amoral patrons. The domain's two Darklords also provide opportunities to explore different types of amoral arrogance and petty obsessions. Characters might become caught between Ivana Boritsi and Ivan Dilisnya's unique obsessions—but could also learn that the best way to undermine these villains is to play them against one another.

The following sections detail the schemes of the domain's nobles and Darklords, while the Borca Adventures table suggests other adventures appropriate to the domain.

BORCA ADVENTURES

d8	Adventure
1	A noble asks the characters to protect their sibling from a mysterious assassin. The killer is Nostalia Romaine, whose blood was replaced with poison by Ivana Boritsi.
2	A scholar requests aid in gaining access to Scholomance. This institution is Borca's elite school of magic and also home to the Rainmaker Society, which is said to control Borcan politics.
3	A young noble befriends the characters and introduces them to the fabulously amoral Levkarest club scene. By the night's end, a character is accused of murder.
4	Half the village of Leoni is arrested by the erinyes-masked Judge Ranziska and marched before Sturben's Faceless Court. The remaining villagers beseech the party to defend their families in court.
5	The eligible noble Vladimir Nobriskov hosts a contest for his affections. Participants turn up murdered, victims of Nobriskov's lycanthropic hunger.
6	A book-collecting noble seeks the party's help in finding a rare text called *The Revelations of the Prince of Twilight*, a tome said to teach the reader to tap into the hidden power of their shadow.
7	The Ocrotire family offers a sizable bounty for anyone who can capture the Lake Balaur Beast, which has escaped from the estate's oceanarium.
8	Members of the Ulmist Inquisition accuse the characters of crimes they haven't yet committed. They relent only if the characters undertake a mission against the **priests of Osybus** (see chapter 5).

NOBLES OF BORCA

From their decadent manors and lofty business offices, twelve prominent noble families rule over Borcan politics, industry, art, entertainment, religion, and every other aspect of life in the domain. The following families are Borca's most prominent, though dozens of lesser branch families orbit each:

Boritsi. The Boritsi name is a mark of quality and innovation, appearing across Borca on perfumes, tonics, and dozens of buildings and theaters. Countless families claim ties to the Boritsis.

Dilisnya. The family defensively guards its prestige, as its wealth is based in agriculture—particularly rearing pigs. Treacherous branch families have warred among themselves since the loss of nearly the entire main family.

Eris. The elderly Tolashara Eris claims to be the last of her line. She pours her family's wealth into supporting art in Levkarest and endlessly building her estate both taller and deeper.

Ivliskova. The Ivliskovas run dozens of orphanages and the elite Ivliskova Finishing School. This boarding school boasts a flawless graduation rate—for those students who don't disappear.

Nobriskov. Pious and formal, the Nobriskovs claim descent from Borca's ancient clans and hide their family's lycanthropic curse.

Nuikin. Every member of this competitive family is expected to become a genius in their respective field. Numerous libraries, museums, and theaters advertise Nuikin accomplishments.

Ocrotire. The Ocrotires descend from respected admirals and seafaring explorers (despite Borca's lack of a coast). Their estate features a vast oceanarium featuring thousands of bizarre sea creatures and a complete megalodon skeleton.

Olzanik. This family of metalworkers obsesses over war. To them, every success is a conquest, but no Olzanik has ever seen battle in national service.

Piechota. The estate of Borca's best ranchers lies half ruined as the result of another family's treachery. Their wealth largely expended, the Piechotas open their home to travelers along the Ruby Road.

Pretorius. The Pretorius estate is a raucous casino surrounded by the Ash Gardens, a region burned in a vast wildfire. Those who can't pay debts incurred at the casino are burned alive and their ashes scattered in the wastelands.

Ritter. The shear-wielding Ritters define the cutting edge of fashion. Their coveted designs change seasonally, and any who create reproductions meet vicious ends.

Tatenna. Bankers and landlords, the Tatennas track debts across the domain. They deal with every family except the Olzaniks, with whom they maintain a generations-old feud.

INTRIGUE IN BORCA

Endless power games play out in Borca. Something as simple as having the right talent or piece of gear could cause a noble to take notice of a character and invite them to an outing or event that leads to further intrigues. These plots initially revolve around small, petty things, but culminate in disasters and true outrages. They often play out in familiar ways.

READY ACCOMPLICES

Characters readily win contacts among Borca's nobility, since the elite seem easily charmed by the adventuring life. Friendly nobles soon embroil new acquaintances in their schemes, asking characters for favors meant to prove friendship or trustworthiness. These requests typically play into characters' action-first inclinations and gradually add up, giving the noble knowledge they can later leverage however they please.

IGNOBLE BONDS

Between adventures, a noble contact might share their problems with a character or seek favors from a character. Roll or choose an option from the Ignoble Request table to determine what the contact wishes. These requests target a specific rival or member of another family, and lead to increasingly dramatic treacheries.

IGNOBLE REQUEST

d6	Request
1	Manufacture a business or social opportunity for the target's confidant, leaving the target isolated.
2	Deliver a lavish gift to the target, such as a large sculpture or a steed, at an inappropriate time.
3	Make the target cry in public.
4	Plant evidence of a crime at the target's home.
5	Orchestrate a false business deal, political alliance, or arranged relationship.
6	Make the target miss their own social event.

LETHAL LEVERAGE

Ever thinking of themselves, the aforementioned noble contact seeks leverage over the characters. The Lethal Leverage table suggests things a noble contact might seek to use against adventurers. Once they have such leverage, the noble contact is no longer a friend, but rather the characters' debt holder or blackmailer. Most such treacherous individuals try to ensure that threats or magic can't easily compel them to relinquish their leverage, such as sending it to a third party or disseminating it within a group of allies.

LETHAL LEVERAGE

d6	Leverage
1	The contact provides the characters with noteworthy gear to use during a request, then collects it afterward as evidence.
2	The contact conveniently "goes out of town," requesting characters report to them in writing.
3	The contact requests magical insurance, such as a *geas* spell preventing mutual harm or committing the characters to a misrepresented act.
4	The contact becomes the guardian of someone close to the characters.
5	The contact holds a powerful magic item for the characters "so it doesn't fall into the wrong hands."
6	The contact has the characters act against a mutual friend "for their own good." The contact then threatens to reveal this act to the friend.

COUP DE GRACE

Once the aforementioned noble has gained leverage over the party, they might make all sorts of demands. It's then up to the characters whether they obey or find a way to escape the noble's schemes. This might even be the point where the noble reveals that they've been an agent of Ivana Boritsi or Ivan Dilisnya all along, and now the Darklord they serve has a use for the characters.

IVANA'S INTRIGUES

Ivana Boritsi's interests lie in manipulating sweeping aspects of Borca's society, asserting her dominance amid an ever-shifting landscape of petty noble schemes. She isn't a spellcaster, but her insights into alchemy allow her to create chemically potent mind-altering effects. Ivana's chemical arsenal includes drinks that convey illusory sensations, perfumes that charm creatures, and dramatic poisons activated by innocuous secondary triggers. Through suggestion and by subtly exposing targets to her chemicals, Ivana convinces victims she's practically omnipotent.

Use the poisons detailed in the *Dungeon Master's Guide* as a baseline for the effects Ivana creates and combine them with the effects of enchantment and illusion spells to design custom, nonmagical toxins for her. The following example combines an inhaled poison and the *dream* spell, creating a tool Ivana uses to manipulate her agents.

Ivana's Whisper (Inhaled). This poison bears a distinct scent and chemical message from Ivana Boritsi. A creature subjected to this poison must succeed on a DC 18 Constitution saving throw or experience the effects of a *dream* spell created by Ivana the next time they sleep. This poison is nonmagical, and Ivana doesn't directly communicate with those affected during the dream. Rather, she creates the illusion of speaking with her intended target by alchemically crafting her message, predicting her target's reactions, and chemically encoding in her responses. She wears this poison as a perfume or hides it within gift bouquets, allowing it to convey her message later.

IVAN'S INTRIGUES

Ivan Dilisnya has a simple desire: companionship. Unfortunately, he's a selfish and controlling individual. To enable his need for attention, the Dark Powers granted him a subtle ability to have the letters he writes magically delivered. Ivan uses this simple power for amoral, cowardly ends. On rare occasions Ivan takes his clockwork coach through communities to watch for passersby worth writing to.

The Darklord's Letters. Ivan's letters are supernatural missives relayed by the Dark Powers. If Ivan writes a letter and addresses it to a creature whose name he knows and whom he's seen before, he can choose to have one such letter vanish at midnight of the following night. That letter then reappears in an unobserved but obvious space near the letter's addressee during their next long rest. The letter might appear among the recipient's mundane mail, on their bedside table, or among their gear. A letter's mysterious means of delivery is never observed. Ivan's letters can reach a target anywhere within the Domains of Dread.

The Darklord Knows. Ivan supernaturally knows the location of every letter he has magically sent within the last month, pinpointed to within 1 mile. As a result, he can tell that one of his letters is in a settlement, but not in which house. He also knows when his letters are destroyed.

The Darklord's Demands. Ivan persistently pesters people with his letters, often fixating on two or three individuals. He writes frequently, using the facade of the recipient's secret admirer, a youngster in need of help, or a distant family member, though his lies fracture over time. His salutations are off-putting or childishly insulting, like "Dear Delicious Knuckle" or "My Preening Pig-Face." His letters' contents typically focus on him rather than the recipient, obsessing over his feelings, distractions, and self-indulgent rants. Inevitably, his cowardly cruelty shows through as the letters grow increasingly possessive and insulting. He initially coaxes recipients to fetch gifts for him or to undermine his foes, but his requests culminate in insisting that the recipient joins him at Degravo, the Dilisnya estate.

The Carnival
Wandering Domain of Wonders

Darklord: Nepenthe
Genres: Body horror and dark fantasy
Hallmarks: Entertainment, fey bargains, misfits, wandering exiles
Mist Talismans: Carnival flier, colorful ticket, strange prize from a Carnival game

Resplendent with bright banners, calliope music, and the smells of rich food, the Carnival promises visitors a surreal wonderland where any dream is possible.

Garish fliers appear before the Carnival's arrival, promising marvels, terrors, and a brief escape from the gloom of daily life. But nothing in the Land of the Mists is beyond suspicion, and the wise know strangers are intrinsically dangerous.

The Carnival doesn't exist to entertain its visitors. Rather, it's a traveling domain, capable of visiting other domains and lands beyond the Mists. Visibly marked as outsiders by birth, circumstance, intention, or talent, the Carnival's troupers trade their unique performances for coin and whatever else they need to survive. Although these entertainers are well intentioned, sinister forces travel in their wake. The longer the Carnival tarries in one place, the greater the threat to the performers and visitors. So the Carnival travels constantly, lest the troupers endanger the lands they visit.

Noteworthy Features

Those familiar with the Carnival know the following facts:

- Fliers advertising the Carnival's impending arrival appear mysteriously in communities before it appears. The Carnival doesn't contribute to their production or distribution.
- Two silver pieces buy a ticket to the Carnival, while the Big Top's shows, the Hall of Horrors, and sideshows have their own entry fees.
- The Carnival wanders endlessly, never staying anywhere for more than a few weeks. Most settlements welcome this traveling diversion, but tragedies follow its path.
- Merchants unaffiliated with the Carnival follow its travels and set up shop alongside it. Known as the Litwick Market, this collection of tents and booths is filled with strange vendors and stranger goods.
- Those seeking an escape from a place or their current lives can join the Carnival. As long as travelers are willing to work and contribute to the community, they're welcome to stay as long as they like.

CARNIVAL CHARACTERS

When players create characters from the Carnival, consider asking them the following questions.

What sets you apart from your birth family? Do you have a unique talent or inborn ability? Do you display a physical difference? Do you carry a curse or blessing? How do you feel about your differences?

Do you perform? Have you devised a way to profit from your circumstances? Are you proud of your performances? Do you have a show mentor or partner? Or do you earn your way in the Carnival as a laborer, as a vendor, or in another role?

How did you join the Carnival? Did you run away to join? Were you an outcast who found a home with the Carnival? Did Isolde or a trouper save you from danger?

Settlements and Sites

This small domain encompasses only a few hundred square yards. A handful of horses and exotic pack animals transport the Carnival's two dozen wagons from site to site.

One of the Carnival's oldest performers, Hermos the Half-Giant, handles the Carnival's day-to-day operations. Hermos is a mountain of muscle half again as tall as most human adults. His deliberate manner and coolheaded demeanor earn him the respect of the Carnival's troupers. Other senior or charismatic figures hold influence over cliquish groups of performers, but few dare openly contradict Hermos since he's favored by the Carnival's leader, Isolde.

The Carnival's arrangement varies depending on where it sets up, but always includes a thoroughfare of games, food, and sideshow stalls leading from the ticketing gate to the Big Top.

Big Top

Standing at the Carnival's center is the Big Top, its largest tent. The Big Top houses spectacular shows, from acrobats and displays of magic to beloved plays. Three coppers buy a visitor admittance for as long as they like, with performances of varying quality running from sunrise until midnight.

Sideshows

Lurid banners with exaggerated art and the calls of barkers advertise the Carnival's unusual performers. For 2 copper pieces, visitors enter a tent and watch a performer's show. The Carnival's best-known attractions include the following troupers (along with the stat blocks they use):

Tindal the Barker. Tindal, the Carnival's cynical, fast-talking lead barker (**mage**), tours the grounds with visitors. At their last stop, he reveals his own uniqueness as the Amazing Soul-less Man: he casts no reflection and claims to lack a soul.

Alti the Werehare. A quick-tongued rapper and dancer, Alti (**wererat**) is a bombastic performer who turns into a rabbit on nights of the full moon.

Amelia the Vampire. Amelia (**scout** with a flying speed of 30 feet) is a cheery acrobat aided in her performances by a pair of leathery wings that allows her to fly. Before stepping on stage, she powders her face, affects a somber accent, and pretends to be undead.

Charlotte the Fire Eater. This juggling daredevil (**veteran**) performs with a dizzying array of flaming knives and other deadly objects. She claims that her blood is flammable and that she's burned the hair off eighteen hecklers.

The Organ Grinder. This somber clown grinds an ornate barrel organ (**scout**). An attendant group of mischievous, half-trained, not-quite-identifiable animals caper to this music. The clown never speaks but allows visitors to guess at the animals' nature for a copper piece.

Silessa the Snake. A dancer and animal tamer, Silessa (**druid**) performs with a collection of rare serpents. She claims she was born a snake and magically transformed into an elf.

HALL OF HORRORS

A severe, bespectacled academic, Professor Pacali runs the Carnival's Hall of Horrors. This sizable, sinister tent contains a maze of taxidermic creatures, cabinets of curiosity, peculiar specimens in jars, and the occasional true wonder. Pacali hides a personal unsettling secret. During his time as a researcher at the Brautslava Institute in Darkon, Pacali was cursed: his worst impulses now grow from his body as terrible creatures. He bottles these murderous homunculi and touts them as "Professor Pacali's Pickled Punks," but every now and then one "escapes." Pacali persistently criticizes Hermos and Isolde, but rarely acts against them directly.

LITWICK MARKET

The Carnival doesn't travel alone. Wherever it goes, fey creatures chase after it, appearing on the Carnival's outskirts as mysterious merchants selling dangerous enigmas and Mist talismans. They peddle lost memories or love potions for peculiar prices, such as the buyer's dreams or ability to speak vowels. Gradually, more dangerous fey arrive—creatures who delight in sabotaging performances or nearby settlements. These tricks and accidents grow increasingly dangerous, potentially culminating in disasters for which the Carnival's troupers ultimately take the blame. All these fey hold a grudge against the Carnival. They light their stalls with eerie colored lanterns and call themselves the Litwick Market.

DECEITFUL FEY LURE THE UNWARY FROM THE CARNIVAL'S MIDWAY.

Isolde and Nepenthe

Isolde, the Carnival's leader, is an eladrin (an elf native to the Feywild). She is a Fey who otherwise uses the **cambion** stat block. She is never seen without her *holy avenger* longsword, Nepenthe, which glows red with hate. Nepenthe, not Isolde, is the Carnival's Darklord.

Isolde

Isolde was a holy warrior devoted to a pantheon of elven deities called the Seldarine. In this role, she defended the Feywild against dragons, demons, and other threats. In time, her heroics caught the eye of an archfey named Zybilna, who had forged secret pacts with some of the fiends Isolde and her companions had slain. Rather than be angry at Isolde, Zybilna was impressed by her. She enlisted a

ISOLDE WITH THE SWORD NEPENTHE

powerful fiend known only as "the Caller" to corrupt and slay all of Isolde's companions, leaving Isolde alone, bitter, and vulnerable. The insidious archfey then befriended Isolde and offered to help her forget her terrible losses. Isolde became the master of a traveling fey carnival that served as a gateway to Zybilna's domain. The carnival did what Zybilna hoped it would do: it brought comfort to Isolde and quelled her thirst for vengeance.

Zybilna and Isolde enjoyed a strong partnership for years, but as time wore on, they grew distant until their relationship finally soured. Eladrin crave change, yet Isolde felt like she was frozen in time. She wished to leave the fey carnival and pursue other dreams, but Zybilna wouldn't hear of it and secretly used *wish* spells to make Isolde place her devotion to the carnival above her desire to leave it.

When Isolde's fey carnival crossed paths with another carnival from the Shadowfell, the eladrin found the escape she longed for. Isolde orchestrated a trade with the other carnival's owners, a pair of shadar-kai (elves native to the Shadowfell). Isolde would become the master of their carnival, and they would become the masters of hers. To appease Zybilna, this arrangement would remain in place only until the two carnivals crossed paths again.

Zybilna was intrigued enough by the shadar-kai to let Isolde go, but not without casting a spell that made Isolde forget about Zybilna and her Feywild domain, thus preventing the eladrin from divulging the archfey's secrets. As a further punishment, Zybilna sent malevolent fey creatures to hound Isolde and her Shadowfell carnival. Isolde doesn't know who is behind this petty torment, nor does she care. Her hunt for the Caller and her thirst for vengeance have become all-consuming.

Nepenthe

The *holy avenger* named Nepenthe was crafted by shadar-kai to mete out justice as an executioner's weapon. In its lifetime, the sword has beheaded thousands of criminals, not all of whom were guilty of the crimes for which they were convicted. The sword cannot distinguish the guilty from the innocent. With each beheading, it hungers for more justice and blood.

Nepenthe came to the Carnival in the hands of a retired half-ogre who moonlighted as a sword-swallower. When the half-ogre died of old age, the sword was deemed the property of the Carnival. It was given to Isolde by the Carnival's previous owners, who claimed that the sword would help her protect the Carnival against any threat.

In Isolde, the sword found a partner who shared its blind malice toward the guilty. Isolde uses Nepenthe to behead anyone found guilty of stealing from the Carnival or inflicting harm upon it.

As soon as Isolde took up the blade, it rekindled the grief and fury she had suppressed for so long, awakening the desire to avenge her long-dead companions by slaying the fiend she knows as the Caller (see "Mist Wanderers" later in this chapter for details). Isolde always chooses the Carnival's stops based on her predictions of the Caller's next steps, and if her pursuit forces the Carnival into danger, so be it. Only by ridding Isolde of Nepenthe can she truly escape the Dark Powers' clutches. But Isolde will never part with the blade willingly, and if it is taken from the Carnival, the sword will always find its way back.

In addition to having the properties of a *holy avenger*, Nepenthe is a sentient, neutral evil weapon with an Intelligence of 10, a Wisdom of 8, and a Charisma of 18. It has hearing and darkvision out to a range of 60 feet. It can read and understand Elvish. It can also speak Elvish, but only through the voice of its wielder, with whom the sword can communicate telepathically. When using its telepathy to speak to Isolde, the sword can mimic the voices of Isolde's fallen companions as it drives her to catch their fiendish killer. Unlike Isolde, whose motives are good, the sword is corrupt and irredeemable.

FREEDOM OF THE MISTS

The Carnival travels through the Mists and between other Domains of Dread as Isolde pleases—though the Dark Powers occasionally send it off course. The Carnival provides one of the few means of escaping from another Darklord's domain, since it ignores the closed borders of other domains. Other Darklords cannot travel with the Carnival to escape their own domains, however.

CLOSING THE BORDERS

Nepenthe can close the borders of its domain, as detailed in "The Mists" at the start of this chapter. With the sword's consent, Isolde can do the same. When the Carnival's borders close, the Mists are filled with eerie, colorful lights and distant music, echoing memories of past carnivals.

ISOLDE'S TORMENT

Isolde is both protector and prisoner of the Carnival. The following truths endlessly weigh upon her:

- The Carnival constantly grows, bringing additional souls dependent on Isolde's guardianship. She's tortured by her obligation toward the Carnival's troupers and her vow to avenge her murdered companions.
- Isolde obsessively plots the perfect confrontation with her immortal quarry, the Caller. But the small concerns of the Carnival nag at her ceaselessly, exacerbated by the fey interlopers drawn to her presence. Her burdens drive her to seek seclusion to keep her legendary temper in check.

- Isolde dreads the day when the Carnival crosses paths with its fey counterpart for a second time. Were that to happen, Isolde would be forced to relinquish the Carnival to its true shadar-kai masters, and Nepenthe along with it.

ROLEPLAYING ISOLDE

The Carnival is the closest thing Isolde has to a family and a home, and she expects everyone who works for her to carry their weight. She endlessly overburdens herself, struggling to protect those around her as her hate for the Caller drives her forward at any cost.

Personality Trait. "We all contribute so that we all benefit. Those who do not carry the burden do not eat."

Ideal. "Those most deserving of aid are those who never ask for it."

Bond. "You share a bond with those you travel with, a bond closer than blood. Choose well who you share the road with, lest you carry them forever."

Flaw. "For my victories and scars, I deserve more than a nursemaid's duty."

ADVENTURES IN THE CARNIVAL

The Carnival deals in fabricated spectacles and cheap surprises, but it disguises actual marvels of a far deadlier sort. Even as the Carnival's troupers astonish their visitors with amazing performances, a surreal world of outlandish beings, dangerous bargains, and deadly tricks encroaches on the festivities, threatening performers and audiences alike. The Carnival provides a safe place for a time, but the longer it lingers, the greater the danger grows—whether from intolerant common folk, jaded troupers, dangerous fey, or Isolde's tireless quest.

Consider the plots on the Carnival Adventures table when planning adventures in this domain.

CARNIVAL ADVENTURES

d4	Adventure
1	One of the Carnival's performers has been arrested by a local sheriff. Hermos asks the party to return the trouper, either to save them or to make them face Carnival justice.
2	A local hires the party to find a loved one who disappeared at the Carnival. The trail leads to a Litwick Market vendor whose trinkets turn people into their favorite animals.
3	The Carnival adopts a new performer escaping their family. The performer asks the party to deter family members intent on bringing them home.
4	The characters find a mirror holding the disembodied reflection of Tindafulus, a **mage** trapped by his own reflection. He wants the party to find his duplicate, who escaped with a mysterious carnival.

DARKON

Domain on the Brink of Destruction

Darklord: None
Genres: Dark fantasy and disaster horror
Hallmarks: Fractured realm, magical ruins, ongoing supernatural catastrophe
Mist Talismans: Ashes of a corpse, coin stamped with Azalin Rex's face, tainted spring water

The domain of Darkon has failed. Across the land, ageless monuments and magical wonders crumble before the Shroud—the Mists turned hungry.

Once the prison of the lich Azalin Rex, Darkon stretched between two oceans, its lands filled with gothic cities and the monuments of forgotten wizard-tyrants. Largely ignoring his role as ruler, Azalin dwelled in seclusion while manufacturing magical atrocities and manipulating prophecies to free himself from the Dark Powers' grip. He finally succeeded, orchestrating a magical event that shook the entire domain: the Hour of Ascension. The Darklord vanished—and Darkon changed.

Since Azalin's disappearance, a strange golden star called the King's Tear hangs in the heavens, and each night the Mists surrounding the domain roil with hidden activity and creep inward. These Mists, now known throughout the domain as the Shroud, erode Darkon's borders. Those fleeing the Shroud report strange shapes and figures within. What happens to the lands claimed by the Shroud is a mystery, and none who enter it return.

Despite facing gradual annihilation, Darkon's living population largely ignores the threat, dismissing reports of vanished regions as rumors and fearmongering. As the domain splits into crumbling islands, ambitious beings vie for Azalin's power, each claiming to be the lost king's obvious successor. These would-be tyrants blame one another for the domain's dissolution, and each believes they alone can save Darkon by becoming its sole ruler.

NOTEWORTHY FEATURES

Those familiar with Darkon know the following facts:

- The Mists consuming Darkon have divided the land into four regions: the Jagged Coast, Lychgate, the Mistlands, and Rexcrown.
- Azalin Rex, King of Darkon, vanished during the Hour of Ascension. Since then, an unmoving golden star called the King's Tear hangs in the sky. The sun and moon pass behind this star daily.
- The Kargat, the nation's secret police, is particularly active in Darkon's largest cities: Martira Bay and Il Aluk.
- The night after any Humanoid dies, its corpse rises as a mindless Undead that shambles into the night. Locals swiftly burn bodies to prevent this.

SETTLEMENTS AND SITES

Darkon is a land of dark wonders and apathy. The ruins of forgotten magical empires and impossible architecture litter the land, but the jaded people ignore these marvels to focus on daily concerns.

CASTLE AVERNUS

In the minds of Darkon's people, Castle Avernus was the sanctuary of their aloof king and the citadel from which he watched over his people. In truth, Avernus was a perilously haunted fortress, home to Azalin's deadliest servants and magical depravities. During the Hour of Ascension, that changed.

Castle Avernus was destroyed in a torrent of otherworldly flame, an explosion that froze partway through its blast. The castle now hangs in midair, its chambers, laboratories, and crypts suspended in disjointed sections. Magic woven into the fortress's stones attempts to heal the shattered castle, causing new halls and rambling stairs to form between fractured floors. These surreal ruins can't conceal the magical radiance hanging at the castle's core—a vestige of the magical force that destroyed the castle and precipitated the Hour of Ascension. This mysterious force now calls to spirits across Darkon, drawing them in to feed an ongoing magical reaction.

Despite the devastation, Castle Avernus isn't empty. Azalin's treasures and former servants survived, including Ebbasheyth, the Darklord's black shadow dragon advisor; a vast library that records the memories of all who die in Darkon; and the tomb haunted by Irik Zal'honen, Azalin's son.

IL ALUK

A city of spires and leering gargoyles, Il Aluk is home to Darkon's elite and presents a facade of cosmopolitan glamor that fails to hide its crumbling

MAP 3.3: DARKON

social order. Cut off from ports elsewhere in the domain, Il Aluk's nobles cling to lies of prosperity while their fortunes dwindle. They have passed their suffering on to their servants, forcing the populace into poverty and inciting a swell of a violence ranging from riots to assassinations. The nobles' rising fear then swept Madame Eris into power; her elitist cruelties and faux reminiscences have precipitated a rash of brutal murders and fabulous balls.

MARTIRA BAY

The foggy port of Martira Bay is no stranger to mystery. A center of trade, the city receives regular visits from eerie vessels from mysterious lands. The oddities these ships bring make Martirans indifferent to miraculous sights. This unflappability helps residents avoid standing out or drawing the attention of the Kargat, Darkon's secret police, who conduct their domain-spanning conspiracies from the city's notorious fortress, the Black Tower (see "Other Groups" later in this chapter for details).

An unprecedented number of serial killers prey on Martira Bay, most infamously the Midnight Slasher, the Spider, and the Weeping Woman. The overwhelmed constabulary has requested aid from spiritualist groups and professional detectives such as the Ray Agency and the Dusklight Detectives.

NEVUCHAR SPRINGS

Colorful chemical lanterns limn the paths of Nevuchar Springs, following carved cliff trails that descend to the Nocturnal Sea and paved stairs rising to the famed cavern pools in the nearby hills. Here the town's elf mystics, known as the Eternal Order, study alchemy and the rare properties of their famed amber hot springs. Secretive traditions veil their methods, but the miraculous effects of their practices are undeniable. Those in need of healing or relaxation visit lavish spas such as the famous Cascana Sanitarium. For all the springs' wonders, some who visit emerge psychologically changed. The locals shrug off these dangers, repeating the local aphorism and spa slogan: "Never wait to wash away the old you."

RIVALIS

Quaint pleasantness is a way of life in Rivalis. This town boasts a population of halfling fishers and culinarians, while old human families keep estates around the nearby lakes. When brigands threaten the town or fishing boats vanish—victims of the lake monster, Wolf-Head Wylie—things are only briefly "unfortunate." Discussing such events at the town's larger public houses, such as Old Nuck's or the Lost Goat Knight, spurs locals to change the subject.

INHERITORS OF DARKON

Since the disappearance of Azalin Rex, Darkon has been without a Darklord. Three individuals strive to claim Azalin's place as the domain's ruler, though none know what that entails. Additionally, these individuals cannot open or close the domain's borders.

ALCIO "BARON" METUS

Alcio was never close to her brother, Baron, even after a Kargat vampire turned them both into undead servants. When her creator was destroyed, Alcio and Baron went their separate ways.

It took Alcio years to learn of her brother's death at the hands of Rudolph van Richten, a doctor from Rivalis (see "Lone Travelers" at the end of the chapter). Furious, she sought revenge, but van Richten had moved on, his trail hidden by the Mists. Alcio sought hints of the doctor's location at Richten House, his family's estate. There, she found the spirit of Rudolph's wife, Doctor Ingrid van Richten. Despite imaginative bargains and threats, Alcio couldn't convince Ingrid to reveal anything beyond psychological diagnoses and bemused mockery. Furious, the vampire sought other avenues in her search for her brother's slayer.

In Martira Bay, Alcio discovered Baron's allies in the Kargat. Through audacity and violence, she adopted her brother's rank and the fiction that he held a noble title. As Baron Metus, Alcio flourished in the criminal and espionage communities the Kargat dominated.

When Azalin vanished, Alcio turned her connections with living criminals against the Kargat's largely vampiric leaders. They quickly fell to her allied gangs-turned-vampire hunters, and the Kargat fractured, with Alcio taking over the Black Tower.

Now, Alcio spreads her agents across Darkon, targeting Il Aluk as the next addition to her territory. She still seeks information on Rudolph van Richten, either his whereabouts or a means to coerce Ingrid van Richten to betray what she knows.

Using Alcio Metus. Alcio is a flashy, passionate, and fantastically violent **vampire**. As the head of the Kargat and the region's criminal operations, she rules the Jagged Coast using information and intimidation. She's quick to punish incompetence and quicker to reward daring, but she reserves her greatest rewards for those who further her plots for revenge against Rudolph van Richten.

DARCALUS REX

During her annual midnight submergence in the deepest of Nevuchar Springs's miraculous baths, Cardinna Artazas—the community's thrice-reincarnated elder mystic—received an apocalyptic vision

ALCIO "BARON" METUS

from the spirit of the pools. Throughout history, the waters had cryptically spoken to members of the Eternal Order. Now Cardinna interpreted their message as a personal mission to prevent the end of the world.

Having heard of the Shroud, Cardinna delved into the libraries of her order. There, she discovered writings alluding to "the land," "the ancient," and their reliance on one another. She surmised that Darkon needed not just a ruler but a heart. Though most thought of Azalin as Darkon's only ruler, there was once another: Darcalus Rex, its first king.

Through magic and chemical manipulation, Cardinna summoned the spirit of Darcalus Rex, the tyrannical wizard-king who ruled prior to Azalin. Cardinna's magic worked, causing a mysterious entity to inhabit her order's sacred pools. Now she dedicates the Eternal Order's resources to what she believes is a necessary evil: nurturing a reborn tyrant who tests her resolve as he demands ever greater magical reagents and sacrifices.

Using Darcalus. Darcalus Rex is a **necrichor** (see chapter 5) who cares little for the survival of Darkon—and might not even be the ancient ruler. The elf **archmage** Cardinna Artazas desperately believes she's doing what must be done—including corrupting her order—to save her homeland.

MADAME TALISVERI ERIS

The members of the Eris family stand proudly as Il Aluk's foremost artisans of the grand craft of lying. Despite its ancient name, the family has long endured crushing debt. Through poise and predatory business dealings, members have clung to their rotted estate, Calasquel. As the fortunes of Il Aluk's elite withered, Talisveri Eris took advantage of her family's duplicitous expertise, peddling empty assurances from the center of a web of credit, gossip, and desperate debtors.

Bubbly and fantastically vain, Madame Eris would appear to be a woman of nearly eighty if her attempts at magical age-defiance hadn't resulted in her permanent invisibility. The result of imbibing a flawed magic elixir meant to make her look younger, Eris's invisibility has persisted for decades. She uses avant-garde fashion and gallons of makeup to create the face she presents publicly, as well as presenting numerous alter egos: fictitious family members such as her miserly cousin, Halpernista; her foppish nephew, Oscanor; and her bewilderingly ancient and perpetually furious sister, Lady Tatsaul.

Madame Eris hosts elaborate balls at Calasquel, outside Il Aluk, during which she privately meets with attendees, learns their woes, and tempts them into exploitative business ventures. She plays the nostalgic, elder aristocrat who themes her events around bygone decades, featuring period entertainments and fare that only she remembers—since they're largely lies of her creation.

On the night of each new moon, Madame Eris hosts a private event, gathering her loyal and indebted associates. She refers to this group as the Family. As she deeply exploits these entitled young nobles, she leads them to believe they're key to restoring Il Aluk's grandeur. During this event, she encourages her guests to drink a cordial called the Spirit of Nobility. This magic elixir grants the drinker the effect of a *greater invisibility spell* until dawn. Madame Eris then encourages her guests to indulge their desire for violence—and commit crimes that further her plots. Residents of Il Aluk stay indoors during the new moon, believing hateful spirits walk the streets then.

Using Madame Eris. Madame Eris is a human **noble**. Her body is permanently invisible, but her cosmetics and clothing aren't. It takes her at least 10 minutes and copious cosmetics to create a visible form. She dresses in a fashion typical of her desired appearance or of a fictitious family member.

ADVENTURES IN DARKON

Darkon presents a dystopian fantasy setting perfect for exploring the darker sides of familiar magic and monsters. Creatures such as dragons and beholders that might be ill-suited to other domains find natural homes among this realm's scattered settlements and ancient magical ruins. The Darkon Adventures table provides suggestions for various adventures in the domain.

DARKON ADVENTURES

d6	Adventure
1	The party learns how to destroy the Heart of the Abyss, a relic held by the Order of the Guardians and hunted by a demon called the Whistling Fiend.
2	The **night hag** Styrix has created a device called the Rift Spanner that she plans to use to escape the Domains of Dread. She just needs to transform a few hundred innocents into larvae to power it.
3	A ship captain offers to take the characters away from Darkon, but only after they deliver a trunk full of alchemical supplies to Madame Eris at her family estate.
4	Merchants hire the party as protection from the pirate ship *Bountiful*. Captain Damon Skragg raids not for loot, but for flesh to feed his **ghoul** crew.
5	Researchers from the Brautslava Institute require assistants to aid in investigations into fields such as necrolinguistics and temporal archaeozoology.
6	Murders plague the wealthy families of Redleaf Lake. Locals seek aid from the characters, unaware the bitter dowager Damita Adler exacts a generations-old revenge from her dilapidated home.

THE DOOMED DOMAIN

Unlike domains that feature claustrophobic, tightly themed horror, Darkon provides a setting for a horror-tinged quest with the highest possible stakes. The specifics of such a campaign involve the characters engaging with a handful of elements: fate, hope, allies, rivals, dread, and a campaign climax. Use this section to generate an outline for a campaign focused on the doom of an entire domain.

THE SECRET OF DARKON'S DOOM

When Azalin Rex disappeared during the Hour of Ascension, Darkon lost its Darklord and the phenomenon called the Shroud began consuming the domain. When preparing your campaign, use the Darkon's Destruction and Azalin's Fate tables to establish an idea of why Darkon is being destroyed.

DARKON'S DESTRUCTION

d4	Destruction
1	With Azalin gone, Darkon has no purpose. The Shadowfell is reabsorbing the demiplane.
2	Darkon is being consumed to fuel magic funneling power from Castle Avernus into the King's Tear.
3	The Hour of Ascension was an attack. Invaders are using the Shroud to disguise their assault.
4	The priests of Osybus (see chapter 5) are draining life from Darkon to empower the imprisoned vestige of a wicked deity.

AZALIN'S FATE

d4	Fate
1	Azalin was destroyed—slain by a failed magical experiment, a rival, or the Dark Powers.
2	Azalin escaped the Domains of Dread and returned to his home world of Oerth.
3	Azalin caused an ongoing conjunction that allows him to walk free so long as Darkon is collapsing.
4	Azalin escaped into his past or drew multiple versions of himself into the present.

THE SHROUD

During the day, the Mists surrounding Darkon can be traversed as normal, allowing creatures to travel between domains or regions of Darkon itself. At night, though, the Mists surrounding the domain turn deadly and encroach on the land—sometimes by infinitesimal degrees, other times in unstoppable floods. The fates of those claimed by these surges is a mystery. If a character experiments with the Shroud, a taste of this threat can take the form of damage, stress (see "Fear and Stress" in chapter 4), or a glimpse of the deadly forces lurking beyond. Don't outright slay characters who encounter the Shroud, but make sure the experience reinforces the threat to all of Darkon.

DARKON'S DELIVERANCE

Darkon can be saved. Characters might discover a possibility on the Darkon's Salvation table, leading them to goals on the Means to Save Darkon table.

DARKON'S SALVATION

d6	Method
1	Find or restore Azalin and return him to Darkon.
2	Present the Dark Powers a worthy new Darklord.
3	Bestow a symbol of rule upon a new Darklord.
4	Free Darkon from the Shadowfell.
5	Merge Darkon with another domain.
6	Trick another Darklord into entering Darkon.

MEANS TO SAVE DARKON

d6	Implement
1	Pieces of Azalin's shattered crown
2	The Rift Spanner, a portal-making contraption
3	A hidden amber sarcophagus that contains the last vestige of a powerful evil being
4	The King's Tear, a floating anomaly or structure
5	The Apparatus (see "Mordent" in this chapter)
6	The blood of Strahd von Zarovich, fundamental to the nature of the Domains of Dread

DESPERATE ALLIES AND RIVALS

The Darkon Allies table describes characters and groups who strive to save the domain, while the Darkon Rivals table notes those who scheme to ruin it.

DARKON ALLIES

d6	Ally
1	Irik Zal'honen, the mournful spirit of Azalin's son
2	The Order of the Guardians, ascetics who isolate dangerous magic and prevent supernatural ruin
3	Cardinna Artazas of the Eternal Order
4	Doctor Ingrid van Richten, a scholarly spirit who haunts Richten House near Rivalis
5	The Ray Agency, investigators based in Martira Bay
6	Skeever, Azalin's imp familiar

DARKON RIVALS

d6	Rival
1	Alcio Metus and the Kargat
2	Darcalus Rex and the Eternal Order
3	Madame Talisveri Eris and the Family
4	Ebbasheyth, Azalin's black shadow dragon advisor
5	A cursed artifact held within an Order of the Guardians monastery
6	Azalin's shadow, an echo of the Darklord

Dread in Darkon

While the Shroud poses a domain-spanning threat, other dooms threaten adventurers in Darkon. Consider the grim omens and lurking terrors on the Dread in Darkon table as recurring threats in your adventures.

Dread in Darkon

d6	Dread Possibility
1	A prophecy foretells the characters' involvement in Darkon's salvation or destruction, and comes with eight unavoidable omens.
2	The characters were involved in the Hour of Ascension and share a Dark Gift (see chapter 1).
3	One of the characters is the perfect vessel for a new Darklord or Azalin's rebirth.
4	The party is forced to work with an evil being, one from the Darkon Rivals table or another Darklord.
5	The dead of Darkon wish to aid the characters, flocking to them in a growing legion.
6	The characters suffer desperate, fractured dreams sent from mysterious allies or their future selves, warning them of calamity.

Darkon's Final Fate

While planning your adventures in Darkon, keep the end of the campaign in mind. Your plans for this climax might change multiple times during the campaign, shifting with the characters' actions and goals. The suggestions on the Darkon Finale table offer conclusions that can guide your adventures.

Darkon Finale

d6	Finale
1	None of Azalin's would-be inheritors are fit to become Darklord. Only by merging their spirits or making one inheritor the vessel for a hidden evil can a new Darklord arise.
2	The King's Tear is a dungeon-sized amber chrysalis that Azalin is using to create a new Dark Power. The characters must find the black shadow dragon Ebbasheyth and convince her to help infiltrate the floating construction and shatter it from within.
3	Azalin believes the only way to escape the Domains of Dread is by shattering their linchpin: the first domain, Barovia. He has escaped Darkon, but the next stage of his scheme must be stopped before he destroys all the domains.
4	Each of Azalin's inheritors holds a piece of the Darklord's crown. Claiming the pieces and bringing them to Castle Avernus allows Azalin's restoration or a new Darklord's ascension.

Castle Avernus, frozen at the moment of its destruction

d6	Finale
5	One of the characters is a clone of Azalin, created as a potential Darklord so the real Azalin could escape. The Hour of Ascension was a distraction to mislead the Dark Powers.
6	Azalin changed time so he never became a Darklord. The characters must follow Azalin into his past and ensure his deeds attract the Dark Powers' notice.

Ultimately, whatever course you choose, the characters in horror stories rarely escape unscarred. Perhaps a character or one of their allies must make a dramatic sacrifice to save Darkon—or become the new Azalin. Or perhaps Darkon is irrevocably, doomed and the characters must choose which piece of the fractured domain will survive. In any case, whether a new Darklord rises or Darkon is otherwise spared, one nightmare's end is likely another's beginning.

DEMENTLIEU

Domain of Decadent Delusion

Darklord: Saidra d'Honaire
Genres: Dark fantasy and psychological horror
Hallmarks: Masquerades, decadent aristocracy, social decay, illusions, impostor syndrome
Mist Talismans: Jeweled or feathered mask, article of well-worn fine clothing, shoe made of glass or gold

Every night brings another glittering affair in Dementlieu, whose citizens live glamorous and exciting lives. They enjoy the finest clothes, elegant jewels, grand ballrooms—and most extravagantly, the Grand Masquerade hosted by Duchess Saidra d'Honaire every seventh day at her island estate. Everyone who is *anyone* attends the duchess's balls, and everyone who longs to be someone tries to wrangle an invitation or sneak in uninvited. But Duchess Saidra's wrath upon those who dare to set foot where they don't belong is truly horrible—and inevitably fatal.

The domain of Dementlieu consists of the city of Port-a-Lucine, which embraces the murky waters of Pernault Bay and Lucine Bay, as well as shifting scraps of fog-shrouded suburban areas around the city. Port-a-Lucine is a festering mire of rot and decay hidden beneath a glittering facade of decadent wealth. Everything appears more valuable, more solid, and more wholesome than the actuality, and everyone behaves as if the illusion of grandeur and prosperity were real.

Everyone in Dementlieu sweats to get by, but admitting to reality means social ruin. The poorest citizens struggle to maintain a middle-class appearance, scrounging through garbage heaps at night to find wares to sell in their shops in the morning. The members of the true middle class pretend to be titled aristocracy, but they wear much-patched and mended clothes, and starve for a week to host a ball that barely passes as lavish—by recycling table scraps into mysterious pâtés and cleverly disguised dumplings. The real aristocracy of the domain exists solely in its Darklord, Duchess d'Honaire.

Anyone who lets the mask slip meets a grisly end. When an "aristocrat" at the duchess's masquerade loses a button from a fraying coat, the duchess pronounces the impostor's doom and the unmasked pretender crumbles to dust. When a struggling merchant fails to keep up appearances, the resulting fall is less public but no less final. Left with no home and no livelihood, these wretches inevitably fall prey to the Red Death. This mysterious spirit haunts the poorest parts of town and drains every glimmer of life from its victims—and is embodied by Duchess Saidra.

NOTEWORTHY FEATURES

Those familiar with Dementlieu know the following facts:

- The city's decadent aristocrats keep a busy social calendar, fluttering like butterflies to multiple events each day: museum and art gallery exhibitions, concerts and play performances, brunches, luncheons, teas, dinners, and especially balls.
- Every week brings the preeminent social event of the city: the Grand Masquerade, hosted by Duchess Saidra d'Honaire. Invitations are coveted, and attendees outnumber the invitations.
- Nothing in Dementlieu is as it appears. Everyone pretends to be wealthier than they are. Magical illusions hide disrepair, and lies great and small fill everyday communication. Everyone knows these truths, but no one dares speak of them.
- The day-to-day administration of Port-a-Lucine rests in the hands of Lord Governor Marcel Guignol. He hears counsel from a group of five advisors drawn from the ranks of the aristocracy, including Duchess Saidra. With this council, he writes laws that a small city watch helps him enforce. He also serves as the sole judge when those laws are broken.
- Decorative masks are a common accessory in Dementlieu, worn at social events and in daily life alike. Many people know their neighbors by their masks better than by their faces.

SETTLEMENTS AND SITES

Port-a-Lucine shines with the veneer of a sophisticated city. It boasts a university, an opera house, a wax museum, and an aquarium, as well as a scandalous cabaret (the Red Widow Theater) and lush gardens. The Zuvich Hospital offers the highest standards of science-based medical care, while the Great Library curates a large collection of supposedly significant but largely repetitive writings.

D'HONAIRE ESTATE

Decorated with fanciful gargoyles and lurid tapestries, the lavish home of Duchess Saidra d'Honaire is the setting of the Grand Masquerade (detailed later in this domain). A small army of energetic, masked ghouls constantly prepare for the upcoming festivities.

MOTHER OF TEARS CATHEDRAL

The Mother of Tears Cathedral is the most honest place in Dementlieu. Dedicated to the god Ezra, the cathedral's teachings put greater emphasis on weeping for the horrors of the world than on taking any action to cure or combat them. The clergy resists acknowledging any kind of distinction of class or rank among the worshipers, despite the stark stratification of society outside the cathedral's walls. All people are desperate wretches in the merciful hands of Ezra, who mourns for and with them all. A magnificent alabaster statue of Ezra, her sword and shield set aside as she weeps into her hands, adorns the sanctuary.

RED WIDOW THEATER

The Red Widow is a cabaret known for lively music, provocative dancing, and shady dealings. A gigantic statue of a spider, painted in garish crimson with a black hourglass shape on its abdomen, adorns the front roof of the building, inviting customers into its decadent web. At this shrine to decadent pleasures, attendees celebrate beauty and life in defiance of the crushing poverty and horror outside.

But the theater harbors horrors nonetheless: shape-shifters use the cabaret's intimate spaces to find prey. Though rumors persist of shape-shifting giant spiders that feast on unwitting customers, they fail to depress attendance at the theater's performances.

THREE ODD GABLES

Under the eaves of the Tenebrarum Woods at the end of Mill Street, a coven of green hags lives in three crooked houses. These fey delight in meddling in the lives of Dementlieu's

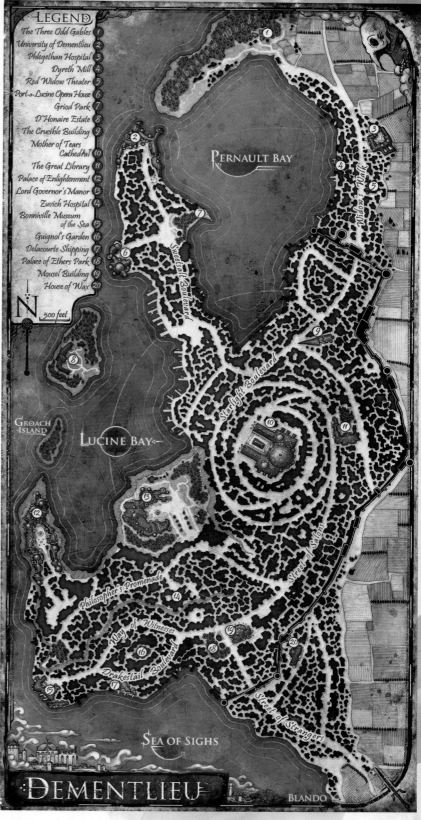

LEGEND
1. The Three Odd Gables
2. University of Dementlieu
3. Phlegethan Hospital
4. Dyreth Mill
5. Red Widow Theater
6. Port-a-Lucine Opera House
7. Griod Park
8. D'Honaire Estate
9. The Crucible Building
10. Mother of Tears Cathedral
11. The Great Library
12. Palace of Enlightenment
13. Lord Governor's Manor
14. Zuvich Hospital
15. Bonniville Museum of the Sea
16. Guignol's Garden
17. Delacourte Shipping
18. Palace of Ethers Park
19. Mousel Building
20. House of Wax

MAP 3.4: DEMENTLIEU

citizens, adopting disguises as kindly grandmothers and using their magic to help impoverished people pass as well-to-do aristocrats or attend the Grand Masquerade. Their price seems perfectly reasonable, until their clients discover a hidden catch.

CHATEAUFAUX

The people of Port-a-Lucine speak as if Dementlieu included a large swath of countryside called Chateaufaux, where nobles summer at their estates and prosperous farms and villages send goods for sale into the city. But no one has been outside the city, no goods arrive from beyond the city, and Chateaufaux does not exist. The Mists creep close to the walls of Port-a-Lucine, occasionally exposing shifting patches of forests and meadows, but nothing more.

SAIDRA D'HONAIRE

Saidra d'Honaire grew up on a tiny farm, living alone with her father after the death of her beloved mother. Her father called her "Duchess," claiming that he was a duke exiled from his rightful home by a vicious younger brother. The young girl took pleasure in lording that fact over other peasant children, proclaiming herself superior by birth despite her present circumstances. Saidra had no friends but many playmates, as she bullied other children into entertaining her.

When Saidra was a teenager, her father married a prosperous merchant with two daughters a few years older than Saidra. Though her father urged the three girls to love each other as sisters, his new wife and her daughters scorned Saidra, mocking her claims to nobility and treating her as a servant. Despite the family's new wealth, Saidra continued to dress in rags and labor from dawn to dusk, acting as a housemaid to her stepmother and stepsisters.

A harder blow descended when Saidra's stepmother casually mentioned the death of a duke who ruled nearby. Saidra asked if this duke was her father's wicked brother, and if his demise meant her father could reclaim his title. Her stepmother and stepsisters laughed at her, and her father admitted the truth. He had been only a servant in the duke's household and fled when he was caught trying to steal silver from the kitchen.

Saidra refused to accept this bitter truth. Fleeing the house, she went to her mother's grave and begged the departed spirit to aid her. A kind, grandmotherly figure appeared and granted Saidra's wish, bestowing on her a magnificent gown and fine jewels to attend the masquerade ball that celebrated the coronation of the new duke. Saidra rode to the ball in a stately conjured carriage, determined to kill the duke and claim his title.

At the ball, the glamour around Saidra made her irresistible to the duke, and they danced together for hours. Saidra began to contemplate an alternative to murdering the duke: she could marry the poor fool and become the duchess she'd always believed herself to be.

But as the clock struck midnight, terror stalked the ball as guests started rapidly sickening and dying. The plague afflicted the duke and Saidra as well. As they lay dying in each other's arms, the duke gasped a fateful confession: he was not the son of the late duke, but of a servant in the duke's household. The duke, unable to have children of his own, claimed the servant's infant son and raised him. Later, that servant was caught stealing from the kitchen and fled the house with his young daughter.

Enraged to discover this "duke" was no more a real duke than her father—and worse, that he was her brother, Saidra drew her blade and drove it into the pretender's heart. She stumbled out of the palace, but the plague claimed her on the stairs.

Saidra awoke on the foggy grounds of her new estate in Port-a-Lucine, a true duchess, as she had always imagined, but also an undead wraith. When she's dressed in elegant gowns and an elaborate mask, those around her accept the obvious lie that she's a living woman. When she isn't hosting her masquerade balls, she sheds her garb and stalks the city as a murderous spirit known as the Red Death. In either form, her goal is the same: to unmask and destroy pompous fools who pretend to be what they are not, aspire to higher station than they deserve, and fail to maintain the appearance of normalcy.

SAIDRA'S POWERS AND DOMINION

Saidra's form is a vaporous as her claims to nobility. She's a crimson spirit with statistics similar to a **wraith**. She can cast the *disintegrate* spell (save DC 18) on any creature that reveals themself to be lying about who they are. In her guise as duchess, Saidra dons a bird-like mask and fashionable scarlet gowns. As the Red Death, she is nothing more than a crimson-tinged shadow.

Closing the Borders. When Duchess Saidra wants to close the borders of her domain, the Mists don't rise. Rather, those who try to leave find themselves roaming the lands of Chateaufaux. Stately houses stand atop gently rolling hills amid lush farmlands and vineyards, but the houses never get any closer, no matter how long one travels. And sooner or later, travelers always find themselves back on the outskirts of Port-a-Lucine.

SAIDRA'S TORMENT

Duchess Saidra is finally the noble she always wanted to be, but a number of circumstances prevent her from enjoying her reign:

- Saidra is plagued by the fear of being unmasked and having the truth of her origins revealed. She projects her insecurity outward, accusing others of her own sin as she delights in unmasking frauds and social climbers.

- While hunting the streets as the Red Death, Saidra seeks her lost family. She resents but longs for her father, but she still fears her stepmother and stepsisters. She occasionally receives vague letters in their handwriting Chateaufaux.
- As a wraith, Saidra is incapable of enjoying the pleasures her station affords her. No matter how lavish her parties, the fact of her true form taints every moment of the charade.

ROLEPLAYING SAIDRA

Duchess Saidra behaves how she believes wealthy people behave. She hides her lack of worldliness behind decadence, which those around her quickly turn into fashion and fads. Her fantastic temper reveals itself whenever she's made to look foolish or finds someone out of their place in the social order.

Personality Trait. "I am imperious with my lessers and any who step out of place."

Ideal. "To everyone a place in society, and everyone in their place. Anyone who aspires to a position they're not entitled to or qualified for must be punished."

Bond. "I have achieved the status I deserve, and no one will take it away from me."

Flaw. "I fear that one day my father, my stepmother or stepsisters, or the mysterious spirit who clothed me for the duke's masquerade will appear and reveal the shame of my true history."

ADVENTURES IN DEMENTLIEU

Duchess Saidra's story presents a warped fairytale rooted in the common anxieties of modern life: fear of missing out and of being "unmasked" as a fraud. As the characters navigate the anxious social scene of Port-a-Lucine, they play out echoes of familiar tales. The green hags who live in the Three Odd Gables serve as "fairy godmothers" to any character who wants to dress up for the duchess's ball, but the hags don't bestow their favors freely. Their gifts comes with strict conditions, such as a requirement to leave the ball by midnight or a demand to humiliate another attendee. The hags scheme to ruin mortal lives for their own pleasure, so their every act of apparent kindness is calculated toward that end. See "The Grand Masquerade" for suggestions of how to run Dementlieu's premier social event.

As adventurers interact with people in Port-a-Lucine, they find everyone obsessed with status. Outsiders new to the city are an unknown quantity, and people try to quickly identify their relative social status. Characters can easily pass as aristocrats, particularly if they flaunt their wealth and claim ancestral lands in Chateaufaux. But if they admit to a lower social status, or if their poor manners reveal their inferior quality, they become targets of derision and the city's social scene closes to them.

For more adventure ideas, consider the plots on the Dementlieu Adventures table.

DEMENTLIEU ADVENTURES

d6	Adventure
1	A shrieky soprano is starring in the new production at the Port-a-Lucine Opera House. Jealous divas hire the party to figure out what magic she used to bewitch her way into a role.
2	A Phlegethan Hospital patient contacts the party, claiming to be the rightful Duke d'Honaire. He has a preternatural ability to bend others to his will.
3	The party runs afoul of the city watch and learns that their captain has been replaced by a devil who's transforming them into a brutal force.
4	People are being replaced by lifelike constructs, while the originals are held captive in the cellar beneath Alexandre du Cire's House of Wax. A party member is the next target.
5	A crusader hunting the Red Death is murdered. The culprit isn't the Red Death, but the family of a recent victim, who don't want the victim's poverty and lies to come to light.
6	A woman claiming to be Duchess Saidra's stepsister arrives in town and makes discreet inquiries about how to best reveal the horrible truth about the duchess: that she is a lowborn fraud.

THE GRAND MASQUERADE

The horror of the Grand Masquerade focuses on the fear of discovery—being forced to interact with people in a setting where you don't belong, and where the consequence of exposure can be catastrophic.

For the people of Port-a-Lucine, attending the Grand Masquerade signals a victory in their ceaseless quest for status. Visiting Duchess Saidra's estate, tasting her refreshments, moving in her social circle, and dancing to the music of her first-class orchestra are delights to be savored—and entirely worth the risk of discovery. To adventurers, though, these delights might not be sufficient motivation to take that risk. The Grand Masquerade is a fantastic adventure backdrop, but not a complete adventure. Adventurers need a good reason to attend; you can give them one by rolling on the Grand Masquerade Objectives table that follows. Link these objectives to larger adventures in Dementlieu, such as those growing from the seeds on the Dementlieu Adventures table.

Grand Masquerade Objectives

d6	Goal
1	Find a specific aristocrat at the masquerade and get information from (or to) them.
2	Prevent a villain from committing a crime at the masquerade.
3	Perform a trivial task in exchange for a favor from the hags of the Three Odd Gables, such as leaving a trinket on a mantle or filching a fruit tart.
4	Protect another attendee, ensuring that person isn't assassinated ... or unmasked.
5	Use the crowd to expose people to an antidote, a curse, or important information.
6	Secure a private audience with Duchess Saidra.

Once the characters have a reason to be at the Grand Masquerade, they face a series of dangerous trials as they navigate the social intricacies of the ball. Common challenges include securing an invitation, acquiring a costume, navigating social niceties, and dancing. Random complications can arise at any point during the ball, heightening the constant risk of unmasking.

Invitations and Costumes

An invitation to the Grand Masquerade is a fiercely coveted item in Dementlieu. Tension builds throughout the week as members of the aristocracy wait to see whether they'll make the list. The duchess's servants deliver invitations two days before the event.

Invitations. If the characters have established themselves in Port-a-Lucine as important, wealthy, and interesting people, they receive genuine invitations. The duchess hears about them if they spend lavishly, or as your adventure demands. Forging an invitation requires a successful DC 10 Intelligence check.

Costumes. A basic costume with a simple mask costs 5 gp. But elaborate costumes are a status symbol, and shoddy costumes attract unwanted attention. Ultimately, the characters decide how much to spend (or the hags of the Three Odd Gables can provide elaborate costumes for "free").

Arriving at the Masquerade. When the characters arrive at the duchess's estate, the Darklord's ghoul servants check invitations and outfits at the doors. They refuse entry to anyone missing acceptable versions of either. Ask the characters to make Charisma (Deception) checks if they present false invitations or have expressed worry that their costumes are subpar, but unless they roll especially poorly, the check simply reinforces the fear of being caught.

Social Niceties

Once inside the Grand Masquerade, the characters must observe a host of unwritten rules of etiquette and act like they know exactly what they're doing at all times. Other guests make idle conversation and assume that characters know people throughout the city. At the first hint that a character might not belong at the masquerade, guests start loudly asking pointed questions, attracting increasing notice.

Allow the characters to employ the following tactics in their interactions at the Grand Masquerade:

- Characters can keep a close eye on how other people behave and mimic that behavior. Use Wisdom (Perception) checks to measure how keenly they observe the partygoers' deportment, and Intelligence (Investigation) checks to deduce the right behavior for a particular situation.
- Characters can apply magic or intuition to discern the response or behavior that a questioner expects. Use Wisdom (Insight) checks unless characters have access to mind-reading spells such as *detect thoughts* or similar magic.
- Characters can fake it 'til they make it. Use Charisma (Deception) checks extensively as characters work their way through the ball. Failed checks draw increased attention; on successful checks, the questioners lose interest.
- Characters can distract watchers to shift attention if things go badly. Use Charisma (Deception) or Dexterity (Sleight of Hand) checks (or any other reasonable skill checks the players suggest) to determine whether they turn the focus away from their errors.

Dancing

Port-a-Lucine's high society has an established canon of dances that everyone knows and performs competently. These include paired dances and group dances, and involve dancing with a bewildering number of people over the course of the evening. Dancing is an opportunity to seize a fleeting connection with an important contact—and a chance to make a fatal error that results in being unmasked.

Characters might try to learn the basic dances as they prepare for the Grand Masquerade, but no outsider can hope to learn every step in as little as a week. Like navigating the social niceties of the gathering, fumbling through a dance involves careful observation and skilled fakery, plus the added ingredients of natural grace and agility. Allow characters to make Dexterity (Acrobatics) or Charisma (Performance) checks to see if they pull off the steps—either through natural agility (Dexterity) or though their ability to make their moves look good anyway (Charisma).

Random Complications

Use the Grand Masquerade Complications table to arbitrarily introduce a new element to the ball and keep the players on their toes.

Grand Masquerade Complications

d6	Complication
1	An angry guest with a costume identical to a character's accuses them of stealing the idea.
2	A flirtatious guest decides these interesting characters deserve to be introduced to the city's elite.
3	The character with the highest passive Wisdom (Perception) score notices a nimble-fingered guest slipping a necklace off their dance partner.
4	An intoxicated guest loudly confesses truths that other guests pretend not to hear.
5	A scream from a different part of the estate pierces the air. Everyone hushes for a moment, then immediately carries on as if nothing had happened.
6	Duchess Saidra enters the room, and sycophants immediately surround her.

Unmasking

If the duchess unmasks someone at the ball, read this text to the players to describe what happens (unless they intervene):

> "You!"
>
> A piercing voice cuts through the noise of the ball. The music stops and conversations hush as all eyes turn to Duchess Saidra and the poor fool she's confronted. The mask falls from his terror-struck face as the duchess raises her hand. "You dare intrude into the sanctity of my home?" she intones. A hunched, ghoulish footman clutching a dustpan scrambles forward. "You defile my Grand Masquerade with your unworthy presence? I condemn you." With those words, a chill wave emanates from the duchess, and the unmasked figure crumbles to dust.
>
> The duchess turns away, the ghoulish footman starts sweeping up the mess, and everyone around you pointedly returns to their own business.

If the adventurers attract the duchess's wrath, they are unlikely to cower in fear as she pronounces her judgment and gathers the energy to destroy them. They might try to flee, which could lead to a chase involving Saidra's servants or guests. If the characters attack Duchess Saidra, even if defeated she won't remain so for long unless she is first unmasked as a fraud. Not doing so terminally hampers the characters' entrance to Dementlieuse society.

Duchess d'Honaire punishes the unworthy who sneak into the Grand Masquerade.

FALKOVNIA

Domain Besieged by the Dead

Darklord: Vladeska Drakov
Genre: Disaster horror
Hallmarks: Dwindling resources, fickle hero worship, impending disaster, suspicion, totalitarianism, zombies
Mist Talismans: Arms marked with the Blood Falcon, bloody spear head, correspondence from Lekar, sample of zombie flesh

The days of the living are numbered in Falkovnia. The people would flee if they could, taking their chances in the Mists, but they aren't allowed that choice. The military has turned against the people, making them prisoners within their own country. With cudgel and pike, the soldiers of Falkovnia force every commoner into grueling labor, rushing them to raise fortifications and scrape scrawny roots from the dirt. Every lash strike, every day of meager rations is necessary—or so the soldiers claim—because time is short and the dead are coming.

Falkovnia is a land besieged. Empty countryside surrounds ruined or crumbling cities. A few desperate pockets of civilization survive, carrying on not out of hope, but out of fear of the land's merciless soldiers. Led by General Vladeska Drakov, Falkovnia's military organizes a desperate and occasionally effective defense against an implacable foe: the ever-growing armies of the dead.

Every month a new zombie legion issues from the Mists. Never emerging from the same place twice, the horde sweeps across the land, drawn to the densest populations of the living. That's currently the Falkovnian capital of Lekar, where unfit and underfed conscripts defend crumbling walls alongside General Drakov and her crimson-armored elite soldiers, the Talons. Causalities stack up during the zombie sieges, but miracles and moments of valor have not abandoned Falkovnia. The people's numbers dwindle, but they soldier on.

In the aftermath of an attack, the Falkovnians burn their dead, repair what they can, and whisper that now might be the time to flee. Invariably, though, someone speaks too loudly and a so-called traitor is impaled upon Lekar's walls. The people might want to abandon their homes, but Vladeska Drakov will not know defeat.

NOTEWORTHY FEATURES

Those familiar with Falkovnia know the following facts:

- Every month, on the night of the new moon, thousands of zombies appear from the Mists and invade Falkovnia.

- Ruins cover Falkovnia—cities and villages crushed by zombie hordes and haunted by undead stragglers.
- Elite Falkovnian soldiers known as Talons patrol the land, hunting for deserters, looters, and strangers to press into service. Talon officers bear the Blood Falcon, the symbol of Vladeska Drakov, tattooed prominently on their bodies.
- There is only one punishment for any crime in Falkovnia: impalement.
- Individuals earn public or military esteem for special acts of heroism. Dubbed "Trueborn of Falkovnia," these national heroes are treated well, but the fickle public turns against them if they're perceived as not doing enough to end the undead invasion.

SETTLEMENTS AND SITES

Falkovnia's settlements lie in ruin, its cities crumbling and unprotected, its villages abandoned and overgrown. Still, bastions of civilization hold out against the undead infesting the land, while dangers more terrifying than zombies lurk in hidden places.

LEKAR

The only city left in Falkovnia, Lekar now bears the brunt of the zombie invasion. The old city outgrew its walls multiple times since its founding, leaving its districts divided by fortifications. During the First Siege of Lekar, General Drakov sacrificed the entirety of the northern River Ward, leaving hundreds of souls to be slaughtered but allowing the remaining defenders to turn back the zombie horde.

MAP 3.5: FALKOVNIA

The city's survivors face harsh conditions. Talon soldiers patrol the walls and the streets, keeping peace in the cramped slums that now fill the city. Troops lead civilians outside the walls to scavenge from ruined settlements and work the fields of abandoned farms, but their harvests are never enough for the city's survivors. Though bitter and desperate, soldiers live marginally better than civilians, being assured of daily rations and housing in the Bastion Ward—the Talons-only district around city hall where General Drakov established her command center. From here, Drakov orders daily public executions as conscripts dispense supplies to the masses, and she plans how to resist the next zombie attack.

MORFENZI

Once a rich rural community, Morfenzi now holds only rubble and graves. The fields surrounding it remain strangely fertile, making them a prime destination for bands of farmers dispatched from Lekar. The Talons keep an outpost hidden beneath the town's ruins, under the command of one of General Drakov's surviving aides, the brilliant arcanist and scientist Vjorn Horstman. Horstman runs the post as his personal laboratory, obsessively striving to create new weapons to help Drakov win her war.

SILBERVAS

Groups of fractious survivors claim sections of this small city's ruins, scavenging and skirmishing over territory and resources. The survivors are unified in their commitment to silence, to avoid attracting the notice of zombies—and whoever makes their home in the ominously lit Dekovan Palace overlooking the ruins.

VIGILA FOREST

Towering black deciduous trees pierce the canopy of Falkovnia's dense, whispering forests. Called "sentries of death," these trees inspire grim stories suggesting that their wood is haunted or their roots reach into the realm of the dead. In contrast, a ring of pale sentry trees stands in the depths of the Vigila Forest. Tales tell that none who enter the ring survive. The zombie plague seems to offer proof of their truth: few undead emerge from the forest, and those that do are entirely skeletonized.

Vladeska Drakov

In the world of her birth, Vladeska Drakov was known as the Crimson Falcon, leader of a peerless mercenary army called the Falcon's Talons. She and her troops executed a thousand ancient grudges and petty atrocities in a land of bitterly feuding royal families. Infamous but respected, Drakov amassed a fortune and planned to retire young, buying a title and a realm to rule.

The sacking of Yeivere changed her plans. During that city's razing, Drakov's mercenaries went a step too far. The Falcon's Talons killed a unique soul during their slaughter. None can say who the soul was—a prince, a saint, a witch, an angel—but with its death, the world turned against them.

The ruling families united to hunt the Talons. Thanks to her tactical genius, Drakov repelled her pursuers and went on the offensive. One by one she attacked her former benefactors, burning villages, pressing citizens into service, and impaling anyone with a drop of noble blood. Though it took years, Drakov forged a bloody empire. But while sacking the burning city of her last remaining foe, Drakov and her troops were engulfed by strange smoke. When it cleared, everything they knew was gone.

Transported to an unfamiliar land, Drakov and her troops wasted little time subjugating it. The realm fell quickly, even easily, and upon taking the city of Lekar, Drakov prepared to name herself ruler of her new empire: Falkovnia.

Then, under a moonless sky, the dead rose against the land's invaders. The surrounding villages fell to the zombies with hardly a sound, and undead claws scraped Lekar's walls before the first alarms were raised. The First Siege of Lekar raged for four days. Drakov's strategies, both brilliant and desperate, eventually turned back the zombie horde, but at the cost of most of her veteran troops.

Since then, Drakov has lost nearly her entire nation. Every month a new desperate battle unfolds. She prepares ceaselessly for each, certain of her plans and ultimate victory, but doubting the mettle of her troops. With threats and public, impalings she tries to keep her people more terrified of her than of the undead. And with every new moon she faces an unconquerable foe, never revealing to anyone that each zombie bears the familiar, rotting face of an innocent her soldiers once put to the sword.

Vladeska's Powers and Dominion

Vladeska Drakov is an experienced military commander with statistics similar to those of a **knight**. While her martial skill is considerable, her true might comes in the form of the obedient army that unquestioningly enacts her every whim.

The Falcon's Talons. Vladeska's military forces are both completely overwhelming and entirely outnumbered. As an occupying force, the Talons are terrifying. Their numbers are relatively few, but they're organized enough to oppress Lekar's ragged survivors and enforce Drakov's totalitarian laws. In the face of zombie hordes, though, they're fighting a losing battle against foes whose numbers only grow. And every time a Talon falls, Lekar's final defeat grows closer. Talon soldiers use the **guard** stat block, while commanders are **veterans**.

Martial Law. Lekar—and, to an extent, all of Falkovnia—is a martial dictatorship. Drakov's troops carry out example-setting impalings as punishment for even the slightest crimes. These executions serve the greater good and impose necessary order, but make it clear that zombies aren't the realm's only monsters.

Only Bad Decisions. There is one simple truth in Falkovnia: the dead are about to kill everyone. This sets the stage for countless bad decisions, from leaders making terrible sacrifices or permitting amoral acts to individuals making fatalistic choices. Everyone in Falkovnia behaves as if it's their last day alive—because it probably is.

Closing the Borders. Unlike most Darklords, Vladeska Drakov can't open her domain's borders, so Falkovnia's borders are usually closed. Anyone who enters the Mists surrounding Falkovnia encounters an endless number of zombies. Even if travelers somehow avoid these shambling corpses, they emerge from the Mists back in Falkovnia, pursued by an undead mob. For one week every month, though, following the night of the new moon, the Mists surrounding Falkovnia are empty of zombies and the borders open. During this time, Drakov sends patrols of Talons to sweep the edges of the Mists for deserters. These patrols are difficult to avoid and battles with them often attract zombies.

Vladeska's Torment

Vladeska Drakov is close to attaining her desired empire, but circumstances keep it ever out of reach:

- Vladeska knows it's only a matter of time until zombies overrun Lekar. She has no time for rest or deliberation; every moment must be used to the fullest before the hordes return. Every wasted second is a life lost.
- Vladeska refuses to flee. She knows doing so could save many of Lekar's people, but it would mean admitting failure—a fate worse than death.
- Vladeska recognizes every zombie's face, knowing they're her own fallen soldiers, the defenders of communities she razed, or murdered civilians. She doesn't understand why this is, but she knows the zombies are coming for her alone.

ROLEPLAYING VLADESKA

Steely and fierce, Vladeska Drakov views softness as weakness and resents having her time wasted. She values cold competency and makes life-and-death decisions mercilessly. Her isolation and the stress of rule weigh heavily upon her, but daily catastrophes keep her focused on her nation's needs and not her failures. She believes a foe from her past is responsible for the endless zombie attacks and quietly looks for trustworthy agents to find the zombies' source.

Personality Trait. "I am the only one capable of making the decisions required for the greater good. This proves my excellence and sets me apart."

Ideal. "Once I've crushed my opposition, I will claim my realm, ruling not as a conqueror but as royalty."

Bond. "All who live in my domain are my troops, and they exist to further my will. Those who deny me are traitors bound for execution."

Flaw. "I and all I command will know death before we show weakness in defeat."

ADVENTURES IN FALKOVNIA

Falkovnia provides the perfect setting for disaster horror, particularly of the zombie apocalypse variety. Characters might be harried by zombie pursuit across the empty countryside or asked to defend the last holdout of civilization against a relentless horde. The zombies could serve as direct threats or motivate others to monstrous deeds, with the ends supposedly justifying the means.

You determine the composition and behavior of the zombie hordes of Falkovnia. The zombies emerge from the Mists on the night of the new moon and trudge toward the last holdouts of civilization. Whether they move in a single wave or scatter into smaller bands, this surge brings a monthly threat to besiege the walls of Lekar.

When creating zombie encounters, consider the average level of your group and what threats you want to represent. The "Zombie" entry in chapter 5 presents a variety of zombie types to complement the shambling **zombie** of the *Monster Manual*, posing greater threats or terrifying surprises. The horde can also include other corporeal Undead such as **skeletons**, **ghouls**, or **wights**. Alternatively, the "zombies" might not be Undead at all but another group attempting to lay claim to Falkovnia—perhaps a forgotten human culture or relentless giants.

Falkovnia is one of the few domains where the characters and the land's Darklord theoretically represent the same side, united against the zombies. The characters might defend Drakov's people and enact her defensive measures, but might also try to subvert her Pyrrhic strategies or attempt to smuggle survivors to safe locations outside Lekar. Consider exploring plots in which the characters rise in the Darklord's esteem as Trueborn of Falkovnia, but then must walk the line of both keeping Drakov's trust and upholding their principles.

Consider the plots on the Falkovnia Adventures table when planning adventures in this domain.

FALKOVNIA ADVENTURES

d10	Adventure
1	The party discovers a town where **zombies** have begun acting strangely: plowing fields, tarrying in shops, and congregating in the crumbling temple. What's causing this odd behavior?
2	In Morfenzi, Vjorn Horstman envisions an army of bestial super soldiers. He works to perfect what he calls his "primal serum," an elixir that inflicts those injected with a random form of lycanthropy. He seeks to use the characters as test subjects.
3	A plague strikes the slums of Lekar. Those killed by the disease rise as **zombie plague spreaders** (see chapter 5).
4	A pack of zombie animals—predominantly wolves, ravens, and cattle—attacks work bands from Lekar and survivors upon the roads. The characters are enlisted to serve as guards.
5	The characters are sent to investigate a fallen star that crashed near the village of Delmunster. The village proves remarkably peaceful and free of zombies, in large part because it's populated by the podlings of a **bodytaker plant** (see chapter 5).
6	A character learns that an influential Talon plans to overthrow General Drakov during the next zombie assault on Lekar by sabotaging the city's defenses and admitting the zombies to the Bastion Ward.
7	The Jimsonweeds, a band of survivors in Silbervas, vanish after attempting to pillage Dekovan Palace. Soon after, the palace's strange lights appear among buildings formerly claimed by the lost survivors.
8	A knight named Gondegal attacks Talon patrols and claims she can lead common folk to a safe holdfast. None who go with her are seen again. The Talons hire the party to hunt down the knight.
9	The characters learn of downtrodden citizens in Lekar plotting to escape into the Mists following the next zombie siege. Are the citizens desperate noncombatants, or are they Talon agents seeking to draw out "traitors"?
10	On the night of the new moon, no zombie horde appears at Lekar's walls. Instead, a undead messenger arrives with a missive for General Drakov.

SIEGE OF LEKAR

Falkovnia's terrors culminate monthly in the zombie assault on Lekar. If you plan to involve characters in Vladeska Drakov's war against the undead, first consider how they become involved. The following examples are just a few of the possibilities:

Forced Conscripts. The characters run into an overwhelming force of Talons and are absorbed into its ranks. When zombies appear at the city wall, the characters are offered their freedom in return for defending the city.

Last Bastion. Far from Lekar, the characters fall in with local survivors who say the city is the country's last safe bastion. Upon arriving, they discover the sanctuary is not what they'd hoped.

Missed Connection. The characters come to Falkovnia having heard tales of it before the land's zombie uprising. An individual or item they seek is now in Lekar, forcing the characters to search the city and then escape.

Mindtaker Mists. The Mists deposit the characters' consciousnesses into soldiers, Talon officers, or unprepared peasants preparing for the siege. Consult the "Survivors" section of chapter 4 for suggestions on how to represent soldiers bound to face the horde.

BEFORE THE SIEGE

However the characters become enlisted in Lekar's defense, they face a hopeless battle. They join hundreds of unprepared defenders, including **commoners** holding clubs or longbows for the first time.

Prior to the start of the siege, determine where the characters will be positioned among the city's fortifications or on the streets. The specifics of these locations don't matter—no precision tactics will change the characters' fortunes against the zombie horde. Allow the characters to strategize however they please, though.

Fortifications. Stairways within Lekar's 40-foot-high towers grant access to the 30-foot-high walls. Parapets guard both, providing defenders with three-quarters cover from those outside the walls. Fortifications around the gates hold controls for massive barred doors and portcullises. Both towers and gates contain suspended cauldrons (detailed in the *Dungeon Master's Guide*).

Streets. The streets are packed with poorly armed commoners and cruel Talon soldiers. Any character who succeeds on a DC 16 Wisdom (Perception) check finds useful materials among the carts and cargo cleared from the streets— weapons, a variety of adventuring gear, or the resources to approximate one gunpowder keg explosive (described in the *Dungeon Master's Guide*).

VLADESKA DRAKOV AND HER TALONS STRUGGLE TO
DEFEND LEKAR FROM ENDLESS ZOMBIE HORDES

During the Siege

Run the siege as a series of encounters rather than one extended battle. As terrible events unfold around the characters, it's up to them to determine who and how they'll help.

Begin the siege with zombies approaching Lekar's walls. The characters might pick off distant zombies or enact plans to destroy dozens at a time. The characters' strategies are likely successful, but the horde soon begins overwhelming defenses nearby. Once the characters defeat a few zombies, roll 1d6 and consult the Zombie Siege Encounters table. The event rolled unfolds within sight of one of the characters. It's up to the characters to either take action or let the event transpire. When the characters complete an encounter, roll on the table again. If the characters ignore one of these events, the defenders' situation worsens. Add +2 to the next roll on the table.

The siege lasts as long as you like. Use frantic rushes between emergencies to describe small horrors and victories while wearing down the characters' resources with brief zombie attacks. If the characters feel completely overwhelmed, Talon **priests** with *potions of healing* might appear, or an officer can enlist characters to deliver orders from General Drakov (likely related to the siege's climax).

As the battle reaches what you determine to be the halfway point, start rolling 2d6 on the Zombie Siege Encounters table and consult the "Concluding the Siege" section to guide the battle toward its climax.

Zombie Siege Encounters

d6s	Encounter
1	Zombies rip apart a soldier, causing those nearby to freeze or flee.
2	Commoners flee the battle. A Talon attacks them, killing deserters to deter further flight.
3	A Talon messenger, bearing orders from General Drakov, struggles to reach a besieged gate.
4	A panicked Talon mage recklessly casts destructive spells, catching zombies and soldiers in the effects.
5	A group of commoners attempts to flee the city, revealing a hidden gap in the wall.
6	Zombie bodies pile up, creating a growing ramp onto a section of wall.
7	Zombies dig through or under the wall, allowing them to flow steadily into the city.
8	Zombies cause a siege weapon to fire into the city or start a conflagration.
9	Fighting breaks out at a building Talon priests use to treat the wounded.
10	Zombies break through a gate and begin scaling the portcullis beyond.
11	Zombies infiltrate the sewers and appear in a supposedly safe part of the city.
12+	Masses of zombies or a botched scheme by defenders causes a wall or tower to collapse.

Concluding the Siege

After several encounters and hours of battle, guide the siege toward its conclusion. Use crumbling fortifications, routed defenders, and surprise zombie appearances to make it clear that a section of Lekar is lost. General Drakov puts a desperate plan from the Zombie Siege Climax table into effect if the characters don't stop her.

Zombie Siege Climax

d4	Climax
1	Breaching the river grates, zombies pour into the city via the Zapadnost River. Drakov orders thousands of gallons of oil emptied into the sewer and then lit. The zombies burn, but flames consume the districts and the river is poisoned.
2	The northern district will be overwhelmed. Drakov plans to destroy the bridges crossing the river using kegs of explosive powder. This will halt the zombies but trap many soldiers and civilians on the other side.
3	Drakov plans to open several gates, admitting the zombies into one populated district. While the zombies feed, the district will be set aflame.
4	Drakov's troops round up civilians and force them out of the city, splitting the zombies' attention. This allows the Talons to shore up defenses and repel a second, less concentrated zombie attack.

Drakov's scheme might be even more alarming, involving magical or monstrous secret weapons.

Once you've determined how the siege will unfold, start foreshadowing Drakov's scheme, giving the characters the opportunity to aid it, enact a less destructive plan, or save innocents. Use missives intercepted from messengers or a *sending stone* taken from a fallen Talon officer to clue the party in on Drakov's strategy.

In the aftermath, the characters are recognized for their heroics, winning esteem among the citizens, with the Talons, or from Drakov herself. This can lead to new daring assignments or even being put in charge of preparing for next month's dire siege.

MARK BEHM

Har'Akir

Domain of the Ancient Dead

Darklord: Ankhtepot
Genre: Dark fantasy
Hallmarks: Ancient tombs, desert perils, lost gods, mummies
Mist Talismans: Canopic jar, lapis lazuli scarab, scroll of hieroglyphics

The sands of time bury the desert realm of Har'Akir. Here, the wonders of fallen empires and pyramids of forgotten pharaohs crumble beneath a merciless sun. Untold generations of tombs and secrets lie beneath the sands, markers of a history the land's few residents know of only in story and song. Their interest in past splendor is smothered, as life is harsh in Har'Akir and the living exist only to serve a deathless god-king.

This realm of fierce deserts and mysterious monuments is ruled by the mummy Ankhtepot, speaker for the gods and immortal pharaoh. From his golden pyramid in the City of the Dead, the Darklord watches over his domain, careless of the passage of mortal lives as he sends his servants in search of his only remaining desire: his *ka*, the missing piece of his fractured soul.

As the pharaoh obsesses over his lost treasure and thoughts of escaping his impossibly long undead existence, his servants plague the domain in his name. In hidden tomb-courts, withered, animal-headed elder mummies known as the Children of Ankhtepot luxuriate as emissaries of false gods. And in the mud brick city of Muhar, the priests of morbid gods oversee all aspects of life, apportioning food and blessings to the worthy and punishing blasphemers. But all the pharaoh's servants also pursue his quest to find his mysterious lost treasure, and are ever desperate for some clue or news to placate Ankhtepot and spare them from the storms of his wrath and his buried legions of the ancient dead.

Noteworthy Features

Those familiar with Har'Akir know the following facts:

- Har'Akir is a land of vast deserts and deadly storms. Water is scarce beyond the land's few oases and the city of Muhar.
- The land is ruled by Pharaoh Ankhtepot, the immortal intermediary between the mortals and the gods. The pharaoh rules from his pyramid, Pharaoh's Rest, in the City of the Dead.
- The people worship a pantheon of strict gods (see "Gods of Har'Akir" later in this section). The priests of these gods oversee all aspects of labor, agriculture, trade, justice, and religion in the pharaoh's name.

Akirran Characters

Characters from Har'Akir claim descent from an ancient culture and have survived in an extreme environment. Most of the land's people have dark hair and a variety of warm skin tones favoring golden to deep brown and black shades, and names with Egyptian inspirations. When players create characters from Har'Akir, consider asking them the following questions.

How do you survive in the desert realm? Are you a laborer in the fields or camps surrounding Muhar? Are you a scribe or priest of Har'Akir's gods? Are you a trader who travels the land or a member of the desert-dwellers known as Sute's Chosen?

What role does music play in your life? Do you prefer to sing, dance, or play an instrument? What animal, hero, god, or past pharaoh is evoked in your favorite song? How do others feel about your performances?

How do the gods feature in your life? Are you a devout follower of all the gods of Har'Akir, or do you favor a single deity? Do you worship only as you must to gain food and protection from the priests? Do you secretly worship a deity other than the gods of Har'Akir?

- The monuments, tombs, and pyramids of past golden ages litter Har'Akir. These countless tombs are interconnected, forming a vast, semi-hidden underground network called the Labyrinth.
- Akirran death rituals call for removing the heart, draining the body of blood, and wrapping the remains in linen. These methods preserve the body so the pharaoh might call it to service. It is a crime to burn the dead.
- Akirrans value music, and many locals are accomplished singers or proficient in playing the reed pipe, goblet drum, or arched harp.

Settlements and Sites

Har'Akir sprawls across a desert bordered in the east by crumbling, canyon-etched mountains. Most locals live around four oases, located in the bed of an immense river that dried up long ago.

The Oases

Four oases hold all the water in Har'Akir, making them focuses of life among the domain's people, beasts, and monstrous inhabitants:

Muhar Oasis. The largest oasis shares a name with the city of Muhar, which sits upon its southern shore. Gazelles and herons frequent its northern shore, often attracting predators such as crocodiles, hyenas, chimeras, and giant scorpions.

Red Oasis. Har'Akir's people say this oasis's waters are poison, as the oasis was given by the gods to the beasts of the land. Prides of cunning lions hunt nearby, frequently washing their kills here.

Sek's Tears. The waters of this oasis are said to be able to heal any affliction, but they are guarded by the sphinxes who dwell in the nearby canyons.

Map 3.6: Har'Akir

White Oasis. Holy to the god Neb, the White Oasis is surrounded by rich deposits of limestone favored in the creation of monuments and tombs. A largely disused quarry nearby now shelters a community of recluses called River's Shelter. All of the residents expect to die soon, for one reason or another, and seek to cleanse themselves with the White Oasis's waters before meeting their end.

MUHAR

With a population of approximately 3,000 people, Muhar is the largest settlement in Har'Akir and the center of trade, agriculture, art, and religion in the domain. The Temple of Ese towers over the city, its limestone walls glinting like a jewel in the sun. Here Akirrans worship, receive food shares, seek justice, and receive medicine or healing, all from the hands of High Priest Isu Rehkotep. The priest claims to speak for Pharaoh Ankhtepot in all matters, and her word is considered both royal decree and divine edict. In truth, though, the pharaoh cares little for the living so long as order is maintained, leaving Rehkotep to run Muhar largely as she pleases. Those who displease Rehkotep or oppose her priest-guards are thrown into the Mouth of Oru, a pit that connects to the Labyrinth.

OUSA'S PYRAMID

A mountain of white limestone rises above the southern plateaus of Har'Akir. This pyramid is known as the spirit home of Ousa, partner of Ese and the god who rules in the afterlife. Akirrans whisper that the interior holds a door between this world and the land of the dead. In front of this wonder, a giant statue of Anu, the Great Jackal, overlooks parched riverbeds. A small order of jackal-masked priests guards entry to the pyramid. The priests follow the commands of Thute, a limber and vicious Child of Ankhtepot with a jackal's head.

THE LABYRINTH

Beneath the Sands of Sute lie generations of hidden tombs, built one atop the other and hidden by the sands of ages. Elaborated upon by the Dark Powers, these endless, entangled crypts are known as the Labyrinth—a vast, dungeon-underworld that connects every tomb and monument in Har'Akir. The Children of Ankhtepot and their undead servants make use of hidden thoroughfares connecting to the City of the Dead. But many less-traveled passages lie throughout the Labyrinth, forming a sprawling wilderness of crumbling, monster-haunted ruins and trap-laden passages. Within the deepest of these secret places lie crypts dedicated to gods that

MIKE SCHLEY

predate Pharaoh Ankhtepot's reign. A traitorous Child of Ankhtepot called Senmet also lurks within these passages, seeking ways to depose Ankhtepot and become the new pharaoh.

THE SANDS OF SUTE

The desert between the old riverbed and the Sun's Throne Mountains is the largest, most inhospitable region of Har'Akir. Two mighty sandstorms rage over the region: the Breath of the Forgotten and the Breath of the False. These storms are said to impose tests from the gods on those who enter them, trials that punish those living lives without consequence or faith. They are also known to stop and rise without warning, obeying Ankhtepot's whims. Religious guides known as Sute's Chosen wander the region; the order's members claim to know how to read and navigate past the storms to reach the City of the Dead by the most expedient route.

PHARAOH ANKHTEPOT ENVISIONS HIS MISSING KA.

CITY OF THE DEAD

The Sun's Throne Mountains are a massive monument to the dead, their cliffs dotted with the cavern-tombs of forgotten heroes and nobles. The densest collection of these crypts lines the monument- and temple-filled canyon called the City of the Dead. This necropolis climbs the canyon walls, where whole cliffs have been sculpted into massive statues of Har'Akir's gods and pharaohs. Among these monuments hide entrances to ancient tombs, many of which belong to past high priests of Muhar and Children of Ankhtepot.

The City of the Dead rises toward the sculpted, golden mountain called Pharaoh's Rest, the massive pyramid of Pharaoh Ankhtepot. From here, the Darklord can see across much of the domain as he sends agents to hunt the missing piece of his soul.

THE BENT PYRAMID

In the northern desert stands a small pyramid that has a curious design: the sides rise from the earth at a steep angle until halfway up, then come together at a shallower angle. The Bent Pyramid, which is encased in black granite, has no interior, no temple, and no obvious reason for existing. Sute's Chosen, however, know it sits atop a well of immense magical power that can be tapped by manipulating sound waves.

ANKHTEPOT

In an ancient country the inhabitants called the Land of Reeds and Lotuses, Ankhtepot served three generations of pharaohs as high priest. When the second pharaoh died, her unworthy son ascended to the throne. The new pharaoh quickly became unpopular among the people and priests. Seeking a remedy for this, Ankhtepot came to believe that the gods wanted another to take the pharaoh's place, one with knowledge of rule and the deities' blessing.

On the day of the ritual that would consecrate the pharaoh's connection with the gods, Ankhtepot rallied his loyal priests and murdered their liege. He had misjudged the peoples' loyalty, though, and they rose up and executed the traitorous priests.

Moreover, Ankhtepot had misjudged the will of his gods. As he stood before them in death, the immortals forsook him, cursing him and denying him entry to the afterlife. Instead, they returned him to the world, but stripped away a piece of his soul, his ka—the vital essence that inspires all living beings. Ankhtepot reawakened, trapped and paralyzed within his corpse as he was mummified along with his treacherous followers. The murderous priest felt the pain of every cut and every organ removed as if he were alive. Then, within an unmarked crypt, he suffered and starved for what felt like an eternity.

Untold years passed, but on the day the last memory of Ankhtepot's name faded from his homeland, a voice intruded on the priest's prison, asking if he still felt he was worthy to rule. Through the ages, Ankhtepot's arrogance hadn't waned, and he answered with certainty. Granted new freedom by the Dark Powers, Ankhtepot emerged from his crypt into the domain of Har'Akir.

In this new land, Ankhtepot found a pious people devoted to the same gods he once served. Immediately he set to wiping out that religion, replacing it with new gods of his own imagining, false divinities for whom he alone spoke. Using blasphemous rites, Ankhtepot resurrected the priests once buried alongside him as powerful mummies, replacing their heads with those of beasts holy to his new faith. These Children of Ankhtepot served him as they did in life, and together the dead conquered the souls of Har'Akir.

The ages have marched ever on. Ankhtepot has known treachery and conquest. He has known divinity and rule. But now he knows only boredom and despair. His sole remaining desire is to recover his lost ka, which he knows remains somewhere in Har'Akir. With it, he hopes to become mortal again, die, and face his original gods' judgment once more. Whether this means peace or oblivion is meaningless to him. Ankhtepot seeks only an end.

ANKHTEPOT'S POWERS AND DOMINION

A fantastically ancient Undead, Ankhtepot has statistics similar to a **mummy lord**. Beyond this, he rules as pharaoh, national leader, and voice of the gods. None in Har'Akir, among the living or the dead, denies his will, but the Darklord's wishes are few. He cares only for order and to find his lost ka.

Children of Ankhtepot. The Darklord is served by many of the same priests who died alongside him in ages past. He resurrected these **mummies** and **mummy lords** with the heads of animals, painting them as spirits and harbingers of his fictitious gods of Har'Akir. As Ankhtepot has grown bored with mortal concerns, the Children of Ankhtepot have pursued their own vices. Many dream and despair in their crypts. Others foment small cults of their own. And still others seek to undermine the pharaoh and claim his position—including the treacherous **mummy lord** Senmet.

The Gods' Law. Although Ankhtepot cares nothing for fragile, short-lived mortals, he has a tyrant's obsession with order and knows the living might be useful in finding his lost ka. To that end, he relies on his priests to maintain peace in Har'Akir and provide for the people. Should the populace grow discontent, Ankhtepot expects the priests to deal with discord swiftly. If they can't, he sends his mummy servants to indiscriminately quell any uprising.

Examples of such massacres fill Har'Akir's history, but they are known only to the domain's priests.

Pharaoh's Priests. The priests of Har'Akir's gods work Ankhtepot's will. Most priests believe themselves to be devout servants of the gods, having no idea that their deities are false. They keep alert for strangers and omens, reporting them to their superiors and, ultimately, High Priestess Isu Rehkotep. The high priestess dutifully watches for signs of a mysterious treasure her pharaoh seeks and orders any strangers in Har'Akir brought to her at the Temple of Ese, but she also relishes her influence and decadent lifestyle. She dreads the day Ankhtepot blames her for not finding what he desires, though she has no idea she's searching for the Darklord's ka.

Closing the Borders. When Ankhtepot wishes to close the borders of Har'Akir, mighty sandstorms rise at the edges of the domain. Those who enter the storms are affected as detailed in "The Mists" at the start of this chapter, but in addition, they take 2d6 slashing damage per round from the scouring sands.

ANKHTEPOT'S TORMENT

The Dark Powers torment Ankhtepot in one simple, all-encompassing way: they won't let him die. Existence is pain for the pharaoh. He vividly remembers every one of his crimes and understands that his ambitions have sustained his corporeal form for untold lifetimes. He seeks his ka and rebirth as a mortal not to prolong his existence, but so his life might finally end.

ROLEPLAYING ANKHTEPOT

Ankhtepot is seen only a few times a year, when his priests bring offerings to Pharaoh's Rest and beseech him for the gods' empty blessings. Those who glimpse the pharaoh describe a withered corpse clad in black linen wrappings and gold adornments, with a voice like sand ground between clashing mountains. The only time he bothers with either the living or the dead is when they actively offend him (such as by trespassing upon his solitude at Pharaoh's Rest), when they bring him hope of finding his ever-elusive ka, or when disappointment kindles his rage.

Personality Trait. "The stirring of a song, the scent of bread, the cool rush of water over skin. I have forgotten it all."

Ideal. "I will regain my ka and stand before the gods renewed, before I face the final darkness."

Bond. "My final age will be peaceful, and my domain will know order."

Flaw. "I will cross any boundary, uncover any secret, shred any soul, if it gains me my death."

ADVENTURES IN HAR'AKIR

If you find terror in trap-laden tombs and ancient curses (explored further in chapter 4), Har'Akir provides them in endless supply. The land's central plot—the search to find Pharaoh Ankhtepot's ka—can lead adventurers to explore mysterious sites as they seek hiding places undisturbed for centuries. Consider running a tour of the domain's most intriguing locales, punctuated with treks across the brutal deserts—landscapes fraught with hazards such as extreme heat, quicksand, and sandstorms whipped up by strong winds, all detailed in the *Dungeon Master's Guide*. In the course of their adventures, characters can learn the truth of Ankhtepot's origins and Har'Akir's original gods. How they use these discoveries is up to them, but each discovery should bring the characters closer to sealing Ankhtepot's doom or their own. "The Darklord's Soul" below provides ideas for running adventures focused on Ankhtepot's obsession, while the Har'Akir Adventures table suggests other plots that might unfold in this domain.

HAR'AKIR ADVENTURES

d8	Adventure
1	The priests of Ese seek adventurers to retrieve someone they condemned from the Labyrinth.
2	The historian Kharafek has excavated a canyon riddled with sealed tombs. She's paying laborers well but is also using them to bear the brunt of the curses the crypts conceal.
3	The hermits settled in River's Shelter accidentally revealed a crypt and released **mummies** that resent being disturbed.
4	The pyramid of a former high priest has vanished. The priests of Neb seek help finding the monument before the pharaoh notices and is displeased.
5	Snefru, a priest of Oru, discovers that the Bent Pyramid responds to song. She seeks aid to assemble a massive chorus to open a path inside.
6	The revolutionary Aliz is secretly a jackal-headed **werewolf** allied with the **mummy lord** Senmet. She seeks to find Ankhtepot's ka to bring the pharaoh's rule to an end.
7	Sute's Chosen seek help rescuing travelers missing in the Breath of the Forgotten. The party must endure the gods' tests to save them from the storm.
8	Nephyr, a cat-headed Child of Ankhtepot, arrives in Muhar. To motivate the living to find the pharaoh's lost treasure, each dawn she curses a number of innocents equal to the days she's spent in the city.

GODS OF HAR'AKIR

Har'Akir's people once worshiped the deities of the Egyptian pantheon—the same deities Ankhtepot once served. But the spiteful Darklord scoured the old religions from his domain, replacing them with parodies that make him and his followers central to the land's faith. Over generations, these deities have become the gods of Har'Akir:

Anu, who judges the fate of the dead
Ese, who presides over life and the living
Neb, who guards the path of the dead
Oru, who orders the heavens and all beneath
Ousa, who controls death and the dead
Sek, who heals the sick and cultivates life
Sute, who sows despair and discord

The Dark Powers have granted a measure of power to Ankhtepot's false gods. Clerics who worship one of Har'Akir's gods or the pantheon as a whole receive power as if they worshiped a true deity that offers the death domain. Despite their distinct roles, traditions, and places within the lives of Har'Akir's people, these gods are all especially aloof, cryptic, morbid, and supportive of the pharaoh's rule.

THE DARKLORD'S SOUL

Above all things, Pharaoh Ankhtepot seeks to retrieve his ka, the missing piece of his soul. Characters in Har'Akir are likely to become involved in the pharaoh's search. Before they do, though, consider the specifics of that search, what form his lost ka might take, how characters might become involved, and what happens if the pharaoh does recover his soul.

THE SOUL'S SHAPE

Before tasking characters with retrieving it, determine what form the pharaoh's ka takes. It might be a physical object, a living creature, or a spiritual concept that needs to be summoned into being. Roll or choose an option from the Ankhtepot's Soul table to determine the form of the Darklord's ka.

ANKHTEPOT'S SOUL

d8	The Ka's Form
1	A **hawk** or **giant eagle** that tirelessly circles the sun.
2	A canopic jar containing the pharaoh's heart hidden within a forgotten tomb
3	Mummified and divided-up heart-meat, a piece of which is hidden within each of the remaining loyal Children of Ankhtepot
4	A blessing granted to those who survive both the Breath of the Forgotten and the Breath of the False

d8	The Ka's Form
5	A set of relics holy to the old gods of Har'Akir
6	The manifestation of a joyous song sung by Muhar's people
7	The soul of an innocent healer who resembles the pharaoh as he was in life
8	The soul of a character, perhaps one with an Echoing Soul (a Dark Gift detailed in chapter 1)

THE HUNTERS' ROLE

Once you know the form of Pharaoh Ankhtepot's ka, determine how the characters become involved with the hunt for it. Events might make finding the soul to be in the characters' best interests, or they might already possess it—making them the Darklord's quarry. In any case, while it's well known that the pharaoh seeks some lost treasure, he doesn't advertise that what he seeks is his own ka, making this revelation part of any successful hunt. Roll or choose an option from the Hunt for the Ka table to determine what form the domain-spanning quest takes.

HUNT FOR THE KA

d6	Hunt
1	The characters come to the attention of High Priest Rehkotep, who demands they aid her in finding the pharaoh's lost treasure or face punishment.
2	Revolutionaries displeased with the priests and the pharaoh search for Ankhtepot's lost treasure in hopes of gaining leverage over the ruler.
3	The sphinxes of Har'Akir know that Ankhtepot is close to finding his lost ka. They hope to find it first and place it outside the Darklord's reach.
4	A Child of Ankhtepot, either a loyal servant like Nephyr or a traitor like Senmet, tasks the characters with finding the lost ka to fulfill their own ends.
5	Murals or hieroglyphs within a tomb the characters discover lead to other ruins, each bearing a clue to finding the pharaoh's missing treasure.
6	After the characters die, Pharaoh Ankhtepot resurrects them (perhaps as reborn; see chapter 1). Their continued existence is contingent on searching for and finding his ka.

THE RESURRECTION RITUAL

Once Pharaoh Ankhtepot's ka is found, he must still heal his fractured soul. Doing so requires a ritual with several components:

- It must be performed in a specially prepared chamber at the heart of Ousa's Pyramid.
- It must be performed for 1 hour, starting when the full moon is at its highest point.
- If the ka exists within another being, it must be released at the ritual's climax, with the possessor being slain and granted the honor of mummification.
- If the ka does not exist within another being, at the ritual's climax a worthy life must be extinguished to seal the ka to the rest of the pharaoh's soul.

The ritual is enacted and watched over by the Darklord's servants, living priests, Children of Ankhtepot, and other deathless guardians. The Darklord and any required victim must remain present for the duration of the rite. If the ritual is disrupted, the ka escapes, fleeing the pyramid and potentially taking on another form. Even if the ka is recaptured, the ritual can't be performed again until the next full moon. In any case, Pharaoh Ankhtepot is furious if the ritual fails, taking his rage out on all present—and perhaps, all of Har'Akir.

THE PHARAOH'S RETURN

If the ritual is successful, Ankhtepot is reborn. Roll or choose an option from the Ankhtepot Reborn table to determine what this means for Har'Akir.

ANKHTEPOT REBORN

d4	Development
1	Ankhtepot is now mortal, but retains all his supernatural abilities. Newly invigorated, the tyrant takes a more active role in Har'Akir's rulership, indulging in decadences and forcing the people to raise vast monuments to his newfound glory.
2	Ankhtepot is only briefly mortal. His body rapidly wastes away, returning him to his Undead state. Furious, he unleashes his deathless hordes, intent on transforming Har'Akir into an afterlife of his own making.
3	Ankhtepot is reborn and soon after dies for good. The remaining Children of Ankhtepot turn against one another, each declaring themself Pharaoh Ankhtepot II.
4	Ankhtepot is reborn, dies, is cursed by the gods anew, and is locked within a hidden tomb. Har'Akir falls to chaos as the land is scoured by squabbling mummies, a fruitless revolution, and harsh storms. Only by returning Ankhtepot to power can the land be saved.

HAZLAN

Domain Doomed by Magic

Darklord: Hazlik
Genres: Dark fantasy and disaster horror
Hallmarks: Amoral spellcasters, magic-ravaged environment, magical experiments, wild magic
Mist Talismans: Eye of Hazlik amulet, gremishka foot, scrap from a red robe

In Hazlan, magic is authority, justification for any excess, and—for those without it—the specter of inevitable doom. This domain is less a nation than a vast magical laboratory, whose wizard overlord Hazlik views every being as either an apprentice or a test subject. He conscripts those he acknowledges as lesser wizards into performing elaborate magical experiments, twisting the fabric of magic and reality until it frays. These experiments endlessly scar a domain drained of vitality, tortured by magical disasters, and overrun with abominations. The greatest wounds affect the invisible flows of magic underpinning the land, turning it erratic and dangerous.

Despite the domain's magical dangers, the ambitions of the spellcasting elite grow more audacious by the day. Paranoid and controlling, Hazlik watches the schemes of his lessers, observing them through the Eye of Hazlik. This pervasive eye-shaped symbol marks structures, decorations, clothing, and individuals, and through these eyes the Darklord sees all. He watches as common folk cower at the passage of his ostentatious apprentices. He watches as monstrosities birthed from strange experiments prowl openly. He watches as ravenous worms from deep within the poisoned land crawl to the surface in search of food. And he watches every new magical innovation, eager to claim it and add the discovery to his list of glorious achievements.

NOTEWORTHY FEATURES

Those familiar with Hazlan know the following facts:

- The wizard Hazlik rules Hazlan. His apprentices have free rein to exploit the land and its people to further their magical experiments.
- Inhabitants claim the eyelike design called the Eye of Hazlik bears Hazlik's blessing and wards off dangerous magic.
- Magic is unreliable in Hazlan, resulting in dangerous side effects.
- The visible effects of magical disasters disfigure the domain, from rivers poisoned by alchemical runoff to craters caused by magical explosions.
- Creatures warped by magical experiments infest the domain, including magic-hungry gremishkas (see chapter 5) and ravenous purple worms.

HAZLANI CHARACTERS

Characters from Hazlan have been exposed to strange magic all their lives. People of all descriptions and races hail from the domain, perhaps living in small communities or having been created by magic. When players create characters from Hazlan, consider asking them the following questions.

What is your relationship with magic? Do you avoid magic, knowing the danger it represents? Did you learn enough to aid in practical activities or to set you apart from those with no magic? Did you embrace magic to join Hazlan's elite?

Has magic altered you? Have you been affected by a magical disaster, pollution, or experimentation? Do you have an obvious Dark Gift or characteristic that sets you apart?

Do you carry an Eye of Hazlik? This symbol of your people is said to ward off dangerous magic. Do you carry one as a talisman or bear one as a tattoo? Or do you hate the mark, viewing it as a symbol of magic-using oppressors?

SETTLEMENTS AND SITES

Hazlan's few remaining communities are populated by hunters, miners, and artisans. They struggle to learn a glimmer of magic to earn a measure of respect from the domain's spellcasters. Mages live wherever they please, in traveling caravan palaces, floating towers, or more fanciful dwellings. Most gather close to Hazlik's palace, Veneficus.

RAMULAI

Thick, sparkling smog chokes the village of Ramulai. The nearby mines yield a host of rare elements useful in magical experimentation, and Hazlik's apprentices have constructed numerous alchemical refineries and dangerous laboratories in Ramulai to take advantage of this resource. The waste from these industries fills the Burning River, named for the regularity with which the pollutants within it ignite, causing the waters to burn with colored flames. These toxins sicken the people of Ramulai, cause transformations among the regional wildlife, and created the swampland known as the Brew.

SLY-VAR

Hazlik's apprentices live in Sly-Var, a settlement composed of a collection of laboratories. Spellcasters obsessed with earning the Darklord's favor raise architecturally discordant towers that defy physical laws by floating, being accessible only by magic, or being larger on the inside than the outside. The town's residents magically create whatever they need, resulting in little need for trade. This leaves the labyrinthine streets and knotted bridges between intertwined compounds eerily empty. Common folk often disappear among these streets, the victims of magical guardians, escaped test subjects,

MAP 3.7: HAZLAN

or wizards who see the magically deficient as stock for their experiments.

TOYALIS

The largest town in Hazlan spreads along the canyon floor where the slow, iridescent waters of the Alterity River and the Strangers' Tears meet. Toyalis boasts a population of poor but hardworking common folk united by their shared pursuit of prosperity and terror of the domain's magic-using elite. Although the townsfolk have no passion for magic, colorful murals and decorations depicting magical creatures, arcane symbols, and the Eye of Hazlik cover the town's rough wooden and adobe structures.

Several times each season, one of Hazlik's apprentices leads a procession of attendants and magical wonders to Toyalis in search of replacement servants, new apprentices, or stock for magical experiments. A carnival atmosphere ensues, with this apprentice displaying their magical accomplishments and setting up competitions to assess the locals. These contests involve tests of magical ingenuity, strangely themed talent shows, and open brawls. When the mage's procession leaves, it takes townsfolk deemed valuable with it.

THE LACUNA

At the center of Hazlan sprawls a mysterious region of persistent, knee-high ground fog. Anyone who steps into the fog falls as though into a ravine. Few who tumble in reemerge.

The vapors of the Lacuna are identical to the Mists that border the domain. The people of Hazlan know that the Lacuna used to be smaller, and that it was created by a magical disaster. The fog has since spread, extending in tendrils toward sources of powerful magic throughout the domain. Originally, the Lacuna reached exclusively toward Veneficus and the Mound of the Worm. Since then, Hazlik's apprentices have placed sprawling magical sigils upon the land, runes that slowed the Lacuna's growth but split its development in multiple directions.

VENEFICUS

Hazlik's crimson-towered palace stands atop the jagged mesa called the Red Rise. The Darklord dwells here alone, attended by a staff of servile constructs and magical creations. Although the palace features impressive audience chambers and decadent pleasure gardens, Hazlik rarely welcomes guests. Only his most accomplished apprentices attend him with any regularity. Apprentices who displease him never return from the Darklord's palace.

HAZLIK

Left to his solitude, Hazlik spends days at a time within his personal meditation chambers, avoiding sleep and using the Eyes of Hazlik throughout the domain to search for useful magic—and to identify any who might be acting against him.

DISASTER SITES

The landscape of Hazlan bears the scars of reckless magical experiments and wizardly rivalries. The following are examples of the bizarre sites that dot the domain:

The Brew. This toxic marsh is poisoned by alchemical pollution from Ramulai and populated by sapient fungi and enraged plant creatures.

The Fleshless Forest. Every plant and creature within this forest was turned to stone. The condition is infectious.

Moonstone Valley. Meteors and otherworldly creatures crash in this wasteland during every new moon.

Mound of the Worm. Land rose from deep underground to form this mesa, unleashing dozens of purple worms upon the surface. The aged albino worm Gravedrinker dominates this region.

The Orbitoclasts. One of numerous floating rock formations in central Hazlik, it bears an uncanny resemblance to tools used in performing lobotomies.

The Playas. These former lakes have been reduced to quicksand-riddled purple worm feeding grounds.

Seething. This region is devoid of life, and its land crumbles away into the Mists.

HAZLIK

The wizard Hazlik always stood one formula away from attaining his dreams. Raised among the merciless Red Wizards of Thay on the world of Toril, Hazlik steadily rose among the ranks of those obsessive, treacherous spellcasters. Eager and encouraged to push past the weakness of mortality, he sought to discover hidden truths of magic and its command of reality. He obsessed over radical pursuits, such as creating the perfect mortal form and visiting dream realms within an individual's psyche.

As Hazlik advanced in power, he developed rivalries with his fellow Red Wizards. Through petty contests, victories, and embarrassments, he grew increasingly arrogant, orchestrating events that left his rivals scarred by his spells or their own backfiring magic. During these feuds, there was one competitor Hazlik was unable to defeat: the Red Wizard Indreficus. Hazlik gradually came to fixate on Indreficus as his true rival. Indreficus shared Hazlik's genius and arrogance, and they spent many seasons as vicious adversaries and passionate lovers. They drove one another to feats of magical brilliance both revolutionary and unspeakable. For a time, the two ambitious wizards knew a wicked peace.

That ended when Hazlik discovered that Indreficus had gained the attention of the land's ruling zulkirs and planned to betray Hazlik to garner their favor. Heartbroken and enraged, Hazlik captured Indreficus and subjected him to a nightmarish experiment that left him permanently transformed into a pain-wracked living portal. Hazlik presented his creation to the zulkirs, planning to impress his people's rulers and gain their patronage.

Instead, the zulkirs revealed that Indreficus had not betrayed him. Rather, the zulkirs had watched the pair's ascent and, wary of their potential, sought to undermine them before they became threats. Moreover, they deemed Hazlik's transformation of Indreficus an abomination. As punishment, they ruled that every rival Hazlik had defeated could exact a penance of their choosing upon him. But even as the first brand-wielding member of the mob of Hazlik's scarred rivals approached to take their revenge, Hazlik fled through the groaning portal that had been Indreficus.

To his surprise, Hazlik emerged in a grim nether-world of fog and hateful visions where Indreficus's condemning voice hounded him mercilessly. Eventually, he escaped those nightmare lands into a realm that knew nothing of magic. He had changed, becoming covered in golden tattoos evocative of symbols that meant "traitor" in his homeland. Undaunted, Hazlik claimed the title of zulkir and dubbed his new world Hazlan.

HAZLIK'S POWERS AND DOMINION

Hazlik is a vain, egotistical overlord, convinced he is the supreme being in his domain. His statistics echo those of an **archmage**, but he favors using an array of magic items rather than his own spells.

Glory Taker. At any given time, Hazlik permits dozens of apprentices to study at his feet. His lessons are infrequent, demanding, and filled with mocking examples. Those who don't impress him don't survive long. He encourages rivalries among his students and drives them to push the boundaries of magical possibilities. His goading results in magical wonders, failed experiments, and the magical disasters that plague the land. Hazlik claims his apprentices' successes as his own, both to hide his lack of innovation and to further his reputation as Hazlan's greatest wizard. His favorite—or least disappointing—apprentices include the masked wizard Yhal the Skygazer, shadow-cloaked Ruzelo, and the daring genius Eleni.

Inside the Experiment. Hazlik realizes that Hazlan doesn't feel as real as the world of his birth, though he's yet to discover why. He pushes his apprentices to chip away at the nature of the land, hoping to find out what lies beyond—and ultimately, to escape. He cares nothing for the domain or its inhabitants, as he's confident he'll be able to leave before Hazlan becomes utterly uninhabitable.

Magic Hoarder. Hazlik's magical ability is impeded, so he covetously pursues magic items. If he learns of a useful magic item, he sends an apprentice to claim it for him or hires adventurers to retrieve it. These items enable Hazlik to hide his limitations and give him a taste of the magic he's lost.

Omnipresent Observer. Hazlik spies on his domain's inhabitants using his personal sigil, the Eye of Hazlik. The details of his pervasive surveillance are detailed in "The Eye of Hazlik" later in this domain description.

Closing the Borders. Hazlik can open and close the borders of his domain at will, as detailed in "The Mists" at the start of this chapter. In addition to the normal effects, these Mists are filled with the results of horrific magical experiments, such as misshapen chimeras, incomplete golems, and droves of gremishkas (see chapter 5).

HAZLIK'S TORMENT

Hazlik's arrogance defines his existence, but various aspects of his imprisonment undermine his ego and force him to doubt himself:

- Since entering Hazlan, Hazlik hasn't been able to learn new magic. No matter how much he studies or researches new magical lore or spells, he cannot master them. He can use and prepare any spell he already knows but can no longer advance the magical research that formerly drove his life.
- Vivid nightmares wherein Indreficus taunts him for his failures compound Hazlik's frustrations, and he avoids sleeping to prevent them. By employing rare herbs and tinctures, he can go for days without sleeping, but his stock needs regular replenishing. This cycle casts Hazlik between extremes of exhaustion, jitteriness, and paranoia.
- Hazlik is terrified of others learning of his limitations. This leads him to berate and betray other wizards, claim magical discoveries as his own, and endlessly spy on both rivals and visitors to his realm.
- Hazlik openly denies the various destructions afflicting his realm. At first, he didn't care that this strange world was being destroyed, expecting to escape it swiftly. As that seems increasingly unlikely, his dread clashes with his refusal to acknowledge that he's ever wrong.

ROLEPLAYING HAZLIK

To Hazlik, everything is a useful tool, an amusement, or a potential spell component. However, he's deeply frustrated by his paralyzed magical ability and lashes out in response to the slightest setback.

Personality Trait. "Morality is a comfortable term for cowardice. Reality bends to those bold enough to learn its secrets."

Ideal. "Knowledge is worth any price."

Bond. "My discoveries will change magic forever, and I will be legendary."

Flaw. "My brilliance knows no rivals."

ADVENTURES IN HAZLAN

While Hazlan's magic-using elite test the boundaries of arcane possibility, the domain around them crumbles. The result is a realm where supernatural disasters wrack the land and magic turns against the characters, forcing them to doubt abilities they previously took for granted. Here, no adventure site is too fantastical. Anything explainable as "an evil wizard did it" fits perfectly, and impossibilities that challenge adventurers of any level can arise. The "Magic in the Dying Domain" section that follows explores the unpredictability of magic in Hazlan, while the Hazlan Adventures table suggests other adventures that might unfold here.

d10	Adventure
1	Hazlik's apprentice Eleni charmed the ancient albino **purple worm** Gravedrinker, using it as a weapon against any who oppose her master. When the worm breaks free of her control, Eleni seeks aid with recapturing it before Hazlik finds out.
2	Castoff magical creations litter the dry lake bed called Obsession's End. A sapient war machine or an **iron golem** escapes the midden and asks the party to help it find a way to live an ordinary life.
3	Innumerable **gremishkas** (see chapter 5) collect in caves along what's known as the Gnawing Path. The creatures plot to overwhelm Sly-Var and will pass through Toyalis in the process. Members of both communities request exterminators.
4	A cult forms around the Philosopher's Egg, an eight-story citrine egg perched atop a mesa in the region called Seething. The cultists hunt for someone who has never been touched by magic to release the unborn antimagic entity within.
5	One of Hazlik's apprentices sends multiple groups to capture a **star spawn emissary** (see chapter 5) that emerged from a meteor in Moonstone Valley. But the shape-shifter disappears, slipping in among its would-be captors.
6	An apprentice of Hazlik yearns to explore the bottomless pit known as Gluttonkettle. He needs a test crew for a vehicle he's devised to traverse impossible distances.
7	A magically talented commoner is kidnapped and forced to become a wizard's apprentice. Their family hires the characters to retrieve them, but the kidnappee has quickly adjusted to the decadent life of an amoral wizard.
8	The moon over Hazlan shatters and plummets toward the ground. Whether caused by a mighty spell gone awry or a domain-spanning illusion, the sight throws Toyalis into chaos. Residents demand that the characters help them flee the disaster.
9	One of Hazlik's apprentices needs agents to search for a suspected fountain of youth said to have formed among the innumerable magical toxins polluting the swamp known as the Brew.
10	Hazlik knows his domain's days are numbered. He attempts to use the characters to recreate the living portal that first brought him to Hazlan, either as its creators or its raw materials.

MAGIC IN THE DYING DOMAIN

Magic is a source of both prestige and terror in Hazlan. Commoners fear it but know it represents a path out of desperation, while the elite equate worth and magical skill. Adventurers in Hazlan are treated as outsiders by the elite and potential threats by the common folk. Worse, visitors who don't understand the dangerous nature of magic in the domain might accidentally unleash magical ruin.

HAZLAN WILD MAGIC

Excessive experimentation has caused the nature of magic in Hazlan to fray, making the entire domain a region of wild magic. Whenever a character in Hazlan expends a spell slot to cast a spell of 1st level or higher or actives a magic item, an additional effect might occur. The character's player rolls a d10. If they roll a 1, roll on the Hazlan Wild Magic table to determine the effect. Only Hazlik is unaffected by the domain's wild magic.

HAZLAN WILD MAGIC

d20	Wild Magic Effect
1–5	The character causes a random effect from the Wild Magic Surge table in the *Player's Handbook*.
6–7	The character is frightened of all creatures until the end of their next turn.
8–9	A number (2d4) of the Staring Cats of Uldun-dar appear within 30 feet of the character. These sapient, hyperdimensional **cats** have uneven numbers of eyes and are not hostile, but they ominously share reports on how the character died in multiple parallel dimensions. The cats vanish after the character's next long rest.
10–11	The character and the creature nearest them both teleport up to 60 feet to random unoccupied spaces of the DM's choice. When they reappear, they are covered in harmless ectoplasm.
12	The character broadcasts their surface thoughts for 1 round, as if all creatures within 30 feet of them had cast *detect thoughts* targeting them.
13–14	A spectral Eye of Hazlik appears, hovering over the character for 1 hour. The eye functions as detailed in the "The Eye of Hazlik" section.
15–16	A portal similar to that created by *arcane gate* opens within 10 feet of the character. It connects to another portal somewhere in Hazlan. The portal remains open for 1 hour, during which creatures from either side can pass through.
17–18	A shrieking, skinless, many-limbed horror that has the statistics of (and vaguely resembles) a **unicorn** appears within 30 feet of the character. It is hostile to them, vanishing after 1 minute.

d20	Wild Magic Effect
19	The character casts *fireball* as a 5th-level spell centered on themself using Charisma as the spellcasting ability. Screams and laughter emanate from the flames.
20	A fog cloud appears, centered on the character. The effect is similar to a *fog cloud* spell and lasts for 10 minutes. The DM can choose to have the fog affect creatures as if they'd entered the Mists.

THE EYE OF HAZLIK

A stylized eyelike design adorns buildings, art, clothing, and talismans across Hazlan: the Eye of Hazlik. Locals claim the symbol wards off dangerous magic and offers protection from magical creatures. It's also said that spellcasters who wear the symbol are less likely to suffer the domain's wild magic effects. Remarkably, it's not all superstition.

An Eye of Hazlik takes a shape reminiscent of the eyelike tattoos that cover Hazlik's body. It can be any size and can be created from any medium: a tattoo, a medallion, an embroidered motif, or even a building-sized mural. Within the borders of Hazlan, an Eye of Hazlik has the following traits:

- An Eye of Hazlik is not magical.
- Anyone who openly wears an Eye of Hazlik on their person or clothing or as a talisman can, once per day, choose not to roll on the Hazlan Wild Magic table.
- Hazlik is aware of any spell cast or magic item used within his domain within 30 feet of an Eye of Hazlik. He is also aware of the spell's level and the rarity of such a magic item.
- At any time, Hazlik can use any Eye of Hazlik in his domain as a stationary eye created by the *arcane eye* spell. He can spy through the eye whenever and for as long as he pleases. The eye radiates magic while Hazlik spies through it.

An Eye of Hazlik taps into the Darklord's mastery of magic within his domain, helping to stabilize the wearer's magic—at a price. Hazlik uses the eyes to keep tabs on magic-users in his domain, spying on those who might be useful or threatening to him. This surveillance enables him to reinforce his reputation as an ever-present, brilliant overlord.

THE WIZARD ELENI'S MOST RECENT EXPERIMENT: DOMINATING THE WORM GRAVEDRINKER.

ROBIN OLAUSSON

I'CATH

Domain Trapped in a Dream

Darklord: Tsien Chiang
Genres: Body horror and cosmic horror
Hallmarks: Endlessly changing labyrinth, deadly
    jiangshi, inescapable dreamworld
Mist Talismans: Scrap of ghost hair silk, small
    golden bell, scroll covered in prayers

When the inhabitants of I'Cath fall asleep, they enter an alternate version of the city they call home—a city dreamed into being by the domain's Darklord. In time, these poor souls can't remember which version is the real I'Cath and which one is the dream.

In the physical world, I'Cath's surreal, knotted streets echo with their emptiness. Within spare, meandering row houses, the majority of the populace slump against walls or sprawl against each other where they fell. These people lie trapped within a collective dream world created by the city's ruler, Tsien Chiang. Within this shared dream they labor ceaselessly, ever striving to create the impossible, perfect city of a perfectionist mastermind.

Within the dreaming domain of I'Cath, Darklord Tsien Chiang rules a golden vision of the city—a place of ultimate beauty and efficiency where all things move according to her design. For her, it is near perfection. For her people, it is a nightmare of inescapable drudgery from which death is the only escape. The dream city's identical, even streets sprawl across a broad hill, atop which rises a glorious palace Tsien Chiang shares with her four perfect daughters. Day or night, the streets are filled with people ever toiling to perfect the buildings, reshape the gardens, and undo the work of the previous days and weeks in favor of new designs. Within the dream, the people don't sleep, eat, or need to attend to any other concerns. They know only their work and the glory of Tsien Chiang.

In the waking world, the truth of I'Cath is starkly apparent. Rows of decrepit, moldy homes merge to line endless, coiling avenues. The streets wind and double back, but eventually climb the rise at the city's center, where the infamous Palace of Bones and the gold-scaled Ping'On Tower loom. By day, the streets are largely empty, except for those few desperate residents of I'Cath who have yet to succumb to the domain's dream. They rush through their days, scavenging what they can in hopes of enduring the coming night.

Every twilight, Tsien Chiang climbs the spirit-infested Ping'On Tower and tolls the Nightingale Bell. This renews the magic of her dream world and

I'CATHAN CHARACTERS

Characters from I'Cath have known wonder and want, and often have remarkable stories about how they left their homeland's dual realities. The domain's residents tend to have dark hair and a range of sandy skin tones. Their names might take inspiration from Chinese names. When players create characters from I'Cath, consider asking them the following questions.

How did you escape I'Cath? Did you discover a secret way out of the city? Did a family member make a bargain with Tsien Chiang that gave you a chance at a better life? Did Tsien Chiang send you forth for a reason?

Whom did you leave behind in I'Cath? Why didn't they go with you? Did you try to forget about them? Do you plan to return to I'Cath for them?

How long were you awake? How did you evade or distract the jiangshi and the hungry ghosts? Did you find or lose something during your wandering? Do you bear a mark or scar from the experience?

keeps her citizens asleep, but it also calls forth the legion of I'Cath's undead ancestors whom she has bent to her will. Nightly these jiangshi (see chapter 5) emerge from their tombs and reshape the city's mazelike streets, striving to match Tsien Chiang's vision with merciless perfection. The Darklord's servants carefully move any sleepers they encounter out of the way of their work, but prey upon any waking souls who cross their paths.

Any whom the Mists carry to I'Cath or who wake from Tsien Chiang's dream find themselves in a gray, haunted, ever-changing city where food is scarce and jiangshi hunt the living. With twilight comes a terrible choice: endure the uncertain terrors of the waking world or succumb to endless servitude in sleep.

NOTEWORTHY FEATURES

Those familiar with I'Cath know the following facts:

- The citizens of the vast city of I'Cath sleep endlessly within their homes.
- Those who wake feel the pangs of starvation. Food is more valuable in the city than gold.
- Jiangshi haunt the streets of I'Cath, tearing down whole districts and rebuilding them.
- Tsien Chiang rules the city from the Palace of Bones. By day, she drafts plans to improve I'Cath. By night, she rules over her people's dreams.
- Tsien Chiang's four supernatural daughters wander the city by day and gather at the Palace of Bones at night.
- The streets and row homes of I'Cath change nightly, making navigation next to impossible. The city has a single exit, the Four Trees Gate, but few know how to reach it.

SITES

The gray homes and windowless walls of I'Cath's real, waking city create a maze that changes nightly. Amid this ever-shifting labyrinth, a few locations remain the same.

GEMSTONE GARDEN

A beautiful park of fruiting trees and glistening ponds filled with bone-white carp covers acres of rich land hidden within the city. A dozen gleaming, gem-colored pavilions give the sprawling garden its name. Waking residents of I'Cath yearn to visit the park to harvest its bountiful trees and pools, but they dare not, since the garden's thousands of shrines and memorials form a massive graveyard. The dead here don't lie quietly, as each marker names an ancient jiangshi. These jiangshi work Tsien Chiang's will throughout the city, but they return to seek vengeance if anyone intrudes in their garden.

GWAI-HUIT CENTER

During daylight hours, the empty stalls of this vast, dismal market hide a handful of tents and shrouded booths where unscrupulous merchants sell wares and talismans for scraps of food—largely stolen from the Gemstone Garden or carried by strangers from beyond the Mists. In return, they offer goods pilfered from the Mansions or rarities such as silk made from ghost hair and vinegar said to ward off jiangshi.

Every dawn, a single stall in the market mysteriously restocks with wilted vegetables. The hope of finding a bit of food attracts desperate, awake individuals from across the city.

THE MANSIONS

The people of I'Cath call the city's countless row homes the Mansions. Sliding doorways grant access to the Mansions' leaky and poorly maintained four-story interior structures. I'Cath's residents inhabit these areas in clusters of sleeping, difficult-to-wake bodies. By night, the long-haired spirits of Ping'On Tower wander the Mansions, searching for homes and families long ago destroyed in the city's renovations.

As characters explore the Mansions, consider how to represent the thousands of perpetually sleeping bodies inside. Do I'Cath's residents lie where they fell? Did the city's jiangshi place them in orderly rows or stacks? Does the dream have a physical manifestation or toll? Do pale mushrooms or webs cover the sleepers? Consider using the helpless sleepers to reinforce body horror themes or the flavors of another horror genre discussed in chapter 2.

THE PALACE OF BONES

The home of Tsien Chiang and her daughters stands upon a hill at I'Cath's center. Its walls and supports are built from the bones of those who died as a result of the Darklord's harsh governance over her homeland. Inside, the grimly beautiful palace displays its splendor with elaborate architecture and bone murals, while revealing its neglect with disrepair and emptiness. Only Tsien Chiang's library sees regular use. The Darklord spends her days here, drawing new plans for her city and analyzing mysterious forces and mystical fortunes in pursuit of the ultimate harmonious design.

Beautiful but poisonous plants fill the palace's courtyard. Among these gardens rise an ancient willow tree and Ping'On Tower.

PING'ON TOWER

A hollow octagonal tower climbs from the grounds of the Palace of Bones, its fourteen levels decorated with eaves bearing furious-looking golden dragons. The topmost floor houses the Nightingale Bell, a broken bell forged from the scale of an ancient gold dragon. Stairs spiral up the structure's hollow interior, but the tower is far from unoccupied. By day, hundreds of spirits, hungry for the offerings and remembrances once provided by their lost families, mournfully drift through the tower. At twilight, when Tsien Chiang climbs the tower to ring the Nightingale Bell, the ghosts scatter to wander the city and fruitlessly wonder why they've been forgotten.

TSIEN CHIANG'S DREAM

Hidden behind the waking reality of I'Cath is a perfect city of precision, obedience, and gold that exists only in Darklord Tsien Chiang's dreams. Through the warped power of the Nightingale Bell, she shares her vision of a sprawling, orderly city run by an obedient, thankful populace. The bell spreads the dream to dominate the sleep of I'Cath's population, causing it to persist even when Tsien Chiang is awake. The dream city is a vision of perfection for Tsien Chiang, but for all others it's a realm of inescapable drudgery and thankless labor.

TSIEN CHIANG

TSIEN CHIANG

When Tsien Chiang was a child, her home was destroyed by a colonizing force, forcing her to flee into frozen mountains where she expected to die. Fortunately, a gold dragon took pity on her and gave her shelter. With nowhere else to go, Chiang promised to serve the dragon.

During the years that followed, Tsien Chiang attended the dragon, learning mysterious magic and medicine. In time, she became an accomplished wizard. Yet when she spoke of avenging her family and reclaiming her people's land, her dragon mentor chided her for holding onto her hatred and refused to teach her dangerous magic.

Eventually, Chiang could deny her revenge no longer. Among her mentor's records, she had learned of a bell that could make its ringer's dreams come true—but creating the bell required the scale of a gold dragon. Knowing her mentor would never provide a scale, Chiang drugged the dragon with a rare herb, planning to steal a small scale while he slept. But in her haste, she mixed the herbal concoction poorly. The dragon's body and everything nearby rapidly aged and decayed, killing her benefactor and destroying a hoard filled with ages of treasures and wisdom. Chiang's home had been destroyed again, but a single golden scale remained. Using the scale, Chiang constructed the Nightingale Bell

and dragged it into her occupied city. Tolling it, she wished for a city devoid of invaders—and instantly they vanished.

Awed and delighted, the nation executed the few invaders lingering outside the city and made Tsien Chiang their queen. Chiang ruled for years, enacting vast reforms and strict but sensible laws in pursuit of creating the perfect empire. She had a family, taking particular pride in her four beloved daughters.

As the memory of Chiang's past victories faded, her people grew frustrated with the queen's stern laws and demanding orders. Though her capital had become a radiant center of learning and art, the citizens revolted. Chiang acted swiftly to quell the uprising with numerous executions, yet the revolution grew. Everything she had wished for fell into flames. She showed no mercy to the rebels, ordering her armies to kill the families of all insurrectionists. In response, assassins struck Tsien Chiang's palace. Although she survived, her family did not.

Distraught, Chiang climbed to the highest tower of her palace, looked out over her burning dreams, and struck the Nightingale Bell. Rather than granting her vengeful wish, the bell cracked and spilled a golden mist across the land. When the mist cleared, Tsien Chiang's perfect city was gone, replaced by the unreal prison-city of I'Cath.

CHIANG'S POWERS AND DOMINION

Tsien Chiang's statistics are similar to those of a **mage** with access to a variety of magic items—her favorite being an ornate robe that functions similarly to a *Heward's handy haversack* and *wings of flying*. She uses this robe to store scrolls detailing her most recent plans for I'Cath's renovation. Additionally, Tsien Chiang enforces her will upon her domain in a variety of other ways.

Dream of Perfection. Tsien Chiang's magical creation, the Nightingale Bell, traveled with her to I'Cath. Soon after the city's rebirth, Chiang used the cracked bell to wish for her perfect city. Instead, her wish created a persistent dream world that occupies the dreams of all who sleep in I'Cath. In this dream, Tsien Chiang's every plan is executed to perfection. As her city moves with brilliant efficiency, Chiang luxuriates with perfect dream versions of her lost daughters.

Renovating the City. Each evening, Tsien Chiang relays her orders for I'Cath's reconstruction to her droves of jiangshi agents, led by Minister Suen. Suen then disseminates these orders to the jiangshi of the Gemstone Garden, who work through the night. Every morning, Tsien Chiang finds some aspect of the city's miraculous changes unacceptable and returns to her palace, where she spends the day assembling new orders for her jiangshi servants.

The Darklord's Daughters. When Tsien Chiang arrived in I'Cath, she used the Nightingale Bell to revive her four daughters, who had been murdered in the uprising against her. The bell created two sets of interpretations of her daughters. The set inside the dream city are perfect recreations of Chiang's lost daughters. Those in the waking city are monstrous interpretations of Chiang's memories, innocent but unnatural beings. The eerie daughters in the waking world hold the key to undermining Tsien Chiang's hold over the city's dreams.

Closing the Borders. I'Cath is surrounded by walls and by the Mists beyond that. Chiang believes everyone in I'Cath has a responsibility to strive for perfection, so she keeps her people imprisoned within the city. As a result, the domain's borders are always closed, as detailed in the "The Mists" section at the start of this chapter. Should Chiang choose to open the domain's borders, the Four Trees Gate appears, and the Mists beyond the walls don't prevent passage.

CHIANG'S TORMENT

Fortune confounds Tsien Chiang in numerous ways, but the following are the most pronounced examples:

- Chiang wishes to make the dream of I'Cath a reality, and though her servants follow her plans perfectly, the city grows endlessly more disordered.
- Chiang relishes the dream vision of I'Cath, but it makes the reality of her city all the more unbearable. She won't let the corruption of her real city invade her dream, and aggressively stamps out any imperfection in the dream realm.
- The loss of Chiang's daughters haunts her. She knows the idealized dream versions of her daughters are fictions, but she still spends as much time with them as possible. She avoids their eerie waking-world versions, whom she fails to love.

ROLEPLAYING CHIANG

Tsien Chiang pursues an unattainable set of goals: a perfect city, a thankful populace, and an ideal family. Yet she is unable to articulate the specifics of her desires and unwilling to compromise. She lashes out at those unable to match her visions of perfection, seeing others' failings but not her own. Only the dream created by the Nightingale Bell offers her any respite.

Personality Trait. "I see what's best for my city and its people. I will lead them to perfection."

Ideal. "Once my city knows harmony, then I can rest."

Bond. "What I want and what's best for my people are one and the same."

Flaw. "Perfection is the only acceptable standard. The flawed must be remade, and the lazy must serve."

ADVENTURES IN I'CATH

I'Cath presents two worlds: a reality of want and desperation, and a dream of beautiful control, both dominated by Tsien Chiang.

The reality of I'Cath is an inescapable ghost city, overrun by jiangshi and ghosts. Escaping means engaging with those who know the city's secrets, whether sleeping residents, wandering ghosts, or deadly jiangshi.

The dream of I'Cath presents a second layer to the prison city. The characters might find ways to move in and out of the dream. I'Cath's people have no such recourse on their own, but if the characters wake individuals or disrupt the dream, they could allow those caught within to escape. (See "The Dream of I'Cath" later in this domain for details.)

Darklord Tsien Chiang and her daughters dwell at the heart of both these worlds. Working with or undermining them provides paths to disrupting the Dream of I'Cath and ultimately escaping. But Tsien Chiang holds great power over both her realms, and if she is convinced that either her city or her dream is beyond redemption, her edicts turn dire.

Consider the plots on the I'Cath Adventures table when planning adventures in this domain.

I'CATH ADVENTURES

d10	Adventure
1	A desperate local needs medicine for a sick spouse, but the only merchant in Gwai-Huit Center with the necessary herbs demands fresh fruit from the Gemstone Gardens. The local entreats the characters to infiltrate the **jiangshi**-haunted park (see chapter 5).
2	A child has gone missing on the streets of I'Cath. The child's parents plead with the characters to find the youngster before dusk.
3	A **spy** known as a criminal in I'Cath's dream city is imprisoned and tormented every time he falls asleep. He begs for the characters' aid to help keep him awake.
4	A group of **bandits** waylay anyone who passes through their territory, demanding fresh meat for passage. Trapped locals seek help in moving through the gang's territory.
5	A melancholy elf is unable to enter Tsien Chiang's dream to join his family. He entreats the characters to help him find a way.
6	A **jiangshi** approaches the characters and asks them to locate one or more of her lost family members within the dream city. She's worried about what's become of her family—their bodies should be in the city, but she's lost track of them.

d10	Adventure
7	A family in the Mansions made offerings of food and remembrances to placate a hungry **ghost**. This has attracted dozens of other ghosts. The family seeks help placating the undead mouths they can't feed.
8	Tsien Chiang's library in the Palace of Bones holds secrets about the border between dreams and reality. The characters must infiltrate the palace, find the information they need, and escape before Tsien Chiang returns at dawn.
9	A desperate **veteran** wakes from the dream and attempts to set I'Cath on fire, believing it's better for everything to burn than to live a lie. The characters must choose how to contend with the murderous arsonist.
10	All but one of Tsien Chiang's daughters have gone missing—and the remaining daughter is either Tsien Seu-Mei or Tsien Lei-An, neither of whom can speak. This daughter crosses the party's path and silently begs for help.

THE DREAM OF I'CATH

For some, the unending dream Tsien Chiang forces upon her populace presents a tempting alternative to the bleak, haunted reality of I'Cath. However, those who succumb to the dream retain little hope of escaping the city.

DREAMS OF PERFECTION

Anyone who sleeps in I'Cath enters Tsien Chiang's dream of a bustling, beautiful city filled with smiling people. But the forced smiles hide desperation from the watchful eyes of Tsien Chiang's stoic jiangshi ministers. The people undertake endless, repetitive tasks—such as scrubbing the city's coinage or counting the seconds. Those who fail to keep up are reassigned to exhausting labor. Those who rebel are either dragged off to lightless cells or slain outright, forcing them to awaken in the real world.

Nature of the Dream. Creatures in the dream of I'Cath have the statistics they do in waking life. If a creature dies in the dream, it takes 3d6 psychic damage, returns to the waking world, and does not receive any benefit from the rest that just ended.

The Nightingale Bell. The Nightingale Bell fuels Tsien Chiang's dream. Chiang must ring the bell once per day to maintain the dream. Otherwise, the dream fades and everyone in the domain wakes. Only Tsien Chiang can use the Nightingale Bell to maintain the dream of I'Cath. However, anyone can ring the bell to enter the dream bodily as though it were a demiplane. A creature that physically enters the dream leaves behind no body, and if killed, dies for real. The Nightingale Bell is protected by the Dark Powers and can't be destroyed.

Dreaming the Dream. A character cannot remove levels of exhaustion by finishing a long rest in I'Cath if they spend any part of that rest in Tsien Chiang's dream. Characters with no levels of exhaustion wake from the dream after 6 hours. Characters with 1 or more levels of exhaustion can try to wake up after every 6 hours they spend within the dream; to awaken, they must succeed on a DC 10 Wisdom saving throw. Those who fail remain within the dream for another 6 hours, after which they can try to escape again. Creatures that do not sleep can choose to enter the dream by meditating. If they enter the dream, they are affected by it as if they were sleeping. Many residents of I'Cath don't attempt to escape the dream, considering existence within it preferable to life in the real city.

TSIEN CHIANG'S DAUGHTERS

In her desperation to be reunited with her daughters, Tsien Chiang used the Nightingale Bell to wish her murdered children back into being. To her shock, each daughter reborn into the waking world took on an unnatural form. Although these young women mirror the personalities of Tsien Chiang's true daughters and their doubles in the dream version of I'Cath, their forms and abilities are radically different. Chiang shuns them, but doesn't do them harm. Now these four strange beings wander I'Cath, curious about the city and eager to please their mother. Every dusk they assemble at the Palace of Bones, hoping for kindness from Tsien Chiang as she hurriedly passes them to ascend Ping'On Tower.

Tsien Chiang's daughters are generally good natured, but anxieties prevent the daughters from sleeping. If offered comfort and kindness so that the four sisters are all equally at ease, the daughters are able to fall asleep (see "Disrupting the Dream").

Tsien Chiang's four daughters have the following names, forms, and simple dreams:

Tsien Lei-An. Voiceless Tsien Lei-An is made entirely of eyes and has the statistics of a **scarecrow**. She wishes for a robe of ghost hair silk or a jiangshi's slippers. She spends much of her time wandering the Mansions, rooting through the possessions of sleeping city-dwellers.

Tsien Man-Yi. Made of pale wood, Tsien Man-Yi must remain near the willow tree in the courtyard of the Palace of Bones, and has the statistics of a **dryad**. She wishes for flowers from the Gemstone Garden or for a friend to fall asleep under her tree's boughs.

Tsien Seu-Mei. Voiceless Tsien Seu-Mei is made entirely of teeth and has the statistics of a **ghoul**. She wishes to eat a delicious dessert or care for one of the fish of the Gemstone Gardens. She often wanders the stalls of Gwai-Huit Center.

Tsien Wai-Ching. Made of living fog, Tsien Wai-Ching is the youngest daughter and has the statistics of a **specter**. She wishes to help a spirit from Ping'On Tower find its family or to play with an incorporeal toy. She regularly explores the memorials in the Gemstone Gardens.

DISRUPTING THE DREAM

Damaging Tsien Chiang's dream undermines her grip on I'Cath, freeing the dreaming populace and opening the domain's borders. Thousands of living people suddenly need to be fed, but they can reclaim their normal lives.

Those seeking to spoil Tsien Chiang's dream can do so in the following ways:

Dreaming Daughters. If all four of Tsien Chiang's daughters in the waking world fall asleep, their sleeping forms replace their doubles in the dream city. This unites them with their mother in her perfect world, exactly as they've always wanted. Tsien Chiang, however, is horrified by their intrusion and flees her dream.

Dreams of Revolution. I'Cath's dreamers and displaced ancestral spirits might be persuaded to revolt against Tsien Chiang. This leads to extreme responses from the Darklord and her servants, but could force her to neglect or end the dream.

Waking Dream. A particularly compelling waking individual, spirit, or goal within I'Cath distracts Tsien Chiang from her dream. Perhaps the spirits of her lost family haunt the Mansions, or an individual directs the jiangshi to perfectly execute the Darklord's plans. Either outcome might lead Tsien Chiang to focus on reality and let her dreams slip away—for a time.

KALAKERI

Domain of Betrayal and Revenge

Darklord: Ramya Vasavadan
Genres: Gothic horror and dark fantasy
Hallmarks: Monstrous leaders, family intrigue, war-torn nation
Mist Talismans: Ornate but rusted talwar, shield emblazoned with a wyvern-and-lotus emblem, a well-polished skull

For untold generations, the Vasavadan dynasty has ruled over the Great Kingdom of Kalakeri. This land was one of stability and prosperity until a barbarous civil war and a queen's dying curse brought low what centuries never could. Once an unrivaled power known throughout the world for its rare resources and vibrant trade, Kalakeri is now locked in an endless storm of violence. At the center of that storm stand the remnants of the Vasavadan: three heirs transformed into unspeakable monsters by their depravity and hatred.

Kalakeri is a deceptively beautiful land of verdant rain forests and an idyllic web of rivers and lakes known as the Backwaters. Rare creatures and extraordinary magical plants are found across the forest peninsula locals call the Harvest Peninsula. At the height of its prosperity, Kalakeri was a robust center of art, commerce, and religion, with foreign merchants spreading wild tales of Sri Raji, the Steaming Lands, the Land at the Heart of the World, and other fanciful names for Kalakeri. Now Kalakeri is a shadow of its past glory, a quagmire of intrigue and despair where fortunes change on a whim.

The people of Kalakeri live in dread, as a single misstep means doom. Schemers and hapless citizens alike are tossed by the tidal forces of the royal family. Following her betrayal and assassination, Maharani Ramya was restored to the world to avenge herself against her treacherous siblings, Arijani and Reeva. Ramya's curse manifests in both her deathless rage and in the monstrous forms afflicting her siblings. Both sides continue to escalate their atrocities against one another, drawing the powerful and the innocent alike into their squabbles. As Arijani and Reeva host murderous galas to entice fiendish allies, the forces of the Darklord search out and execute anyone they consider treasonous, adding their skulls to Ramya's ever-growing Tower of Traitors.

NOTEWORTHY FEATURES

Those familiar with Kalakeri know the following facts:

- Two factions struggle to lay claim to Kalakeri's Sapphire Throne: the soldiers and loyalists of

Maharani Ramya, and the nobles and merchants who support the younger royal siblings, Arijani and Reeva.
- The vast city of Jadurai performs multiple duties as Kalakeri's capital, the site of the royal palace, and a battlefield where factions struggle to claim or hold it as a symbol of rule.
- Fierce followers of each faction scour the land, murdering any who oppose their faction.
- Refugees from the strife hide in the Backwaters, and rebel groups there organize against the entire Vasavadan family.
- The Tower of Traitors is a dizzying, skull-studded structure that grows daily. Some say its completion will cleanse the nation of evil, while others believe it will summon the gods' wrath.

SETTLEMENTS AND SITES

Kalakeri is dominated by tropical rain forests that surround hundreds of miles of inland waterways. Farming and fishing villages line these waterways and the coast.

JADURAI

This city is thousands of years old. Here ancient structures with the architecture of previous dynasties stand alongside modern buildings. Hardly a month passes without locals rediscovering a forgotten chamber or catacomb.

The colorfully canopied Lakshma Market trades in everything from betel leaves to the eggs of wyverns, which are common near the mountain spires known as the Lesser and Greater Vochalam. People of all social classes flock to the market, moving past the flower-petaled kolam that ward the entrances of the high temple of Kalakeri's gods.

Map 3.8: Kalakeri

Jadurai retains its splendor, but the conflict between Ramya and her siblings takes an enormous toll. Sections of the city lie in ruins, and the slums encroach farther every day as misery and squalor consume Jadurai from the inside.

THE BACKWATERS

An extensive web of brackish rivers and lakes crisscrosses the Harvest Peninsula. Houseboats travel their lengths, ferrying food and wares between thriving trade towns, rural villages, and the estates of regional nobles.

Refugees from the ongoing war and the rampant poverty of Jadurai seek haven in the Backwaters. Those brave enough to fight the tyranny of the Vasavadan scions organize into rebel bands that prepare desperate, dangerous attacks on the royal family.

Kalakeri's most fearsome predators inhabit the Backwaters, including basilisks, hydras, stone giants, and cloud giants.

CERULEAN CITADEL

The Cerulean Citadel is the palace of the royal family. The jewel in Jadurai's crown, it derives its name from the sky-blue sandstone used to construct its outer walls. The octagonal Citadel encompasses one hundred acres. Within its defensive walls and strategic bastions lies a complex of beautifully designed marble quarters and pavilions, arranged between courtyards, baths, ponds, and gardens. Bas-reliefs adorn the buildings, depicting the history, heroes, and legends of the kingdom, some of which remain mysteries to the wisest scholars. The central domed court houses the Sapphire Throne and is the hub of political activity in the Citadel. Beneath the Citadel, vast tunnels for storing supplies and secretly moving troops also hide the magical troves of forgotten rulers.

TOWER OF TRAITORS

The Tower of Traitors is an ever-expanding structure on the outskirts of Jadurai, situated on the battlefield where Arijani and Reeva murdered Ramya, precipitating the creation of Kalakeri as a domain. Row upon row of skulls, all taken from Ramya's fallen enemies, fill depressions set into the stone tower. Two skulls hold places of special prominence: the original human skulls of Arijani and Reeva. Ramya's skeletal soldiers continue to build the tower as part of her plan to rid Kalakeri of evil and receive the gods' blessings.

THE VOCHALAMS

Two treacherous mountains jut from the forest-cloaked hills and cliffs of southwestern Kalakeri. The Greater Vochalam and the slightly smaller Lesser Vochalam are home to vast numbers of wyverns. Legends say that temples crown both mountains and that an ancient deity placed a treasure able to grant wishes in one of them. Whoever claims the treasure in the wrong temple, though, is turned into a wyvern loyal to Kalakeri's true leader.

THE ASHRAM OF NIRANJAN

Another Domain of Dread hails from the same lands as Kalakeri. Those who sail into the Mists of the Sea of Spears often find this shadow-haunted domain of Niranjan, which is detailed further in the "Other Domains of Dread" section later in this chapter.

RAMYA VASAVADAN

The Vasavadan dynasty has ruled over Kalakeri since ancient times. Ramya Vasavadan was hand-picked by her father to succeed him, but on the bleak day of the maharana's death, Ramya's brother, Arijani, declared himself the new maharana. Allied with ranas hungry for unearned power, Arijani tried to force Ramya to relinquish the Sapphire Throne.

Ramya refused to yield. Moving swiftly, she organized her allies, met her brother in battle, and captured him. She intended to execute Arijani, but her sister Reeva counseled her to be merciful. Ultimately, Ramya forgave the rebel faction, Arijani was imprisoned, and Ramya ascended as Kalakeri's maharani, Queen of Kings.

A golden period in Kalakeri's history followed as Ramya promoted learning and upheld justice. Meanwhile, Reeva secretly coordinated with Ramya's foes. After years of resentment and plotting, the rebels freed Arijani and spurred nobles across the nation into open revolt.

The resulting conflict swiftly turned vicious. Regretting her past mercy, Ramya captured enemy ranas and executed them using flame and ravenous tigers, while her loyalists put anyone suspected of treason to the sword. The maharani's brutality increased distrust in her rule, and the fighting spread.

After numerous battles, Reeva begged her sister to meet her brother and negotiate an end to the war. Ramya, who remained ignorant of Reeva's part in freeing Arijani, trusted her sister—and walked straight into their trap.

Ambushers slaughtered Ramya's royal guards and captured the maharani. In the central courtyard of the Cerulean Citadel, Arijani sentenced his sister to death. As the court strangler's garrote crushed her windpipe, Ramya cursed her brother and sister, calling them bloodthirsty beasts. Arijani and Reeva denied their sister the honors befitting a maharani, dumping Ramya's corpse into the sea. As they did, a terrible monsoon struck the Harvest Peninsula, bringing with it walls of supernatural mist that closed around Kalakeri.

The storm lashed Kalakeri for weeks, and when it reached its height, Ramya emerged from her watery grave. Reborn with terrifying power, she called upon those who had been slaughtered in her service. Loyal in death, a corpse legion joined the revitalized maharani. They stalked the streets of Jadurai, tore down the gates of the Cerulean Citadel, and slaughtered those who had betrayed Ramya. They dragged Arijani and Reeva into the courtyard where their sister died, and there Ramya declared them traitors. The treacherous pair clawed and howled like beasts as undead elephants crushed them to death. Their wails of terror left Ramya unmoved.

Arijani and Reeva's plots didn't end with their lives, however. They too were reborn, transformed into fiends with animalistic features by their souls' ravenous desires. And so the conflict gripping Kalakeri continues, trapping the nation in an endless war and forcing its people to swear loyalty to monsters.

RAMYA'S POWERS AND DOMINION

Reborn as a **death knight**, Ramya desperately tries to hold on to or retake the Sapphire Throne in a cycle of victory and loss with her equally uncompromising siblings. Although an illusion disguises her deathless state, Ramya constantly feels the chill in her bones and her own crumbling flesh. Her existence has becomes one of constant struggle, doubt, and defeat as her obsessions shape all of Kalakeri.

War Leader. Ramya eagerly leads her troops in battle. She rides into combat upon a war **elephant** or **wyvern** and carries the legendary talwar (longsword) and longbow of the Vasavadan dynasty's founder. The Vasavadan coat of arms, a golden wyvern clutching a white lotus in its talons, emblazons her armor and that of her soldiers.

Merciless. Ramya demands loyalty from her subjects. She and her soldiers kill anyone who she considers a traitor, a status extended not only to those who back Arijani and Reeva, but even to those who don't support her vociferously enough. Her paranoia makes her ruthless, leading her to slaughter countless innocents.

Deathless Loyalty. Kalakeri's armies and the guards of the Cerulean Citadel obey Ramya without question, despite thousands of them having died in her service. These soldiers' loyalty follows them into death. Any living soldier who dies in Ramya's service returns to life as an Undead warrior—a **skeleton** or **wight**—on the night of the next new moon and rejoins the maharani's army. Ramya's living followers consider this deathless state an honor and the ultimate mark of loyalty.

Blood Relatives. Ramya never compromises with her siblings Arijani and Reeva. She constantly struggles to quell the rebellion they lead, as detailed in "Treachery in Kalakeri" later in this domain.

Closing the Borders. Ramya can close or open Kalakeri's borders as detailed in "The Mists" at the start of this chapter, but she can do so only while she controls the Sapphire Throne. If her faction is driven out of Jadurai, the domain's borders remain in their current state until she regains control.

RAMYA'S TORMENT

The Dark Powers endlessly conspire to confound Ramya, most persistently in the following ways:

- Ramya's treacherous siblings, Arijani and Reeva, endlessly contest her reign and sow discord across Kalakeri. Ramya both loathes and loves her siblings, so despite their perpetual deceptions, she remains vulnerable to their promises and lies.
- Ramya can manipulate her domain and control its borders only while she controls the Sapphire Throne. If she is ousted and one of her siblings controls the Cerulean Citadel, doubt and despair weaken her influence over her domain until she retakes her seat of power.
- An illusion masks Ramya's Undead state. Her true nature is revealed only by the chill of her skin and in her withered reflection. Ramya permits no mirrors in her presence, lest her curse be revealed.

ROLEPLAYING RAMYA

Ramya is distant and aloof, though she craves connection. Those who speak with her find her measured in conversation, and capable of kindness and humor. However, a vein of paranoia runs through all her actions, and she reacts to any hint of suspicious words or deeds with creative and potentially lethal tests and punishments.

Personality Trait. "There is loyalty, and there is treachery. In rule, there are no half measures."

Ideal. "I will regain my deserved glory even if I must scour the world with my wrath."

Bond. "I still love those who oppose me. The flames of righteousness provide the swiftest path to renewal."

Flaw. "None are truly trustworthy. I am utterly alone."

MAHARANI RAMYA VASAVADAN

ADVENTURES IN KALAKERI

Kalakeri is trapped in an unbreakable spiral of suffering and hate. The common folk exert no control over the struggle for the Sapphire Throne and are forced to maintain the appearance of loyalty toward rival terrors.

Every part of Kalakeri holds secrets and dangers, and nowhere is untouched by its rulers' war for dominance. When planning adventures in Kalakeri, consider who currently controls the Sapphire Throne—Ramya or Arijani and Reeva. Either faction is likely to notice the party and court them as potential allies. The characters then walk the fine line detailed in the "Treachery in Kalakeri" section later in this domain description.

The wilds of Kalakeri might also fuel terrifying adventures. The land holds all manner of perilous ruins and mysteries, from the secrets of lost rulers to the practices of forbidden magical sects. Without a steady, reliable presence on the throne, ancient cults, deadly beasts, and opportunistic demagogues are free to unleash dooms upon isolated villages. Your adventures might lead characters into Kalakeri's deepest wilds to rediscover lost secrets, save innocents, or curry favor with a faction.

Consider the plots on the Kalakeri Adventures table when planning adventures in this domain.

KALAKERI ADVENTURES

d10	Adventure
1	**Bandits** takes over the village of Neelakurinji, claiming Ramya or Arijani as their leader. In truth they serve neither and are opportunistically robbing those who fear disobeying the factions. An escaped villager entreats the characters for help.
2	The **stone giant** guru Jalendu claims to know a path to religious enlightenment. Those who fail to prove their devotion to his teachings turn up petrified.
3	The sea boils around an ancient, submerged ruin called the Drowned Altar. With constant upheaval, no one has performed the rites necessary to placate what dwells in the deep.
4	Dozens of servants were hired to help host a grand gala thrown by Arijani. The event was a success, but none of the servants returned home. Their families entreat the characters to seek answers.
5	The rare ralvanji spice has miraculous medicinal properties, but by royal edict it is grown only in the gardens of the Cerulean Citadel. Estavan, a mysterious **oni** merchant, offers to pay good money for the spice and even more for the seeds.
6	A parent asks the characters to bring their runaway teenager home, not knowing their child joined Ramya's army, died, and returned as a **wight**.

d10	Adventure
7	Reeva employs the party to find the forbidden ruins of Bahru, said to lie somewhere in the Ashwagangha Mountains. She believes her ancestors imprisoned a powerful force there, which she hopes to awaken and bend to her service.
8	The shadows of people in Meenakara are disappearing, and the shadow-bereft soon sicken and die. A local leader claims that the strange plague's cure lies among the hidden isles known as the Ashram of Niranjan (detailed in "Other Domains of Dread" later in this chapter).
9	A commoner begs the characters to prove their sibling's loyalty to Ramya. Time is short, since the sibling was arrested and taken to the Tower of Traitors to face execution.
10	Ramya desires a consort to cement her rulership and bring stability to the kingdom. A character who is a capable warrior catches her attention.

VASAVADAN TRAITORS

Maharani Ramya's rule over Kalakeri is constantly jeopardized and undermined by her deceitful siblings' endless pursuit of power. Arijani and Reeva promise their followers wealth, freedom, and a chance for unprecedented social ascension, but in truth, their agendas are entirely self-serving, and they care for nothing but control. Whether or not the characters agree with these rebellious royals' agendas, they present the most significant opposition to Ramya's ruthless control of Kalakeri—while defeating them is the swiftest route to gaining Ramya's favor.

ARIJANI

Arijani is the charming face of resistance for all who oppose Ramya's control of the Sapphire Throne. Like Ramya and Reeva, Arijani was given a second life by the Dark Powers. Now a **rakshasa**, Arijani uses his mastery of illusions and Reeva's insights to manipulate Ramya and his other foes. He's gregarious and enjoys the finer things in life, traits that ingratiate him with the wealthy and influential supporters he seeks to attract to his cause. These traits also allow him to cultivate a persona of vacant decadence, which he uses as a mask so his foes will underestimate him and reveal themselves. Arijani has faked his and Reeva's deaths on multiple occasions, after which they always return "resurrected," leading Ramya to believe they can never be truly defeated.

ARIJANI AND REEVA VASAVADAN CONSPIRE
IN A COURTYARD OF THE CERULEAN CITADEL.

REEVA

Reeva remembers a time when she loved Ramya, before her sister eclipsed her in their family's esteem. Unable to overtake Ramya in leadership skills, she sought more subtle methods. Her interests in intrigue and magic intensified when she discovered a hidden library beneath the Cerulean Citadel—a repository of insidious magic hearkening back to the rule of certain tyrannical Vasavadan ancestors. Reeva uses what she discovered there to further Arijani's ambitions and yearns to gain control over the citadel so she can unearth its deepest, most insidious secrets.

After her murder, Reeva was reborn as an **arcanoloth**, a state that horrifies her. When frustrated, she vents her rage by instructing her servants to abduct someone she considers beautiful and then overseeing that beauty's destruction. Reeva is a cunning plotter, strategist, and manipulator. She applies these talents to her magic, entreating fiends for aid and using them to hasten the day when no one will

underestimate her again. Many of Arijani's allies don't trust Reeva. Behind her back, they mockingly call her charismatic Arijani's opposite, or "Inajira."

TREACHERY IN KALAKERI

The struggle between the heirs to the Sapphire Throne drives the conflict in Kalakeri. Both Ramya's loyalists and Arijani and Reeva's rebels are fanatics, eager to report or act against those they consider traitors to the nation's rightful ruler or rulers. Meanwhile, the common folk in areas under a faction's clear control extol their loyalty to the local power loudly; in less stable areas, most keep their allegiance secret. While exploring the domain, characters regularly face questions about their loyalty—and in this conflict, neutrality is tantamount to betraying both sides. The characters' answers eventually earn them the attention of one side or the other, with members of that faction trying to dragoon them into the conflict.

Renown in Kalakeri

Judgment follows everything the characters do in Kalakeri. Those who support either of the domain's factions earn enemies and allies. Those who don't support a faction draw suspicion. Those who play the factions against one another might earn the favor of both—but for how long?

Using the renown system from the *Dungeon Master's Guide*, track the characters' standing with Kalakeri's two factions. Every character begins with 0 renown score with each faction. Characters gain or lose points as they act against or in the service of either faction. As they do so, their standing with the factions changes, granting them access to favors or provoking reprisals. Characters adjust their renown score once per adventure, and rarely by more than 5 points. The Renown in Kalakeri table notes activities that increase or decrease a character's renown score.

Intrigue and Horror. When dealing with Kalakeri's factions, every option or choice has ramifications. Give the characters opportunities to meet, interact with, and rise in the esteem of Ramya, Arijani, and Reeva. As they do, highlight the monstrous nature of the three villains and that dealing with them involves hard choices. The renown system requires the characters to become active participants in the horrors of Kalakeri, encouraging them to ally with evil beings or make uncomfortable concessions to win greater victories later. Perhaps the characters betray Ramya in a way that evicts her from Jadurai for years, or cause one of Arijani and Reeva's political alliances to crumble. How far will they go for such opportunities?

Benefits of Renown. Whether the characters back Ramya or Arijani and Reeva, or seek to play both sides, those who advance in their standing with a faction advance in that side's esteem, gaining favor with that faction's leader or leaders and influence over their plots. Use the examples of these benefits in the following sections to guide you in creating further rewards and concessions appropriate to the characters' standing.

Losing Renown. A character's renown score with a faction can drop to less than 0. A faction mistrusts and actively opposes the suggestions of characters with a renown score of –1 or lower. Those with a renown score of –5 or lower are actively hunted by a faction's members and considered enemy agents.

Recovering Renown. It's possible for characters to gain renown with a faction, betray the faction, and still maintain a measure of respect with the group. Characters might thus thread the needle of serving both groups. Relationships constantly shift in Kalakeri, and grudges rarely last long. As a result, the characters might walk the razor's edge of loyalty and betrayal in hopes of furthering their own goals.

Continual Conflict. Kalakeri's factions are locked in a stalemate, their victories and losses forgotten within days or weeks. Characters who interact with the factions might change this balance. But if either faction firmly controls Kalakeri, the leaders enact their monstrous agendas upon the land, leading only to continued suffering. The Dark Powers ensure that the defeated faction doesn't remain quelled for long, though. The characters might instead try to gain influence with Ramya or with Arijani and Reeva to curb the villains' atrocities and mitigate the wickedness in Kalakeri. Such actions put the characters at risk, but if they don't intercede, who will?

Renown in Kalakeri

Adjusted Renown	Activity	Faction
+1	Advancing the faction's interests	Either
+1	Revealing a traitor	Either
+1	Attaining victory over a rival through martial skill	Loyalists
+1	Evicting rebels from a community	Loyalists
+1	Attaining victory over a rival through duplicity	Rebels
+2	Completing a mission assigned by the faction	Either
+2	Executing a traitor	Either
+2	Evicting loyalists from a community	Rebels
+2	Gaining a rich or powerful ally for the faction	Rebels
+2	Offering rare occult lore to Reeva	Rebels
+3	Recovering Arijani or Reeva's skull from the Tower of Traitors	Rebels
+4	Ousting foes from the Cerulean Citadel	Either
–1	Being accused of treachery	Either
–2	Being caught aiding a rival faction's agenda	Either
–2	Failing at an assignment	Either
–2	Offending Arijani's ego	Rebels
–3	Discovering a faction leader's true form	Either
–5	Openly betraying the faction	Either

LOYALISTS OF KALAKERI

The Kalakeri military and traditionalists throughout the domain back Maharani Ramya's claim to the Sapphire Throne. Ramya tries to eliminate her siblings and the rebels supporting them through dramatic military actions and merciless trials and tests of loyalty. The loyalists covet Jadurai as a center of power and revere the Tower of Traitors, which serves as a command center and a symbol of undying loyalty.

Benefits of Renown. Those who gain certain thresholds of renown with the loyalists can make requests of that faction and Maharani Ramya. These requests and the threshold at which they'll be entertained are detailed on the Loyalist Benefits table—along with how the request adjusts the character's renown score with the faction, if applicable. Ramya treats those with a renown score of 25 or higher as trusted advisors and reveals her undead nature to them.

LOYALIST BENEFITS

Renown Threshold	Request	Renown Adjustment
1	Moving unimpeded through loyalist-controlled territory	—
1	Learning the location of the bulk of Ramya's armies	—
3	Learning where a particular skull is in the Tower of Traitors	−1
3	Learning where a specific soldier in Ramya's army is stationed	—
5	Gaining an audience with Maharani Ramya	—
10	Pardoning someone accused of being a traitor	−2
10	Gaining command of a contingent of Undead soldiers to fulfill a mission	−2
15	Convincing the faction to heed advice	−2
15	Convincing Ramya to relinquish a skull from the Tower of Traitors or dismiss a soldier from her army	−2
20	Convincing the faction to heed advice seemingly counter to its interests	−5
25	Convincing Ramya to leave Jadurai	−5

REBELS OF KALAKERI

Since Arijani and Reeva's murder and monstrous resurrection, control of the Sapphire Throne has passed between Ramya and Arijani multiple times. Using their influence among the ranas and merchants in the western part of Kalakeri, Arijani and Reeva have repeatedly driven Ramya out of the capital or into shocking defeats. When in control of the Cerulean Citadel, Arijani hosts decadent parties to spread his influence among Kalakeri's elite and those who further his interests. These events serve a secondary role in concealing private feasts featuring obscene delicacies and mortal flesh, allowing Arijani and Reeva to satisfy their fiendish hungers.

Benefits of Renown. Those who gain certain thresholds of renown with the rebels can make requests of that faction, Arijani, and Reeva. These requests and the threshold at which they'll be entertained are detailed on the Rebel Benefits table—along with how the request adjusts the character's renown score with the faction, if applicable. Arijani and Reeva never reveal their true natures to anyone.

REBEL BENEFITS

Renown Threshold	Request	Renown Adjustment
1	Moving unimpeded through rebel-controlled territory	—
1	Learning if a wealthy individual has been courted by the rebels in the past month	—
3	Learning where Arijani and Reeva are encamped	—
5	Gaining a private audience with both Arijani and Reeva	—
7	Gaining a private audience with either Arijani or Reeva	—
10	Obtaining an invitation to one of Arijani and Reeva's galas	−4
15	Convincing the faction to heed advice	−2
15	Convincing the faction to heed advice seemingly counter to its interests	−5
20	Obtaining an invitation to one of Arijani and Reeva's private feasts	−5
25	Convincing Reeva to reveal secrets hidden under the Cerulean Citadel	−5

KARTAKASS

Domain of Tarnished Dreams

Darklord: Harkon Lukas
Genres: Dark fantasy and gothic horror
Hallmarks: Hidden identities, dangerous performances, exploitative ambitions, werewolves
Mist Talismans: Handbill advertising remarkable performances, rustic woodcut of hunting wolves, wolf's tooth necklace

Kartakass is a vast stage that serenades the ambitious with promises of fame. Performance is a way of life in this forested domain, with everyone from the bards of Skald to the actors of Emherst pursuing dazzling dreams. Here, the people live by a simple rule: never let an audience grow bored.

To outsiders, life feels staged and surreal in Kartakass, as every plant and beast, every peasant and performer strives to prove their greatness. Trees and flowers burst into bloom and then wither after their extended spring, while songbirds sing themselves hoarse. And every local, from the youngest child to the most venerable elder, knows that dreams, fame, and immortal adulation are theirs for the taking—if they prove worthy.

In Kartakass, individuals strive for glory. Where talent and expertise fail, obsession and duplicity reign, leading to repeating cycles of triumph, betrayal, and despair. Predators of all sorts flourish in this land of consuming passions and vicious secrets. With each full moon, the truth of Kartakass is exposed, and lycanthropes reveal their hunger for dominance and for blood.

NOTEWORTHY FEATURES

Those familiar with Kartakass know the following facts:

- Kartakass has no unifying government. Instead, each settlement is governed by a meistersinger, who is acknowledged as the mayor and embodiment of local art. Meistersingers maintain creative rivalries with each other, largely for show.
- Settlements pride themselves on performative traditions, such as distinctive dress or song stylings.
- Wolves roam the land freely. Few venture outside during the full moon, fearing werewolves.
- A sourceless song whispers through the mystical Wildersung Wood, always fading before it ends. Although no one knows its conclusion, all Kartakans know the beginning: "Sing of the trees, give voice to the breeze, and stave off the bloom of doom. While the wise sing their song, guilty necks stretch long, and ..."

KARTAKAN CHARACTERS

Characters from Kartakass are quick to smile—and quicker to be suspicious of others' smiling faces. The domain's population is comprised of a variety of peoples who have broad ranges of rich skin and hair colors. The use of dyes and cosmetics to accent one's features and memorability is common among all genders. When players create characters from Kartakass, consider asking them the following questions.

What artistic skill do you idealize or have a talent for? Is it a natural skill? Is it your family's preferred art form? Did you learn it from an idol or mentor?

What do you use your talents, work, or travels to hide? Does insecurity or doubt drive you to excel? Did someone best you in your field of mastery? Does a vice, curse, or rumor color your reputation?

What does success mean to you? Do you pursue wealth, fame, love, or acceptance? What extremes would you embrace to gain success?

SETTLEMENTS AND SITES

Kartakass is a gentle land of rolling hills, light forests, and clear lakes. The domain welcomes strangers. Small bands of merchants roam along the Lost Chord road or visit the quay at Point Hallucination in hopes of welcoming visitors and directing them to the domain's festively decorated communities.

EMHERST

Upon the cave-threaded, wooded rise known as the Fox's Theater stands the idyllic village of Emherst—and beneath it lies the true Emherst. On the surface, Emherst is an elaborate, immersive stage. Every "resident" is an in-character actor, and most are younger than thirty, including those playing aged roles. These are students of the Emherst School of Living Theater located in the Understage, a network of caverns beneath the village. This underground "backstage" connects every structure in the village via tunnels and hosts elaborate elevators and special-effects devices. Incredibly devoted to their craft, the instructors, students, and support staff of Emherst continually improvise performances, taking seven weeks to prepare before performing uninterrupted through an eighth "live" week. As actors refuse to break character, outsiders find the performances changing around them to incorporate their interactions with the community. Ruthless competition for prime roles leads to tragedy, the appearance of tragedy, or individual breaks with reality.

HARMONIA

Among the oldest settlements in Kartakass, Harmonia is considered the heart of the land's musical traditions. Entertainers pursuing the "true" music of Kartakass train and perform in the town's numer-

MAP 3.9: KARTAKASS

ous venues, such as the Harmonic Hall school of music and the acoustically complex Amphitheater of Harmonia, which projects whispers in some areas and silences screams in others. Artists vie for opportunities to present their work at the supremely popular Crystal Club, a members-only venue inside a cave that features a stage constructed from a massive natural geode. The club is known for its dramatic decor and overly critical clientele, and it's widely rumored that performers who fail to impress at the exclusive club go into exile. The bloodier truth reflects the fact that the club's membership is restricted to lycanthropes. This echoes the secret of Harmonia: its vaunted traditions, such as night performances, fur-trimmed clothing, and grisly woodcuts, are inexorably intertwined with bestial curses.

MEDRIA

The fishing village of Medria sits on the southern shore of Tragedy's Stage, a lake known for its notoriously choppy waters. The community's residents are uniquely inured to apocalypse scenarios, since early morning sound blasts, wandering puppets, and lurid but heatless explosions regularly emanate from the studios of local dramatic effects artists and their apprentices. Magic and theatricality blur in Medria, leaving the locals numb to both wonder and danger.

SKALD

The largest community in Kartakass, Skald presents itself as a bustling hub of commerce and creativity that boasts the best of everything in the land. The lure of overnight celebrity, glowing marquees, and fawning crowds attracts the ambitious to Skald, aspiring to the fame of stars such as the renowned bard Akriel Lukas. Yet behind the facade of creativity and freethinking, business owners and aging celebrities prey on youth and creativity, while critics and struggling performers create a culture of desperate deceptions. Vice, criminality, dark bargains, and supernatural predators flourish in Skald, like a pack of wolves hiding behind glamorous masks.

WILDERSUNG WOOD

The straight-limbed trees that make up this wood bear bark that causes sounds to echo. Wildlife lurks restlessly in the Wildersung Wood, stalking travelers with unusual boldness. And each day at twilight, a sourceless chorus drifts through the trees. The voices always sing the opening verses of the same song, but fade before it ends. Legends warn that any who hear the song should raise their voices and join the chorus. Those who don't risk meeting a terrible fate—strangers or those who refuse to sing are regularly discovered with inexplicably broken necks.

HARKON LUKAS

HARKON LUKAS

Harkon Lukas's life companions are ambition and blood. Born amid a community of lycanthropes, he dreamed of commanding not just a pack, but a whole army, a nation, even an empire of born predators. Early in life, he sought to unite his reckless werebeast family and turn them into tools of his ambition. When they failed him, though, Harkon lashed out, ultimately driving the lycanthropes to turn on him. The would-be leader murdered dozens but barely escaped alive, fleeing into a nation of humans.

In the years that followed, Harkon learned how to blend in with other peoples, how to manipulate those he considered his inferiors, and how to turn adoration into a weapon. He decided that if rule over a nation of hunters wasn't possible, he would force an empire of sheep to dance to the howling of wolves. Harkon Lukas became a legend, a performer, a teacher, a scoundrel, and a luminary. People flocked to bask in his remarkable presence.

Eventually, though, the land's rulers realized the threat Harkon posed. Officials tried to quietly imprison him for invented crimes, but the people defended him. When royal agents came for him en masse, the lycanthrope feigned his death. Outraged, the celebrity's followers rioted, and as the news spread, their outrage inspired a revolution. Within a week, the nation's government had crumbled, its defenders fleeing before an army that bore the red-stained coffin of Harkon Lukas at its head. As the rebel forces neared the walls of the royal palace, they were met by a contrite monarch, who gave a heartfelt speech, begging forgiveness and outlining concessions and a way for the nation to move forward. The rebels agreed to further negotiation.

At that moment, Harkon Lukas ended his ploy, bursting from his crimson coffin in wolf form and devouring the monarch before thousands of followers. Drenched in blood, the "resurrected" Harkon returned to his human form and donned a battered crown amid the roaring cheers of a nation of fans. But before the reign of the wolf could begin, the Mists rose amid the assembled throng and closed around their champion. When they cleared, the sovereign-wolf was no longer a step away from rule, but a stranger in an unfamiliar provincial land called Kartakass.

HARKON'S POWERS AND DOMINION

A born liar and shape-shifter, Harkon Lukas orchestrates elaborate manipulations. He has statistics similar to a **loup garou** (see chapter 5) but is never forced to change shape, either by the moon or by other external factors. He prefers his human form, but explores different physical details as the mood strikes him. He's rarely seen without his signature wide-brimmed hat; wolf's tooth necklace; and violin, which he calls Bleeding Heart.

Hungry for Fame. Despite being Darklord, Harkon Lukas numbers among the least feared of Kartakass's people. He ever seeks to win esteem and influence among the domain's people, but the locals constantly forget he's a relevant modern performer. They remember his works fondly but vaguely, ever distracted by new novelties. In response, Harkon reinvents himself time and time again, striving to win the domain's love. To this end, he often exploits ambitious and naive new talent. He collects promising up-and-coming performers, becomes their mentor, traps them within the bond of lycanthropy, and then uses them as tools (see the "Insatiable Hungers" section later in this domain for details). Such alliances rarely last for more than a few months before Harkon grows bored and steals his protégés' performance ideas, their wealth, and their lives.

The Lukas Clan. Harkon Lukas uses and manipulates all those around him with two exceptions: his eldest adult children, Akriel and Casimir. Both children aren't lycanthropes and have complicated relations with their father, seeking to both earn his favor and surpass his greatest triumphs. Akriel idolizes Harkon and mimics his performing style to fuel her own career. As the Dark Powers don't torment her as they do Harkon, her reputation steadily grows—much to her father's resentment. Casimir, on the other hand, wants nothing to do with Harkon and seeks to make his own way in life. Whether at the whims of his father or the Mists, though, he always finds his way back to Kartakass.

The Old Kartakan Inn and Taverna. Lukas owns this intimate, traditional tavern in Skald. Nightly, either Harkon Lukas (if he's in town) or new artists under his tutelage perform here. Any newcomer who performs on the Old Kartakan's stage is sure to become Skald's newest celebrity, with all the adulation, opportunity, and jealousy that inspires. Harkon keeps a private suite in the taverna. Those who come here seeking him must first talk their way past the taverna's heavily tattooed head bouncer and mixologist, the werewolf Haldrake Moonbaun.

Closing the Borders. When Harkon chooses to close Kartakass's borders, a soothing song fills the Mists. The Mists function as detailed in "The Mists" at the start of this chapter, but in addition, any creature in the Mists that has its speed reduced to 0 by exhaustion falls unconscious and is teleported out of the Mists. The creature awakes at the Mists' edge back in Kartakass 1d6 hours later.

HARKON LUKAS'S TORMENT

The Dark Powers endlessly stymie Harkon's quest for fame, assaulting his ego in the following ways:

- Harkon is obsessed with spreading his fame and travels Kartakass endlessly. Whenever he returns to a community, though, he finds he has been forgotten. Semi-polite variations of "I thought you'd retired" ever torment him.
- Harkon believes he just needs to find the right act, styling, or inspiration to finally cement him in the hearts of Kartakass's people—and from there, take control of the nation.
- Although Harkon is unable to build his own fame, he has a peerless eye for talent. His protégés swiftly attain stardom, and with it, Harkon's resentment.
- Harkon's frustration eventually gives way to indulgences of his lycanthropic hungers. Bloody slaughters of his students and rivals often precede him moving on to another town.

ROLEPLAYING HARKON

Harkon Lukas thrives on compliments and control. The lycanthrope skillfully reads other people, anticipates their ambitions and desires, and readily exploits them. He has a talent for flattery and making others feel like the center of the world. But he's a natural liar, and his seeming earnestness disguises double meanings and lies.

Personality Trait. "My words are beauty, my deeds are power, and my aspirations will change the world."

Ideal. "Everyone wants to love me. I'll make them realize that."

Bond. "I share my passions broadly and intensely, but everyone understands that the most dazzling flames die fastest."

Flaw. "Anyone who spurns my love will know my hunger."

ADVENTURES IN KARTAKASS

The desires and secrets of Kartakass's people run in parallel with those of the lycanthropes that flourish here. The domain's residents consider lycanthropes to be legendary threats, but in truth any resident who gives in to their vices might be consumed by the beast within. Numerous types of lycanthropes might flourish in Kartakass, or the curse of lycanthropy could spontaneously manifest in people who can't control their passions. Use or customize the lycanthropes in the *Monster Manual* to create cursed individuals transformed by desire and vice into bestial hybrids.

Kartakass also presents a fantastic domain in which to explore surreal twists on nature. The Dark Powers might give animals and plants friendly voices and welcoming aspects, but every being in the domain has an agenda. The cycle of life, as framed by predators and prey, takes on a grisly cast when a songbird's aria is cut short by lupine jaws.

Consider the plots on the Kartakass Adventures table when planning adventures in this domain.

KARTAKASS ADVENTURES

d8	Adventure
1	The characters arrive in Kartakass and immediately meet a friendly local: Harkon Lukas.
2	A foe carries an invitation to Harmonia's Crystal Club. If the characters visit, they find themselves the only non-lycanthropes in the crowd.
3	A set dresser in Medria used "tamed" **mimics** during a stage production. Now the audience is trapped inside a theater overrun by the monsters.
4	The party investigates a murder in Emherst. The victim is an actor who played a character murdered daily in the ongoing immersive play.

d8	Adventure
5	Akriel Lukas hires the party to "borrow" her father's violin so she can accurately model her own violin, Sundered Heart, from it.
6	A scholar named Radaga seeks the characters' aid in recovering a mysterious relic—an ancient crown—from a skeleton-haunted canyon in the Martello Hills.
7	The party is invited to participate in a fighting tournament in the goblin-overrun hills known as the Catacombs. Upon arriving, they find that **goblins** organized the event under the oversight of the flamboyant **gladiator** Nym Pymplee.
8	A brewer in Harmonia hires the party to deliver a cart of meekulbrau—a local berry wine that soothes the throat and improves vocal performances. A band of thieves hijacked the last two deliveries, and the brewer wants to make sure this latest delivery reaches its buyer, Harkon Lukas.

AKRIEL LUKAS

INSATIABLE HUNGERS

In Kartakass, characters can effortlessly earn reputations as heroes and luminaries. Their smallest feats become exaggerated in stories and song, opening the door for greater connections and opportunities. Depict the public's interest in the characters by using the renown system presented in the *Dungeon Master's Guide*. Start the characters with high renown scores, but let their renown scores decay if they don't work to keep the public's interest. At the height of their fame, characters might be recognized by strangers on the streets, given free room and board, or invited to lavish social events. As their novelty fades, though, they'll find passersby snickering behind their backs and social circles closing to them. There are ways to alter the characters' social trajectory, though, such as embracing a relationship with Harkon Lukas.

THE DARKLORD'S BETRAYAL

Harkon Lukas approaches the characters as an ally who eagerly sponsors their adventures and rise to fame. Although he does this in hopes of benefiting from the characters' triumphs and stealing their celebrity, the Darklord can be a powerful ally. Ultimately, though, all of Harkon's relationships walk a familiar path.

Meeting the Darklord. Through sycophants and werewolf allies, the Darklord learns of noteworthy characters before they hear of him. By manufacturing a chance encounter, Harkon takes the opportunity to be impressed by or indebt himself to the characters. He then uses tactics on the Favors for Harkon Lukas table to share a goal with intriguing characters. However Harkon comes to need or employ the characters, he encourages and compliments them. Afterward, he seeks to employ the characters further, either on personal jobs or by tipping them off about grander quests.

FAVORS FOR HARKON LUKAS

d4	Favor
1	Harkon is expected to debut a new song, "Just Like the Wind," but his backup performers and entourage are missing. The Darklord asks for the characters to fill in as entertainers and personal security.
2	Harkon expects to be attacked by a toxic former student or lover at a public event. The Darklord asks the party to intercept this stalker.
3	Harkon feigns fear of being mobbed by fans. The Darklord asks the party to disguise him and escort him to an event.
4	In the wild, Harkon's entourage is slain by wolves or by bandits. If the party saves him, the Darklord feigns helplessness and asks to travel with them.

ERIC BELISLE

The crowds at the Crystal Club in Harmonia have a vicious reputation. Some performers learn why firsthand.

Bite of the Darklord. After gaining a measure of the party's confidence or singling out a character as a useful favorite, Harkon Lukas asks his eccentric signature question: "May I bite you?" He does this while removing his wolf tooth necklace and offering to place it around a character's neck. By doing so, he marks the character as his protégé. If the character refuses, Harkon respects their decision but hopes they will reconsider. If the character accepts, the Darklord gives them *Harkon's Bite* (see the description below). Harkon acknowledges that the necklace carries minor magic to bless the wearer's performances. However, he doesn't mention that it also curses the wearer with lycanthropy. The Darklord can create one new necklace every week.

The Darklord's Pack. Harkon curses protégés with lycanthropy to force them into a circle of confidence. During the first full moon after a character receives *Harkon's Bite*, the Darklord lingers nearby to "discover" their transformation. He promises to keep this secret and reveals his own lycanthropy. The Darklord then uses this shared secret to gain leverage over the character and pushes them to embrace the curse. Harkon is initially patient with those who refuse his aid but manufactures perils that push the character to rely on him.

The Darklord's Betrayal. Inevitably, the Darklord grows tired of his protégés. Harkon begins treating them as minions or expendables to be used in his schemes. Those who resist find their reputations destroyed, their secrets revealed, and wolves dogging their steps. The only recourse is to flee Kartakass, upstage the Darklord, or somehow reveal Harkon Lukas as a monster.

Harkon's Bite
Wondrous item, uncommon (requires attunement)

A dire wolf tooth dangles from this simple cord necklace. While you wear it, the necklace grants you a +1 bonus to ability checks and saving throws.

Curse. Attuning to *Harkon's Bite* curses you until either Harkon Lukas removes the necklace from you or you are targeted by a *remove curse* spell or similar magic. As long as you remain cursed, you cannot remove the necklace.

Upon donning or removing the necklace, whether you are attuned to it or not, you are afflicted with werewolf lycanthropy as detailed in the *Monster Manual*. The curse lasts until the dawn after the next full moon. If you are still wearing the necklace at this time, you are afflicted with the lycanthropy again.

MARK BEHM

LAMORDIA

Domain of Snow and Stitched Flesh

Darklord: Viktra Mordenheim
Genres: Body horror and gothic horror
Hallmarks: Amoral science, bizarre constructs, frigid wilderness, mutagenic radiation
Mist Talismans: Animate finger, glowing minerals, preserved limb

Life is cheap in Lamordia. As far as the land's esteemed scholars are concerned, the spark that animates flesh is merely the result of chemical accidents and the proper formulas. Golems, homunculi, and other constructed beings groan to life to support a populace desperate to survive in this frigid realm.

Frozen bogs and glacial expanses surround Lamordia's smog- and machinery-filled cities. Unpredictable blizzards plague the long winters, and the chill summers last only a few weeks. Those who brave the wilds must contend with starving predators, from wolf packs and giant owls to isolated Humanoid clans struggling to subsist outside the domain's iron-walled cities. The cruel environment and populace threatened by starvation make Lamordia a crucible of desperate innovations. Claiming to work for the greater good, innovators and scholars push beyond the limits of morality. Their scalpels turn scientific pursuits into butchery, as their experiments reach beyond what is necessary for health to grasp after the secrets of existence. Flesh is Lamordia's most abundant natural resource, exploited for both desperate purposes and vain ambitions. And no ambitions have led to greater evils than the work of the domain's Darklord, Dr. Viktra Mordenheim.

NOTEWORTHY FEATURES

Those familiar with Lamordia know these facts:

- Lamordia is a frigid land of barren mountains, frozen swamps, and icy seas. Its ruler, Baron von Aubrecker, hasn't left his estate for years, though he issues proclamations and sends agents to collect taxes.
- Steam power driven by boiling sewers fuels clockwork inventions and massive cranes in the city of Ludendorf. The necessity of such innovations in fending off starvation and the frigid environment encourages the scientists at Ludendorf University to push the boundaries of science and morality.
- The reclusive genius Dr. Viktra Mordenheim created or inspired Ludendorf's greatest innovations.
- Few voluntarily trek into Lamordia's wilderness, fearing freak blizzards, starving beasts, and creatures warped by strange radiation.

LAMORDIAN CHARACTERS

Characters from Lamordia are typically direct, skeptical of superstition, and inured to cold. Humans and gnomes are the domain's primary residents, with white hair and skin, often tinged blue or gray, being common. German conventions inspire many names in the region. When players create characters from Lamordia, consider asking them the following questions.

Where and how were you raised in Lamordia? Were you a whaler, clerk, or factory owner in Ludendorf? Were you a miner, hunter, or prospector in Neufurchtenburg? Or if you lived outside these communities' walls, how did your family survive?

What is your relationship with Ludendorf University? Were you educated there? Have you used tools created by its scientists? Were you hired to participate in a doctor's or student's experiments? Did you sell them the flesh rights to your body?

How has the land scarred you? Have you suffered from frostbite in the wilderness? Do chemical or radiation burns scar your body? Did you sell a body part for coin? Did someone steal an organ from you while you slept?

SETTLEMENTS AND SITES

The bulk of Lamordia's population is divided between two smoke-belching communities, Ludendorf and Neufurchtenburg. Few dwell outside these settlements, since life is short in the frigid wilderness.

LUDENDORF

The city of Ludendorf is a morass of steam-powered factories operating at the behest of morally bankrupt barons. Boiling sewers and steam tunnels thread the city's foundations, heating cramped tenements and powering the cranes needed by the city's fleet. These ironclad, ice-breaking whaling vessels dare the Sea of Secrets to bring back massive beasts that provide vital food and fuel for the city.

Ensconced in the city's heart, Ludendorf University supports many local industries. Funded by corrupt entrepreneurs and wealthy but immoral benefactors, the university's vast curriculum boasts esoteric programs such as alchemical combustion, chemical sentience, and speculative anatomy. The sciences reign here, and students and faculty alike push to discover technologies that will net lucrative contracts from the city's wealthy overlords. The university continually needs new subjects for experiments and hires volunteers or pays individuals for "flesh rights"—ownership of their cadavers once they die. A secret society within Ludendorf University idolizes Dr. Mordenheim and follows the reckless paths laid by her lesser-known early works.

NEUFURCHTENBURG

Neufurchtenburg is a hardy town of bent-backed miners and desperate fortune-seekers. Tapped-out mines provide shelter for the residents, while the

MAP 3.10: LAMORDIA

iron-walled city hosts the smoking refineries necessary to process minerals harvested from the mountain range known as the Sleeping Beast. These rarified, little-understood elements are then shipped to Ludendorf's factories. Radiation-warped monsters and dangerous Humanoids from the nearby bogs roam the town's borders, mounting assaults to steal minerals and disrupt mining operations. Neufurchtenburg's hardy populace uses hulking clockwork machines, cutting-edge firearms, and destructive alchemy to fend off these incursions.

SCHLOSS AUBRECKER

The von Aubrecker clan has ruled Lamordia for as long as anyone remembers, from their ancestral home—a wind-whipped castle on a remote island. But Lamordia's ruler, Baron Rudolph von Aubrecker, has not made a public appearance in the two decades since he alone survived a tragic shipwreck with the help of Dr. Mordenheim. Those who have business with the baron are welcome for a brief stay, but they interact only with his perpetually smiling butler, Gerta. Visitors never enter the castle's west wing, where the baron—transformed into a **brain in a jar** (see chapter 5) by Mordenheim's experiments—works to rebuild his lost body and exact revenge upon the doctor.

SCHLOSS MORDENHEIM

This imposing complex perches on a dramatic cliff overlooking the icy sea and serves as the abode of Dr. Viktra Mordenheim, Lamordia's Darklord. The doctor lives in a small portion of the castle, a high turret that holds her multi-level laboratory and personal chambers. The rest of the castle is home to her assistants and to servitor creations said to be generations beyond the inventions of Lamordia's other scientists. Dr. Mordenheim doesn't receive guests, but once a year she petitions Ludendorf University to send her its most promising student to serve as her new lab assistant. The doctor also regularly hires mercenaries, supposedly to find rare components for her experiments, recover stolen inventions, or fend off the mysterious figures that lurk in the lands around her home.

THE SLEEPING BEAST

Overgrown with bizarrely warped forests, this jagged mountain range stretches for miles along the domain's southern border. A blanket of eerie calm hangs over its peaks, the result of high levels of radioactivity in the strange mineral deposits that vein the region. Warped beasts with lopsided anatomy, extra heads, and stranger qualities roam here, ambushing the desperate miners. The mountains' name stems from the legends originating with the bog-dwelling precursors of Lamordia's people who believed that the range was actually a single unfathomably large creature, and the veins of strange minerals were the beast's bones and blood. They punished anyone who harvested minerals from the Sleeping Beast, since doing so risked waking the beast and precipitating an apocalyptic disaster.

VIKTRA MORDENHEIM

A child prodigy from a minor noble family, the brilliant Viktra Mordenheim became obsessed with the complexities of Humanoid anatomy at an early age. She taught herself medicine as a child, and as a teen earned both a doctorate and an appointment as a preeminent researcher at a local university. Despite her genius, though, the young Dr. Mordenheim lacked empathy, compassion, and moral qualms. She pursued medicine solely to satiate her burning intellectual curiosity, never to aid her patients. She perceived magic as stealing the powers of otherworldly beings and cheating the laws of nature, and sought instead to use her mind to master the world.

Eventually, Dr. Mordenheim became convinced that she could do more than create life—she could defeat death! She wished to breathe sentience into dead flesh and produce sturdier shells than the bodies of fragile, temporary mortals. She added corpse theft to her repertoire, employing thieves to procure specimens for her tests. This was how she met Elise, a beautiful but reckless body snatcher who was charmed by the doctor's aloofness and whose spontaneity entranced the methodical surgeon.

When Elise began showing signs of an incurable wasting disease, it was the first time either woman had felt the pangs of despair. In the months that followed, Dr. Mordenheim desperately hastened her experiments, employing anyone who would bring her bodies—both newly dead and still living. On her operating table, victims were killed, returned to life, and died again as Mordenheim sought to glimpse the secrets hidden in the instant of death.

One moonless night, Elise fell into a sleep from which she wouldn't wake. Bringing Elise to her lab, Dr. Mordenheim worked feverishly for days to save her, pouring what she'd learned from a thousand deaths into saving one life. Elise became the recipient of the doctor's masterpiece, the end to disease and death: an artificial organ Mordenheim called the Unbreakable Heart. But as she stitched the miraculous device into place, constables burst into the lab and accused the doctor of facilitating numerous murders. As Dr. Mordenheim struggled against arrest, smoking chemicals and arcing electricity filled the laboratory. Before she lost consciousness, she saw Elise rise from the table, the Unbreakable Heart glowing within her behind golden stitches.

Dr. Mordenheim awoke in Lamordia, an unfamiliar land where her genius was celebrated. Elise and the Unbreakable Heart were nowhere to be found, but the doctor soon heard rumors of a glowing woman wandering in the icy wastes. Since then, Mordenheim has continued her experiments on the dead and living, striving to recreate her successes and failing every time. Between disappointments she searches the hinterlands, hoping to find Elise—and with her, the miracle of the Unbreakable Heart.

MORDENHEIM'S POWERS AND DOMINION

Dr. Viktra Mordenheim dresses in functional, bloodstained lab wear. Her statistics are similar to those of a **spy**, but her focus is on science and her medical genius is unmatched. From her laboratory at Schloss Mordenheim, Dr. Mordenheim uses her scientific genius to pursue and pervert the secrets of life. Eschewing magic, the doctor uses unfathomable scientific secrets to achieve goals known only to her. While this might lead to plots involving all manner of amoral science, the doctor's work includes the following routine abominable operations.

Construct Creation. Dr. Mordenheim can create any Construct or corporeal Undead by working in her laboratory for a number of uninterrupted days equal to the creature's challenge rating. At the end of the final day, the creature is complete and obeys her will. She uses this ability to create **flesh golems** and **homunculi**, as well as **zombies**, **death's heads**, and **brains in jars** (see chapter 5).

Reborn Maker. A side effect of Dr. Mordenheim's experiments is the creation of reborn (see chapter 1). It takes her 1d4 days and the dead bodies of two Medium or Small Humanoids to create one reborn.

Brain Swap. Dr. Mordenheim can place a creature's brain or head into another body, moving it from a donor to a recipient. The process requires the donor to have a brain and either be incapacitated or to have been dead for less than 24 hours. In an operation that takes 1 hour, the doctor transfers the donor's brain or head from their body to the incapacitated or dead corporeal body of a creature without a brain. The donor awakes 1 hour later with control of the recipient's body.

While controlling the recipient's body, the donor retains their alignment, Intelligence, Wisdom, and Charisma scores. They otherwise use the recipient's body's statistics, but don't gain access to the recipient's knowledge, class features, or proficiencies. Dr. Mordenheim can swap a donor's brain or head back from the recipient's body to their original body through this same process, as long as the original body exists and no more than 1 week has passed. This period can be extended if steps are taken to preserve the original body, such as by keeping it in cold storage or under the effect of a *gentle repose* spell.

WITHIN ELISE'S UNDYING BODY BEATS DR. MORDENHEIM'S GREATEST CREATION: THE UNBREAKABLE HEART.

Closing the Borders. When Dr. Mordenheim closes Lamordia's borders, temperatures across the domain drop below 0 degrees and driving snow scours the land (detailed in the _Dungeon Master's Guide_). Those who reach the Mists find they function as detailed in "The Mists" at the start of this chapter.

MORDENHEIM'S TORMENT

Although Dr. Mordenheim doesn't show her emotions, she's vexed by the following circumstances:

- Mordenheim cannot remake the miracle of scientific immortality embodied by the Unbreakable Heart. She relentlessly tries to understand and repeat the circumstances of its creation, but fails every time.
- Elise evades Mordenheim's attempts to find her.
- The people of Lamordia view Mordenheim as a luminary and savior. She does not understand why and loathes the distractions they create.

ROLEPLAYING MORDENHEIM

Dr. Mordenheim's most chilling feature is her absolute disregard for others' well-being and autonomy. Her lack of empathy is immediately apparent to any who meet her. She views people as mere collections of neurons and meat, and she considers herself so superior that others' lives mean nothing to her.

Personality Trait. "The body holds so many secrets. If you've nothing else useful to offer, your body's secrets will reveal themselves on my slab."

Ideal. "The perfect form and mind do not exist because I've not created them yet."

Bond. "My genius is a blessing. Those who walk from my laboratory are reborn blessed."

Flaw. "No one will ever approach my levels of genius. I simply cannot be matched."

ADVENTURES IN LAMORDIA

Themes of body horror pervade adventures set in Lamordia. Here characters might become victims of Dr. Mordenheim's experiments or uncover terrible truths underlying the domain's strange science.

In the latter case, Lamordia's sinister steampunk veneer offers a perfect setting for a grotesque flavor of gothic horror, focusing on lives enslaved to machines, the worth of flesh, and the cult of scientific advancement at any cost. The harsh landscape feeds into this with both brutal cold and deadly creatures. Are the "whales" the mighty steamships of Ludendorf hunt for food and fuel truly whales, or perhaps dinosaurs, dragon turtles, or abominations created from people's flesh? At the other extreme, how do Lamordia's original inhabitants—the spirits of forgotten tribes, icy Fey spirits, or the Sleeping Beast—feel about the land's exploitation?

IRINA NORDSOL

The monsters that roam Lamordia are lab-crafted horrors or mutated beasts, but use the statistics of creatures from the *Monster Manual*. A monstrosity burned by radiation might use the stat block for a cyclops, while a scientist's winged flesh-blob assistant might use a homunculus's stat block.

Beyond these possibilities, consider the plots on the Lamordia Adventures table when planning adventures in this domain.

LAMORDIA ADVENTURES

d10	Adventure
1	Sapient lab animals escape Ludendorf University and need help finding a new home. One, however, is eager to improve upon its form and the forms of its fellows.
2	Medical student Emil Bollenbach strives to craft revolutionary **flesh golems**, such as ones made entirely of doppelgangers or beholders. His patrons enlist the party to aid his research.

THE BRAIN OF BARON RUDOLPH VON AUBRECKER CONSTRUCTS A NEW BODY.

d10	Adventure
3	A murderous, jaundiced whale is hunting Ludendorf's ships. The superstitious Captain Furschter of the city's navy asks the party to learn why by seeking Winter's Mouth, a crack in the ice where the sea supposedly whispers its secrets.
4	Three brilliant Ludendorf University students compete to become Dr. Mordenheim's new assistant. Each seeks the party's assistance in ensuring they're chosen for the opportunity.
5	A wave of warped monstrosities is preparing to assault Neufurchtenburg. The metallurgists at the Giesbrecht Automatic Armaments company have created a new weapon or vehicle that could save the town, but they need someone to test it.
6	Ruprekt Schaller stood to inherit his dying father's factory in Ludendorf. Instead, Udo Schaller paid assassins to murder his son and had his brain transplanted into Ruprekt's young body, with the help of Dr. Mordenheim. Udo's daughter and sole surviving heir, Varissa Schaller, wants to avenge her brother's murder and begs the party to help destroy her father.
7	Prospectors seeking rare gas pockets discover numerous well-preserved bog mummies dating back to Lamordia's ancient druidic peoples. They seek help when the mummies vanish and undead animals begin terrorizing their camp.
8	Baron von Aubrecker writes to the party, asking them to recover the body of a "relative" from the *Haifisch*, a shipwreck impaled on a spire of ice.
9	The Sleeping Beast is experiencing an increasing number of earthquakes. The overseers of the Pulstein Mine call for aid, believing that strange creatures are causing the quakes to steal the "marrowstone" they're mining.
10	Scholars at Ludendorf University learn of the Unbreakable Heart and claim a monster stole it. The characters and dozens of other hunters are sent to the Isles of Agony to recover the device.

MORDENHEIM'S MONSTERS

The horror at Lamordia's heart is Dr. Mordenheim's bizarre experiments and ceaseless search for Elise.

ELISE AND THE UNBREAKABLE HEART

Above all else, Dr. Mordenheim's objectives are finding Elise and recovering or re-creating the Unbreakable Heart.

Elise. Dr. Mordenheim's supposed beloved and greatest achievement, Elise is a confused, frustrated soul who never wished for her current circumstances. She's now a **flesh golem** with the following adjustments:

- Elise does not have the Berserk or Aversion of Fire traits.
- She has immunity to cold damage.

Elise's heart has been replaced with the Unbreakable Heart. If this device is removed, Elise dies, even if it is replaced with another heart. Elise is horrified by what Dr. Mordenheim did to her and tries to avoid the doctor and all strangers, fearing they might kill her to learn the Unbreakable Heart's secrets. She roams without destination but keeps a hidden sanctuary at Hope's Heart on the Isles of Agony. Although she has tried to leave Lamordia, the Mists prevent her from doing so.

The Unbreakable Heart. The Unbreakable Heart is a nonmagical scientific wonder that replaces a creature's heart. The device installs itself, connecting to a creature's anatomy and stitching itself into place if positioned in a cavity where the creature's heart used to be. A creature with the device inside them is immune to disease, ceases to age, and does not die of old age, though they can still die in other ways. The glowing device sheds light in a 10-foot radius and dim light for an additional 10 feet. While inside a creature, the device causes the creature to shed dim light in a 10-foot radius.

Re-created by the Doctor

If the characters oppose Dr. Mordenheim, they face droves of her bizarre creations. They also risk becoming her newest experimental subjects.

Dr. Mordenheim's experiments provide an opportunity to put players in control of strange creatures or unique bodies. Either as part of an adventure or a longer campaign, the characters might awaken with their minds transplanted into terrifying new forms. Such a plot comes with both opportunities and pitfalls. On the one hand, waking up in Mordenheim's laboratory, either recently changed into reborn (see chapter 1) or about to undergo that process, could be an exciting way to start an adventure or whole campaign. On the other, players might not appreciate losing access to their characters or having their bodies held hostage to Dr. Mordenheim's plots. Before running an adventure where players lose control of their characters or decisions about those characters are made for them, ask the players if they're comfortable with such possibilities. It's better to tip your hand about the plot than to lose a player's investment in the game.

When delivering characters into the Darklord's clutches, employ scenarios where the party is actively involved, not merely abducted in their sleep. Consider using any of the following events that might lead to plots involving Dr. Mordenheim.

Overwhelmed. Constructs created by Dr. Mordenheim attack the party or their allies (at the doctor's command or otherwise). These foes are more powerful than the characters, who might defeat the majority of the attackers before being overwhelmed.

Self-Sacrifice. A massive sea beast attacks the characters' ship. The characters save the other passengers but fall into the icy water. They awake to discover that Dr. Mordenheim has "saved" them.

Worse Than Death? The characters are legitimately defeated during another adventure. Rather than the campaign ending, they awake in Dr. Mordenheim's clutches, delivered there by the Mists.

Mordenheim's Designs

Once the characters become subject to Dr. Mordenheim's schemes, consider what she wants of them and what bodies she fashions to ensure that her new agents can fulfill her goals. While she could create a device or a chemical dependency that encourages the characters to serve her, holding their original bodies hostage is probably enticement enough. The Serving Dr. Mordenheim table suggests schemes the doctor might coerce the party to take part in. Whether she intends to fulfill her promises or keep her new agents hostage forever is up to you.

Serving Dr. Mordenheim

d4	Mission
1	The doctor desires a cutting-edge discovery from a factory in Neufurchtenburg. To acquire it, she has kidnapped the factory owner's family and put the characters' consciousnesses into their bodies. Until the characters deliver the discovery, she holds their bodies and the family's brains in cold storage.
2	Wishing to spy on Ludendorf University, Mordenheim mounts the characters' heads onto suits of **animated armor**. The characters will get their bodies back when they return with the information the doctor desires.
3	Agents of Baron von Aubrecker attack Schloss Mordenheim and wreak considerable damage. Dr. Mordenheim places the characters' brains into **flesh golems** and sets them loose to punish the baron.
4	Dr. Mordenheim wants Elise found and returned. Using various monster parts, she creates unique hunter bodies with the statistics of **flesh golems** or other monsters. She places the characters' minds into these bodies, promising to restore them when they bring her Elise.

MORDENT

Domain of the Haunted

Darklord: Wilfred Godefroy
Genre: Ghost stories
Hallmarks: Ancestral curses, haunted mansions, mist-shrouded moors, vengeful spirits
Mist Talismans: Broken jewelry, death mask, faded love letter, family portrait

When death occurs in Mordent, it doesn't signal a passage to a state of rest, or an end to the struggle of mortal existence. Death here heralds the beginning of a haunted afterlife as a restless spirit. The dead earn no rest, no finality, no peace—just a passage into a shadow world of wispy phantoms, mournful groaning, and clanking chains.

At first glance, Mordent is a quiet domain of peaceful country estates that sprawl across rolling moors. Landowners of the aristocratic class maintain a pretense of being the benevolent custodians of the land and its hard-working farmers, fishers, and laborers. From the loftiest families to the lowliest workers, Mordent's people cling to traditions that define the order of society and each person's place in it. They do things "the way they have always been done," because the old ways offer stability and security in an uncertain world.

Beneath that peaceful veneer lies a troubled society trapped in the ghostly grasp of its ancestors. The past can't be forgotten or left behind, because the spirits haunting the land embody that past. The social order can't change, because the restless dead enforce the old ways to maintain that order.

In Mordent, the dead who have unfinished business or a strong tie to a place or a family line manifest as all manner of spectral terrors. But not every unquiet spirit haunts the living. Isolated spirits wander the moors and ignore the living, or melt slowly into the Mists until at last they forget their identities. An unlucky few become trapped in the magical experiments of twisted scholars or bound to the service of the Darklord of the domain, Lord Wilfred Godefroy. And those with a personal connection to the Darklord are inevitably drawn to his manor on Gryphon Hill to become part of his endless torment.

NOTEWORTHY FEATURES

Those familiar with Mordent know the following facts:

- Most of Mordent's people live in quaint communities, the largest of which is the seaside town of Mordentshire.
- The estates of wealthy families dot the Mordentish countryside. Most residents live private lives adhering to vague strictures of what is proper or polite.

> ### MORDENTISH CHARACTERS
>
> Characters from Mordent are typically earnest and practical. Humans are the domain's primary residents. Locals have varied hair colors and a range of skin tones from black to pink, often with reddish undertones. Celtic and English conventions inspire many names in the region. When players create characters from Mordent, consider asking them the following questions.
>
> **Who your family?** Ancestry matters in Mordent. Are you from a landed family? Or were your parents tenant farmers, fishers, laborers, or in service to one of the noble estates?
>
> **What are your family secrets?** In Mordent, a secret shame, dismal curse, or gruesome haunt accompanies every family name. How much do you know about the skeletons in your family's closet? What guilt or misfortune do you carry with you?
>
> **What's your experience with the supernatural?** Have you encountered a ghost or spirit, or heard a firsthand account of a haunting from someone close to you? How did that experience affect you?

- The spirits of the dead don't rest quietly in Mordent. Each denizen of this realm can relate a story of a terrifying haunting that they or someone they know experienced personally.
- The House on Gryphon Hill is the most famous haunted house in Mordent, known to be occupied by the spirit of Lord Wilfred Godefroy—an evil man who murdered his wife and daughter.
- The proximity of the spirit realm spurs local eccentrics to investigate spiritualism and the nature of the soul.

SETTLEMENTS AND SITES

The lands of Mordent are carved into estates passed down through hereditary lines, accompanied by minor titles of nobility. These estates—including Gryphon Hill, Heather House, and Westcote Manor—number among the most notable landmarks in the domain. The tenant farmers who work the land pay a portion of their crops to the landowners as rent. A small but relatively well-off middle class populates the handful of towns and villages scattered across the domain, most notably the town of Mordentshire.

MORDENTSHIRE

Perched atop a chalky cliff overlooking a quiet harbor, the small town of Mordentshire is the domain's center of trade—and thus, a place that the well-to-do aristocratic families of the countryside visit as little as possible. A cold wind blows in constantly from the sea, frequently escalating into howling storms. When the winds die down, they're replaced by a shroud of bone-chilling fog, which the locals call "the breath of the dead."

Mordentshire's businesses largely cater to local laborers, with a few remarkable exceptions. Saulbridge Sanitarium provides a refuge for the ill while

MAP 3.11: MORDENT

also secretly hosting a cell of the Ulmist Inquisition (see "Other Groups" later in this chapter). There's also the herbalist shop of the scholar Rudolph van Richten. When van Richten is away, his shop is run by local mystery enthusiast Beatrice Polk or by twin sisters Gennifer and Laurie Weathermay-Foxgrove (see "Travelers in the Mist" for information on van Richten and the Weathermay-Foxgroves).

HEATHER HOUSE

In Mordentshire, the Weathermay family are respected local paragons of virtue and good sense—despite some family members' unfortunate proclivity for adventuring. The head of the family, Alice Weathermay, serves as mayor of Mordentshire and maintains her family's cliffside home, Heather House. The manor has known joy and tragedy, and reflects both in its ivy-shrouded stone and sharp gables. Within, the house is a museum of family trophies and heirlooms, including a grand rosewood harpsichord and the wheelchair of Lord Byron Weathermay, the house's architect, who ensured that clever lifts made his home fully accessible. At the edge of Heather House's grounds is the Weathermay Mausoleum, the resting place of generations of Weathermays—and the location of a secret magical laboratory guarded by the quasit Tintantilus.

IDLETHORP

In the shadow of Punchinel Manor lie the ruins of a small, abandoned hamlet that once functioned as a crossroads trading post of minor importance in the western part of Mordent. The last owner of Punchinel Manor was an artificer who crafted unique miniature flesh golems from stitched-together body parts—a pair of hands attached directly to a head, for example. He was murdered by his creations, and the manor has remained unoccupied for years.

SIGIL LAKES

Viewed from above, three lakes in southwestern Mordent appear to form a mystical symbol, though as far as anyone can tell, the triangular shape of the lakes and their peculiar arrangement are entirely natural. Recently, a circle of druids gathered in the nearby village of Glaston to plan a rite using the lakes to create a magical passage to similarly shaped sites in other lands. The fate of the druids is unknown, but the region is now haunted by a terrifying variety of ghostly animals that delight in hunting the living.

Van Richten's Herbalist Shop in Mordentshire

Wilfred Godefroy

Lord Wilfred Godefroy was an unremarkable minor aristocrat who inherited the estate of Gryphon Hill near Mordentshire centuries ago, after murdering his father. An angry and abusive man throughout his life, he also murdered his wife, Estelle, and young daughter, Penelope, in a fit of rage. The two rose that night as mournful phantoms and haunted him with their wailing and condemnation. Every night for the next year, the spirits appeared and tormented him, until in desperation he took his life on the anniversary of their murder.

But Lord Godefroy's suicide didn't stop his torment. His spirit lingered in Gryphon Hill, and the ghosts of his wife and daughter haunted him day and night. Moreover, the spirit of his murdered father soon appeared to join the chorus of condemnation. Lord Godefroy possessed an adventurer and attempted to use the living body to put his family's spirits to rest—but the adventurer died, and then *his* ghost began to haunt Godefroy as well.

In desperation, Lord Godefroy sought out a different kind of help in the world of the living. He began haunting an alchemist named Rastinon, urging him to pursue research into mortal souls. Rastinon crafted a terrible artifact he called the Apparatus, which could separate the soul from a living body, translocate souls from one body to another, and otherwise manipulate the substance and energy of spirits both living and undead. Lord Godefroy hoped the Apparatus would send all spirits (including him) to their deserved rests, but the artifact had the opposite effect: its necromantic energy washed through the region around Mordentshire, killing every living being in it. As the Mists rose, Lord Godefroy became lord over a land of ghosts, haunted by the spirits whose deaths he had caused. Now, all living souls that dwell in Mordent are doomed to haunt the domain's Darklord long after the demise of their mortal bodies.

Godefroy's Powers and Dominion

Lord Wilfred Godefroy rules his own personal afterlife. His statistics are similar to those of a **ghost**, and he is one of the most powerful spectral Undead in the domain. From the House on Gryphon Hill, Godefroy forces throngs of the dead to serve his will and to seek out a path to their true, final deaths.

Lord of the Dead. After 24 hours, the spirit of anyone who dies in Mordent reappears as a **ghost**, a **specter**, or another incorporeal Undead near where they died. These spectral dead can be magically returned to life as normal, but those who aren't restored to life linger as Undead until they're destroyed or the Mists claim them. Spectral agents of Lord Godefroy remain alert for useful souls that might be enlisted into the Darklord's service.

Gryphon Hill. The House on Gryphon Hill, just outside Mordentshire, is home of Lord Wilfred Godefroy. Hundreds of spirits are bound to the house and the surrounding grounds, and all serve the lord of the house and struggle to keep in his good graces. Those spirits who rebel are punished, either forced to face Godefroy's kennel of spectral hounds or dragged to the deepest recesses of the house, which even the eldest spirits fear. Any spirits capable of possessing the living are permitted to do so only when Lord Godefroy commands it. The Darklord rarely allows the dead to experience life like this, and when he does, it's to possess those who can work his will elsewhere in the domain or to expand the eclectic structure that is the House on Gryphon Hill.

The Apparatus. Lord Godefroy has not given up hope that the bizarre device called the Apparatus might allow him to escape his torment and reach a more peaceful afterlife. Godefroy's servants have spent centuries abducting magical geniuses, possessing them and convincing them to recreate the Apparatus again and again, often with unpredictable or catastrophic results. The magical device has caused all manner of inexplicable teleportations, mergings of living beings, duplications of souls, and strange manipulations of the Mists. At any time, Godefroy's servants are working to perfect the Apparatus somewhere in Mordent.

The Living and the Dead. Lord Godefroy eagerly seeks news of anyone with the ability to exorcise spirits, learn secrets from those long dead, or slip beyond the boundaries of the Mists. His most useful contact in learning news and keeping tabs on the living is Alice Weathermay, mayor of Mordentshire. Godefroy manipulates her to pass on information and do his bidding by holding the spirit of her dead husband, Daniel Foxgrove, hostage.

Closing the Borders. When Godefroy wishes to close his domain, fog rolls in off the sea and blankets the land. Everything in the domain that's outdoors is heavily obscured by the fog (see the *Player's Handbook*). Characters who reach the domain's borders through this fog are affected as detailed in "The Mists" at the start of this chapter.

Godefroy's Torment

Lord Godefroy is an abyss of grief and rage, tormented by the following circumstances:

- Godefroy is concerned only with his own misery; the suffering of the other spirits in Mordent merely fuels his torment.
- Exceptionally arrogant, Godefroy brooks no opinions or criticisms from his inferiors, and blames every failure on his spirit servants.
- Godefroy's family still haunts the House on Gryphon Hill. Although he wishes for their love, he avoids the floor of the house where they dwell, resenting their rightful condemnation.
- Godefroy is convinced the Apparatus is the key to escaping his undead existence. However, he can't grasp even its basic workings and is frustrated by every delay and malfunction related to the device.

Roleplaying Godefroy

The thinnest veneer of gentility covers Lord Godefroy's boundless rage. Arrogant, impatient, and quick to offer mockery, the Darklord seeks any opportunity to vent centuries of frustration. He eagerly uses threats and violence to manipulate the living and the dead, eagerly taking advantage of any connection he perceives—especially ties to family.

Foundations of Horror

Three years after the 1983 release of the adventure *Ravenloft*, the sequel adventure, *Ravenloft II: The House on Gryphon Hill*, debuted. The adventure pulled back the Mists on the domain of Mordent, a realm of terrors beyond Barovia, and introduced such characters as Lord Byron Weathermay, the mesmerist Germain d'Honaire, the tragic Godefroy family, the lycanthropic Timothys, and Azalin the lich—names you'll find throughout this book. With the *House on Gryphon Hill*, Barovia and Mordent paved the way for Ravenloft to become a vast and varied setting encompassing dozens of Domains of Dread.

Personality Trait. "I have no patience for insult, disrespect, or provocation, and I respond with violence to any affront."

Ideal. "My perspective and concerns are the only ones that matter."

Bond. "Gryphon Hill is my ancestral home. I am deeply bound to that site, its history, and my ancestral line."

Flaw. "I'm surrounded by idiots, and few people are more insufferable than the living."

Adventures in Mordent

Mordent is the realm of the classic ghost story. In tone and trappings, the domain resembles the countrysides of Gothic literature: lands dotted with haunted manor houses, stalked by packs of ghost hounds, and troubled by the spirits of dead warlocks that cause trees to rot from the inside out.

Any kind of ghost story adventure (as described in chapter 2) fits in Mordent. This domain is particularly appropriate for stories that deal with the lingering influence of the past, the oppressive weight of tradition, and the ongoing effects of generational curses. The restless spirits enforce an archaic and repressive social order where everyone knows their place, and those who step out of line are punished—sometimes gruesomely.

Consider the plots on the Mordent Adventures table when planning adventures in this domain.

Mordent Adventures

d8	Adventure
1	An alchemist discovers a way to "burn" spirits to provide fuel for magical fire. Several spirits seek the party's aid in preventing their second death.
2	A noble seeks help as an undead ancestor tries to prevent the noble's marriage to an "unsuitable" partner.
3	The spirits of two lovers whose families prevented their union begin exacting revenge on the living.
4	A pair of rival fiends, Athos and Diche, break loose from idols in the collection at Heather House. Members of the Weathermay family call for aid.

d8	Adventure
5	The citizens of the village of Crawford spread tales of a gigantic raven. Sheriff Perkins hires the characters to hunt down the creature, which is actually a **wereraven** (see chapter 5) protecting the community from a greater threat.
6	A curse has afflicted Westcote Manor for a hundred years. The surrounding bog encroaches on the house, and howling bog hounds draw ever closer to the estate's beleaguered lord.
7	The baronet of a small estate is forced to commit increasingly heinous crimes each day or face unspeakable torment at the hands of his ghostly ancestors, who suffered under the same curse.
8	Someone has rebuilt the infamous Apparatus and is using it to transpose vicious souls into the bodies of mild-mannered citizens of Mordentshire.

HAUNTING MORDENT

Crafting an adventure around a haunting is similar to building any other adventure. The "Ghost Stories" section of chapter 2 provides a good starting point for detailing elements of a ghost story. This section supplements that material with advice specific to building an adventure reminiscent of a classic ghost story, focusing on three key elements of such tales: history, tragedy, and romance. Throughout this section, consider the word *ghost* synonymous with any sort of spirit or incorporeal Undead.

HISTORY

Because elements of a ghost's mortal life define and foreshadow the course of their death and undeath, a common aspect of a ghost-story adventure involves piecing together the history of the ghost's life to figure out how to put the spirit to rest. This gives any ghost story characteristics similar to a mystery. Be generous in planting clues to the ghost's history throughout the adventure, assuming that the players will miss several of them. You can use the Ghost's History table to determine how long the ghost has been Undead.

GHOST'S HISTORY

d6	Ghost's History
1	The ghost died so recently that they might not yet fully realize they are dead.
2	The ghost died recently enough that people who knew them in life are still around.
3	The ghost died years ago, and few people who knew them in life are still alive.
4	The ghost died a generation ago; folks remember rumors or stories told about the person's life.

d6	Ghost's History
5	The ghost died multiple generations ago, and only local folklore or histories preserve their memory.
6	The ghost died a very long time ago, and no one knows anything about their history.

TRAGEDY

Ghosts embody the pain and grief that surround death. To build an effective ghost story adventure, present either the ghost or those they haunt as the tragic victims of painful circumstance. The Tragic Elements table offers suggestions, framing each as a tragic element for either the ghost or their victims.

TRAGIC ELEMENTS

d10	Tragic Element
1	The ghost aches from a broken heart.
2	The ghost interferes with the romantic life of their victim.
3	The ghost was falsely accused and convicted of a crime.
4	The ghost makes an innocent person appear to be guilty of the ghost's crimes.
5	In life, the ghost was cut off by family members and denied a rightful inheritance.
6	The ghost refuses to acknowledge any living heirs as family members and tries to prevent these heirs from inheriting what is rightly theirs.
7	Society shunned the ghost unfairly in life.
8	Association with the ghost causes their living victim to be shunned by society.
9	In life, the ghost's efforts to do good led them to be cursed by a hag, fiend, or powerful spirit.
10	The ghost foils their victim's efforts to do good.

ROMANCE

Issues of love and romance are intimately bound to the tragic elements of a ghost story, or can supplement those elements to make the ghost sympathetic. The Romantic Elements table offers suggestions.

ROMANTIC ELEMENTS

d8	Romantic Element
1	The ghost hopes to be reunited with another ghost—the spirit of someone they loved in life.
2	The ghost haunts someone they loved in life, who still returns that love.
3	The ghost haunts a place they loved in life, perhaps their home or a memorial to one they lost.
4	The ghost haunts someone they loved in life, who is trying to move on.

ALL WHO DIE IN MORDENT BECOME CAPTIVES
TO THE WILL OF LORD WILFRED GODEFROY.

d8	Romantic Element
5	The ghost haunts someone who looks like a person the ghost loved in life (possibly a descendant of that person).
6	A person who loved the ghost in life refuses to let the spirit leave.
7	The ghost was murdered by someone they loved in life.
8	The ghost seeks vengeance on someone who spurned them in life.

PUTTING THE PIECES TOGETHER

Once you've thought about the roles of history, tragedy, and romance, you might already have a clear idea of where you want to go with your ghost-story adventure. If you need inspiration to put the pieces together, consider these questions.

Who's the villain? A D&D adventure often revolves around the activity of a villain, but the villain in a ghost story might or might not be the ghost themself. If you've built a tragic ghost who's deeply in love with the person they're haunting, the villain might be someone else entirely—someone obsessed with the haunted person, perhaps, who goes to great lengths to keep the ghost away.

What's the beginning of the story? While a ghost's history frames how the story plays out, the adventure doesn't begin until a group of adventurers becomes involved and entangled in the ghost's undeath. At the beginning of the adventure, let the players know about an eerie occurrence and give them a reason to care about it. The party might encounter the ghost right away, but even if destroyed, the ghost keeps returning until their business is resolved.

What resources are available to the characters? The bulk of a ghost-story adventure involves learning about the ghost and their haunting while continuing to deal with escalating supernatural manifestations. Characters might interview locals; read letters, diaries, or historical records; or examine objects found at the haunted site to piece together the information they need to put the ghost to rest.

How does it end? In Mordent, the spirits of the dead don't naturally pass on to a final rest, but characters can prevent the restless dead from interfering any further in the affairs of the living. That often involves completing whatever business a ghost left unfinished, resolving the ghost's attachment to something or someone in the living world, or finding a way to destroy the ghost so they can't return, which is usually a matter of exploiting their attachment to people or a location.

RICHEMULOT

Domain of Disease, Isolation, and Wererats

Darklord: Jacqueline Renier
Genres: Disaster horror and gothic horror
Hallmarks: Contagion, crumbling infrastructure, martial law, rats and vermin, wererats
Mist Talismans: Plague mask, rat's tail, snake-oil curative

Like a pendulum, Richemulot swings perpetually between hope and despair. Some days, the sun rises over Pont-a-Museau as if it were an ordinary city, and not one in which many of the buildings stand empty and abandoned. On those days, people move freely through the open gates, and the silent, heavily armored guards of the Casques Silencieux watch over calm promenades and markets. But a day or a week or a month later, the first telltale cough cracks amid the crowd. As people evacuate the streets and lock their doors, rats crawl from the sewers in tremendous numbers. Shortly thereafter, the gates slam shut. No doctors come, and no information arrives; the populace is left to die.

The Gnawing Plague stalks Richemulot, arriving without warning. It comes with the rats, but it doesn't leave with them. For weeks or months at a time, life becomes an interminable wait as people peer out from between slatted windows and wonder how long the plague will last this time. Inevitably, frustration and fear beget superstition and violence.

Eventually the gates open, signaling that the city is safe again. How the Casques Silencieux know is a mystery, but their judgment always proves correct. And so the cycle goes, from ruin to relief and back again, with de facto ruler Mademoiselle Jacqueline Renier ever above it all, tirelessly working to pull her realm back from the brink of total collapse.

NOTEWORTHY FEATURES

Those familiar with Richemulot know the following facts:

- The Gnawing Plague, or simply "the Gnaws," is a deadly, recurring ailment that afflicts Richemulot.
- Richemulot's royal family died of the plague. Mademoiselle Jacqueline Renier, the nation's most prestigious aristocrat, rules as temporary warden.
- When the plague swells to epidemic proportions, the state police, the Casques Silencieux, enacts martial law and quarantines whole cities.
- The government organizes no food or medical aid for quarantined communities, leaving residents to contend as best they can.
- Richemulot's cities contain an inexplicably large number of buildings, an amount greater than their highest populations would have ever warranted.
- Rat swarms prowl city streets like packs of dogs.

RICHEMULOISE CHARACTERS

The people of Richemulot know how unexpectedly death can arrive. The domain is predominantly populated by humans and halflings with dark hair colors and various rich skin tones, many of whom bear the marks of childhood diseases or medical treatments. When players create characters from Richemulot, consider asking them the following questions.

How do you avoid the Gnawing Plague? The Gnawing Plague visits Richemulot regularly. When the plague comes and the cities face quarantines, how do you stay safe? Do you keep a stockpile of food and other supplies for the inevitable lockdowns? Do you rob your neighbors or rely on their kindness?

Are you a survivor of the Gnawing Plague? Did someone tend to you while you were sick? Did you undergo a remarkable treatment? What scars or painful memories do you have from the experience?

How did the Gnawing Plague change your destiny? Did your chances for education, travel, or apprenticeship vanish? Were you a noble who lost all they had? Were you banished from your community when you got sick?

SETTLEMENTS AND SITES

The majority of Richemulot's population is divided between its three walled cities, Mortigny, Pont-a-Museau, and Saint Ronges, though villages and isolated farmsteads dot the swampy countryside.

PONT-A-MUSEAU

The capital of Richemulot, Pont-a-Museau straddles the Musarde River, its buildings dominating both banks and the islands and bridges between. The city's abundant space could easily house twenty thousand souls, but although it's Richemulot's most populous city, fewer than half that number live here. Still, Pont-a-Museau's casual sophistication hints at a cosmopolitan past. Indeed, the sprawling, foreign architecture gives rise to one of Richemulot's most widespread folk tales—that the people living here now aren't the land's first inhabitants.

The citizens of Pont-a-Museau share their city with rats. These vermin are a ubiquitous presence, and visitors become accustomed to the flash of sudden movement at the periphery of their vision. Some say they are Jacqueline Renier's spies. This rumor might contain truth, as many who whisper it vanish in the night and are never seen again.

Chateau Delanuit. Upon an island in the center of the Musarde sits Chateau Delanuit, the hereditary Renier estate. From here, Jacqueline Renier rules Richemulot. She holds audience from her parlors and public courtrooms, but her private residence is sacrosanct, and few outside her family ever visit it.

Unknown to all but the Renier family and their staunchest allies, Chateau Delanuit stands above the inscrutable Inverted Court, a downward-spilling palace that connects to the vast sewer system of

Pont-a-Museau and beyond. This is the epicenter of Richemulot's polity, the clandestine home of its wererat families, and the true capital of the domain.

SAINT RONGES

Though Saint Ronges shares the same mysterious origin as the rest of Richemulot's cities, the cause of its depopulation is well known: the Plague strikes harder here, and for longer, than anywhere else in the domain.

This was not always so. When Jacqueline Renier first ascended to the throne and imposed her law upon the land, the people of Saint Ronges resisted her rule. Renier granted the city its freedom, absent the support and infrastructure of the state. To this day that remains the case, though the dwindling People's Council of Saint Ronges has long since learned its lesson. The council has repeatedly petitioned Mademoiselle Renier for mercy. For now, she is still considering.

MORTIGNY

Mortigny is both the smallest of Richemulot's three cities and the most overcrowded; its streets are congested and its buildings strained to capacity. The town resembles an extended tenement, with new construction built atop old and hastily thrown together shanties lining the inside of its walls.

Mortigny is quickly quarantined during surges of plague, but anyone is allowed to enter the city so long as they do so with the understanding that they can't leave. Small communities across the domain send their sick to Mortigny, both to be rid of them and because the city has Richemulot's largest concentration of medical practitioners. The best of these healers work at Mortigny West Clinic under Doctor Simone Temator. Doctors across the city fight tirelessly to aid the sick and research new treatments for the Gnaws, but ultimately their work does little to curb the disease. Many desperate practitioners have turned to unconventional methods to halt the plague's spread.

JACQUELINE RENIER

A century ago, Richemulot was a lively place. In those days, not a building stood vacant as merchants from both ends of the Musarde set up shop along the broad boulevards of Pont-a-Museau. As wealth trickled into the merchants' coffers, those of low birth began to taste the benefits of nobility.

Renier saw how the city was changing and tried to convince her family of the danger it

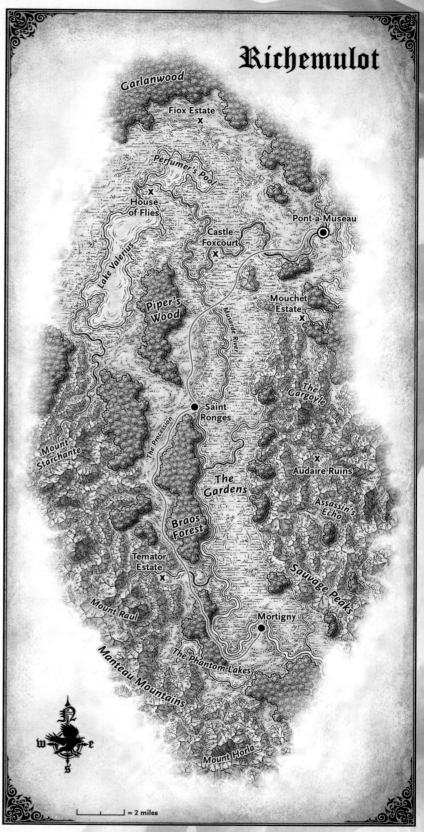

MAP 3.12: RICHEMULOT

JACQUELINE RENIER

her family. Only her twin, Louise, resisted, for which Jacqueline disfigured her and cast her out.

Next, she bent her wererat allies to her vicious pursuit of control, unifying the country's verminous hordes. Within the sewers of Pont-a-Museau, the wererats concocted a roiling pestilence incubated in the filth of the bourgeoisie. Disease was not unknown in Richemulot, but the virulence of this new Gnawing Plague sent panic through the populace. The disease killed indiscriminately, wiping out the nation's royal dynasty and leaving power vacuums filled and then quickly emptied by ailing nobles. Only the Reniers proved immune, and eventually Jacqueline stood as the highest-born noble in the land, and the nation's de facto leader.

The people begged Renier for help. Disgusted by the masses, she deemed them unworthy merely for the circumstance of their birth and the scarcity of coins in their pockets, Renier let them die. As the last human soul expired in Pont-a-Museau, the Mists rose, drawing Richemulot into the Domains of Dread.

JACQUELINE'S POWERS AND DOMINION

Although Jacqueline Renier has statistics similar to those of a **wererat**, she assumes her hybrid or rat form only when forced to defend herself or when pushed to the brink of rage. She is rarely without guards, be they members of the Casques Silencieux, wererat bodyguards, or hidden swarms of rats.

Casques Silencieux. The Darklord's silent state police guard Chateau Delanuit and enforce her quarantines across Richemulot. Rather than the soldiers they appear to be, these troops are **animated armor** filled with rats that mindlessly and mercilessly enact Jacqueline Renier's will. If a guard is defeated, the armor collapses, releasing a **swarm of rats**.

Plague Seasons. The Inverted Court beneath Chateau Delanuit holds hidden sewer laboratories where wererat alchemists endlessly brew evermore-virulent strains of the Gnawing Plague and even worse maladies. Rats are then infected with these diseases to spread them across the domain. As each strain is subtly different, creatures might fall victim to the Gnawing Plague again and again.

Rat Queen. Jacqueline Renier can understand and magically command any rat within 120 feet of her using limited telepathy. All rats in Richemulot are especially intelligent and eagerly obey Renier's will. This typically involves spying for her: eavesdropping on conversations, tailing individuals, and reporting back.

Closing the Borders. When Jacqueline Renier wishes to close her domain's borders, the Mists rise at the edge of the lands, as detailed in "The Mists" at the start of this chapter. Additionally, the Mists

posed. The burgeoning middle class sapped her family's authority, transforming them from lords over the commoners into mere landlords. But Renier's family surrendered to the times. Her grandfather grew infirm over the years and less able to look out for the family's interests, and the others—even her twin sister, Louise—seemed oblivious to the threat. It fell to Jacqueline to correct their failings.

Finding like-minded souls took Renier years, but she finally became aware of the mysterious Trueblood Council, a secret society of Richemulot's eldest and most esteemed families. Expending a fortune, Renier aggressively pursued membership. Finally she was granted an invitation to join the society's members at their meeting place hidden among the sewers of Pont-a-Museau. But when Renier arrived, she found a throng of filthy commoners, not the dramatic masterminds she'd expected. As she cursed them and set off to fetch the guards, the council members revealed their true wererat forms. That night, she was inducted into their ranks.

Renier swiftly accepted her new life as a wererat and her status as a member of Richemulot's first inhabitants. Her spite toward the lowborn turned instead toward non-wererats. Her first major act consisted of conferring the gift of lycanthropy upon are filled with **swarms of rats**; endless waves of them attack any creatures that enter the Mists.

JACQUELINE'S TORMENT

As Darklord and de facto steward of Richemulot, Jacqueline Renier stands at the height of society. However, when Richemulot was claimed by the Mists, its populace consisted mostly of commoners once more. Rather than ruling a land dominated by her wererat peers, Renier now endures various torments:

- Renier has no taste for ruling, yet feels obligated to keep up appearances to maintain her power. Her decrees are rash and self-serving.
- Renier's schemes killed most of the finer aspects of Richemulot's society. She endlessly craves the decadence she once took for granted.
- The people talk of establishing a new government when the threat of the plague passes. Renier and her wererat allies must constantly create new strains of the plague to maintain power.

ROLEPLAYING JACQUELINE

Jacqueline Renier believes she's infallible. Proper rule by the Reniers benefits all, and she is obviously the greatest of the Reniers. On some level, she knows that her certainty is born of unchecked privilege and vanity. These flashes of clarity frustrate her, leading her to impose cruel edicts and public displays of her superiority, such as city-spanning punishments and dramatic executions.

> **Personality Trait.** "The commoners think they're the future. I'll show them how much they need me."

> **Ideal.** "Nothing is more important than the preservation of power."

> **Bond.** "Those who show their obedience are my true subjects. All others have a chance to prove their loyalty. Is that not mercy?"

> **Flaw.** "I will let everything rot in the streets before I give up one bit of what I was given."

ADVENTURES IN RICHEMULOT

Adventurers might be accustomed to defeating foes using sword and spell, but such weapons hold little power against a nation-spanning plague. The characters might even be able to handle maladies when they afflict one or two members of the party, but their magical resources are quickly expended in the face of relentless contagion that's intentionally spread. The "Cycle of the Plague" section later in this domain explores how to use an ongoing disease as a backdrop to your adventures, while the Richemulot Adventures table suggests other plots that might unfold in the domain.

RICHEMULOT ADVENTURES

d6	Adventure
1	At the command of Jacqueline Renier, **swarms of rats** nightly slip into homes and murder the resident cats. Distraught pet owners entreat the characters for aid.
2	A desperate rogue seeks the characters' aid when the rest of her band is trapped within the abandoned Fiox Estate by a haywire security system.
3	A band of students plot a revolution against Jacqueline Renier in the valley called Assassin's Echo. They're convinced one among them is a traitor but don't realize there's a **wererat** in their midst.
4	A constable requests the characters' aid in solving murders in which the victims have been drained of blood. The murderer is a **strigoi** (see chapter 5) that haunts a sunken chapel in the swamp known as the Gardens.
5	Doctor Temator of Mortigny believes she can create a cure for the Gnawing Plague and enlists the characters to find subjects who have never had the disease. Rumors soon spread that the doctor and characters are actually spreading the plague.
6	Louise Renier seeks the characters' aid in infiltrating a ball Jacqueline is holding at Chateau Delanuit. She aims to infuriate Jacqueline so that she reveals her **wererat** nature before her guests.

THE GNAWING PLAGUE

The Gnawing Plague, also known as "the Gnaws," is known in every corner of Richemulot.

> **Transmission.** The Gnaws is spread when a creature is bitten by a **rat**, **giant rat**, **swarm of rats**, or **wererat** that carries the disease, or by coming into physical contact with an infected creature.

> **Infection.** Creatures exposed to the disease must succeed on a DC 10 Constitution saving throw or become infected. The DC of this saving throw can increase depending on the severity of the plague's spread (see "Cycle of the Plague" below).

> **Symptoms.** It takes 1d2 days for the Gnawing Plague's symptoms to manifest in an infected creature. The infected creature then gains 1 level of exhaustion, regains only half the normal number of hit points from spending Hit Dice, and regains no hit points from finishing a long rest.

The plague's symptoms include buboes, fatigue, splotchy rashes, sweats, and shaking, particularly facial tremors. Locals liken these twitches to the sniffing of rats. Sufferers often have scraps of leather placed in their mouths to prevent their teeth from clattering, though they inevitably gnaw through these scraps.

Recovery. At the end of each long rest, an infected creature must make a DC 10 Constitution saving throw. On a failed save, the creature gains 1 level of exhaustion. On a successful save, the creature's exhaustion level decreases by 1. If a successful saving throw reduces the infected creature's level of exhaustion below 1, the creature recovers from the disease.

Immunity. All forms of rats and wererats are immune to the Gnawing Plague.

CYCLE OF THE PLAGUE

The Gnawing Plague is an ever-present threat in Richemulot. At any given time, every community in the domain is in one of four stages of the plague. Whenever characters find themselves in a community, determine what stage that community is experiencing and if it's different from the day before.

PROGRESSING STAGES

The plague's progress begins at stage one, advances to stage four, and then either wanes back to stage one or ends when everyone in a community is dead. Each stage can last for days or weeks, as appropriate for your adventures.

Alternatively, if you'd like to have the plague play out more randomly, roll a d20 each day. If you roll 2 or lower, the stage decreases by one. If you roll a 17 or higher, the stage increases by one. If the characters spend at least 1 hour during the day working to treat the sick, the stage decreases by one if you roll a 4 or lower.

Let the plague's cycle proceed for as long as your adventures demand, waxing or waning whenever it's most dramatic. The plague will never kill everyone in Richemulot; there will always be miraculous cures or reasons for Jacqueline Renier to withdraw her infected rat swarms. The cities then repopulate swiftly, with new residents emerging from the Mists to little notice. This ensures that after a period of relative peace, the plague's next wave is just as devastating as the last.

STAGE ONE: THREAT

At its calmest, the plague isn't obvious in the population. The plague behaves as detailed in "The Gnawing Plague" section and isn't likely to spread unless an influx of the Darklord's rats causes it to.

STAGE TWO: OUTBREAK

Coughing can be heard in the streets. Furtive looks pass between strangers, and the Casques Silencieux appear in increasing numbers. During this stage, whenever a character goes out in public, roll or choose an encounter from the Stage Two Encounters table. If exposed to the Gnawing Plague, a character must succeed on a Constitution saving throw to resist the disease with the DC listed in the table entry for that encounter.

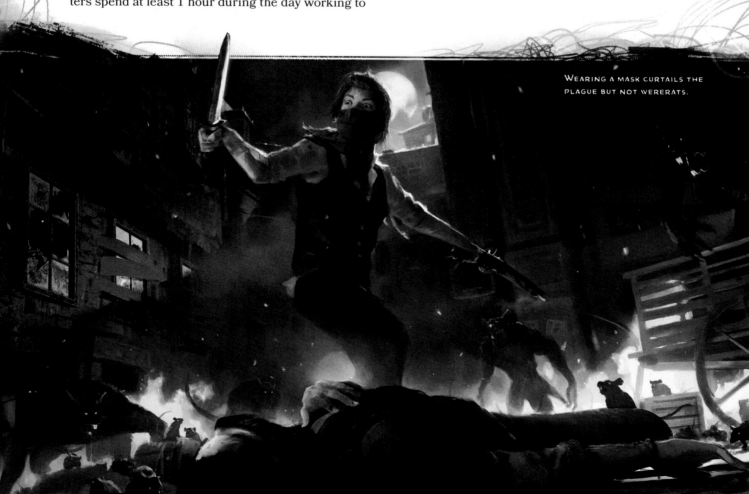

WEARING A MASK CURTAILS THE PLAGUE BUT NOT WERERATS.

STAGE TWO ENCOUNTERS

d6	Encounter
1	The character avoids direct contact with anyone who might be infected.
2	How many people brush up against the character as they push through the crowds? The character must succeed on a DC 12 Constitution saving throw or contract the Gnawing Plague.
3	A nearby person turns and coughs directly on the character, who must succeed on a DC 14 Constitution saving throw or contract the Gnawing Plague.
4	A **rat** scurries across the character's foot. If the character isn't wearing metal armor, it scratches them and they must succeed on a DC 12 Constitution saving throw or contract the Gnawing Plague.
5	A sobbing child is separated from their parents in a crowd. A character who physically interacts with the child must succeed on a DC 14 Constitution saving throw or contract the Gnawing Plague.
6	A cutpurse tries to pick the character's pocket. If the character tries to physically stop the criminal, they must succeed on a DC 12 Constitution saving throw or contract the Gnawing Plague.

STAGE THREE: ILLNESS

All businesses close, and the gates to walled communities are sealed. The Casques Silencieux usher anyone on the streets back into their homes. Those without shelter congregate in alleys, where the rats grow bold. During this stage, whenever a character goes out in public, roll or choose an encounter from the Stage Three Encounters table. If exposed to the Gnawing Plague, a character must succeed on a Constitution saving throw to resist the disease with the DC listed in the table entry for that encounter.

STAGE THREE ENCOUNTERS

d6	Encounter
1	A dead body lies in the character's path. A character who touches the body must succeed on a DC 12 Constitution saving throw or contract the Gnawing Plague.
2	A retching **commoner** tries to grapple the character, begging for any help. Anyone the commoner touches must succeed on a DC 16 Constitution saving throw or contract the Gnawing Plague.
3	Three Casques Silencieux (**animated armor**) gesture for the character to get indoors immediately. They turn hostile if the character resists.
4	Several mangy **giant rats** attack. Anyone bitten by a giant rat must succeed on a DC 14 Constitution saving throw or contract the Gnawing Plague.

d6	Encounter
5	A **swarm of rats** shadows the character as they travel. If confronted, the swarm attacks. Anyone bitten by the rats must succeed on a DC 14 Constitution saving throw or contract the Gnawing Plague.
6	A young, well-heeled couple cavorts openly, oblivious to the quarantine. These **wererats** don't reveal their true nature unless they must, and then only to blend in with the swarms of rats.

STAGE FOUR: PESTILENCE

The dead lie in the streets. Neighbors shun one another. Everyone hears the gnawing sounds in the dark, but no one searches out the source. During this stage, whenever a character goes out in public, roll or choose an encounter from the Stage Four Encounters table. If exposed to the Gnawing Plague, a character must succeed on a Constitution saving throw to resist the disease with the DC listed in the table entry for that encounter.

STAGE FOUR ENCOUNTERS

d6	Encounter
1	A desperate group of **commoners** tries to break through a sealed gate to escape quarantine. Anyone who tries to aid or deter them must succeed on a DC 16 Constitution saving throw or contract the Gnawing Plague.
2	Three thieves attack someone who cries out for help. If a character intervenes, all four thieves reveal themselves to be **wererats** and attack.
3	A squad of Casques Silencieux (**animated armor**) marches through the street. If the Casques Silencieux spot a character, they try to force the character into a home where the residents are all dead.
4	The character spots several rats in an alley using trash to enact a miniature courtroom drama. If a character interrupts or is critical of the rats' play, the rats become a **swarm of rats** and attack.
5	The character notices a **giant rat** about to throw alchemist's fire at an inhabited home. If they intervene, the rat flees. Whether or not it escapes, the character's lodgings are soon the target of arson.
6	A celebration takes place in a nearby house. Six **wererats** openly cavort in hybrid form, dancing and carousing with the corpses of the home's former owners.

Tepest

Domain of Nature's Cruel Secrets

Darklord: Mother Lorinda
Genre: Folk horror
Hallmarks: Fey bargains, nature worship, rural festivals, secret sacrifices
Mist Talismans: Bloodstained farm implement, dried crown of white camellias, straw doll

All is well in Tepest. Fields shine with the golden hues of a bountiful harvest, and horned village children happily recite sing-song rhymes. But those who linger among this land's pastures and colorful cottages can't escape the feeling of being watched, or the impression that the idyllic fields have a distinctly somber cast. The locals dismiss such worries as the tricks of scheming fey, but their smiles fail to mask the desperation in their eyes.

Brutality wears a welcoming face in Tepest—a truth embodied by the ancient hag Lorinda, who betrayed her coven in pursuit of a daughter to love. Taking the guise of a deity called Mother, Lorinda has adopted the entire village of Viktal, protecting its people from nature's whims so they can feed her accursed offspring. Meanwhile, lingering in forests and hiding beneath the earth, resentful fey watch and plot, offering cruel bargains to those who wander beyond Mother's sight.

The people of Viktal, Tepest's only remaining community, do what they must to survive, using tradition and faith to cloak their fear of the wilds and their complicity in a cycle of murder. Strangers are symbols of hope to them—either as a promise of a life free from terror, or as potential sacrifices for the next necessary slaughter.

Noteworthy Features

Those familiar with Tepest know the following facts:

- Viktal is the only noteworthy community in Tepest. The idyllic village's residents devoutly follow the optimistic, naturalistic faith of the god known as Mother. Supposedly, no one born there ever wants to leave.
- The frequent festivals in Viktal include a fertility celebration called the Tithe, which occurs once each season.
- The most zealous of Viktal's faithful are Mother's Minders. These devotees sacrifice their left eyes to Mother to show their faith.
- Caves dot the land, connecting to deeper caverns where dangerous fey dwell. The people of Viktal fear the fey and blame them for every accident and ill.
- Few children are born in Tepest. Determined would-be parents must bargain with Mother or the fey to bring them a child.

Settlements and Sites

The forested valley of Tepest stretches between ranges of rugged mountains etched with dramatic cliffs and mysterious vales. Rocky soil and unpredictable weather make much of the region ill-suited to agriculture, and deadly predators, murderous goblins, and cunning fey haunt the wilds. Despite this, the land around the community of Viktal is a haven of peace and bounty. Most people in the domain live here, though scattered homesteaders and hermits take their chances in the wilds.

Viktal

Tales of the days before Mother arrived claim that the families of Viktal barely scraped enough from the earth to survive, and often lost livestock and children to malicious fey. Today, Mother ensures peace in Viktal. Wicker scarecrows guard the rich fields, and friendly people go about their business with idyllic simplicity. Families in the community share their crops and resources equally. The cheery villagers welcome visitors, showing eager interest in their stories and lodging them free of charge at the village inn, the Fisher's Rest. Visitors are welcome to stay for as long as they like, especially as one of the seasonal Tithe festivals approaches.

The Gurgyl

Those who venture into the wilds on a moonlit night might see a massive shape silently lumbering through Tepest's woods. The Gurgyl, a structure of thorns, wicker, and giants' bones, appears as a misshapen, towerlike nest balanced on three skeletal dragon legs. Lorinda and her daughter Laoirse dwell inside this mobile fortress, which holds Lorinda's kitchen-laboratory, Laoirse's nursery-oubliette, and the Old Cauldron, a plugged pot where Lorinda's coven-sisters languish. The Gurgyl ranges across Tepest at Lorinda's will and

MAP 3.13: TEPEST

might appear anywhere. The villagers of Viktal know the Gurgyl serves their god in some way, but sighting it portends bad luck.

KELLEE

The gates to the walled village of Kellee hang open, and its crumbling houses stand empty. Lorinda first sought to spread her worship here, but something went terribly wrong. Now, one of hag's forsaken creations haunts the abandoned village, and neither Mother nor her followers dare approach the place.

THE LOST COURT

This serene valley lies in the shadow of Mount Arak. By day, its woods throng with fat, happy animals. By night, the ground turns to mud and brambles from which the transformed victims of deadly magic rise. A sanctuary from the terrible night beckons on the shore of Lake Lenore—the sturdy walls and warm hearth of the Nobody's Inn. The fey and their servants avoid the inn and its skeletal innkeeper, Bryonna, at all costs.

MOUNT ARAK

Miles of tunnels run beneath Tepest's forests and vales, all of which eventually lead to vast hidden caverns beneath the dramatic peaks of Mount Arak.

The fey create their homes in a realm of glowing crystals and mist-filled fissures. Dozens of different species live here, under the seelie Queen Maeve and the unseelie Prince Loht. These siblings jointly rule their hidden realm together despite a strained relationship.

The inhabitants of Arak resent the people of the surface for ancient slights and view them as dangerous. They avoid the folk of Viktal but eagerly play malicious tricks on those who venture into the wilderness. The fey could easily overwhelm the surface dwellers, but Maeve and Loht hold them at bay to avoid the hag Lorinda's ire. The fey monarchs believe Lorinda's followers possess a weapon capable of unleashing a deadly force and that it is locked beneath the three-peaked mountain called Gwydion's Claw.

MOTHER LORINDA

Lorinda, Laveeda, and Leticia, the Mindefisk sisters, were gifts from the faeries to their lonely mother, a kind, honest woman who wanted daughters to cherish. Their brutish father and brothers resented the girls, whose sufferings grew worse after their mother died. Desiring a better life, the sisters began preying upon travelers who passed by their secluded

MOTHER LORINDA

home. They murdered wealthy strangers, stole their valuables, and disposed of the bodies in their family's stewpot. The sisters' wickedness was revealed and when they squabbled over a stranger they all fancied and ultimately murdered the traveler. When the rest of the family discovered their terrible deeds, the sisters killed their father and brothers. As their murder spree unfolded, the Mists rose. When they cleared, unfamiliar mountains in a land called Tepest surrounded the sisters' simple valley home, and their true nature as vicious hags manifested.

From the strange fey of Tepest, the three hags learned magic that they used to prey upon the humans of the nearby valleys. Over generations, they became known as fickle sages and weavers of dooms and miracles. Strangers sought them out, begging for bountiful crops, potent medicines, or the children that fate denied them. The hags sowed blessings and despair in equal measure. Numerous hexblood children originated from the hags' cauldron. In time, the hag Lorinda asked her sisters to help create a child of their own. But Laveeda and Leticia refused, loathing the idea of sharing their magic and secrets.

In secret, Lorinda assembled a creature of animal parts, brambles, and foul magic. With its help, she ambushed her sisters and trapped them inside their own magic cauldron. Soon after, Lorinda's creation fell apart, and she has used magic stolen from her imprisoned sisters ever since to create flawed, hungry beings she calls children (see "Lorinda's Children" below). She manipulates the people of Tepest to provide excellent meals for her daughter.

LORINDA'S POWERS AND DOMINION

Lorinda is a **green hag** of extreme age. In her true form, she carries her darling family—three grim dolls she calls Laveeda, Leticia, and Laoirse. When dealing with the residents of Viktal, she takes on her benevolent illusory guise as Mother.

Mother. Lorinda wears the guise of Mother to manipulate the people of Viktal. In this illusory form, she appears as a matronly figure wearing a cloak of moth wings and bearing a branch burning with torches. Using her control of the land as Tepest's Darklord, Mother brings bounty to fields and flocks, or curses farms with famine and aberrant livestock. Those in her service rarely produce offspring and so petition her for hexblood children (see chapter 1). All Mother asks of her followers in return for her blessing is that they love her best, remain watchful for those of weak faith, and offer seasonal sacrifices (see "Viktal and the Tithe").

Mother's Minders. Servants of Mother prove their faith through song, rustic art, and small sacrifices. The most devout, called Mother's Minders, each undertake a ritual in which they pluck out their left eye, gifting its sight to Mother. Lorinda can see through her followers' empty eye sockets as though they were *hag eyes* (detailed in the *Monster Manual*). Additionally, she can teleport at will from the Gurgyl to an unoccupied space adjacent to any Mother's Minder. On the rare times she does, she appears to physically crawl out of her follower's empty eye socket.

Laveeda and Leticia. Lorinda's sisters are imprisoned in a fat cauldron that serves as the engine for their animated home, the Gurgyl. Lorinda can use her sisters' prison to cast any of the spells shared by a hag coven (detailed in the *Monster Manual*). If the cauldron is unsealed, Laveeda and Leticia seek swift revenge against their sister.

Lorinda's Children. Lorinda pushes the limits of her foul magic to turn sticks and carcasses into her own children. She loves these monstrous beings, naming them all Laoirse and treating them as if they were the same individual. These creatures rarely live for more than a few weeks—except when a villager is sacrificed to Mother during the Tithe, which extends Laoirse's life by a few weeks. Lorinda dotes on her children, rarely letting them leave the Gurgyl, and wreaking horrible vengeance on any who harm them.

LORINDA'S TORMENT

Lorinda endures various miseries, the following chief among them:

- Lorinda desires to have a family, but her inherently controlling, murderous nature leads her to destroy whatever she creates.
- She constantly doubts the adoration she receives from her daughters and worshipers. Lorinda requires constant proof of their love.
- Lorinda can create hexblood children for others, but any being she fashions for herself is monstrous, ravenous, and short-lived.
- Lorinda fears that her sisters will one day escape their captivity and take revenge on her.

ROLEPLAYING LORINDA

Lorinda loves the trappings of motherhood and is off-puttingly maternal toward all those she encounters. She's quick to dote on others, calling them unsettling pet names like "lostling," "caterpillar," or "sweetskin." She insists that others call her some variation of "mother." Lorinda relishes the worship of Viktal's people but treats them as livestock, guarding them fiercely only to slaughter them as she wills. In her Mother guise, she maintains an air of benevolence, claiming to ask for little despite her followers' supposed sloth and ingratitude. She will do anything to prevent the villagers from learning her true nature.

Personality Trait. "I'm the greatest parent in the world. I just need children worthy of my love."

Ideal. "Good children get rewards. Bad children get punished."

Bond. "My sweet Laoirse is my world."

Flaw. "The children can't know what I was—what I am."

ADVENTURES IN TEPEST

The horror of Tepest rises from its mysterious wilderness and the seemingly idyllic community of Viktal. Here, dread lies in contrasts. Tree branches grasp like claws while every cottage exudes a warm glow. Smiles come readily but last too long. Wildflowers grow from the carcasses of mutated lambs.

The Mists deposit visitors to Tepest near Viktal, whose folk encourage strangers to partake of the village's hospitality. Will characters accept a welcome respite, or will they be suspicious of their hosts? Do they ask about Mother? If they discover the horror of the Tithe, do the characters view the villagers as victims or monsters? The following section, "Viktal and the Tithe," explores how to draw characters into the village's eerie traditions.

Beyond Viktal, the inescapable hostility of the natural world holds sway. Harsh weather casts a pall over the land, and predators and dangerous plant creatures haunt the forests. Any kind of Fey creature might dwell in the domain—or beneath it in the realms of Arak. Even whimsical fey take on a malicious tinge in Tepest, whether as thieves, kidnappers, deal-makers, or collectors of eerie trophies. Like the land itself, the fey have strange powers, and villagers pushed to desperation seek them out in the hopes of bargaining for what fate has denied them.

When planning adventures in this domain, consider the plots on the Tepest Adventures table.

TEPEST ADVENTURES

d10	Adventure
1	Toxic, vision-inducing fungi taint the ruined village of Briggdarrow. Recently, homesteaders outside Viktal discovered the fungus on their properties and claim it's being spread by strange fungus-covered bipeds (**myconids**).
2	A hermit who once lived in the abandoned fortress on Cas Island hires the party to retrieve an heirloom she left behind. But she warns that the Avanc, a dangerous lake monster, swims nearby.
3	A shepherd's youngest child went missing after a sinkhole opened in a nearby pasture, revealing a glowing cavern that leads into the tunnels of Arak.
4	The Parrish family fled Viktal in fear of Mother. They seek help revealing her malice to their former neighbors before she finds them.
5	Mother's Minders nail wicker dolls over the doors of a dozen houses in Viktal. Soon after, both the dolls and the inhabitants of those houses vanish.
6	A druid seeks aid in reclaiming their people's holy site from an ancient, evil **treant** called Blightroot. The druid doesn't mention that the surrounding forests are a clonal colony of the villainous plant.
7	A grieving villager begs the characters to take their deceased loved one to the Cauldron, a pool said to restore life to a corpse bathed in its waters. The villager says nothing of the terrible price the pool's magic exacts.
8	Two young lovers go missing from Viktal. One is found days later, unable to remember anything, aged fifty years, and desperate for help to find their partner.
9	A character's reflection on the water warns of impending doom. The image insists they find the Seer's Glass, which can reveal the past and future.
10	A strange old woman claims to have lost her child and begs the characters for help. Thus disguised, Lorinda hopes to have the party track down her runaway Laoirse.

Viktal and the Tithe

Those who come to Tepest inevitably arrive near the domain's lone surviving settlement, Viktal. There, they find welcoming people, warm food and beds, and an unsettling sense that the daily life and traditions of the villagers conceal horrible secrets. What starts as glimpses of strange behaviors or rustic decorations culminates in learning the village's secrets firsthand during the seasonal Tithe. This section explores the village of Viktal and provides guidance on how the Tithe unfolds.

Welcome to Viktal

The rustic community of Viktal consists of a few dozen simple cottages surrounding a market square, a meeting hall, and an inn. Farms and fishing shacks cluster around the village, shying away from the shadows of the surrounding woods and mountains. Those who visit Viktal soon meet Mother's faithful, who appear at first to practice a local, naturalistic faith. But as the characters explore, they notice especially pious villagers with missing eyes called Mother's Minders and other locals engaging in unsettling behavior.

The villagers are curious about strangers, and eventually someone invites the outsiders to the Fisher's Rest for a free meal and to share their stories. The villagers encourage new arrivals to become part of the community, since that's what Mother teaches them to do—and to broaden the pool of sacrifice fodder for the next Tithe.

When the characters visit Viktal, roll or choose options from the Sights in Viktal table to set the tone of the village's strangeness.

Sights in Viktal

d8	Sight
1	Locals weave flowers into crowns and sew cuts of meat into cloaks, creating traditional garb for an upcoming festival.
2	Most children in town are hexbloods (see chapter 1). Evasive locals refuse to say why.
3	Villagers harvest wings and chrysalises from caged moths, which are powdered and used to make "shift spice"—a pervasive ingredient in local dishes.
4	A group of young people dramatically sob at the window of an old woman, who tosses horned wicker dolls to those who sob loudest.
5	A local fisher teaches knife-wielding youngsters how to debone live eels and create festive "elver-crowns," a grim local decoration.
6	With adult approval, youngsters affix hornlike sticks to a terrified animal's head.
7	A lovingly carved door or mural depicts a woman's face made of moth wings, watching over an explicitly detailed scene of butchery or surgery.
8	Villagers sing and dance in a circle around someone undergoing a ritual to have their left eye removed.

The Tithe

The Tithe festival takes place in Viktal four times each year, during the equinoxes and solstices. During this day-long celebration, Mother's followers revel in the bounty of nature and new life. The villagers spend weeks in preparation for the celebration, and villagers eagerly explain that the Tithe is a commemoration of nature's abundance during which a measure of the town's bounty is returned to Mother. In truth, the a festival is meant to prepare one of the villagers for slaughter at the hands of Lorinda's child, the latest Laoirse.

Tithe Celebration. The Tithe's festivities start early in the morning, when the town's elders lead everyone in a parade to a prepared festival ground in a field outside town. The assembled villagers spend the day partaking in contests, feasting, dancing, and song.

Tithe Events. Celebratory events on the day include traditional entertainment and competitions. Everyone is encouraged to participate and live life to its fullest. Events end with contest victors receiving small tokens as rewards, and whoever wins the most before dusk is named Mother's Favorite. These events involve simple challenges and ability checks, though elaborate events might run as chases (see the *Dungeon Master's Guide*) or combat with weapons customized to deal low or no damage. Roll for or choose two or three activities from the Tithe Events table to determine what events the characters might participate in during the Tithe.

Tithe Events

d6	Event	Token
1	**Crooked Joust.** Participants use stilts strapped to their arms and legs to topple one another.	Five-legged sheep figurine
2	**Powrie Chase.** Pursuers dress as wicked faeries, donning tattered red cloaks and using sharp darts in a game of tag.	Red wooden ring
3	**Lost Siblings.** Blindfolded participants identify other players by touching their hair.	Sheaf of black wheat
4	**Gossamer Glutton.** Whoever eats the most live moths wins.	Glass butterfly wing

d6	Event	Token
5	**Hungry Sister.** A dozen players with a rope tied around them try to stop someone from getting past them and stealing a pear from a bowl.	A dried length of pear skin
6	**Never Naughty.** Participants take turns flattering three elderly villagers, who decide who wins and who gets paddled.	A reed switch

Mother's Blessing. At dusk, the town's leader names Mother's Favorite and grants them a crown of white camellias prior to an hours-long, communal feast. Then, near midnight, the celebrants move farther into the fields to receive Mother's blessing.

At midnight, amid ceremony and solemnity, Mother appears to her worshipers. Mother's Favorite is instructed to carry a bowl of food and gifts to Mother. As they do, the latest Laoirse—viewed by the villagers as a manifestation of nature's hunger—appears and attacks. All assembled expect Laoirse to slaughter the victim, spilling their blood and bringing fertility to the fields for another season—and gaining an extra few weeks of life before inevitably decaying like all Mother's prior children. As Laoirse drags away her meal, Mother blesses her faithful and vanishes. The villagers merrily return to their homes, having completed the Tithe for another season.

The particulars of how this ritual plays out are up to you, but it always culminates in Laoirse's attack. Whether a character is chosen as Mother's Favorite or the party tries to defend the victim, roll or choose an option from the Lorinda's Daughter table to determine what horror arrives at the ritual's climax. Creatures on the table marked with an asterisk are detailed in chapter 5.

LORINDA'S DAUGHTER

d6	Laoirse's Form	Statistics	CR
1	Giant upright-walking ram	**Minotaur**	3
2	Humanoid made of wicker	**Shambling mound**	5
3	Dozens of stitched together corpses	**Zombie clot**＊	6
4	Shivering, hairless, rabbit-bear	**Abominable yeti**	9
5	Bipedal wolf-elk	**Loup garou**＊	13
6	Giant, shrieking, bipedal sheep	**Goristro**	17

MARK BEHM

VALACHAN
Domain of the Hunter

Darklord: Chakuna
Genres: Gothic horror and slasher horror
Hallmarks: Diabolical traps, hostile wilderness, survival games
Mist Talismans: Displacer beast skin, poisonous flower blossom, rusty foot trap

In the jungles of Valachan, survivors must guard their hearts lest something monstrous eat them. For some, that risk is worth the reward of the unusual plants and magical creatures this land is home to. But Valachan is fiercely protected by its Darklord, the devious and immortal hunter Chakuna. She roams the jungles hunting dangerous beasts—and when she grows dissatisfied with simpler prey, she draws sapient quarry into a fatal contest.

Pitted against other conscripted players in a game of cat and mouse, Chakuna's prey struggle to survive the deadly Valachan rain forest and one another, all while being pursued by the Darklord. Treacherous quicksand and other deadly hazards cover the terrain, and populations of stealthy werepanthers support the Darklord. But desperate contenders might also find unlikely allies who oppose Chakuna and her horrific hunts.

Valachan has villages but contains no cities or towns, since the forest doesn't allow them to be built. Every shivering leaf and every creature's eyes hold an eerie awareness. The forests watch, and they whisper what they see to Chakuna.

A mystery that ties the Darklord to her domain could shatter her power or plunge the land into utter catastrophe. The secret pulses in the breath of the forest, timed to the heartbeat of its master. Those who survive long enough in Valachan to discover its secrets might end up twisted into the predator they oppose.

NOTEWORTHY FEATURES

Those familiar with Valachan know the following facts:

- Valachan is a land of dense rain forests, sandy shores, and forest-covered mountains. This wilderness is fantastically dangerous, but the people who dwell here have long flourished.
- Valachan hosts the Trial of Hearts, a battle royale conducted during certain full moons by the land's greatest hunter, Chakuna.
- Any wild plant or creature in the jungles of Valachan might turn hostile toward explorers.
- Packs of displacer beasts roam the jungle, led by Yana, a preternaturally cunning displacer beast that serves Chakuna.

VALACHANI CHARACTERS

Characters from Valachan typically hail from small, rain forest communities. The domain's people are predominantly humans with dark hair and a range of warm, brown skin tones. Some names take inspiration from Mesoamerican languages. When players create characters from Valachan, consider asking them the following questions:

How did you avoid or survive participating in the Trial of Hearts? Did you flee Valachan to evade the hunt? Did you somehow escape Chakuna after being selected? Did you volunteer to protect somebody else?

Why aren't you a werepanther? Are you from one of the outlying villages, like Shuaran? Were you adopted? Were you born without the gift, or do you display a different manifestation?

What secret of the land do you know better than anyone else? Is it the existence of the grotto filled with healing flowers? The secret way out of a box canyon? How to get a giant parrot to like you?

SETTLEMENTS AND SITES

Valachan is beautiful, lush, and wild. Every kind of colorful creature and vibrant bloom flourishes here, and from its deep gulches to its heady mountain ridges, the domain teems with life. Rumors of this land's rare abundance often escape the domain, enticing traders, herbalists, beast tamers, and seekers of magical reagents to search it out. But visitors must tread lightly and take their plunder sparingly, or the wrath of the Darklord will surely find them.

Valachan has no established roads, but well-traveled game trails snake through the dense forest, marked out by generations of inhabitants. These paths are easily spotted by those who know how to look for them.

Every living thing in Valachan generates wily camouflage, venom, spines, tricks, or traps. Nothing here is safe, defenseless, or as it seems.

EIRUBAMBA RIVER

Wildflowers, enticing fruits, and medicinal herbs grow in the forests and upon the shorelines around the Eirubamba River. Most rain forest predators won't approach the river, though, fearing the territorial giant wasps that swarm among the rare plants.

OSELO

Darklord Chakuna's home village, Oselo appears prosperous and relaxed, and the people are friendly to traders and visitors. Nothing strange occurs during the day. But at night, everything changes. Hunters shift into the forms of panthers and ocelots, forming packs that roam deep into the jungle and return with meat after assisting Chakuna on her hunts. In the aftermath, an underlying disquiet permeates the entire village. A spiritual struggle torments the community, the people torn between wanting to live in peace and obeying Chakuna's will.

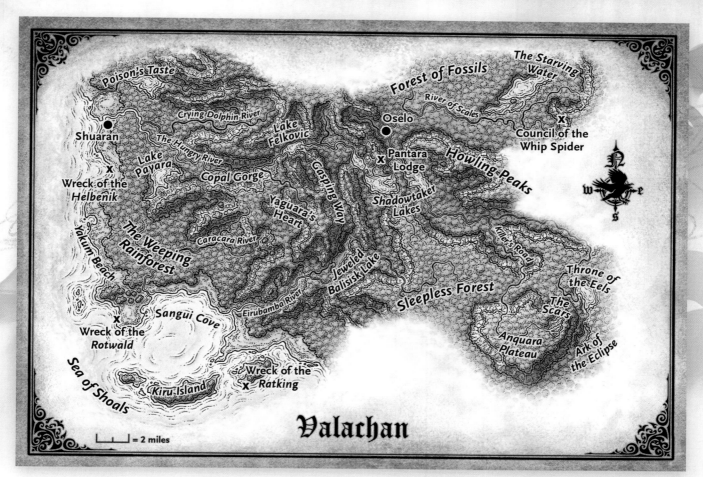

MAP 3.14: VALACHAN

The Oselo people occasionally adopt wayward outsiders, granting them protection from the Trial of Hearts. Once adopted into the village, individuals must prove themselves by undertaking initiation ceremonies focused around surviving in the forest for a week with no tools.

PANTARA LODGE

The seat of power in Valachan, Pantara Lodge is a series of thatch buildings strung together high in the forest canopy, suspended above the overgrown ruins of a castle reclaimed by the jungle. Chakuna's home holds only the bare necessities: an armory, an infirmary, and a stable of displacer beasts. Chakuna's displacer beast hunting partner, Yana, remains by her side here.

Those who listen closely while at Pantara Lodge hear muttering in the night. These whispers issue from the head of Urik von Kharkov, Valachan's deposed former Darklord, who spews curses and secrets from a chamber hidden at the lodge's heart.

SHUARAN

The skilled warriors of Shuaran village don't shape-shift like the Oselo, though Oselo refugees who believe Chakuna's rule is cursed and shun her protection can be found here. Opposed to the

rule of Chakuna, the Shuaran fear her deeply and might aid those who resist her, defining their relationships with strangers through a prickly, easily offended sense of honor. The Shuaran constantly guard against a local shrewdness of howling apes to the south near Yakum Beach. A soft and menacing whooping in the distance can be heard in the village at all times.

YAGUARA'S HEART

The most secret of secret places in Valachan, Yaguara's Heart lies at the center of a maze of mountains southwest of Pantara Lodge. Within this canyon lies a small, crumbling temple nestled among treacherous cliffs and grasping forest. In the blood-painted caverns hidden beneath the temple lies a stone altar bearing the still-beating heart of Darklord Chakuna. Here, an aspiring Darklord can perform a ritual to consume Chakuna's heart and take her place as ruler of Valachan, or destroy it and loose the sapient rage of the rain forest on anyone trapped within the domain's borders. Only Chakuna, the displacer beast Yana, and von Kharkov's remains know the location of Chakuna's heart and how to claim her power.

CHAKUNA

In Valachan, the fall of one Darklord led inevitably to the rise of another. For Chakuna, caught in a cycle of bloodshed and trapped by the forest that lends her power, the tools of the oppressor became the means of her bitter domination.

The Darklord Urik von Kharkov ruled from the now-ruined Castle Pantara, a fortress of tyranny and torment from which he hunted the people of Valachan for sport. Over untold years, the hunt grew in complexity, and von Kharkov sought out the rarest, most dangerous prey. Chakuna's people, the Oselo, became his favorite targets.

The Oselo are hunters and people of the jungle. But by the light of the moon, many grow fur, claws, and fangs, revealing their true nature as watchful and dangerous lycanthropes. By the time Chakuna was a teenager, von Kharkov had fine-tuned the horror of his hunts into a regulated tournament. He hunted her people to the brink of extinction, preventing their escape by closing the domain's borders and trapping them within the Mists.

Chakuna swore to save her people. She entered the tournament freely, determined to turn the tables on von Kharkov or die. She vowed to sacrifice whatever it took to defeat the Darklord—but learned quickly that it takes monstrosity to beat a monster. Chakuna found von Kharkov's weakness, burned Castle Pantara to the ground, and kept the former Darklord's head.

CHAKUNA'S POWERS AND DOMINION

Chakuna gained her status as a Darklord when she defeated Urik von Kharkov. In so doing, though, she discovered a terrible truth about the nature of Valachan, and she now lives to maintain the domain and the cycle of predator and prey. Chakuna has statistics similar to a **weretiger**, but her animal and hybrid forms have the appearance of a panther.

Heartless. Chakuna has no heart—literally. At the height of her contest with von Kharkov, she ripped it out of her chest with her fingers and placed it at the center of the Yaguara Mountain maze, then replaced it by taking and eating von Kharkov's heart. Doing so, she co-opted von Kharkov's powers and accursed immortality and claimed Valachan as her own. Within Yaguara's Heart, the sacred nexus of the maze, Chakuna's heart still beats as one with the land, infinitely connected and as robust as the rain forest. But like anything that lives, her tie with the domain she's claimed must be maintained. Life eats life. And so Chakuna sacrifices the blood of the hunted to the land to maintain her grip on power. If she doesn't, the plants and animals of the domain grow hostile, threatening to wipe out all who dwell there.

The Trial of Hearts. Chakuna has formalized the slaughter she must commit to maintain her tie with the domain as a ritualized battle royale known as the Trial of Hearts (detailed below).

Closing the Borders. When Chakuna chooses to close the borders of her domain, the seas grow rough and the Mists rise. In addition to their normal effects (see "Influence of the Mists" at the start of this chapter), the Mists of Valachan are home to displacer beasts and other deadly predators that attack all creatures they meet.

CHAKUNA'S TORMENT

Chakuna's tie to Valachan is different from the domain bonds of most other Darklords, as hers is a willing bond. She must endlessly steep the land in blood to ensure her survival and protect her people from the vicious land, so that the hunts she vowed to stop now continue in her name. She shields her people from the slaughter, but the rest of Valachan is fair game.

ROLEPLAYING CHAKUNA

The whole web of life in Valachan bends to a singular malevolent consciousness that demands Chakuna prove her worth as its keeper and apex predator, lest it rise up to consume her people. In response, Chakuna is canny, remorseless, and vindictive. She's come to enjoy playing with her food—and she has a whole domain to feed.

Personality Trait. "I owe nothing to those I hunt. They are nothing more than prey."

Ideal. "If I'm cleverer than you, then I deserve to live, and you deserve to die."

Bond. "My people are the strongest people, and I ensure they survive."

Flaw. "Everyone and everything lies. Only by expecting treachery will a hunter survive."

ADVENTURES IN VALACHAN

Valachan forces adventurers to survive in a wilderness that's not merely hostile, but is actively trying to destroy them. Other terrors in the Domains of Dread take the form of vicious villains or terrifying monsters. But in Valachan, the land is the greatest threat, and the domain's murderous Darklord hones that threat like a weapon.

The Trial of Hearts anchors the terror in Valachan, but the domain's dangerous wilderness threatens anyone who explores the land. In addition to natural rain-forest predators, dinosaurs and displacer beasts roam the domain. Its varied Plant creatures include wicked twig blights, cruel treants, and manipulative dryads all expressing the land's underlying blood thirst. The people of the land—the werepanthers of Oselo, the Shuaran, and remote groups of lizardfolk—might provide assistance to outsiders, but they don't tolerate those who insult their ways or bring Chakuna's wrath upon them. Parties without experience exploring dangerous wilds can enlist a guide to aid them, a service that the Oselo are particularly willing to provide.

Valachan provides the opportunity to exaggerate everything the players and characters know about the threats of nature. The Survival skill proves invaluable in navigating the rain forest, determining what kind of creature mauled a corpse, and understanding how different venoms afflict a jungle survivor. The primal power of the land manifests as environmental hazards such as sudden storms, cliff walls made of vertical quicksand, and naturally occurring pit and snare traps. Whispering hollows, carnivorous plants, and cursing winds can overtly reveal the wilderness's hunger.

Consider the plots on the Valachan Adventures table when planning adventures in this domain.

Valachan Adventures

d8	Adventure
1	The Oselo joyously adopt a new member into their community, but the ceremony erupts in strife when Chakuna appears and demands that all newcomers participate in the Trial of Hearts.
2	Shuaran warriors seek help in slaying a massive **saber-toothed tiger** killing their people. They don't mention that they recently lost the *Cat of Felkovic*, a sentient magic item similar to a *figurine of wondrous power* that conjures a feline killer.
3	A sapient **giant spider** emerges from the caverns known as the Council of the Whip Spider. It demands that the Oselo provide it a sacrifice, or every arachnid in Valachan will attack the village.
4	The **tyrannosaurus rex** called Mother Heartless rampages from the Forest of Fossils, incensed by something amiss in her hunting grounds.
5	The **lizardfolk** of the lakes surrounding the Anquara Plateau discover a submerged ruin and unleash an **aboleth** that now holds them in thrall.
6	Beast-shaped **treants** animate and lay siege to Pantara Lodge, obeying Urik von Kharkov's will.
7	The merchant ship *Zodiac* runs aground on Kiru Island. The sailors seek help salvaging other shipwrecks and escaping back to sea—preferably before Chakuna notices them.
8	A pack of displacer beasts washes up dead in Sangui Cove. An enraged Chakuna prowls the jungle, slaying anyone she suspects of being involved.

The Trial of Hearts

Those who venture into Valachan unprepared risk running afoul of Chakuna and becoming her quarry in the deadly Trial of Hearts. Scenarios like the following might lead to the characters becoming involved in the trial:

Unwitting Criminals. The characters come to Valachan seeking a miraculous plant, rare creature, or unique item—and are captured when they discover their prize is sacred to the domain's people. To redeem themselves, outsiders must participate in the Trial of Hearts.

Deadly Detour. While traveling elsewhere, the party is shipwrecked or ambushed by a deadly predator. The characters awake in Valachan, where Chakuna treats them as trespassers.

Mindtaker Mists. The Mists deposit the consciousnesses of each of the characters into guests at Pantara Lodge. Whether the guests are recreational hunters, unsuspecting foreign nobles, or skilled local warriors, they soon discover that Chakuna's hospitality has a deadly ulterior motive. Consult the "Survivors" section of chapter 4 for options to represent those destined to become prey.

Rules of the Trial

On the night of certain full moons, Chakuna selects fifteen souls within her domain who she considers worthy prey. She leads the participants to Pantara Lodge, shows them every courtesy, and then sets out the rules of her test:

- Contenders may divide into small groups or choose to participate alone.
- Once groups are established at the trial's start, alliances between contenders are not permitted.
- Contenders must reach one of two shrines: either on Kiru Island or between the lakes called the Scars atop Anquara Plateau.
- Contenders may leave Pantara Lodge at dawn the next day. Later that day, at dusk, Chakuna pursues the contenders with hunting partners of her choice, attempting to slay anyone she encounters outside a shrine.
- Contenders may kill one another for any reason—particularly to take a shrine.
- The trial does not stop for any reason until Chakuna arrives at both shrines and acknowledges the winners there.
- Winners are escorted to Shuaran, and from there, out of Valachan.
- Losers rot where they fall in the jungle.
- Violations of the rules are punishable by death.

CHAKUNA CORNERS HER PREY IN THE HEART OF VALACHAN.

Chakuna closes her domain's borders while the trial is underway and can change the hunt's rules on a whim. For example, if she catches a competitor too soon, she might offer to release them if they sacrifice an arm to feed her beasts.

TRAVEL IN VALACHAN

Impenetrable rain forests, jagged cliffs, and deadly rapids fill the wilderness of Valachan, and characters exploring the domain or participating in the Trial of Hearts must travel through these deadly wilds. Maps of Valachan can be obtained from the Oselo, the Shuaran people, or from Chakuna.

The domain's jungles are difficult terrain, reducing a party's pace by half. This means characters can move through most of the domain at a normal pace of 1½ miles per hour and 12 miles per day. Characters can move at a fast or slow pace, with effects as detailed in the *Player's Handbook*.

Characters able to fly find their flight slowed by strong winds (effectively difficult terrain), and might face deadly airborne creatures such as **chimeras**, **harpies**, and **pteranodons**. Chakuna might also

add rules to the Trial of Hearts that deem flight and magical travel off limits. If she does, the Mists aid in enforcing these rules.

As Darklord of Valachan, Chakuna isn't impeded by difficult terrain in the domain's wilderness. Instead of tracking how Chakuna follows characters participating in the hunt, have her appear to watch and toy with other participants, then confront the characters at the most dramatic moment.

DANGERS OF THE TRIAL

Valachan offers thousands of ways to die, and characters can encounter many of them during the Trial of Hearts, including jungle predators, animated plants, and displacer beasts. Those who choose Kiru Island as their goal must cross treacherous waters to reach it, while those who head for the Scars must climb the towering Anquara Plateau. Additionally, each hour the characters travel through the domain, roll on the Valachan Hunt Complications table for an encounter. Characters traveling at a fast pace roll twice on this table and use the lower result. Characters traveling at a slow pace roll twice on the table and use the higher result.

Completing the Trial

At both Kiru Island and the Scars, a shrine on stilts offers the only safety during the Trial of Hearts. When Chakuna arrives at a shrine, whoever she finds inside wins the trial—or so she claims. Whether Chakuna abides by the rules of her trial is up to you.

Ultimately, escaping Chakuna requires finding her heart and destroying it. This prevents Chakuna from recovering if slain. If the characters learn the secret of how Chakuna consumed von Kharkov's heart and took his place as Darklord, any of them might seek to follow a similar path. Doing so requires replacing Chakuna's heart with a character's own heart, or the land utterly rebels and tries to kill all sapient beings in the domain. Those who take Chakuna's mantle can ensure their allies' safety, but Valachan becomes their eternal prison.

Valachan Hunt Complications

d20	Complication
1	Chakuna appears and attacks. Roll a die. If you roll an even number, this occurs during another complication and you can roll again on this table. If you roll an odd number, Chakuna attacks suddenly without another complication.
2	Dense foliage, swampy ground, clouds of insects, or thick fog slows the party's travel to a crawl. The party chooses one character, who must succeed on a DC 14 Wisdom (Survival) check or the party's travel speed is reduced by half for the next hour (this is in addition to any speed reduction from difficult terrain).
3	The area is riddled with traps set by Chakuna. A random character must succeed on a DC 15 Wisdom (Perception) check or fall into a spiked pit (see the *Dungeon Master's Guide*).
4	**Chuuls**, **vine blights**, or **zombie plague spreaders** (see chapter 5) ambush the party.
5	The characters find a tree bound in rope. One or more withered, oversized hearts hang from cords attached to its branches. Roll a die. If you roll an even number, the hearts look grim but are harmless. If you roll an odd number, the 1d6 hearts have the statistics of gnashing **death's heads** (see chapter 5) and attack.
6	Clouds of insects, persistent leeches, or other parasites torment the party. Each character must succeed on a DC 16 Wisdom (Survival) check or gain 1 level of exhaustion. Creatures immune to disease suffer no ill effects from the parasites.
7	The party encounters a **druid**, **green hag**, or **displacer beast** that is not part of the hunt. If a character succeeds on a DC 16 Charisma (Persuasion) check, that creature shows them a route that allows them to move at double their speed for the next hour and avoid rolling on this table at the end of that time.
8	An individual or a group of competitors—**gladiators**, **scouts**, or **tribal warriors**—attempts to ambush the party.
9	Whispers in the Druidic language issue from the boughs of trees and cracks in the earth. They repeat one word: Blood.
10	A desperate competitor appears. Roll a die. If you roll an even number, the competitor is gravely wounded, incoherent, and suffering from hallucinations. If you roll an odd number, the competitor offers to help the party break the trial's rules and is struck dead by an arrow from the forest seconds later.
11	Dinosaurs, **giant poisonous snakes**, or **hydras** attack the party.
12	A rope bridge provides the only method of crossing a river or ravine. Each character must succeed on a DC 10 Dexterity (Acrobatics) check to cross the bridge or fall 60 feet into the jungle or water below. The bridge has AC 11, 16 hit points, and immunity to poison and psychic damage.
13	The party discovers an overgrown ruin. A character who succeeds on a DC 18 Wisdom (Perception) check spots a relief carving of a wicked-looking figure ripping out its own heart.
14	A random character must succeed on a DC 14 Wisdom (Perception) check or fall into quicksand (see the *Dungeon Master's Guide*).
15	**Panthers**, **displacer beasts**, or werepanthers (**weretigers**) attempt to ambush the party.
16	The characters discover the corpse of a competitor. Roll a die. If you roll an even number, the corpse has a *potion of healing*. If you roll an odd number, the corpse's heart has been removed.
17	The party chooses one character who must succeed on a DC 16 Wisdom (Survival) check. On a failed check, the party becomes lost. It takes the characters 1 hour to realize they are 1d4 miles away from their assumed location in a disadvantageous direction.
18–20	No complication

OTHER DOMAINS OF DREAD

The Land of the Mists comprise more than the domains presented in this chapter thus far. Countless domains drift through the Mists. The following lands hint at the multitudes of additional domains that make up the Domains of Dread. Detail and explore these domains in your adventures as you please, or use them as examples when creating your own domains using the guidance in chapter 2. Not all domains need to be elaborately detailed settings. As the domains in this section demonstrate, creating a simple concept for a Darklord and the horrors surrounding them can be a perfect starting point for further development over the course of your adventures.

While exploring the Domains of Dread, should the Mists carry characters to a mysterious domain, roll on the Domains of Ravenloft table to randomly determine where the Dark Powers have guided the party. Domains marked with an asterisk are described earlier in this chapter.

DOMAINS OF RAVENLOFT

d100	Domain	d100	Domain
01–04	Barovia*	55–56	Markovia
05–06	Bluetspur*	57–59	Mordent*
07–09	Borca*	60–62	Nightmare Lands
10–12	Carnival*	63–64	Niranjan
13–14	Cyre 1313	65–66	Nova Vaasa
15–18	Darkon*	67–69	Odaire
19–21	Dementlieu*	70–71	Rider's Bridge
22–24	Falkovnia*	72–74	Richemulot*
25–26	Forlorn	75–76	Risibilos
27–28	Ghastria	77–78	Scaena
29–30	G'henna	79–81	Sea of Sorrows
31–33	Har'Akir*	82–83	Shadowlands
34–36	Hazlan*	84–85	Souragne
37–39	I'Cath*	86–87	Staunton Bluffs
40–41	Invidia	88–90	Tepest*
42–44	Kalakeri*	91–92	Tovag
45–47	Kartakass*	93–95	Valachan*
48–49	Keening	96–97	Vhage Agency
50–51	Klorr	98–99	Zherisia
52–54	Lamordia*	100	DM's design

CYRE 1313, THE MOURNING RAIL

Darklord: The Last Passenger
Hallmarks: Escape from disaster, lightning rail

The disaster known as the Mourning numbers among the greatest tragedies to befall the world of Eberron—a mysterious calamity that killed nearly everyone in the land of Cyre. In the nation's capital of Metrol, some citizens foresaw the coming devastation and sought to escape upon lightning rails, elemental-powered engines capable of pulling trains of passenger carriages. As scared innocents packed Metrol's last lightning rail, known as Cyre 1313, the evacuation was delayed at the demand of a late-arriving VIP. Hundreds were forced from passenger carriages to admit and maintain the secrecy of this last passenger and their retinue. When the lightning rail did finally depart, it was too late. The disaster of the Mourning overtook the train and its hundreds of escapees. But even as it did, the Mists claimed Cyre 1313 and all aboard it. Now, the last lightning rail from Metrol hurtles through the Mists as a traveling domain. Those on board fear the disaster pursuing them, the mysterious passenger seated in the train's foremost carriage, and the necrotic energy now infusing the engine's elemental spirit. Yet none of the passengers realize their endless escape is pointless, as Cyre 1313 carries only the dead.

FORLORN

Darklord: Tristen ApBlanc
Hallmarks: Life and death, strange invention

Tristen ApBlanc was born amid tragedy, the son of a vampire father and a human noble. His parents were murdered by fearful villagers, leaving Tristen to be adopted by local druids. But during his teenage years, Tristen's dhampir nature revealed itself (see chapter 1). When the druids discovered the youth's hunger for blood, they cast him out, but Tristen grew enraged and slaughtered the druids, draining them all. The sacred waters of the druids' rituals had infused their blood, though, making it poison to the half-vampire. Tristen died with his adopted family, but as the Mists closed in around their sacred stone circle, he rose a ghost. Unexpectedly, with the dawn, Tristen's dhampir body was restored. Now, Tristen lives by day, a perpetually young, charming, invention-obsessed dhampir dwelling in Castle Tristenoira, the smoking fortress his goblin servants built over the druid circle of his one-time family. At night, though, the young dhampir dies a painful death, in his spectral form, and seeks to scour all that is green and vibrant from his land.

CYRE 1313, THE MOURNING RAIL, THUNDERS THROUGH DOMAINS, EVER TRYING TO ESCAPE THE DISASTER THAT SLEW ITS PASSENGERS.

GHASTRIA

Darklord: Marquis Stezen D'Polarno
Hallmarks: Cursed art, dour population

A notorious hedonist, Marquis Stezen D'Polarno was popular among his noble peers but craved immortality. A mysterious artist offered him eternity by painting D'Polarno's portrait upon a magical canvas. But the artist didn't mention that the painting would strip D'Polarno of his love of life and natural charm. The marquis has discovered a reprieve from his now-dulled existence, however—once every season, when he shows the painting to an audience, it consumes their souls and refreshes his thrill for life. D'Polarno's artistic predations captured the attention of the Dark Powers, which drew his lands into the Mists. Now, Ghastria is a fertile island that, like its lord, lacks an essential vim except for once a season when vigor fleetingly returns.

G'HENNA

Darklord: Yagno Petrovna
Hallmarks: Corrupt theocracy, false deity

Born of a Barovian family, Yagno Petrovna went missing upon the slopes of Mount Ghakis as a youth. As a violent storm rose, he took shelter in a mysterious ruin and was found wandering the hills weeks later, babbling about an amber idol and the god he'd discovered, Zhakata the Provider and the Devourer. His family sought to help him, but when they discovered Yagno secretly sacrificing people to his fictitious god, they chased him into the Mists. When Yagno emerged, the domain of G'henna sprawled before him.

Life is hard in G'henna, a rocky land home to fierce, starving animals. The domain's people worship the bestial god Zhakata and regularly travel to the cathedral-city of Zhukar. There, they offer their crops in sacrifice and hear Zhakata's will through the words of revered prophet Yagno Petrovna.

INVIDIA

Darklord: Gabrielle Aderre
Hallmarks: Bad parents, possessed children

Gabrielle Aderre is convinced that her son, Malocchio, is destined for greatness. From her estate outside the village of Karina, she employs an endless string of servants to provide Malocchio the best possible upbringing. Inevitably, though, every servant flees or vanishes, either as a result of Gabrielle's unreasonable expectations or the deadly tricks and accidents that frequently occur around the child. Gabrielle isn't content to leave her son's grand destiny to chance, though. Using her precious bone spirit board, she calls upon supernatural forces to guide and protect her son. Spirits, angels, fiends, and worse answer her summons, but as long as they chart Malocchio's path to glory, Gabrielle eagerly accepts their gifts.

ROBIN OLAUSSON

KEENING

Darklord: Tristessa
Hallmarks: Banshee, silent village

The forbidding land of Keening is dominated by Mount Lament, at whose base lies the village of Anwrtyn, where all the residents are deaf. This is no accident, for the locals purposefully deafen themselves so they won't hear the shrieking of the banshee Tristessa, a mournful spirit who roams Mount Lament and whose wail carries through the night. In life, Tristessa dwelled under Mount Arak in Tepest (detailed earlier in this chapter), but she was exiled for crimes against her people. In death, she endlessly seeks to be reunited with the family slain by her misdeeds.

KLORR

Darklord: Klorr
Hallmarks: Impending doom, surreal environment

Klorr is the end of worlds. Here, shattered islands drift through a misty netherworld, caught in a swirling spiral that ends at the unignorable, burning eye called Klorr. Thirteen stars orbit this sun-like sphere, one winking out every hour. Each time one of the stars dies, one of the domain's ruined islands is drawn into Klorr and consumed by flames. With it, each other island wrenches ahead, then halts, one hour closer to the same doom.

Those who dwell upon the crumbling land masses trapped in the domain constantly count the hours until their end. Few know how they came to Klorr or when new islands are added to the cycle, only that the Mists closed in and doomed them. Amid the realm's surreal skies float the ruins of lost and failed domains—among them, a tower like a blackened rose and a city of skulls—as well as timeless echoes of domains that yet exist. Those cast away amid this orderly apocalypse grow ever more desperate to defy the doomsday clock and the will of a hidden Darklord, the obsessed clockmaker named Klorr.

MARKOVIA

Darklord: Dr. Frantisek Markov
Hallmarks: Depraved science, sapient animals

Dr. Frantisek Markov is a genius—but less so than yesterday. His Markov Formula grants him unparalleled intellect, but it insidiously steals more than it gives, making him increasingly dull-witted and bestial in form. Despairing, the doctor fled to a tropical island he dubbed Markovia, where he tests new versions of his formula on the local fauna in hopes of recovering his waning genius. As a result of these tests, animals across Markovia now possess sapience and have been deluded into believing Markov is their god.

THE NIGHTMARE LANDS

Darklord: The Nightmare Court
Hallmarks: Nightmares, reoccurring dreams

Any who sleep might close their eyes and become forever trapped in the Nightmare Lands, a phantasmagoric realm whose features shift endlessly. Those who visit and escape speak of malicious wildernesses; the empty city called Nod; and uncountable drifting spheres, each containing a stranger's unending nightmare. Insidious entities called the Nightmare Court rule the domain. None know how many members compose the court, but they include the tragically graceful Ghost Dancer, the tomb-bound Hypnos, the witch Mullonga, the trickster Morpheus, and the embodiment of terror known as the Nightmare Man. These beings are artisans of nightmares, visiting terrors upon any whose sleeping minds brush against the domain.

The Nightmare Court's members share one commonality: all are the living nightmares of Caroline Dinwiddy, a potent psychic who repressed memories of her own heartless deeds. These memories torment her sleeping mind, creating the Nightmare Court. Deep within the City of Nod, inside a warped reimagining of the clinic where she once worked, Dinwiddy sleeps without waking, refusing to face the terrors her dreams unleash upon innocents across the multiverse.

NIRANJAN

Darklord: Sarthak
Hallmarks: Asceticism, brainwashing, shadows

An island chain that once belonged to the domain of Kalakeri, the Ashram of Niranjan was a vibrant *vihara*, or monastery, for ascetic scholars who practiced Ramsana, a way of life whose central tenet advises nonattachment to the material world. Now only a small, reclusive group of these scholars remains, led by the elderly *sadhu* (holy figure) Niranjan. In truth, Niranjan is Sarthak, a wicked bronze dragon who send agents into the Mists bearing his philosophical writings. These works promise escape and peace to any who adopt their teachings and search the Mists for their source. Anyone who comes to the ashram must divest themselves of worldly goods, which are added to Sarthak's hidden hoard. The false sadhu then helps his victim enter a blissful trance that causes their soul to slip away from their body over the course of days. Sarthak consumes this soul and replaces it with a shadow, leaving the victim's body under his control.

NOVA VAASA

Darklord: Myar Hiregaard
Hallmarks: Nomadic riders, transformation

An unparalleled warrior, Myar Hiregaard united the nomadic tribes of the vast plains of Nova Vaasa. But, while respected as a soldier, Myar made a poor peacetime leader. When brutal games could no longer keep her interest, she incited hostilities between two of her vassal tribes, then led her own forces to crush them. Subtly, she did this again and again. After Myar's greatest massacre, the Mists enfolded all of Nova Vaasa, splitting Myar's personality in two when they did. Now she rules her people with strict fairness, but when her bloodlust is piqued, she transforms into the raging knight called Malkan and sows discord across the plains.

ODAIRE

Darklord: Maligno
Hallmarks: Evil toys, village of children

The toymaker Guiseppe had his wish for a family granted when his creation, the marionette Figlio, came to life. A proud father, the toymaker presented his son to all the other people of his village, Odaire. The local children loved Figlio, but their parents were skeptical, saying the marionette was nothing but a toy. Over time, this doubt enraged Figlio, and the marionette convinced Guiseppe to craft siblings for him. Then, when the time was right, Guiseppe's creations did away with all the adults in Odaire. Claimed by the Mists, Odaire is a village populated only by children and ruled by the carrionette Figlio, who now calls himself Maligno. (See chapter 5 for details on carrionettes.)

THE RIDER'S BRIDGE

Darklord: The Headless Rider
Hallmarks: Haunted bridge, murderous legend

Nearly every domain knows some version of the apparition called the Headless Rider. It appears as a mercenary in dark armor in Mordent, a ghostly cataphract in Har'Akir, and a mutated centaur in Lamordia, but in each incarnation certain details remain true: the rider is missing its head, it appears upon a prominent bridge, and it decapitates victims as it endlessly searches for its own head. Should someone escape an encounter with the Headless Rider, they might find a different domain on the opposite side of the spirit's bridge. (See the dullahan in chapter 5 for more details on headless riders.)

RISIBILOS

Darklord: Doerdon
Hallmarks: Misdirection, ventriloquism

The Risibilos is a small music hall, similar to those found in any decent-sized city. Its lord, Doerdon, was once a king—one so thoroughly humorless that he forbade his subjects the privilege of laughter,

THE GHOST DANCER VISITS NIGHTMARES UPON A SLEEPING VICTIM.

PIETRA VAN RIESE

he gave them what they craved. By the play's end, Lemont had joined the play and viscerally murdered every member of the cast while the crowd roared their approval. As the show ended, the playhouse broke from Dementlieu, and Scaena was formed. Comprising a single playhouse, the domain can create any reality Lemont desires upon its stage. The Darklord's immersive performances are somewhat predictable, though, as they always end in slaughter.

Sea of Sorrows

Darklord: Pietra van Riese
Hallmarks: Island domains, nautical horror

The murderous pirate Pietra van Riese, captain of the *Relentless*, had an unsavory reputation for attaching her captives to ropes and dragging them through the water until they drowned. She never removed the detritus of her victims, even though some returned to life as zombies. The *Relentless* was ultimately sunk by rival captains, but death couldn't keep Pietra. She awoke in the Sea of Sorrows, water in her lungs and sea creatures making their homes in her flesh. Her crew stirred with her, now fish-eaten corpses. When Pietra sought to speak with them, her voice emerged from their mouths.

The *Relentless* sails a domain that can overlap any body of water in any other domain. Some domains border the Sea of Sorrows, while others have their own names for these mysterious waters. Those who venture into the Mists by boat might find themselves amid an endless, debris- and sargassum-choked expanse of eerie beasts and shifting islands, including the following:

Blaustein. This island-fortress domain was once ruled by the notorious Bluebeard, but his spectral wives overthrew him and now endlessly torment him.

Dominia. The asylum of the vampire Dr. Daclaud Heinfroth rises upon this stormy island. The asylum's patients are all dramatically different versions of Heinfroth inspired by who he was at various points during his lengthy life.

Isle of the Ravens. A storm of ravens surrounds this forested islet. Hidden amid the feathered gale, an impossibly tall tower stretches into the sky. This is the home of the Lady of Ravens, and any who offend her join her ebon-winged flock.

The Lighthouse. Otherworldly light shines from atop this twisted spur of bizarre fossils. Anyone who enters finds that the light doesn't call out to the sea, but down to what lurks in the pit hidden within.

Vigilant's Bluff. An undead paladin holds vigil atop this drowned island. Weary travelers can find refuge here if they're respectful of the paladin's faith. The bones of those who were not litter the surrounding coral.

upon pain of death. He is now cursed to entertain others, a task he is utterly unqualified for.

Fortunately, the Mists delivered him a partner, a ventriloquist's dummy carved in the likeness of Strahd von Zarovich. The eerie dummy has a mind of its own, insisting that it is the real Strahd and that the creature currently sitting upon the throne of Castle Ravenloft is a mere impostor. It rages at the audience and makes audacious promises to any who will help it regain its station. This is hilarious to anyone with the slightest inkling of who Strahd is, and their peals of laughter are agony to Doerdon's ears.

Scaena

Darklord: Lemont Sediam Juste
Hallmarks: Reality-manipulating theater

Lemont Sediam Juste fancied himself a serious playwright, and he achieved popular, if not critical, acclaim throughout Dementlieu for his works of grisly horror. But he craved respectability, and with his new play *Apparitions*, Lemont believed he would find it. The night of the premiere, when the audience signaled their boredom, the playwright was crestfallen. His supporters wanted blood, so

THE SHADOWLANDS

Darklord: Ebonbane
Hallmarks: Falls from grace, heroic sacrifice

Within this forested land of peasants and heroes dwells an order of questing knights known as the Circle. These knights seek to vanquish evil, following the example of their founder, the paladin Kateri Shadowborn. Even long generations after Kateri's death, members of the Shadowborn family still number among the Circle, their heroics known across the Shadowlands and in other domains. Yet despite their victories, the foes and failures of these knights are ever drawn back to the Shadowlands, filling it with vengeful souls and monsters. These include villains such as the necromancer Morgoroth; the fallen paladin Elena Faith-hold; and Ebonbane, Kateri Shadowborn's accursed sword.

SOURAGNE

Darklord: Anton Misroi
Hallmarks: Imprisonment, swamp magic

In society, Anton Misroi presented himself as an upstanding gentleman. But within the walls of the prison over which he was warden, he was a sadist who believed righteousness was on his side. When his torturous punishments finally drove the prison's inmates to rise up, the bloody riot that ensued drew the attentions of the Dark Powers. During the uprising, Misroi was drowned in the swamps surrounding the prison. But he rose again soon after, an undead warden in search of inmates.

Beyond Misroi's prison, alligator-filled swamps cover the domain of Souragne right up to the sinking settlement of Port d'Elhour and Marais d'Tarascon, a village where above-ground crypts outnumber the residences of the living.

STAUNTON BLUFFS

Darklord: Teresa Bleysmith
Hallmarks: Endless warfare, repeating history

Eerily faceless mercenary regiments sweep the countryside of Staunton Bluffs. Burning villages and killing helpless residents, they push ever eastward toward Castle Stonecrest, hereditary home of the Bleysmith family. Teresa Bleysmith, spurred by jealousy of her brother, Torrence, gave her family's foes the intelligence they needed to raid Staunton Bluffs. The attack was never supposed to go so far, but the duplicitous mercenaries stormed through the countryside to take Castle Stonecrest within a day. Teresa survived the attack, but when she surveyed the damage done and found her family dead by her own designs, she threw herself from the bluffs. Now she haunts her own domain, where she repeatedly relives the day of her betrayal.

TOVAG

Darklord: Kas the Bloody Handed
Hallmarks: Undead military dictatorship

Notorious across the planes, the vampire Kas was once the champion of the lich Vecna. Wielding the artifact that bears his name, he betrayed his master, and the resulting battle supposedly destroyed them both. In truth, Vecna escaped and grew in power over ages and across worlds. Kas, though, was claimed by the Mists, and in his wasteland domain of Tovag, he believes his war with Vecna rages on. Patrols of prisoner-soldiers under undead commanders scour the land, dragooning strangers to serve in Kas's armies and to manufacture bizarre war machines. When Kas deems the time right, he sends his forces into the Mists, believing that Vecna's realm lies just beyond. Invariably, those troops never return, leaving the vampire to rage, rebuild his forces, and continue his search for the *Sword of Kas* (detailed in the *Dungeon Master's Guide*), which he considers his key to victory.

VHAGE AGENCY

Darklord: Flimira Vhage
Hallmarks: Detective work, memory loss

Everything inside the office of the Vhage Agency appears as a monotone gray. Anyone who passes the frosted glass door that leads into this single-room domain is expected by Flimira "Flintlock" Vhage, the detective agency's owner. From this hub for occult detective adventures (see chapter 2), Vhage collects mysterious correspondence relating to mysteries all across the Domains of Dread. She enlists agents to investigate these cases, and then report back to her. However, she never reveals her own past as a detective turned criminal, her involvement in every case her agency investigates, or that the Vhage Agency exists entirely within her mind.

ZHERISIA

Darklord: Sodo
Hallmarks: Serial murderers, urban decay

Each day, the city of Paridon in Zherisia erupts in riots over food scarcity, taxation, and citizens who go missing by the dozens every night. At least one murderer stalks Paridon: the ancient doppelganger Sodo, who has impersonated so many people that it now finds it impossible to hold a form for more than a few days at a time. As Sodo's flesh runs like hot wax, it staves off dissolution by consuming the organs of humanoids. Paridon's streets serve as the doppelganger's hunting ground, and those who enter the sewers risk attracting the notice of countless carrion stalkers (see chapter 5) and their monstrous Hive Queen.

Travelers in the Mists

Adventures in the Domains of Dread often indulge in a single domain's distinctly frightful themes. But if you plan to run whole campaigns set in the Land of the Mists, creating narratives that span domains can prove challenging if every realm is a world unto itself. Individuals who willfully brave the Mists to travel between domains are especially useful in your broader horror stories.

While it's true that most residents of the Domains of Dread never leave their home domains and wisely don't fixate on what lies beyond the Mists, some daring souls do. Many such inquisitive individuals simply vanish, the Mists delivering them to deadly domains from which they never return. But others manage to band together, learning the ways of the Mists, how to travel through them, and how to survive their dangers. Those who travel between domains might have the Mist Walker Dark Gift (see chapter 1) or know how to employ Mist talismans (detailed at the start of this chapter). Such travelers can provide the following services adventurers might find useful:

- Evidence of other domains
- News, rumors, and requests for help
- Information on Mist talismans
- Guidance or traveling companions

The characters in your adventures should feel special if they travel the Mists, as few have the courage to do so. When characters encounter travelers from other domains, those individuals should likewise be remarkable or have a desperate reason to have braved the Mists. Learning about such wanderers can drive the characters from a single adventure into a larger campaign that explores other domains.

The following sections present groups and individuals who routinely travel the Mists. The Strangers in the Mists table also suggests the kinds of people characters might encounter amid the Mists.

Strangers in the Mists

d6	Encounter
1	Someone from another world who's just been drawn into a domain by the Mists
2	Someone fleeing the Darklord of another domain
3	A raven carrying a message from the Keepers of the Feather
4	Curious members of the Keepers of the Feather led by a **wereraven** (see chapter 5) in disguise
5	A band of Vistani
6	A spirit that cries out before being yanked back into the Mists, leaving behind a Mist talisman

Keepers of the Feather

When asked about the origins of their society, the members of the Keepers of the Feather speak of their traditions originating long ago and beyond the Mists. This is true, but most who repeat that story are only trying to layer a mystical facade over their dilettante spiritualism.

Only the group's highest-ranking members know that the Keepers of the Feather began in Barovia as a small sect of wereravens (see chapter 5) dedicated to opposing the evils of Strahd von Zarovich. Though their numbers were not enough to oppose the Darklord directly, they sought useful lore and aided brave souls from the shadows, manipulating fortune to confound some of Strahd's more diabolical plots. Over generations, the wereravens' hidden resistance to Strahd continued in Barovia, but some among them learned of other lands suffering beyond the Mists. Unwilling to let the innocents of those lands fend for themselves, some of the Keepers of the Feather ventured forth, hoping to share their wisdom and their subtle resistance to evil with those who needed it most.

However, the Mists find a way to twist even the best of intentions. In the cities of urbane domains like Borca, Darkon, and Dementlieu, the mystical writings and talismans the wereravens carried from Barovia came to the attention of the bored elite. Fascinated, these socialites became obsessed with the occult, seeking out esoteric works, hiring doubtful fortune-tellers, and hosting parlor séances. In most cases, the results were passing fads. In some, they were catastrophic—the unprepared successfully

---

Keeper Characters

Characters playing members of the Keepers of the Feather have access to contacts with interest in spiritualism and the occult, including hapless dilettantes, reclusive scholars, correspondents from other domains, and hucksters. At any time, members of the organization might call upon their contacts to uncover some esoteric secret, engage in a supernatural investigation, or even explore another domain.

When players create Keeper of the Feather characters, ask them the following questions.

What sparked your interest in the occult? Did you encounter a mysterious being that you want to understand? Is membership a family tradition? Are you trying to contact someone beyond the grave? Do you seek some other knowledge?

What esoteric knowledge most interests you? Are you curious about archeology, astrology, divination, cryptozoology, electricity, or spiritualism? How has this gotten you into trouble?

Who aids your investigations? Is another Keeper your mentor? Do you and other Keepers meet regularly? Do you correspond with a Keeper in another domain? Did this person give you your Mark of the Raven talisman?

summoned fiends and angry spirits into their salons. But a few earnest amateur spiritualists genuinely sought to learn more about the secrets beyond their homes, their lives, and the Mists. In these would-be occultists, the wereravens saw potential.

KEEPER SOCIETIES

Beyond Barovia, where the eldest wereraven members of the Keepers of the Feather keep a low profile, Keepers organize into small social clubs with shared interests in occultism. Some members are actual invested scholars, while others are simply bored rich folk. But all have a strong interest in séances, fortune-telling, secrets of the afterlife, sightings of mysterious creatures, metaphysical theories, and tales of the macabre. Among their misinterpretations and outright flimflam—like round planet theory and dikesha dice—Keepers also possess hints of truth and the tools wereravens have long used to combat evil. Among these are spirit boards (detailed in chapter 4), tarokka decks, Mist talismans, and piecemeal occult writings from various domains. Some among the Keepers don't know the true power of these tools, but this doesn't dull their enthusiasm.

Knowing the threats that Darklords and other evils pose, wereravens of the Keepers typically don't reveal themselves to those not of their kind. Rather, they infiltrate Keeper societies as reclusive members, traveling experts, or foreign scholars. Some Keepers also tell of sightings or visitations involving giant raven-like beings that appear, speak some prophecy or deliver some message, then vanish, often presaging either wonder or disaster. The wereravens take little issue with these exaggerated tales from those who've witnessed their hybrid forms, and they willingly play into the tales of the Keepers if it means spurring them to action.

The Keepers of the Feather are a loose organization, incorporating members who operate alone or in small groups, as well as elite social clubs or secretive societies. In all cases, Keepers identify each other by the Mark of the Raven, a sunburst emblem worn as a pin or amulet. Drawn from esoteric writings, this mark is a recreation of the *Holy Symbol of Ravenkind*, a storied religious artifact from Barovia. Though these reproductions carry no magical properties and most non-wereraven Keepers don't know the symbol's origin, many foul forces instinctively recognize the symbol as an emblem of good.

KEEPER ROOKERIES

Keeper cells strive to correspond and share discoveries between communities and domains. To facilitate this, the wereravens have taught some Keepers how to raise messenger ravens capable of delivering letters through the Mists. Most non-Keepers who

HOLY SYMBOL
OF RAVENKIND

learn of this consider it a trick, or fear what it means to receive messages from beyond the Mists, encouraging the Keepers to offer this rare service only to group members and their allies. Keeper ravens as a means of correspondence is detailed in "Life in the Domains of Dread" earlier in this chapter.

KEEPER ADVENTURES

The Keeper Adventures table offers ideas for strange events that can touch off stories involving the Keepers of the Feather.

KEEPER ADVENTURES

d6	Adventure Hook
1	Keepers invite the characters to a social gathering where fortunes are told and attendees sample rare imported mumia—powdered mummy.
2	A Keeper delivers a letter to the characters that arrived by raven. The message has no sender.
3	Orphir Brindletop, a Kalakeri gnome occultist, is surprised to meet one of the characters, as he received a message for them in a séance long ago.
4	The characters are invited to help a Keeper stake out a graveyard in hopes of spotting a legendary creature said to dwell there.
5	The party is hired to collect a parcel from the Blue Water Inn in the Barovian town of Vallaki, which is secretly run by wereravens. They must not open the package and must get it out of Barovia swiftly.
6	A character glimpses a raven-like figure. When they investigate, they find only the mysterious talisman that it left behind.

VISTANI

Known throughout the Land of the Mists, Vistani (singular: Vistana) are a people with a unique understanding of the Domains of Dread and the hidden paths between them. Following itinerant traditions, many Vistani travel between domains, learning much of hidden lands, the many faces of evil, and the strange wonders of the Mists. A people unto themselves, Vistani refuse to be captives of a single domain, the Mists, or any terror.

VISTANI CULTURE

Unlike the denizens of individual domains, Vistani are inhabitants of the Land of the Mist as a whole. Although they trace their origins to the same world as Barovia, many Vistani look toward the future, learning from their traditions and from one another to better face whatever lies ahead.

Vistani bands consist primarily of one or more extended human families who can trace their heritage back to age-old Vistani clans. Over generations of exploring the Mists, though, individuals of other ancestries have been accepted into some clans and now are full-fledged members of Vistani culture (see the "Vistani Characters" sidebar for details).

As they travel, members of a Vistani band walk, ride on horseback, and drive ledge wagons, stopping at night to set up camp. Vistani bands occasionally camp near welcoming communities to trade and resupply, but rarely stay more than a week—though this can be complicated if a Darklord closes a domain's borders. Most bands make their living primarily through craftwork (especially delicate silver-smithing), horse rearing, and trading wares carried between domains.

Meetings between Vistani bands are opportunities to trade, catch up with friends, and share both news and warnings of dangers ahead or behind.

VISTANI MAGIC AND THE MISTS

Vistani pass their varied teachings through their families as stories and songs, detailing lessons learned from generations of travelers, warnings specific to visited domains, and traditional magic. Spellcasters aren't uncommon among Vistani bands, with many favoring divination magic for the practical help it provides in avoiding danger. Spellcasters often incorporate their people's traditional divination tools into their spellcasting, including the fortune-telling cards called tarokka decks.

With their experience navigating the Mists, many Vistani understand how to employ Mist talismans (detailed at the start of this chapter) to reach specific domains, or possess the Mist Walker Dark Gift (see chapter 1), allowing them to make their way between domains. Vistani don't enter the Mists lightly, though, knowing that each such passage holds

VISTANI WAYFARERS EMERGE FROM THE MISTS INTO A NEW LAND.

inherent danger. Caravan leaders ensure that every family member is accounted for before moving on, ensuring no one gets lost in the Mists.

VISTANI KNOWLEDGE

Vistani travelers have a holistic perspective on the Domains of Dread and know the following secrets:

- The Mists are more than weather and are manipulated by forces that seem fickle and often cruel.
- The Mists can carry travelers between lands and can be coerced but never controlled.
- Evil is real and embodied by individuals of terrible power.
- Time, reality, and memory don't always move in reliable ways, particularly between domains.
- One might glimpse their fortune, but such things endlessly shift. Every soul makes their own fate.

VIEWS OF VISTANI

Their travels across domains bring many Vistani into contact with a wide range of people. As the only outsiders that some remote communities see in the course of a year, the news and goods Vistani bring ensures a genuine welcome and renewal of long-standing trade relationships. Some more dismal communities view Vistani with suspicion, though, being wary of anyone who emerges from the Mists. But even these communities often find the lure of news and trade too tempting to forgo entirely.

Most people who live among the Domains of Dread know the following things about Vistani:

- They don't fear the Mists and can travel safely through the Mists to other lands.
- They carry goods and stories from far-off lands.
- They're protective of their families, which includes members of other caravans.
- Most don't discuss their culture or beliefs with outsiders.
- Their travel routes are unpredictable, and a community might go years without seeing a Vistani caravan.

TRAVELING WITH VISTANI

Members of Vistani bands understand the disorienting, dangerous nature of the Mists better than anyone. Vistani caravans sometimes take pity on those who ask them for help, especially strangers from unfamiliar lands hopelessly searching for home, allowing such wayfarers to travel with them as far as the next settlement. In rare cases, a clan might even adopt a gracious, helpful traveler.

Characters who befriend or do right by members of a Vistani band might be allowed to take shelter or travel with a caravan for a time. But Vistani

---

VISTANI CHARACTERS

Being a Vistana makes a character part of a larger family and cultural tradition. Most Vistani are human, but many bands incorporate other peoples, particularly halflings, wood elves, orcs, and tieflings. Vistani have a range of skin, eye, and hair colors. When players create Vistani characters, consider asking them the following questions.

Did you leave your clan's caravan? If so, are you seeking to right a wrong done to them, or to spare them from harm? If not, how do you balance your adventures with your family's travels? Are there ways you and your family keep tabs on one another?

How much do you know about navigating the Mists? Do you know how to travel between domains? Do you use divination magic to guide your fate? Or do you know little about it, having left navigation to others?

How do you feel about being away from your people? Do you enjoy socializing with a variety of people? Did you seek a settled life? Do you want to finish your tasks quickly and return to your family?

---

travelers quickly share tales of danger and of those who've wronged them with other caravans, and those who slight one Vistana often meet others who share a grudge against them.

FAMED VISTANI

Some Vistani are legends among their people, and their bands might be encountered anywhere. The individuals noted here number among the most famous Vistani band leaders:

Hyskosa. A renowned poet and storyteller, Hyskosa leads a caravan that embraces the Mists and goes where they lead it. As a result, his clan is unmoored from time and reality, appearing in different ages, in strange versions and configurations of domains, and even on worlds beyond the Domains of Dread. His lyrical accounts of his travels are often viewed as prophecies.

Madame Eva. A controversial figure among Vistani, Madame Eva made a bargain with the vampire Count Strahd von Zarovich. As a result, the evils that lurk in Barovia avoid Vistani. However, Madame Eva and her followers occasionally ally with the infamous count, giving them a sinister reputation. Madame Eva and her unique band of Vistani are detailed in the adventure *Curse of Strahd*.

Mother Luba. The halfling Mother Luba is known for putting unquiet spirits to rest and transporting wayward souls through the Mists to their rightful homes. Those wicked spirits beyond her aid she trapped within her tarokka deck, which became known as *Luba's Tarokka of Souls* (detailed in *Tasha's Cauldron of Everything*).

OTHER GROUPS

Representatives of various organizations have their own reasons for exploring the Mists and might be encountered in multiple domains.

CHURCH OF EZRA

Pious souls in various domains pray to Ezra, an aloof god who embodies the Mists (as detailed at the start of this chapter). With no domain-spanning organization, the church serves largely as a formalization of local superstitions, whether in modest rural temples or urban cathedrals. When many common folk give voice to their hopes or seek to ward off evil, it's to Ezra they pray.

THE CIRCLE

The heroic knights of this order quest from the Shadowlands (detailed in "Other Domains of Dread") in search of evil to vanquish. Bold and proud, many members of the Circle inadvertently race toward dramatic tragedies. The more successful knights venture back to the Shadowlands with evidence of their victories, often carrying evil back to their homeland. The knights of the Circle regularly provide bold—and ill-fated—assistance to other would-be heroes.

THE KARGAT AND THE KARGATANE

Darkon's secret police, the Kargat, is composed of vampires and others supernaturally disposed toward intrigue. Since Azalin's disappearance (see "Darkon" earlier in this chapter), the Kargat enforces the will of fractious, power-hungry leaders. The organization is in turn served by the Kargatane, a cultish lower echelon of mortals drawn to service with promises of wealth and supernatural power. Long-serving members of the Kargatane earn transformation into dhampirs (see chapter 1), the first step toward becoming a member of the Kargat and attaining immortality. Agents of both groups wander Darkon and beyond, creating shadowy conspiracies to gain magical power and control by any means possible.

ORDER OF THE GUARDIANS

This network of scholars and monastic caretakers hunts down and puts an end to dangerous supernatural objects, cursed items, and stranger anomalies. In the case of dangers they can't destroy, the Guardians hope to prevent calamities by containing them within hidden, heavily warded, vault-like monasteries. Over generations, these sites have become repositories of incredible secrets and great evil that members of the order struggle to contain. Guardian monasteries are hidden in multiple domains, with the best known being Watchers' Stronghold in Darkon. Power-hungry groups and unscrupulous lore seekers, such as the Kargat and the priests of Osybus, often target these ancient vaults, seeking powers few can hope to control. The Guardians might share goals with characters trying to prevent supernatural dangers, but they just as easily could consider characters threats themselves.

PRIESTS OF OSYBUS

These cultists channel the might of the Dark Powers and steal souls to gain the ability to transcend death. With their foul immortality, they work to unshackle the first Darklord, Strahd von Zarovich, from the Domains of Dread. This inspires them to learn all they can about the nature of the Mists and its deepest mysteries. The priests spread their teachings, forming shadowy cults that draw adventurers into their schemes. These villains are further detailed in chapter 5.

ULMIST INQUISITION

The three branches of the Ulmist Inquisition trace their origins to Malitain, a mysterious, cult-infested city from the same world as Barovia. These inquisitors employ varied psionic powers to stamp out evil, but their zeal and willingness to peer into others' minds mean that many fear them just as much as the villains they oppose. Cells of the Ulmist Inquisition might be found within any domain and often ally with the Church of Ezra while opposing the priests of Osybus. Ulmist inquisitors might ally with characters against evil, but they are just as likely to see corruption within adventurers' souls. These inquisitors are further detailed in chapter 5.

MIST WANDERERS

The individuals in this section travel the Mists, carrying with them rumors and mysteries that can lead characters from one domain to the next. Any of these travelers might use Mist talismans or other methods to aid characters in undertaking their own journeys.

ALANIK RAY AND ARTHUR SEDGWICK

Known as the Great Detective, Alanik Ray possesses an unrivaled deductive mind. The century-old elf has a knack for seeing through falsehoods, a talent aided by decades of experience and science-driven deductive methods.

As a young detective in Darkon, Alanik revealed his father's criminal empire and oversaw its destruction. His success launched his career as a private detective, embroiling him in the intrigues of Martira Bay's nobility. During this time, he met the young physician Arthur Sedgwick, who became his partner and saved Alanik's life countless times. The pair's adventures—including several deadly encounters with the Kargat—eventually led them to relocate to Port-a-Lucine in Dementlieu. A mystery involving a shape-shifting serial killer resulted in a fall from a roof that paralyzed Alanik's legs. Within the following month, the pair created a custom wheelchair for Alanik, and they married.

Today, Alanik Ray and Arthur Sedgwick investigate mysteries wherever need and novelty take them. Arthur lends his practicality and martial skill to Alanik's dazzling intellect during the pair's exploits. Sedgwick also chronicles their adventures and has published two volumes to date: *The Life of Alanik Ray* and *The Casebook of Alanik Ray*.

ALANIK RAY'S TRAITS
Ideal. "Logic is a guide but also an illusion. Order and reason don't supersede what is right."

Bond. "I have the perspective to see depravities others can't. I use my insight to reveal wickedness and make the world a better place."

Flaw. "Most people are dangerous, manipulative liars and not to be trusted."

ARTHUR SEDGWICK'S TRAITS
Ideal. "The sicknesses of the world are vast, but I can help others find the medicine they need."

Bond. "I can't withhold care, no matter how ill a soul might be."

Flaw. "I focus so much on others that I often don't see what's afflicting me."

ADVENTURES WITH ALANIK AND ARTHUR
Alanik Ray is an exceptional investigator with an uncanny ability to notice detail and make deductive leaps. Despite his experience with the paranormal, he relies on his husband Arthur to keep him out of true supernatural peril. Still, the detectives manage to find trouble wherever they go. Use the statistics of **spies** to approximate both Alanik Ray and Arthur Sedgwick. Consider the following plots when featuring the detectives in your adventures:

- Alanik is confounded by a murderer preying on a family. Arthur discovers that these murders repeat in a centuries-long cycle and seeks detectives with greater supernatural experience.
- Alanik exposes a community's constabulary, whose members accuse individuals of crimes before the offenses occur. He seeks help in dismantling the dangerous system.
- A serial killer called the Midnight Slasher leaves behind gory messages such as, "I live in your city" and "I lurk in your nightmares." When the characters meet Alanik, he reveals that these messages appear at crime scenes in multiple communities, on the same nights.

THE CALLER
Folktales of the Caller carry a cold, cruel authenticity, hinting of a vicious mythos too specific to be fiction. The Caller numbers among the most notorious supernatural figures in the Land of the Mists, and where it walks, doom inevitably follows.

The Caller appears as a comely individual of any gender, which takes disarming forms to gain the trust of a specific individual. Whether as a friend, paramour, mentor, or rival, the Caller isolates its target, leading the victim to depend on it emotionally or materially. Over time, the Caller coerces or outright forces its victim to acts of deepening selfishness and immorality. Then when the target reaches a peak of depravity or despair, the Caller abandons its mark, leaving them to face the consequences. The suffering the Caller causes is never isolated, triggering a tragic chain of events that can throw a family, a community, or a whole domain into anguish. Those investigating the history of a calamity might discover generations-spanning cycles of the Caller's manipulations. These schemes shape a mysterious agenda—one gradually molding the Land of the Mists to a nefarious purpose.

THE CALLER'S TRAITS
The Caller's true agendas and disposition are unknowable to mortals. As the ultimate mimic, it can change its personality to reflect whatever most appeals to its current victim.

ADVENTURES WITH THE CALLER
The Caller uses statistics similar to a **succubus/incubus**, and no matter how many times it's defeated, it always returns. Use the Caller to create adventures involving secret histories, domain-spanning conspiracies, and truths hinting at the nature of the Dark Powers. Consider the following plots when featuring the Caller in an adventure:

- One of the characters' allies requests they check in on the ally's brother. This pious or artistic soul has been convinced by a charming peer (the Caller in disguise) to attend a retreat that is secretly a meeting of the priests of Osybus.
- An old friend reappears in a character's life. Likable and knowledgeable but shy, this friend assists the character without recompense. Eventually, the friend (actually the Caller) gets into trouble and needs the character to do them a number of increasingly unscrupulous favors.
- A powerful individual such as Firan Zal'honan (see below), Isolde (see "The Carnival" earlier in this chapter), or a domain's Darklord summons the party and requests they hunt down the Caller. This figure provides their agents with a device that allows the bearers to travel to whatever domain the Caller is currently in.

ERASMUS VAN RICHTEN

Kidnapped by criminals, transformed into a vampire, slain by his father: Erasmus van Richten's teenage years haven't been pleasant. They haven't been entirely terrible, either.

The ghostly son of Ingrid and Rudolph van Richten (detailed later in this section) follows his father, trying to aid him and ever wishing he could let his father know he's okay. But the interaction of Rudolph's curse and Erasmus's unique nature prevents the elder van Richten from perceiving his son's ghostly existence. Erasmus could have become a sorrowful bystander, but his unfaltering empathy and the circle of kind souls in van Richten's orbit have kept him engaged over the years.

Erasmus is a unique spirit. His behavior and rare appearances mark him as a thoughtful, art-loving teenager. He can't express himself as fully as he'd like, since he can appear for only a few minutes every day and can't speak. However, he can manipulate ectoplasm to paint colorful, floating symbols and images. When possible, he depicts information and conveys emotions or warnings. Erasmus's art is fleeting, though, vanishing in seconds. Sadly, his father cannot perceive him or any manifestation he creates.

While traveling with his father, Erasmus bonds with Rudolph's allies. Aromantic yet deeply affectionate, Erasmus delights in frequenting the rooms of those he cares about, leaving behind colorful greetings. He never pushes others to reveal his presence, though, since attempts to do so only cause Rudolph pain.

ERASMUS VAN RICHTEN'S TRAITS

Ideal. "I've been given a second chance, and I'll make sure it has a purpose."

Bond. "I lost my family, but I can embrace a new one. Anyone who needs me and means well is welcome."

Flaw. "I've been the source of so much trouble. I never want to be a bother."

ADVENTURES WITH ERASMUS VAN RICHTEN

Erasmus is a **ghost** and the heart of the van Richten family. Consider the following plots when featuring Erasmus in an adventure:

- Erasmus understands the unquiet dead. Through devices such as tarokka decks and spirit boards, he reveals the histories and intentions of spirits.
- An overzealous priest detects the undead presence hovering near Rudolph van Richten and threatens Rudolph, Erasmus, or both.
- A powerful spirit, such as Lord Godefroy of Mordent, kidnaps Erasmus to manipulate his father.

EZ D'AVENIR

Born Ezmerelda Radanavich but preferring the name Ez, this young wanderer first encountered monsters among her manipulative family, who posed as Vistani to prey upon travelers. Eventually, they kidnapped Erasmus van Richten and sold him to his death at the hands of the vampire Baron Metus. In the brief time she knew him, Ez befriended Erasmus and heard him speak lovingly of a different sort of family than the one she knew. When Erasmus's father, Rudolph van Richten, tracked her family down and delivered her mother to justice, Ez didn't stop him.

In the years that followed, Ez joined a Vistani band, adopted the name Ez d'Avenir, and traveled far but never found the belonging Erasmus described. Eventually she sought out someone she knew could tell her more: Rudolph van Richten. After a wary introduction, Ez met van Richten and studied with him for a time, learning all she could of hunting deadly creatures. Although her and Rudolph's personalities clashed, Ez was surprised to reconnect with Erasmus, now a ghost. She and the spirit renewed their friendship and ultimately discovered paths beyond Rudolph van Richten's obsession. Rather than let her relationship with the doctor turn sour, Ez departed Mordentshire to hunt evil and find a family on her own terms.

Since then, Ez has changed much, learning the ways of the Mists and replacing her leg with a splendid prosthetic after a werewolf attack. She hopes that her explorations and her old mentor's wisdom eventually allow her to create a place that feels safe enough to call home.

EZ D'AVENIR'S TRAITS

Ideal. "Evil that feeds on the innocent is the worst of all evils and must be destroyed."

Bond. "I've known little of family, but I hold those I care for close, and one day I'll consider them a family of my own."

Flaw. "I go where angels fear to tread."

ADVENTURES WITH EZ D'AVENIR

Use the statistics of an **assassin** to represent Ez, or you can use her stat block from *Curse of Strahd*. Consider the following plots when featuring Ez in an adventure:

- Ez discovers an incarnation of the tragic soul Tatyana (detailed in the "Barovia" domain). While investigating ways to keep her safe, she accidentally alerts Strahd's agents to her existence.
- From a cell in Il Aluk, Ez's mother Irena Radanavich manipulates a web of lies to bring her daughter back into the family.

FIRAN ZAL'HONAN

A mask of charm and congeniality conceals one of the most ingenious and utterly ruthless intellects to stalk through the Mists. A wandering scholar, Firan Zal'honan is quick to claim his descent from a noble pedigree. In another life, he claims, he could have ruled as a wizard-king. But his brilliance led him along a stranger path: seeking to escape the Mists into the "true realities" beyond. Firan keeps the basis for his strange theories secret, but his ambitions drive him to travel the domains; visit accursed sites; and investigate inscrutable prophecy cycles, temporal conjunctions, and an unknown figure he calls "the escapee."

For all his arrogance, Firan dreads the Mists and seeks assistance traversing them. His most noteworthy partner is the Vistani leader Madame Eva, who secretly allows him to barter strange secrets for her agents' guidance through the Mists.

Firan is an enigmatic and abrasive expert, but his knowledge of the domains and their secrets is without peer. His research causes him to regularly cross paths with other sinister scholars, such as the priests of Osybus, a group he's equally likely to aid or oppose as his investigations demand. Firan's eccentricities include loathing the domain of Darkon, an almost-personal hatred for Barovia's Count Strahd von Zarovich, and his earnest fear of the Mists—he claims that if he entered them unguided, he would never escape. However, those who prove useful to him can earn a valuable temporary ally.

FIRAN ZAL'HONAN'S TRAITS

Ideal. "Secrets are power. No foe can hide their mysteries from me."

Bond. "None of this is real. I will endure this test. I will reap my reward. I will have my revenge."

Flaw. "My genius is immortal and has been tested like no other."

ADVENTURES WITH FIRAN ZAL'HONAN

Firan Zal'honan is an arrogant, pragmatic, amoral genius. Furthering his schemes or adopting him as a patron can draw a party into conflict with the most prominent villains in the Domains of Dread. Use the statistics of a human **archmage** to represent Firan. He is accompanied by an **imp** named Skeever, who appears as a piebald raven. Consider the following plots when featuring Firan in an adventure:

- The characters happen upon Firan, who claims to be waiting for them. He offers insight into rare magic or their ongoing quests if they'll assist him in investigating an infamous ruin nearby.
- A thief stole Firan's prized amulet—a chain bearing a tiny gold dragon skull. Uncharacteristically agitated, he offers the characters any knowledge he possesses if they retrieve the amulet swiftly.

FIRAN ZAL'HONAN'S MYSTERIOUS RESEARCH LEADS HIM TO DISCOVER AN ACCURSED AMBER SARCOPHAGUS.

Jander Sunstar

Born on the world of Toril, the high elf Jander Sunstar was an adventurer tragically transformed into a vampire. After defeating his master, he wandered far, struggling against his vampiric urges and eventually falling in love with an adventurer named Anna, who claimed to be from another world. When Jander revealed his true nature, Anna's companions assisted her in fleeing him. In a rage, Jander slew all those he blamed for keeping him and Anna apart. In the aftermath of the slaughter, the Mists gathered around Jander, transporting him to Barovia. There, Jander met Strahd von Zarovich and lived in Castle Ravenloft for a time. When the elder vampire sought to make Jander his servant, Jander tried to slay the count, failed, and fled into the Mists.

In the centuries that followed, Jander wandered as a mysterious adventurer, secretly seeking a cure for vampirism. He's discovered multiple remedies, but none work for him. In recent decades, his attempt to save a fellow adventurer resulted in the birth of Savra Sunstar, a dhampir (see chapter 1) who Jander considers his daughter. Savra loathes him, though, and has devoted her life to hunting him and all vampires.

This estrangement pushed Jander to seek more radical methods of expunging his vampirism. Assisting in the experiments of a mysterious alchemist in Mordent, he became the first to test a prototype of the enigmatic Apparatus (see "Mordent" earlier in the chapter). But the machine malfunctioned; instead of purging his vampirism, it created myriad copies of him, scattered across the planes. All believe they're the real Jander, though an improbable number of them have already achieved semi-tragic ends. At least one Jander remains trapped in Ravenloft, forever seeking a peace he'll never deserve.

Jander Sunstar's Traits

Ideal. "Vampirism is a curse that must be eradicated—from myself most of all."

Bond. "I will suffer nobly, enduring my curse so I can bring about an end to history's greatest scourge."

Flaw. "My insights and pain carry more weight than those of younger, more naive beings."

Adventures with Jander Sunstar

Jander Sunstar is a **vampire** and one of Ravenloft's foremost experts on vampirism. He aids characters hunting vampires and recruits allies to protect him from others of his kind. Consider the following plots when featuring Jander Sunstar in an adventure:

- Jander needs assistance in destroying another vampire: one of his duplicates.
- Jander asks the characters to help him save a monster hunter who opposes an overly powerful foe. Within the villain's lair, the characters discover the hunter is Jander's daughter, Savra, who neither requests nor requires aid.

Larissa Snowmane

Captain Larissa Snowmane pilots the paddleboat *River Dancer* along the rivers and coasts of Ravenloft's domains, righting wrongs and ferrying those in need to new homes. Larissa is a legend, known for her icy-white hair, dancing skill, and mezzo-soprano signing voice. As she approaches her seventieth year, she remains one of the domains' most widely traveled explorers. When danger threatens her vessel and crew, Captain Snowmane reluctantly uses a magical performance known as the Dance of the Dead, a forbidden song and dance that keeps Undead creatures at bay but slays living beings who witness it, then reanimates them as zombies. Larissa avoids rival riverboat captain Nathan Timothy and his ship, *Virago*, as well as the swampy domain of Souragne, where she learned her deadly magic from grim forces that consider her debt unpaid.

Larissa Snowmane's Traits

Ideal. "Everyone needs help from time to time. I'll help those who have no one else."

Bond. "My ship, my crew, and those in my care are my home, and I'll risk my life to protect them."

Flaw. "I've seen terrors but have risen above them. I can triumph over any evil—except my past."

Adventures with Larissa Snowmane

Larissa Snowmane is a human **druid** with exceptional insight into navigating the waterways of the Mists. Her handsome, multilevel paddleboat *River Dancer* provides an exciting base of operations for wayfaring adventurers. Consider the following plots when featuring Larissa Snowmane in an adventure:

- *River Dancer* appears when the characters desperately need to escape a domain, but the Mists make their next stop even more dangerous.
- *River Dancer* pulls into port with only Captain Snowmane aboard. Larissa needs a crew, but she doesn't mention that her last crew died when she used the Dance of the Dead.

Rudolph van Richten

A scholar and monster hunter, Rudolph van Richten has traveled to dozens of domains, investigating reports of monstrous beings and documenting them in a series of published guides, the best known of which is *Van Richten's Guide to Vampires*.

In fairer days, Rudolph lived with his wife, Ingrid, and son, Erasmus, in their family home outside Rivalis in the domain of Darkon. Brash and recently established as a medical doctor, Rudolph ran afoul of the Radanaviches, a family using Vistani traditions as a cover for brigandage. When the doctor refused to treat one of the family's mortally ill members, the group's leader, Irena Radanavich, ordered her band to kidnap Rudolph's son and then sold the young man to the vampire Baron Metus. Rudolph pursued the Radanaviches, shattered their criminal operation, and brought Irena to justice, but not before suffering her curse: "Live you always among monsters, and see everyone you love die beneath their claws." In the weeks that followed, the curse took hold. Before Rudolph could track down and slay Baron Metus, the vampire murdered both Ingrid and Erasmus.

In the decades since, van Richten has hunted monsters and armed others with the knowledge they need to confront the dark. Though he's made many devoted allies, he keeps them at arm's length, fearing the threat of his curse. When not traveling, van Richten lives out of his herbalist's shop in Mordentshire in the domain of Mordent.

RUDOLPH VAN RICHTEN'S TRAITS

Ideal. "Evil cannot go unpunished."

Bond. "To protect those I love, I must keep them at a distance and hidden from my enemies."

Flaw. "I am cursed. I will never find peace."

ADVENTURES WITH RUDOLPH VAN RICHTEN

Van Richten readily provides mentorship to characters devoted to fighting the creatures of the night. To represent him, use the stat block for a **priest** from the *Monster Manual* or **Rictavio** from *Curse of Strahd*. Consider the following plots when featuring van Richten in an adventure:

- Long ago, van Richten slew a supernatural villain who terrorized a community, but now that evil has returned. The party must seek out the doctor, since only he knows the secret of defeating the creature—hopefully for good this time.
- One of van Richten's foes captures the doctor and uses his name to correspond with adventurers, luring those who would learn his secrets into a deadly trap.

THE WEATHERMAY-FOXGROVE TWINS

The daughters of the mayor of Mordentshire, Alice Weathermay, twins Gennifer and Laurie grew up as inseparable hellions. Just before their sixteenth birthday, the twins' uncle, renowned monster hunter George Weathermay, returned to Mordent with his fiancé, Natalia Vhorishkova. The twins realized that Natalia was manipulating their beloved uncle, eventually exposing her as a werewolf who was using George to pursue one of Mordent's other famous residents, Rudolph van Richten. After the twins saved van Richten and their uncle from the werewolf, both George and van Richten encouraged their investigative instincts, training them as monster hunters.

Ever since, Laurie and Gennifer have been relentless adventurers. Laurie, taking after her uncle, trained in martial techniques to combat the undead. She rarely travels without her companions Joan and Tirran, the grown pups of her uncle's foxhounds, and her uncle's magic sword, Gossamer.

Gennifer, working closely with van Richten, learned the medicine and traditions of numerous domains. She's conducted in-depth studies of lycanthropy to assist her and her sister in pursing Natalia Vhorishkova, who remains at large. Secretly, Gennifer fears she's infected with lycanthropy, and despite never exhibiting any signs of the curse, she takes medication of her own concoction to ward it off.

GENNIFER'S TRAITS

Ideal. "There's a solution for everything; I just have to be clever enough to see it."

Bond. "My family has endured so much, and now I have to hold my own."

Flaw. "I'll never be as strong as my relatives, so I'll have to be smarter."

LAURIE'S TRAITS

Ideal. "There's a solution for everything. I just have to take your chance when it arises."

Bond. "Deeds, not words, will maintain my family's respected place in society."

Flaw. "I'll never be as smart as my relatives, so I'll have to be stronger."

ADVENTURES WITH THE TWINS

Gennifer and Laurie are skilled and well-prepared adventurers who have the statistics of a **druid** and a **veteran**, respectively. Consider the following plots when featuring the twins in an adventure:

- The characters have gotten in over their heads, and the Weathermay-Foxgrove twins—pursuing the same quest—come to the rescue. Afterward, the sisters encourage the party to participate in a training expedition to an infamous locale.
- Gennifer has vanished. Laurie seeks aid, fearing that Natalia Vhorishkova kidnapped her. In truth, Gennifer's fear of turning into a lycanthrope has led her to head off on her own—and into greater danger.

DURING A SÉANCE, A SPIRIT MAKES ITSELF KNOWN TO THE
KEEPERS OF THE FEATHER.

CREATING YOUR OWN HORROR ADVENTURES is like crafting any other D&D adventure with one exception: your goal is to horrify your players in the most fun way possible. Frightening adventures benefit from an atmosphere of dread, conceived through a combination of terrifying narratives, dramatic presentation, and game elements encouraging fear. Drawing out the anxiety and anticipation of players requires deliberate consideration, though. The tools and techniques in this chapter provide ways to make sure your game is both spooky and safe in ways right for your specific group. A toolbox of horror-focused rules also provides options for what sort of grim adventures you might create. At the end of this chapter, a horror adventure puts these methods to use and leads characters on their first steps into the Domains of Dread.

PREPARING FOR HORROR

Before you run a horror game, consider the following steps to ensure the willingness and full engagement of your players. If a group gathers to play a fun, low-stakes adventure but is immediately thrust into unexpected horror, the game can feel like a trap. You should avoid this. Rather, set expectations with your players about what a horror-focused game means, and determine what topics and themes will encourage or discourage players' participation.

UNDERSTANDING HORROR

Your primary goal as a DM running a horror adventure is to facilitate a fun D&D experience. This book assumes you and your players enjoy the thrill and suspense of scary stories. The audience of a horror movie can enjoy the menace on screen because they know it can't harm them (and they have an idea of what to expect from the film's trailer). In the same way, your players count on you to make sure an adventure's terror doesn't target them personally or otherwise step beyond the game. Your goal is never to make players feel uncomfortable or threatened. As D&D adventures aren't scripted, unexpected elements can arise during play. If your whole group can agree to the terms outlined in this section, everyone should have an exciting, enjoyable experience.

SET EXPECTATIONS

Well before you assemble a group around a game table, pitch the adventures you're thinking about running to your prospective players. Note the types of conflicts that might arise, the tone, and major themes. Telling players what to expect prepares them as they imagine what sorts of characters they could create and launches conversations about content to be embraced and avoided. You don't need to reveal the major plot points or twists in your story, but share the kinds of monsters and general themes you're interested in using, other horror stories you're inspired by, and which genres of horror from chapter 2 interest you. Being transparent with your players allows them to decide if this is a game they want to play, which is best to know before play begins.

HORROR CONTENT SURVEY

Take advantage of the time before your first game session to learn about your players' thoughts related to horror adventures. To do this, create a brief list of questions focused on the following topics. After preparing this survey, distribute it to your players as an e-mail, physical handout, or otherwise before gathering to play. Keep the survey's results anonymous, but use them to guide what sort of adventures you'll create.

CONTENT AND THEMES QUESTIONS

Start your survey by listing common story and horror elements to determine your players' comfort with them. The following list is not exhaustive; customize your list to include elements you imagine could arise during adventures. End the list with a space where players can add other topics to avoid or that they're interested in. For each of these topics, ask whether it should be included or avoided:

- General phobias and common fears, such as clowns, needles, or spiders
- Descriptions of gore or visceral violence
- Romantic in-character dialogue
- Themes of mental and physical health involving the body and the mind
- Real-world religion and politics, or analogs of them
- Topics related to real-world social or cultural injustices and discrimination
- Game-specific content, such as dangers, monster types, and setting details you might use
- Specific genres of horror, like those in chapter 2

If you're not comfortable adding any of these topics to your game, don't include them as options, and use them as the starting point for a list of elements that your adventures won't include.

GAMEPLAY QUESTIONS

After your list of topics, use the following questions to query players about gameplay considerations:

- How scary do you want the game to be? Do you enjoy being creeped out as a player, or should the characters alone experience fear?
- How difficult do you want the game to be? Should there be a high, average, or low threat of death?
- How do you feel about effects that take away your ability to control what your character does?
- Do you want to allow phones or other distractions at the game table, or should they be set aside?
- Are there any specific stories or rules you'd like to see highlighted during the game?
- Are there general events or experiences you don't want to see during the game?
- Do you have any accessibility needs that would make the game more enjoyable, such as captions for video calls or a specific kind of seating?
- Do you have any other notes or concerns?

Once you've completed this survey, distribute it to your players, give them a window of time to respond, then collect the results. Use this information to inform your adventure planning and to create an anonymized list of content that will not be featured in your game. Bring this list to your session zero.

SESSION ZERO

After you learn what topics your players are excited about, it's time to discuss what you've learned with your potential players during a preliminary, before-play gathering or "session zero." *Tasha's Cauldron of Everything* outlines how to run session zero discussions, but in general, use this session to discuss the game's content, social contract, and house rules, and to create characters.

REINFORCE EXPECTATIONS

Make it clear that D&D is a group storytelling game. As the DM, you have a role in crafting adventures and arbitrating rules, but you aren't solely responsible for how much fun the group has. Everyone is responsible for the group's enjoyment of the game. By the same token, the whole group has a role in determining how scary the game is and how far that frightful content goes. Chapter 1 provides guidance for players participating in horror adventures. Make sure you and the players are aware of this and use it to inform character creation and play.

ESTABLISH BOUNDARIES

Review your takeaways from the content surveys. Then, informed by players' survey responses, present your list of content the game will not feature. These are your game's boundaries and will not be included. Emphasize that boundaries aren't negotiable, and neither you nor any of the players should bring them into the game.

Note that boundaries may change during play. Encourage players to bring any additions to you, privately or in the moment, so you can add them to the list. When this happens, don't refer to past survey data, defend past choices, or ask players to explain their boundaries. Trust that players know their needs best, and update the game accordingly.

Let players know that this list of boundaries will be accessible during every session and that by playing, they agree to respect these boundaries. Make it clear that players who don't respect these boundaries will have to leave the game.

CUSTOMIZE YOUR EXPERIENCE

During session zero, the group can discuss ways to customize the game in the following ways:

Discuss Genre. If there are horror genres that players gravitated toward in the survey, see if there are elements players would like to use to inspire their characters.

Discuss Campaign Themes. If you already have ideas for the sorts of adventures you plan to run or your own Darklord and domain, share the general concepts you're interested in and see what players get excited about.

Create Player Characters. If players want to discuss their characters or create them collaboratively, now is a great time to do so.

Choose Optional Rules. If there are optional rules—like those presented later in this chapter—that you're amenable to using, determine which ones work best for the group.

Running Horror Games

While preparing and running frightening adventures, keep in mind the ebb and flow of suspense. Atmosphere, pacing, description, and player involvement all influence a game's tension and directly contribute to how scary your adventures feel.

Horror Atmosphere

Atmosphere is the overall mood of your game. It's the sense of levity, excitement, or dread that stems from a story's content and players' perception of it. Atmosphere can be challenging to build and easy to disrupt, but any D&D game—particularly scary games—benefit from your work to cultivate an atmosphere consistent with the experience you're trying to create. Consider the following elements to influence your game's atmosphere and create moody trappings for your horror adventures. Customize what you can and don't fret about what you can't.

Accessibility

When choosing the space you'll be playing in, review any accessibility needs communicated in the content survey. Accommodate what you can; communicate what you can't as early as possible. Enlist players for help. Players may have difficulty with low light, loud background music, small printed text, strong odors, cramped spaces, specific allergens, or challenges with programs (if playing online). If any player identified these as an issue, don't use them to create an unnerving atmosphere. Recognize the difference between creating a moody atmosphere and making it difficult for players to participate.

Location

If possible, play in an area with minimal visual or auditory distractions. Favor surroundings that appropriately reinforce your desired atmosphere and have little non-player traffic. If space is shared, negotiate with non-players to reserve the space in advance. You can also reduce distracting stimuli by turning screens off, covering decorations, and moving unnecessary objects away.

Music

Consider what fills the pauses in the game's action or other quiet moments. Lulls breed distractions. Subtle music, though, can fill such instances while reinforcing the game's atmosphere. Search for ambient, atmospheric, or instrumental music. Choose options without lyrics and that aren't recognizably tied to popular media. Create playlists in advance. If you can subtly control volume, slowly raise it when you want attention, and lower it when players are talking. Experiment with how volume and tempo influence whether a scene feels subdued or energetic.

Lighting

Dimming the lights can transform your game space, causing distractions to fade and making it look unfamiliar. If the lighting's easy to control, you might adjust it to suggest a setting's light level. More elaborate techniques might involve using colored lights or using patterned cut-outs to cast eerie shadows. Whenever manipulating lighting, though, always ensure players have enough light to read by.

Props

Props can serve as artifacts from your game's world, atmospheric focus pieces, or complete distractions. The first rule of creating props for your game isn't to overdo it. Props can be nice to have, but shouldn't become chores to create, reasons to delay game sessions, or distractions from play. Props can be as simple as a whiteboard for notes or sharing pictures of characters or monsters to increase their memorability. Furniture, whether by its arrangement or removal, can suggest a specific location. Props can even represent game mechanics, such as tracking hit points with crimson flat glass marbles in clear goblets. Ravenloft in particular has a history of featuring props in its adventures (see "Tarokka Deck and Spirit Board" section later in this chapter). The world of creating custom props is endless, but don't compare your game to performances with whole production budgets.

Distractions

A distraction for one player may be a necessity for another. Discuss compromises that benefit everyone. Maybe food and non-game items are kept away from the play space. Perhaps phones and tablets are permitted as long as they are silenced and used away from the table. Additionally, not everyone is comfortable being photographed or identified in public discussions of a game, whether in real-time or after a session, so ask about the place of social media in the game before making assumptions.

The Dungeon Master

You have incredible control over your game's tone and atmosphere. Model the behaviors you want players to emulate by staying focused on the game, letting others speak in turn, heading off encroachment on boundaries, and complimenting exciting choices. Stand or pace during intense moments. Speak faster or sound anxious when something scary is happening. Raise the volume of your voice during pitched battles and whisper during tense or conspiratorial moments. Allow yourself to sound uncertain, correct yourself, or pause as if you heard something outside. Ask players, "Are you sure?" Engaging with the suspenseful atmosphere you want to create helps bring it into being around you.

Horror Pacing

Pacing is the speed and energy with which your story unfolds. This relates to the amount of action in your game and, in a horror adventure, the tension or frequency of suspenseful moments. Everything can't be scary, and continuous terror is unsustainable. Before players grow numb to endless tension, create opportunities for them to catch their breath and regain a temporary feeling of calm. The best horror adventures are like roller coasters, ratcheting up suspense and releasing it before building toward the next harrowing moment. Also, mix up social interaction, exploration, combat, and other types of encounters to create interesting and engaging pacing. Ensure that scenes are always somehow relevant to your story and move characters toward their goals.

Logistics

You often have less time to play than you think once late starts, food breaks, and other interruptions are all taken into account. When planning your adventures, account for less time than your full game session.

Undermine Reality

Dread and uncertainty are keys to engaging horror adventures. Horrific experiences or supernatural settings undermine assumptions about what can or can't happen. Have a character wake from a prophetic nightmare with a fresh scar. Have a threat characters are fleeing appear ahead of them. Make candles gutter, paintings cry, animals whisper curses, or gigantic eyes peer through windows. Did these things actually happen, or are characters' senses turning against them? The answers often don't matter, particularly when the Mists provide explanations for all manner of casually dreadful impossibilities.

Idle Uneasiness

Occasionally slow your adventure's pace to draw out the tension you've established. Linger on describing sensory details. Ask players to describe what their characters are thinking, feeling, or fixating on. Detail the ways objects could be used violently, words could be lies, and shadows could hide monsters. Ask players what they think is the worst possible thing that could happen right now. Describe feelings of being watched. Hint that the characters are being hunted. Let characters respond to these stray thoughts. Sometimes these impressions should just be their nervousness getting to them. But sometimes it's the calm before a threat strikes.

Out of Time

When the time for action comes, make your narration feel urgent. Speak quickly and in short bursts. Focus less on senses and more on descriptions of impact—a splash of crimson, who knows where it came from? Split the characters' attention. Role-play other creatures begging, panicking, and trying to escape. Politely demand players react quickly: "There's no time to debate—what do you do?"

Parallel Scenes

Occasionally encourage players to split the party. When characters are separated, cut back and forth between them. Encourage everyone to watch even scenes their characters aren't in. Keep these split scenes short, and when an exciting event occurs, cut away and make the players wait for resolution. Give characters things to tell one another when they meet again. Players can then decide whether or not their characters trust such reports.

Reliability and Trust

Reliability and trust are just as important to your horror adventures as lurid shocks. Frequent betrayals encourage paranoia that can paralyze players. Emphasize that certain people and locations will never turn on the characters through repeated positive encounters. The players can trust these allies, but can they keep them safe?

Just Enough Hope

Fear without hope tempts paralysis and apathy, which can ruin the game. Reward characters who behave dramatically, heroically, or in ways that increase the game's frightful atmosphere. Rewards might include brief scenes focused on a character's actions, opportunities to regroup and rest, clues to adversaries' weaknesses, and discoveries of actual treasure. To maintain character agency, avoid having strangers or allies of the group rescue characters from problems they got themselves into. By the same token, don't throw characters into impossible situations. Never let hope die.

End on Cliffhangers

Leave players excited to play again. When ending a session, implement one of the following to conclude on a cliffhanger: hint at a new threat, impose a complication on existing plans, increase the stakes, introduce a new mystery, have a foe appear, have the world change, or otherwise shock the characters, then call for a break before players can react.

Describing Horror

The horrors populating your adventures can take endless forms, whether they be foes, impending events, or magical forces. Rather than just naming what the terrible thing is, inspire your players' imaginations by describing a horror indirectly in stages. Chapter 5 features advice or making familiar monsters more frightful. Also consider the following elements when describing terrors:

Before It Arrives. Foreshadow the horror's approach. How do the environment, nearby animals, the weather and nature, and the light and shadows react?

Approaches. What sounds does it make as it moves? What parts do characters see before the whole comes into view?

Up Close. What does it smell like? How does it breathe? Does it cool the air around it or bring heat wherever it goes? How does it stand? When it reaches out to grab a character, what does it feel like?

Attacks. How does it attack? Does it have weapons, or does it use its body to fight? Does it have sharp claws that rake across flesh, or is it a supernatural force that warps what it comes in contact with?

Wounded. When it's wounded, how does it react? What does its blood look like? What is inside it instead of flesh and blood? When it becomes desperate, how does it react?

LET PLAYERS FILL GAPS

Invite players to turn their imaginations against themselves. Leave details intentionally blank, describing just enough to reveal gaps that inspire horrific implications. Fixate on a specific trait, like only describing a vampire's eyes as it attacks.

Alternatively, directly ask players to fill in details. Ask questions like these: What does the way it moves remind you of? It emits the worst smell— what is it? Something falls free and, for an instant, what are you certain it is? Players' responses don't need to control the narrative; it's up to you whether they're true or just one perception.

HORROR GAMEPLAY

Just as you consider how you'll tell your tales of terror, keep in mind what you can do to make the experience of playing the game more suspenseful.

HORROR THREATS

While horror traditionally nullifies heroes' strengths, doing so can remove the players' agency and undercut their enjoyment. Beyond the *Dungeon Master's Guide* advice for creating dangerous encounters, consider the following techniques to make combat feel more menacing:

- Feature monsters that are immune to tactics characters often use but that are vulnerable to other strategies the characters could employ.
- Have foes spend combat actions doing things that are fundamentally creepy, like chanting to sinister gods or regurgitating their last meal.
- Use another creature as the opening act for the true threat. A notorious monster is all the scarier when it emerges and rips apart something the characters assumed was their true antagonist.

SUBVERT CLICHÉS

When characters and worlds feature clichés, they become dull and predictable. If your favorite horror story features outdated tropes, your fondness doesn't redeem them. To create dynamic and compelling characters, consider the following options:

- Avoid drawing inspiration from stock characters in fiction or film.
- Treat characters as real people with real motivations. Put yourself in their shoes. What would you do?
- Show how multiple people from the same culture are different.
- Feature members of different genders, ethnicities, and sexualities, as well as people with disabilities and of varied beliefs, as having broad roles, professions, interests, and outlooks. Endlessly work to quash stereotypes.
- Don't use cliché accents, especially to represent marginalized people.
- Matter-of-factly provide opportunities for everyone to be exceptional. Magical settings bear no resemblance to real-world history, and character creation rules presuppose no standard bar for heroics.

- Have foes play dead, only to "return to life" after characters think things are safe.
- Make use of the techniques detailed in the "Horror Monsters" section of chapter 5.

ENCOURAGE SPACE

A typical D&D session is longer than a typical horror movie, and it can be hard to sustain the atmosphere for hours on end. Plan to take breaks during your game session, and encourage players to step away from the table if they need to. If you feel like the game has gotten intense or taken a turn someone's not enjoying, ask, "Is everyone comfortable with continuing?" before proceeding. If anyone's not, thank the players for their honesty and hasten the game to a cliffhanger. Before the next game session, talk with the group about the best way to move

forward in a way everyone can enjoy. Work to create a supportive environment where players can admit to being uncomfortable without fearing that they're going to ruin everyone's fun. As DM, you can model this behavior by noting when you're shying away from a creepy idea that comes to you or thanking players who uphold the game's boundaries.

Beyond impromptu checks, once during a session, after a scheduled break, check in with the group and consider asking the following questions:

- What do your characters hope will happen?
- What do your characters worry might happen?
- Do you want to update any content boundaries?
- Is there anything that would make the game more enjoyable for you?

Ask Permission

Players put considerable thought and investment into their characters. Don't impose rules on characters that might make players not want to play them anymore. For example, characters might gain any of the lineages and Dark Gifts from chapter 1 during play. If there's an opportunity for a character to gain one of these options, ask that character's player if they'd be comfortable with such an adjustment before imposing it. If the player says no, consider other options.

Beyond rules considerations, some actions also require special consideration before they occur in game, such as these examples: romance between characters, violence between characters, one player's character influencing or controlling another player's character, and yelling. All players (including the DM) must ask and gain permission from everyone playing—not just the affected players—before introducing this content. Without any explanation or debate, if a single person gives a thumbs down or doesn't respond, this action shouldn't be performed. Players may change their minds at any time. If a topic was listed as a boundary, it is off the table entirely.

Content Tools

Content tools enable you and your players to adjust the game's content as you play. Since D&D is improvisational, the game can go in unexpected directions. If a direction makes the game a worse experience for anyone, use these tools to correct course.

Many content tools exist, but a popular one involves passing a blank note card to each participant,

(including the DM) and instructing everyone to draw an X on their card. One uses their X-Card to signal to everyone else in the game that a boundary has been crossed. If you are playing remotely, players can lift the X to the camera, type X in a chat window, or cross their arms to form an X. In any case, this is a sign that something that just happened is off limits. The person touching the card can comment on what they want adjusted, or whoever's narrating the scene can walk back what just happened, try something else, or leave the scene with a vague ending (like in a film where things fade to black). The person using the content tool doesn't have to explain why the content is objectionable, nor should anyone question it. Instead of a debate, thank the person for being honest about their needs and move on.

Make it clear to players that if a person doesn't feel comfortable using a content tool, they can wait for a break to check in or talk to you privately. Players may also give a friend permission to use the card on their behalf. As the DM, lead by example. Treat content tools seriously and use them to adjust how your shared story plays out.

Engaging Players

If players seem disengaged, check in with them. Ask them what they would like to see happen next. If they don't know, write two or three options down, hand them the options privately, and ask them to choose one. If issues remain, call for a break, and privately ask what you can do to make the game more engaging.

After the Horror

It's always a good idea to check in with players at the end of a session, but this rings especially true for adventures where tensions run high and the stories can elicit strong emotional responses. At the end of a horror game session, leave time to check in with players and ask them how the game went, how they're feeling, and what they liked about the session. You might ask the following questions:

- What unsolved mysteries do you want answers to?
- Did you find anything confusing or off-putting?
- What are you looking forward to in the next session?

These answers can help you craft the next session to create a game your players enjoy.

If players give short or vague answers or you suspect that trust at the table has been broken, try creating an anonymous space to receive feedback. It's important to hear honest feedback from players so you can ensure everyone is fully immersed in the story and you can address any issues that might prevent them from enjoying the next game session.

Tarokka Deck and Spirit Board

Ravenloft has a tradition of adventures featuring setting-specific props and memorable, set-piece encounters. Such atmospheric scenes immerse players in an experience unique to the Land of the Mist. Two fateful tools used in such encounters are detailed here, the tarokka deck and spirit board. Consider including these mystery-steeped props in your own Ravenloft adventures, or use them as inspiration to create other immersive experiences.

Tarokka Deck

In both 1983's adventure *Ravenloft* and 2016's adventure *Curse of Strahd*, the plot changes in accordance with cards drawn from a tarokka deck. A tarokka deck contains fifty-four tarot-like, fortune-telling cards, each one bearing one of the following symbols:

Crowns. The portentous cards of the high deck are marked with crowns but are not themselves a suit. The figures on these fourteen cards represent distinct forces of fate, change, and despair.

Coins. The ten cards of this suit symbolize avarice and the desire for personal gain.

Glyph. The ten cards of this suit symbolize faith, spirituality, and inner strength.

Stars. The ten cards of this suit symbolize the desire for personal power and control over mysterious forces.

Swords. The ten cards of this suit symbolize aggression and violence.

Tarokka decks allow you run encounters where fortune-tellers predict characters' fates. Once you're familiar with the cards and their meanings, you can interpret them in ways that tie in to the characters' pasts or events in your adventures. You can also use the results of tarokka readings to guide your campaign and make sure predictions come to pass.

The tarokka hails from the same world as the domain of Barovia, but it and its users have since spread throughout the Domains of Dread. Further details and a complete tarokka deck appear in the adventure *Curse of Strahd*.

Spirit Board

Spirit boards are tools to contact and divine the will of spirits or other mysterious forces. Upon placing their fingertips on a planchette set atop the board, assembled users feel forces move the planchette toward letters and symbols, gradually revealing a cryptic message. The spirits boards common in the Land of the Mists were first created by members of the Keepers of the Feather (see chapter 3), and feature half-understood images from their occult studies and Barovian lore. These markings include symbols from the tarokka deck, which carry the same meanings as they do upon those cards. All manner of mysterious beings consider a spirit board's use an invitation to communicate with the living, resulting in messages shared from beyond the grave and frightful revelations.

This book's appendix provides a depiction of a spirit board to use in your adventures, while a planchette to be used with it appears here. The adventure "The House of Lament" later in this chapter features séances employing a spirit board. When making use of this game prop, you take the role of the forces guiding the planchette. Move the planchette subtly to reveal mysterious messages appropriate to your adventures.

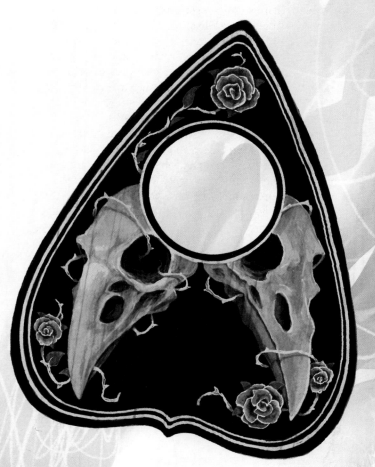

Horror Toolkit

Setting the stage for horror isn't entirely a product of good storytelling. As highlighted throughout this book, any rule might take on a terrifying cast, whether you present it as having some grim source or you customize it with ominous new options. This section goes a step further, providing options to make existing rules more terrifying and presenting systems that encourage unique horror experiences.

Curses

An ancient warning echoes in a tomb robber's mind. A lost treasure bears a magical affliction, assuring it remains lost. A dying priest's last breath carries a portent of doom. Curses come in myriad forms, presaging terrifying tales and distinctive dooms.

This section provides guidance for creating dramatic curses, either distinct from or as part of curses resulting from magic, monsters' actions, or other effects. These curses provide ominously poetic responses to fateful choices and afflictions that last until they're alleviated by specific remedies. Spells at the characters' disposal might relieve these curses' effects temporarily but can't lift them completely. The price must be paid.

A DYING PRIEST OF EZRA CURSES HIS MURDERER.

Laying Curses

Curses aren't something to throw around lightly. They should be dramatically appropriate responses to meaningful choices characters make. If every goblin or bandit coughs out a dying curse, the narrative impact fades. There should always be a way to avoid a curse, and a curse's effects should clearly arise from wrongdoing. Here are some examples of actions that warrant a curse:

- Defiling a sealed tomb
- Desecrating a temple
- Slaying a villain who is backed by a powerful entity such as a demon lord or a deity
- Murdering or grievously harming an innocent
- Stealing a treasure that is meaningful to an entire culture

In cases where the curse arises from a creature, such as a dying villain's last breath, the pronouncement of the curse is clear. When there is no wronged party present to lay the curse directly, the curse should be obvious in some way, such as a warning of dire consequences carved into the wall of an ancient crypt or relayed by a spell such as *magic mouth*.

Components of a Curse

Most curses have three distinct components: pronouncement, burden, and resolution. Whatever form these take, at least one of them, especially the burden or resolution, should have an ironic connection to the action that triggered the curse.

Pronouncement

The first component of a curse is the pronouncement, which amounts to a threat. It promises suffering to those who dare to perform or have already performed a specific offensive act. The pronouncement can be a standing warning against taking some action, or it could be a declaration in the moment. The following examples suggest just a few possible pronouncements:

- A widely spread story explaining that a particular action tempts terrible punishment
- A warning spoken on the cusp of a deadly battle, assuring dire consequences for the victorious
- A poem, rhyme, or song foretelling doom
- A carved epitaph on a gravestone discouraging robbers
- The last words of a dying person—either a powerful villain or a wrongly slain innocent
- Swearing a vow to refrain from or undertake some action on pain of great suffering

Burden

A curse's burden is the effect that causes hardship and suffering to the curse's victim. A burden is often reflective of what caused the curse in the first place, twisting the transgressor's action against them. The burden takes effect immediately, along with a vague sense of foreboding—such as a chill down the spine or a wave of nausea. The victim might not notice the curse's effect until a situation arises to make it obvious. For example, a character cursed with clumsiness that manifests as disadvantage on Dexterity checks might not notice anything until they make such a check. Burdens can take many forms, such as the following:

- The victim has disadvantage on attack rolls, ability checks, saving throws, or some combination of the three. This can be tied to a single ability score or applied generally.
- The victim can't communicate using language, whether through speaking, sign language, writing, telepathy, or any other means.
- The victim gains 3 levels of exhaustion that can't be removed while the curse endures.
- When the victim finishes a long rest, they must succeed on a DC 15 Constitution saving throw, or their hit point maximum is reduced by 1d10. If this reduces their hit point maximum to 0, the victim dies, and their body crumbles to dust.
- When the victim takes damage, they take an extra 1d10 necrotic damage. This effect can't happen again until the start of the victim's next turn.
- The victim gains a Dark Gift (see chapter 1) appropriate to the circumstances surrounding the curse.
- The victim gains vulnerability to one damage type.
- The victim's Strength, Dexterity, or Constitution score is reduced to 3, and the victim can't be raised from the dead while the curse lasts.
- A monster hunts the victim relentlessly. Even if the monster dies, it rises again or a new one takes its place 24 hours later.

Resolution

Sometimes a curse can be ended by making restitution to a wronged party (or their closest kin in the case of a death) or reparation if something was stolen or destroyed. The resolution might be declared as part of the pronouncement, or it may be left to those who suffer the curse to make amends on their own. Research and divination can offer clues or even reveal the exact steps needed to resolve the curse.

While more general curses can lifted by a *remove curse* spell, more specific or dramatic curses can't be permanently lifted through spells. Magic can offer temporary respite, though. A *remove curse* spell cast on the victim of such a curse suppresses the burden for 1 hour. A *greater restoration* spell suppresses the burden until the victim finishes a long rest. Death usually ends a curse, but the curse returns in full force if the cursed character returns to life without resolving the curse.

Persistent Curses. When a curse is resolved, its effects usually end immediately. Some more insidious curses might linger beyond the resolution but can then be removed by a *remove curse* spell or similar magic if the victim succeeds on a DC 15 Charisma saving throw when the spell is cast. If the save fails, it can be repeated after a specific interval passes, usually 1 month, with the curse ending on a successful save. Adjust the DC of a particularly weak curse to 10 or that of a stronger one to 20.

Here are some examples of curse resolutions:

- Protecting a loved one dear to the person who laid the curse from some dire threat
- Returning every piece of a stolen treasure hoard, down to the last copper coin, to the place where it once rested
- Slaying the head of a dynasty that has long held power in the region
- Accomplishing a seemingly impossible task, such as raising a castle above the clouds or making the sun cross the sky in a different direction

Sample Curses

Provided here are several example curses and the circumstances surrounding them. Change the details of any of these examples to customize them to your adventures.

Ancient Seal

This curse protects the resting place of a long-dead ruler and punishes any who disturb the ruler's remains or plunder the treasures.

Pronouncement. Carved into the stone of the crypt door are the words "Relentless death follows those who disturb the sovereign's rest."

Burden. Each character that gains the curse is hunted by a **wraith** that appears at sunset and vanishes at dawn, pursuing the single-minded goal of slaying the cursed individual. The wraith manifests in an unoccupied space within 30 feet of its victim. Destroying the wraith grants a temporary reprieve; it doesn't reform for 10 days. You can scale this curse for lower- and higher-level characters by choosing another kind of creature.

Resolution. The cursed character sets right what they disturbed; stolen treasure must be returned, and if the ruler's body was disturbed, it must be reinterred with proper observances.

In Har'Akir, an ancient curse awakens
the Children of Ankhtepot.

Broken Vow

A character breaks a solemn vow. The consequences stem from the powers that observed the oath's swearing.

Pronouncement. Whatever vow the character made, it came with an implied warning that guilt and restlessness would beset anyone who broke the oath.

Burden. The character is plagued by restless sleep and recurring nightmares featuring those the character swore to protect. The character gains 3 levels of exhaustion that can't be removed until the curse ends.

Resolution. The curse lasts until the character upholds the broken oath. That might require the character to wait until the circumstances arise again or, more questionably, to engineer the circumstances.

Final Breath

A deity's favored servant lies dying and calls down divine wrath.

Pronouncement. The dying creature declares to the killer, "May your mind grow dim in battle until the sun sets forever."

Burden. The character has disadvantage on attack rolls brought on by brief, sporadic bouts of confusion.

Resolution. To lift the curse, the character must cause a symbolic setting of the sun or an empowering of the night to appease the slain creature's deity. The character might prevent a festival dedicated to a sun god or perform a ritual that shrouds an entire settlement in magical night for 24 hours, thus ending the curse.

Innocent Blood

The tragic situation came to pass where a character killed an undeserving person, who laid a vengeful curse in punishment.

Pronouncement. The dying victim spits final words: "You shall spill innocent blood until laid low by the moon's bite!"

Burden. The character is cursed with loup garou lycanthropy (see chapter 5).

Resolution. This curse can't be broken until the character is reduced to 0 hit points by a silvered weapon. If the character survives, the curse can be broken as described in the "Loup Garou Lycanthropy" section of chapter 5. Treat the character as a werewolf whose loup garou progenitor has been killed.

FEAR AND STRESS

Terror takes a toll. The ramifications of frightful experiences might be an instant of instinct-triggering shock or a lasting, traumatic echo. The *Dungeon Master's Guide* presents options for fear and horror to help reinforce terrifying themes in play. This section presents an alternative system, exploring reactions personalized to individual characters and offering incentive for players to embrace roleplaying moments of fear. Options exploring fear provide guidance to create frightening moments for a character outside of spells or monster abilities, while rules for stress model the lingering toll such events can take. None of these options are required to create an enjoyable horror roleplaying experience, but they provide ways to measure the effects of characters facing and overcoming their fears.

SEEDS OF FEAR

Aside from supernatural sources of dread and monsters who strike terror in their victims, fear is subjective and often quite personal. A battle-hardened warrior and a reclusive scholar might not deal with frightful circumstances in the same way. During character creation, a player can choose up to two Seeds of Fear to represent things their character finds truly frightening. The Seeds of Fear table offers some examples. These can change over time as characters grow, overcome old fears, and discover new uncertainties. Work with players to determine when their Seeds of Fear might change.

A character never has more than three Seeds of Fear; if you gain a new seed and already have three, choose which of your old fears is replaced by the new one.

SEEDS OF FEAR

d12	Seed
1	"I can't stand dark places."
2	"I'm terrified of a particular kind of animal."
3	"Deep water will be the death of me."
4	"I can't stand heights."
5	"I hate being stuck in tight spaces."
6	"Being around crowds unnerves me, for I always feel judged."
7	"I hate feeling isolated or being alone."
8	"Storms and extreme weather rattle me."
9	"Being followed chills my blood."
10	"Sudden noises or appearances fray my nerves."
11	"I can't be comfortable around creatures larger than I am."
12	"Reflections always seem like they're looking straight through me."

USING SEEDS OF FEAR

When a character encounters one of their Seeds of Fear, and interacts with the situation in a way that reinforces the seed, such as screaming or stumbling back from a horrid event, consider giving the character inspiration for their fear-focused reaction (see "Inspiration" in the *Player's Handbook*). Once a character gains inspiration in this way, they shouldn't be able to do so again until they finish a long rest.

For example, imagine that a character has the Seed of Fear "I hate being stuck in tight spaces" and must squeeze through a narrow crack in a cave wall to continue an adventure. If the player portrays the character's response in a way that reinforces that fear, such as refusing and finding another way around, taking time and making noise to widen the crack, or portraying some other fearful response, these would be perfect opportunities to reward the player's consideration of a Seed of Fear by granting their character inspiration.

FEAR

An overwhelming foe or horrid monster doesn't need magic or some supernatural ability to strike fear into the most stalwart adventurers. During any frightful encounter, you can call on a character to make a saving throw to resist being scared. The character must succeed on a DC 15 Wisdom saving throw or become frightened until the end of their next turn.

Any of the following circumstances might be reasons to have one or more characters make saving throws to resist being frightened:

- The character experiences one of their Seeds of Fear.
- An enemy is immune to the character's attacks or spells.
- An enemy demonstrates it can deal enough damage to reduce a character to 0 hit points in one blow.
- A creature is alien or monstrous in ways the character never could have imagined.
- An object undermines a character's understanding of reality.

STRESS

Charging headlong into terrifying situations is the stock in trade for adventurers. Among the Domains of Dread, though, periods of respite between harrowing experiences can be rare. Even the hardiest adventurers find themselves worn down over time, their performance suffering as they struggle to cope with the dread and despair.

Various circumstances might cause a character stress. Stress can be tracked numerically as a Stress Score, increasing in trying situations and decreasing with care. At your discretion, a character's Stress Score might increase by 1 when one of the following situations occurs:

- A tense, dramatic moment, especially one involving one of a character's Seeds of Fear
- Every 24 hours the character goes without finishing a long rest
- Witnessing the death of a loved one
- A nightmare or darkest fear made real
- Shattering the character's fundamental understanding of reality
- Witnessing a person transform into a horrid or unnatural creature

When a character makes an attack roll, an ability check, or a saving throw, they must apply their current Stress Score as a penalty to the roll.

REDUCING STRESS

A character who spends an entire day relaxing or in otherwise calm circumstances reduces their Stress Score by 1 when they finish their next long rest.

The *calm emotions* spell effect used to suppress the charmed and frightened conditions also suppresses the effects of one's Stress Score for the spell's duration.

A *lesser restoration* spell reduces the target's Stress Score by 1, and a *greater restoration* spell reduces a character's Stress Score to 0.

HAUNTED TRAPS

Like other traps, haunted traps represent threats leveled toward trespassers. They originate in an area spontaneously, often resulting from overwhelming negative emotions, tragedy, or evil. Just as some terrible fates might cause a tormented individual to rise as an undead creature, so might supernatural evil and violent emotions manifest more generally as one or more haunted traps. Such traps provide a way to theme the dangers and monsters of a haunted place to reveal a grim history or frightening tale. When creating haunted traps, consider what events brought them into being and how the trap's effects suggest those origins.

DETECTING HAUNTED TRAPS

Every haunted trap has an emanation, which might be as subtle as a drop in temperature or as overt as an object moving of its own accord. A haunted trap's emanation occurs before the trap takes effect. A character notices the emanation if their passive Wisdom (Perception) score equals or exceeds 10 + the trap's Haunt Bonus. A character who notices the haunted trap has until the start of their next turn to react, which might include fleeing to avoid the trap or attempting to disarm it (see the following section). Class features and spells, such as Divine Sense and *detect evil and good*, that discern desecration also detect haunted traps.

DISARMING HAUNTED TRAPS

Characters who notice a haunted trap before it activates can attempt to disarm it. Typical methods of disarming traps, such as thieves' tools and *dispel magic*, don't affect haunted traps. However, the Channel Divinity class feature and the *remove curse* spell can disarm a haunted trap.

To use Channel Divinity to disarm a haunted trap, a character uses an action to present their holy symbol and speak a prayer. To use *remove curse* instead, a character must cast the spell and touch an object that is part of the trap. Whichever disarming method is used, the trap itself then makes a saving throw against the character's spell save DC, adding its Haunt Bonus to the save. On a failure, the trap is disarmed for 24 hours. If the trap fails the save by 10 or more, the trap is disarmed permanently.

Depending on the haunted trap's origins, certain spells might also affect the trap. For example, a haunted trap with a fiendish origin might be permanently disarmed by the spell *dispel evil and good*.

Some haunted traps might also be disarmed in nonmagical ways related to the history of a haunted area. Such methods might be as simple as wearing the clothes of a haunted house's former owner or singing a lullaby that soothes a restless spirit.

Haunted traps disarmed in such ways typically remain disarmed for 24 hours.

SAMPLE HAUNTED TRAPS

Several haunted traps are presented here in alphabetical order. Customize them to create terrifying traps appropriate for your adventures.

DANSE MACABRE
Haunt Bonus +4

This haunted trap affects a 20-foot-radius sphere centered on an ancient but pristine instrument. When a creature enters the area, the trap's emanation manifests as the sound of distant, mournful music. A round later, a phantom performer appears and begins playing the instrument for the next minute. While the performer plays, any creature that enters or starts its turn in the haunted trap's area must succeed on a DC 14 Wisdom saving throw or float 20 feet into the air and be affected by the spell *Otto's irresistible dance*. There they are joined by illusory dancers as they dance for the remainder of the performer's song. As an action, a dancing creature can repeat the saving throw to end the effect on itself, whereupon it falls 20 feet and takes 2d6 bludgeoning damage. If a creature's saving throw to resist the trap or to stop dancing is successful, the creature is immune to the haunted trap for the next 24 hours.

While the phantom performer plays, any creature within the haunted trap's area can use an action to try to convince the performer to stop playing, doing so with a successful DC 14 Charisma (Persuasion) check. When the performer stops playing, all creatures affected by the haunted trap are freed from its effects and float to the ground safely.

FACELESS MALICE
Haunt Bonus +2

This haunted trap affects a 15-foot-cube in front of an ornate mirror hanging on a wall. When a visible creature enters the area, the trap's emanation manifests as the creature's distorted reflection in the mirror. If that creature is still in the area at the start of its next turn, it must succeed on a DC 12 Wisdom saving throw or be blinded, deafened, and rendered unable to speak for 1 minute. Additionally, an illusion makes it appear that the creature has had its face erased. The *remove curse* spell ends this effect, as does destroying the mirror. The mirror has AC 12, 10 hit points, vulnerability to bludgeoning damage, and immunity to poison and psychic damage. After a creature fails its saving throw against the trap, the trap won't activate again for 24 hours.

ICON OF THE LOWER AERIAL KINGDOMS
Haunt Bonus +6

This haunted trap is tied to the 10-foot-radius sphere surrounding an ominous, 1-foot-tall statue of a menacing, four-winged, birdlike figure. Once per day, when a creature enters the area, the trap's emanation manifests as the sound of distant flapping wings and a rush of warm air. If that creature is still in the area at the start of its next turn, it must succeed on a DC 16 Wisdom saving throw or be charmed and incapacitated for 1 minute. These conditions last until the creature is damaged or someone else uses an action to shake the creature. If the affected creature remains charmed for the full minute, they are then affected as per the spell *magic jar*, their soul entering the statue and being replaced by the spirit of a disembodied fiend. This effect ends when *dispel evil and good* or a similar spell is cast on the affected creature, or when the statue is destroyed. The statue has AC 17, 15 hit points, and immunity to poison and psychic damage.

This haunted trap manifests as the result of a fiendish influence. Casting *dispel evil and good* on the statue permanently disarms the haunted trap.

THE FACELESS MALICE HAUNTED TRAP CLAIMS A VICTIM.

IRINA NORDSOL

MORBID MEMORY
Haunt Bonus +0

A morbid memory trap presents little danger, but it proves useful in revealing important and unsettling glimpses into an area's past. This haunted trap affects a single room or 30-foot-square area. When a creature enters the area, the trap's emanation manifests as faint, disembodied whispers. If that creature is still in the area at the start of its next turn, an illusory scene plays out, repeating some terrible event that happened in the area. This vision typically lasts 1 minute. When the vision ends, all creatures in the area that saw the illusion must succeed on a DC 10 Wisdom saving throw or become frightened of the area for the next 1d4 rounds. Frightened creatures must take the Dash action and move away from the haunted area by the safest available route on each of their turns, unless there is nowhere else to move. After the haunted trap is activated, it won't activate again for 24 hours.

SURVIVORS

Terror doesn't come just for the brave and prepared—often quite the opposite. Some of the most harrowing horror stories involve the least likely heroes, individuals who find their simple lives transformed into waking nightmares.

In most horror adventures, your players will employ familiar, adventure-ready characters. That doesn't need to be the case, though. Instead, for short, low-power adventures, immersive retellings of tragic events, out-of-body experiences, or other unique tales, consider providing players with temporary, stand-in characters called survivors.

This section provides guidance for using survivors, characters designed for one- to three-session adventures focused on survival rather than saving the day. Using survivors helps create horror experiences focused on the dread inherent to having limited resources and facing impending doom without forcing players to risk their favorite characters.

USING SURVIVORS

Survivors are premade characters that are simple and easy for players to master, while being customizable enough to fill broad roles in your adventures—whether they be farmers or bored nobles, constables or babysitters. Adventures employing survivors are meant to be asides within broader campaigns or otherwise short experiences.

CUT SCENES, DREAMS, AND MEMORIES

Use survivors to provide information to players in the form of a self-contained adventure. Even if it doesn't make sense for a campaign's characters to be present for an event, survivors can provide players with perspectives they wouldn't otherwise have. For example, you might use survivors in the following ways:

- Survivors serve as the first constables on the scene during a serial killer's crime. Afterward, when the players' other characters get involved in the investigations, the players know the details.
- Survivors give every player a part to play in one character's ominous nightmares, such as those resulting from encounters with the mind flayers of Bluetspur (see chapter 3).
- Survivors provide players front row seats to important historic events. It's one thing to hear about the massacre at Castle Ravenloft following Strahd von Zarovich's transformation into a vampire, but it's another to play it.

MINDTAKER MISTS

The Mists frequently kidnap characters from across the multiverse, dragging them into the Domains of Dread. They don't always claim their victims bodily, though. Rather, the Mists might steal characters' minds, placing them into survivors involved in specific terrifying scenarios. Perhaps characters suddenly find themselves mentally recast into someone defending against a zombie siege in Falkovnia, attending a ball in Dementlieu, or exploring the tombs of Har'Akir (see chapter 3 for details on such adventures). Whether the characters survive or meet spectacular ends doesn't matter, as death might mean a return to the character's original body, a second chance to try again, or a stranger fate.

TERRIBLE FREEDOM, DELIGHTFUL DOOM

Make sure your players know how long you plan to use survivors and that they'll be playing their usual characters again soon. Also let them know that survivors are designed to engage with terrifying circumstances, but their triumph over such threats is not assured. Players' decisions will certainly impact the survivors' fates, but if it seems like doom is in store, encourage the players to embrace it and make sure their survivors meet unforgettable ends.

WHAT'S OLD IS NEW

Dwindling resources contribute to terrifying situations. When a group runs out of hit points, spells, food, or other vital reserves, tension and dread increase. High-level characters, though, have such resources in spades. By running an adventure using survivors, you can recapture some of the same tension adventurers experience early in their careers, encouraging players to use their wits and make desperate choices powerful characters can avoid.

TOOLS FOR TERROR

Survivors allow you to control how players will engage with a horror adventure. The stat blocks in the following section are designed to be easy-to-use characters with a hint of talent but little that makes them remarkable:

Apprentices have a minor talent for magic and tend to be well-read.

Disciples faithfully adhere to the tenets of their chosen religions and receive spells from the deities they worship.

Sneaks survive by their wits and are often charlatans or petty thieves.

Squires possess a modicum of martial training and are stalwart companions.

Determine how you want to use survivors in your adventure. If it's important to the story, perhaps all the players use the same stat block, representing their shared experience—a group of Sneaks might all be detectives while a band of Disciples might face a terror unleashed upon a monastery. You can also allow players to choose their own survivors, as any survivor might fill a general role like noble, villager, or sailor with a touch of talent. Make use of these ready-made characters in whatever ways suit your adventure best.

CREATING A SURVIVOR

When you plan a session using survivors, determine how you'll use the **Apprentice**, **Disciple**, **Sneak**, and **Squire** stat blocks that appear in the following section. Once you've determined what survivors to use, take a few moments to individualize them. If the survivors have particular roles in your adventure, provide that information to players along with their survivors' statistics; otherwise, let them come up with their own details. Players can give their survivors names, personalities, and lineages, but these details don't affect the survivors' stat blocks.

LEVELS

Survivors don't possess classes as detailed in the *Player's Handbook*. Despite this, you can make a survivor marginally more powerful by increasing its level. The stat blocks present the survivors as they are at 1st level. Rather than gaining experience points, a survivor increases in level whenever it makes sense for your adventure. When a survivor gains a level, it gains the benefits on the Survivor Progression table. A survivor that advances from 1st to 2nd level and from 2nd to 3rd level gains access to the player's choice of Survivor Talents (see the section below).

FOR SURVIVORS, ANY FOE MIGHT BECOME THE FOCUS OF ITS OWN HORROR ADVENTURE.

SURVIVOR PROGRESSION

Level	Feature
1st	See the appropriate stat block
2nd	Survivor Talent
3rd	Survivor Talent

HIT POINTS

Whenever a survivor gains a level, it gains one Hit Die and its hit point maximum increases. To determine the amount of the increase, roll the Hit Die (the type that appears in the survivor's stat block), and add the survivor's Constitution modifier. It gains a minimum of 1 hit point per level.

If a survivor drops to 0 hit points, it falls unconscious and subsequently makes death saving throws just like a normal player character.

DAWN CARLOS

Survivor Talents

At 2nd level and again at 3rd level, a survivor gains their choice of one of the following talents. A survivor can't gain the same talent more than once, unless a talent's description says otherwise. If a talent has a prerequisite, the character must meet it to gain the talent.

Adrenaline Surge

At the start of your turn, you can choose one creature you can see within 30 feet of you. Until the start of your next turn, you are frightened of that creature and your walking speed is doubled.

Desperate Scream

Whenever you make a saving throw, you can summon your desire to live into a desperate scream. You gain advantage on the saving throw, and the scream is audible up to 100 feet away. You can scream in this way twice, and you regain all expended uses when you finish a long rest.

Divine Guidance

Prerequisite: Disciple survivor

You learn one 1st-level spell of your choice from the cleric spell list. It must be a spell you don't already know. You can cast the spell once with this talent, and you regain the ability to do so when you finish a long rest.

You can select this talent more than once. Each time you do so, you must choose a different spell.

Magical Talent

Prerequisite: Apprentice survivor

You learn one 1st-level spell of your choice from the wizard spell list. It must be a spell you don't already know. You can cast the spell once with this talent, and you regain the ability to do so when you finish a long rest.

You can select this talent more than once. Each time you do so, you must choose a different spell.

Resilience

Choose one ability score. You gain proficiency in saving throws using the chosen ability.

Sacrificing Shield

Prerequisite: Squire survivor

When a creature you can see makes an attack against a target you can see within 5 feet of you, you can use your reaction to become the target of the attack instead. If you are wielding a shield, you can reduce the damage by 1d10. Once you use this talent, you can't do so again until you finish a short or long rest.

Skillful

You gain proficiency in two skills of your choice.

Slip Away

Prerequisite: Sneak survivor

When a creature you can see within 5 feet of you hits you with an attack roll and deals damage to you with the attack, you can use your reaction to give yourself resistance against that damage. You can then move up to half your speed without provoking opportunity attacks. Once you use this talent, you can't do so again until you finish a short or long rest.

Survivors are everyday people thrown into terrifying situations.

APPRENTICE

Medium Humanoid

Armor Class 10
Hit Points 7 (2d8 − 2)
Speed 30 ft.

STR	DEX	CON	INT	WIS	CHA
8 (−1)	10 (+0)	9 (−1)	13 (+1)	11 (+0)	12 (+1)

Saving Throws Int +3
Skills Arcana +3, History +3
Senses passive Perception 10
Languages any one language (usually Common)
Challenge —   **Proficiency Bonus** +2

ACTIONS

Quarterstaff. *Melee Weapon Attack:* +1 to hit, reach 5 ft., one target. *Hit:* 2 (1d6 − 1) bludgeoning damage, or 3 (1d8 − 1) bludgeoning damage if used with two hands.

Burning Hands (1st-Level Spell; 2/Day). You shoot forth a 15-foot cone of fire. Each creature in that area must make a DC 11 Dexterity saving throw. A creature takes 10 (3d6) fire damage on a failed save, or half as much damage on a successful one.

The fire ignites any flammable objects in the area that aren't being worn or carried.

Fire Bolt (Cantrip). *Ranged Spell Attack:* +3 to hit, range 120 ft., one target. *Hit:* 5 (1d10) fire damage. A flammable object hit by this spell ignites if it isn't being worn or carried.

Spellcasting. You cast one of the following wizard spells (spell save DC 11), using Intelligence as the spellcasting ability:

At will: *minor illusion*
2/day: *grease*

SNEAK

Small Humanoid

Armor Class 13 (shield)
Hit Points 9 (2d6 + 2)
Speed 30 ft.

STR	DEX	CON	INT	WIS	CHA
8 (−1)	13 (+1)	12 (+1)	11 (+0)	12 (+1)	9 (−1)

Saving Throws Dex +3
Skills Sleight of Hand +3, Stealth +3
Senses passive Perception 11
Languages any one language (usually Common)
Challenge —   **Proficiency Bonus** +2

ACTIONS

Dagger. *Melee or Ranged Weapon Attack:* +3 to hit, reach 5 ft. or range 20/60 ft., one target. *Hit:* 3 (1d4 + 1) piercing damage.

BONUS ACTIONS

Disengage. You take the Disengage action.

DISCIPLE

Medium Humanoid

Armor Class 11 (shield)
Hit Points 9 (2d8)
Speed 30 ft.

STR	DEX	CON	INT	WIS	CHA
12 (+1)	9 (−1)	10 (+0)	11 (+0)	13 (+1)	9 (−1)

Saving Throws Wis +3
Skills Perception +3, Religion +2
Senses passive Perception 13
Languages any one language (usually Common)
Challenge —   **Proficiency Bonus** +2

ACTIONS

Mace. *Melee Weapon Attack:* +3 to hit, reach 5 ft., one target. *Hit:* 4 (1d6 + 1) bludgeoning damage.

Sacred Flame (Cantrip). You target one creature you can see within 60 feet of you. The target must succeed on a DC 11 Dexterity saving throw or take 4 (1d8) radiant damage. The target gains no benefit from cover for this saving throw.

Spellcasting. You cast one the following cleric spells (spell save DC 11), using Wisdom as the spellcasting ability:

At will: *guidance*
2/day: *cure wounds*

SQUIRE

Medium Humanoid

Armor Class 12 (shield)
Hit Points 11 (2d8 + 2)
Speed 30 ft.

STR	DEX	CON	INT	WIS	CHA
13 (+1)	10 (+0)	12 (+1)	8 (−1)	11 (+0)	9 (−1)

Saving Throws Str +3
Skills Athletics +3
Senses passive Perception 10
Languages any one language (usually Common)
Challenge —   **Proficiency Bonus** +2

ACTIONS

Longsword. *Melee Weapon Attack:* +3 to hit, reach 5 ft., one target. *Hit:* 5 (1d8 + 1) slashing damage, or 6 (1d10 + 1) slashing damage if used with two hands.

BONUS ACTIONS

Shove. While wielding a shield, you try to shove one creature within 5 feet of you.

THE HOUSE OF LAMENT

"The House of Lament" is an adventure for a party of four to six 1st-level characters, who will advance to at least 3rd level by the adventure's conclusion. The adventure's climax serves as a springboard into future adventures in the Domains of Dread, should you wish to take your campaign into those haunted lands.

STORY OVERVIEW

Ages ago, the vicious warlord Dalk Dranzorg ravaged the countryside at the head of a bandit army. After conquering the lands of Count Cordon Silvra, he took the lord's fortress, Castle Laventz, as his own.

Months later, the relentless knight Mara Silvra received word of her father's defeat. Calling in debts and intimidating mercenaries, Mara forged a small army during her grueling march home. Upon arriving, she expected to find her homeland's nobility ready to rise to her cause, but they'd been cowed and terrified by reports of Dranzorg entombing captives and rivals in his castle's walls. Calling them cowards, Mara drove her troops harshly on, suffering daily ambushes and desertions. When Castle Laventz finally came into view, Mara led less than a dozen irresolute knights. Shouting her frustrations into the night, Mara was answered by a voice from the shadows. This sinister force would give her the power to take back her home and rule her lands, but she would never leave Castle Laventz again. Without hesitation, Mara accepted the arrangement. In the same instant, Dranzorg's troops swept in and took Mara and her knights captive.

Within the castle, Dranzorg showed Mara and her followers the hollow walls where they'd be buried alive. Mara's troops pleaded for their lives. Wickedly, the warlord promised to spare them if they watched their leader's entombment and spread the tale of her failure. As they agreed, Mara unleashed her rage with a supernatural, ear-bloodying scream. She slew Dranzorg barehanded and then, taking up his axe, felled the warlord's troops and her own traitorous followers.

Soon after, local nobles received invitations to come to Castle Laventz and celebrate Mara's victory. When each aristocrat arrived, though, they discovered they were the sole guests within a crimson-stained castle. Passing judgment on each noble for abandoning her family, Mara bricked them into her castle's walls. Rumors swiftly spread of Mara's vengeance and the castle whose walls cried. Mara was never seen again, and Castle Laventz came to be called the Castle of Lament.

Centuries passed, and Castle Laventz fell to ruins. Eventually, the successful merchant Loren Halvhrest purchased the land. By then, only one of Castle Laventz's towers remained. The frugal Halvhrest incorporated the tower into the construction of a lavish manor for his family. The Halvhrests lived peacefully in their new home for several years before mysteriously vanishing. Those who investigated found no trace of the family but were deeply unsettled by the house. Grim tales rapidly resurfaced, providing the roots for all manner of ghastly tales and a new name for the structure: the House of Lament.

RUNNING THE ADVENTURE

The following adventure requires the fifth edition D&D rulebooks (*Player's Handbook*, *Dungeon Master's Guide*, and *Monster Manual*). You should read an entire adventure before attempting to run it. If you'd prefer to play this adventure, you shouldn't read any further or you risk spoiling it.

The *Monster Manual* contains statistics for many of the creatures found in this adventure. When a creature's name appears in **bold** type, that's a visual cue pointing you to the creature's stat block in the *Monster Manual*. If the stat block appears elsewhere, the adventure's text tells you so.

> Text that appears in a box like this is meant to be read aloud or paraphrased for the players when their characters first arrive at a location or under a specific circumstance, as described in the text.

ADVENTURE SUMMARY

The characters arrive at the House of Lament after a mysterious message leads them into the Mists. At the door, they meet investigators who invite them to participate in an exploration of the building. As the party initially surveys the house, it manifests subtle hauntings. The characters are then invited to participate in the first of several séances, allowing them to commune with the spirits of the house.

Depending on the spirit summoned during the séance, the characters learn about one of the tragedies that transpired in the house. Additional séances and discoveries ultimately wake the collective spirits and sinister forces lurking in the manor, trapping the characters inside the house. Escape requires the party to defeat an ageless evil. If they don't, they'll become another group of lost spirits imprisoned within the House of Lament.

THE HAUNTINGS OF HALVHREST HOUSE

The House of Lament is a catastrophically haunted structure. It doesn't rush to reveal its terrors, though. Rather, its history, threats, and phantasmal inhabitants reveal themselves gradually and in a variety of ways. Before leading your adventurers into the house, familiarize yourself with the varied ways the house's hauntings manifest.

THE HOUSE'S DOMAIN

The House of Lament is both a domain and a Darklord, a collective of tortured spirits trapped within a single structure. The majority of these shades are nothing more than faint, rageful impressions, but a few powerful personalities remain. These remnants belonged to inhabitants of the house, desperate individuals like Mara Silvra and Dalk Dranzorg. Fractured and angry, the collective spirits within the house brood amid bitter dreams. Yet when strangers enter the domain, the spirits gradually wake, energizing the one instinct they share: to add to the number of souls bound within the house's walls.

The House of Lament is capable of imposing itself over other lands and can appear in other Domains of Dread. A version of the house stands in western Borca (see chapter 3), and the structure can be accessed there no matter where else it appears. The house travels at the whims of the Dark Powers and might appear and linger for days or years before vanishing.

When the House of Lament closes the borders of its domain, a powerful thunderstorm surrounds it, bringing with it strong wind and heavy precipitation (detailed in the *Dungeon Master's Guide*). Anyone who braves the violent storm discovers that the Mists surround the house in all directions. The Mists affect those who enter them as described in chapter 3.

THE ENTITY

A mysterious malevolence lies beneath the House of Lament (see area 31). More a force of nature than an individual being, the Entity is a bodiless intellect that nudges those in the domain toward wickedness. As characters explore, use the Entity as a lurking manifestation of the Dark Powers, a vague glimpse of a terror even the house's spirits fear.

TYPES OF HAUNTINGS

When the party enters the house, few menaces initially present themselves. As characters explore, though, spirits gradually stir to life, transforming the house into a supernatural deathtrap. The haunting within the house has two states:

Dormant. When living beings arrive at the house, the haunting is dormant. During this time, the unassuming structure seems typical of an abandoned house. Impressions of past events and subtle, ambient haunts transpire during this time (see "Ambient Haunts").

Awakened. In the course of the adventure, the activities of the living alert the house's spirits. Once this occurs, the House of Lament closes the domain's borders, surrounds itself with the Mists, and conjures a powerful storm. Dangerous haunts occur throughout the house at this time.

WAKING THE HOUSE

The house reveals its full haunting at a dramatic moment. The adventure notes events that wake the house, many surrounding the events of the third séance (see the following "Séances" section). Use ambient haunts and the atmosphere-building tips from earlier in this chapter to drive the adventure toward a dramatic scene where it feels appropriate for the house to reveal its full malevolence.

If characters prove especially persistent (or destructive), the house might wake earlier. If this occurs, the adventure's horror takes on a more in-your-face slasher quality, but there's nothing wrong with that—ditch the subtlety and go for wild shocks. Triggers that wake the house early include deliberate damage inflicted by its visitors and entering and then leaving area 24.

After waking, the House of Lament will not become dormant again for several weeks.

AMBIENT HAUNTS

Even while dormant, the house is haunted. During this time, the spirits of the house drift and sleepwalk through a structure that's changed radically over generations. Ambient haunts are glimpses of these phantasmal impressions. They're subtle and reveal themselves to only a single witness. They exist to help you develop the house's supernatural ambience and the spirits trapped within.

Using Ambient Haunts. An ambient haunt is unsettling but can't harm characters. Use ambient haunts whenever you please to heighten the creepiness of a situation. Avoid overuse, however. If characters experience frequent haunts, the manifestations become mundane or ignorable.

THE SPIRIT OF LADY
THEODORA HALVHREST

Witnessing Haunts. Ambient haunts are fleeting visions that last scant seconds and that only one character ever sees. They appear when a character is alone or the last one to leave a room, or they are simply imperceptible to all but one character. They never manifest for the entire group. Haunts may favor appearing for certain characters, perhaps due to Dark Gifts or backgrounds individuals possess.

Suggested Haunts. Some encounter areas suggest ambient haunts specific to that location. Don't hesitate to save these haunts for the party's later visits to an area.

Creating Ambient Haunts. The following tables offer glimpses of specific spirits haunting the house. To generate a random ambient haunt, roll on the Spirits of the House table to determine what spirit manifests, then the Spectral Activity table to reveal what the spirit does. You can also personalize ambient haunts to involve characters' fears. Don't hesitate to review these tables and prepare ambient haunts to have ready during the adventure.

Spirits of the House

d20	Spirit
1–5	**Lost Spirit.** Someone bound to the house, such as a noble Mara entombed in the walls, a past investigator, or someone a character knows
6–8	**Newes.** The Halvhrests' off-kilter family pet (an animal of your choice)
9–10	**Victro Belview.** The Halvhrests' stoic, nearly 7-foot-tall butler
11–12	**Loren Halvhrest.** An affable merchant who loves to sing (despite being not particularly good at it)
13–15	**Theodora Halvhrest.** The lady of the house, who loves her family, gardening, and dancing
16–17	**Dalk Dranzorg.** A cruel tyrant who wears a skull-faced helmet and frequently lies
18–19	**Mara Silvra.** A vengeful knight who expects betrayal and tries to expel trespassers
20	**The Entity.** A shadowy malevolence that manifests as grasping limbs or wounded masses within the house's walls and floors

Spectral Activity

d20	Activity
1–3	The spirit causes an object in the room to animate in a whimsical or unsettling manner.
4–6	The spirit leaves a brief message, threat, or question, perhaps asking where someone is or suggesting how one might hasten their demise.
7–9	The spirit walks through a wall or character.
10–11	Only a portion of the spirit appears—such as a hand, eye, heart, nervous system, or skull.
12–13	The spirit uses the room as they might have in life. If the room didn't exist when they were alive, the spirit interacts with a space others can't see (such as a stable, stairwell, or training hall).
14–15	The spirit lurks in an unexpected place, such as in a cabinet, under a bed, or in character's pack.
16–17	The spirit sees a character. It draws near, whispers a question, or flees.
18–19	The spirit recreates a terrifying moment: either its own death or someone else's visceral end.
20	The spirit is soundlessly ambushed by shadowy limbs that drag it into the floor or walls.

Nightmares

Whenever the party takes a long rest in the house, one character suffers a nightmare. Choose a character at random or one who has a Dark Gift or background that makes them sensitive to visions of the past. If none of the characters sleep during a long rest, one of them experiences a waking vision that plays out like an ambient haunt. These nightmares gradually reveal details from the "Story Overview." Relate these specifics to the character experiencing the nightmare, embellishing them or presenting them as intense but half-remembered visions. Characters might witness any of the following events:

- A warlord in a skull-shaped helmet (Dranzorg) cackles as wicked soldiers brick a captive into a stone wall.
- A desperate knight (Mara) forces tired soldiers to march toward an ominous castle (Castle Laventz).
- A knight (Mara) howls her frustrations into the night. Shadows rise, surrounding her in a crimson aura.
- A screaming knight (Mara) slays a warlord (Dranzorg) and proceeds on a murderous rampage through a castle.
- A terrified aristocrat shrieks as they're bricked into a stone wall by a bloody knight (Mara).

Waking from a nightmare can be worse than the dream itself. Unless someone watches each character for the entirety of the time they're resting, the character who experiences the nightmare vanishes. Plausibly they could have wandered off in their sleep, but in truth they're teleported elsewhere by the house. Roll on the Nightmare Awakening table to determine where the character wakes, or choose another unsettling locale.

Nightmare Awakening

d6	Waking Location
1	Standing on a railing on the widow's walk (area 25)
2	In the tub of the master bath (area 17), facing a mirror smeared with blood that repeats the words "Bloody Mara" three times
3	Inside an empty cask in the wine cellar (area 27), which is easily mistaken for a coffin from the inside
4	Sprawled on the table in the dining room (area 11), surrounded by illusory diners draped in sheets
5	Seated in the office (area 18) before an illusory, phantom accountant who measures sins and virtues as ghostly coins on a merchant's scale
6	Under the bedcovers in one of the bedrooms (area 14 or 21) while something approaches in the dark

Haunted Traps

Several of the house's hauntings manifest as haunted traps. Characters can use the Channel Divinity class feature to exorcise these magical traps. See "Haunted Traps" earlier in this chapter for details on these hazards.

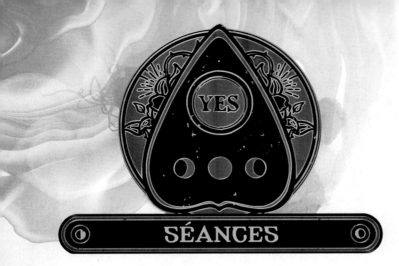

SÉANCES

At certain times in the adventure, characters have the opportunity to commune with the House of Lament's spirits, contacting them directly through a series of séances involving a spirit board (see the appendix). These séances reveal the goals of the house's spirits but also determine the adventure's climax and how the party might ultimately escape the domain. These details are presented here for ease of reference, as the séances occur at multiple points throughout the adventure.

Prior to running a séance, choose or randomly determine which spirit the party will contact. The key spirits, the tone of their communication, and what they fixate upon include:

Dalk Dranzorg. This manipulative murderer wants the party to trust him so they'll free his corpse from area 5a. He gives his name as "Garland Kordz," an anagram of his actual name.

Mara Silvra. This rageful spirit expresses her anger at traitors and trespassers. She urges characters to find area 31, hoping to trade their lives for her freedom from a bargain she made with the Entity.

Theodora Halvhrest. The sorrowful former lady of the house hides the spirits of her children in area 24. She's wary of trespassers but sees them as a way to free her children.

Consult the "Escaping the House" section at the end of the adventure for details on the specific climaxes each spirit drives the plot toward.

RUNNING A SÉANCE

Séances reveal the mysteries of the House of Lament through atmospheric encounters. These events all take place in the house's parlor (area 3). Before a séance, consider how you'll run the encounter and what information it should convey.

Timing. They occur at points noted throughout the adventure or when you feel is appropriate to the tension of the story. The spirits of the house are willing to be channeled only once per day, so the party must wait until after the following dawn to conduct another séance.

Preparation and Ambiance. Plan for séances in a way that creates a safe, moody atmosphere. Prepare the spirit board and any other props ahead of time. Consult "Running Horror Games" earlier in this chapter for advice on creating atmosphere.

Conducting a Séance. One of the investigators detailed in the following "Guests of the House" section leads each séance. Narrate the start of the séance and encourage each character to ask a question. As they do, you control how the spirits within the house respond. To do this, subtly guide the planchette on the spirit board or otherwise make the spirits' intentions known. Use the investigator who isn't running the séance to ask basic questions or ease the party into engaging. Provide short, mysterious answers.

Séance Pacing. None of the spirits immediately blurts out their desires. The characters are strangers in the spirits' house, and before the dead accept the trespassers, these spirits try to build a rapport through at least three interactions. The séances described in the following sections outline the information conveyed in these encounters. You may run more séances as you see fit.

Unanswered Questions. Decide what questions a spirit will or won't answer. If a spirit chooses not to answer a question, they might affect the parlor's lighting or decorations in some ominous but noncommittal way. A character can ask another question if a spirit doesn't answer. Alternatively, if you're using a prop spirit board, don't move the planchette and see if the players unconsciously guide the planchette to a response.

FIRST SÉANCE

The investigator running the séance explains that they plan to use the spirit board in area 3 to contact the spirits to learn why they linger here. The investigators invite the party to sit at the parlor table and join them in touching a planchette atop the spirit board. The lead investigator then starts the séance, saying:

> "Spirits of this house, we are strangers who come openly and without malice. We seek only to know your stories and to help you find peace. We entreat you: make your presence known."

The spirits wait long enough for the characters to wonder if the ceremony worked. Then the room grows cooler, the lights dim, and the planchette moves to the word "Greetings."

One of the investigators asks the first question: "Who are we speaking to?" The spirit replies by spelling out the first name of the spirit you chose to contact (Mara, Theodora, or "Garland" for Dranzorg).

The spirits answer questions as guided by their aforementioned goals and personalities. All of them know the house's history and anything characters have seen or done in the house. By the end of the first séance, the spirit conveys an unprompted message (with ellipses denoting pauses):

Dalk Dranzorg: "HELP U ... UNDER PORCH".
The planchette then moves to the sword symbol. Dranzorg is trying to win trust by leading the party to his lost weapon buried in area 1.

Mara Silvra: "EVICT THE CHIMNEY WITCH".
The planchette then moves to the skull image at the top of the spirit board. Mara wants to use the characters to free her consciousness from the house. She tests them first, setting the characters after the Chimney Witch detailed in area 10.

Theodora Halvhrest: "SEEK THE WITCH STONE". The planchette then moves to the candle image. Theodora tests the characters' willingness to help by having them light a candle detailed in area 25.

When every character has asked a question and the spirit conveys its message, the presence moves the planchette to the word "Farewell" and departs. The investigators are pleased with the progress and eager to contact the same spirit again. They encourage the party to continue their exploration of the house with the spirit's words in mind, but they don't feel the need to rush things, planning to pick up the investigation after resting and further research.

If characters have not already reached 2nd level, they gain a level when this séance ends.

Second Séance

The investigators conduct the second séance likely after the party has explored most of the house and followed the lead they received from the first séance. Preferably, the house has not yet awakened. If the party has not yet fulfilled a spirit's request from the first séance, consider repeating the spirit's request from the first séance at least once.

An investigator starts the second séance as they did the first one, and the same spirit from the first séance answers. By the end of the séance, the spirit conveys a personal message, even if not asked:

Dalk Dranzorg: "SHE MURDERED ME ... TRAPPED ... COLD". Dalk plays for sympathy and hopes to pit the characters against Mara. It's possible the players have realized who "Garland" is, but at this point he denies it.

Mara Silvra: "EVICT LEAPER NEXT". Mara offers a new message only if the characters battled the Chimney Witch. She now asks the characters to combat the Leaper in area 5b.

Theodora Halvhrest: "RESTORE HER SHIELD". Theodora offers a new message only if the charac-

ters acted on her last request. If they did, she ends her message by having the planchette circle the flowers and vines on the spirit board's frame, suggesting the way to open the door to area 24.

After this, the séance ends as the first one did, and the investigators encourage the party to complete its investigations. If the players are enjoying the séances or are taking their time exploring, feel free to run this encounter multiple times, allowing the characters to ask more questions.

If the borders to the domain are not yet closed, a storm begins brewing at this point.

Final Séance

This séance occurs whenever you choose to run it, likely after the party has fulfilled any requests made during the second séance. At its end, the house wakes, shifting the party's objective from investigation to survival.

An investigator starts the final séance as they have previously. The same spirit answers this call, but its demeanor has changed. Their effect on the room is more severe, causing it to grow darker and colder or causing portraits to animate in unsettling ways. By the end of this séance, the spirit has either set the party on the path to wake the house or has done it themselves:

Dalk Dranzorg: "SHE IS COMING ... FREE ME ... UNDER STAIRS". Dalk has lost his patience with the party. He demands they free him from area 5a. If the characters realize who he is, he doesn't deny it and insists they'll never escape without his help. The séance ends with Dalk's message followed by the house awakening and the sound of Mara's distant scream.

Mara Silvra: "FIND ME BELOW". Mara offers a new message only if the characters battled the Chimney Witch and the Leaper. She encourages them to come for her next. Mara opens the path in area 28. At this point, the rest of the house's spirits think Mara is attempting to escape and awaken the house to prevent this.

Theodora Halvhrest: "GET THEM OUT". Theodora shares a vision with all the characters in the room. Spectral images of the dragon and knight toys from area 24 hover in the air before dissolving into vapor. She wants the characters to get the toys her children haunt away from the house.

When the séance ends, review what happens when the house wakes and look ahead to "Escaping the House" at the end of the adventure. Unless otherwise noted, should the party try to conduct additional séances at this point, the spirits are unhelpful or aggressive.

If characters have not already reached 3rd level, they gain a level when this séance ends.

Starting the Adventure

"The House of Lament" serves as an introduction to the Domains of Dread and can serve as the first adventure in a longer horror campaign. As players make characters, use the following details to encourage them along the path leading into the Mists.

Leaving the Past Behind

Before beginning the adventure, ask each player to contemplate where and how their character lives. Their answers don't need to be specific or rooted in the Domains of Dread. If you plan this adventure to be the first in an ongoing horror campaign, recommend characters avoid strong ties to their homes, as they might never see them again.

Mysterious Message

Once each player has conveyed their broad thoughts about their character's situation, inform them that their character has come to possess a cryptic message and directions to an unfamiliar but nearby meeting place. Work with the players to decide the message's contents, how each character mysteriously receive the message, and why they've decided to follow the directions. The message should be vague but enticing to the character, such as "They need your help," "Prove yourself," or "Reclaim what you've lost."

Meeting in the Mists

Once the players are ready to begin, explain that they've each chosen to follow the message's directions. Then read the following boxed text:

> Following the directions in the cryptic message you received, it doesn't take long before they lead you from familiar roads onto a disused trail overgrown by weeds and the roots of spindly trees. A light drizzle begins to fall as you travel. As you approach a wooded crossroads, the leaden rain makes the cloaked form standing there seem all the more unreal.

All the characters see this same sight, though they don't see one another. Ask how each character reacts to what they see. Regardless, the figure responds in the following way:

> The figure's head snaps up, glaring with piercing, yellow eyes. What you took for a cloak spreads around it, revealing itself to be a pair of mighty black wings. With one powerful motion and a blast of chill air, the wings sweep and the vague figure is gone.

The characters have no way of knowing this for certain, but they've just glimpsed a **wereraven** (see chapter 5). They have no way of stopping the mysterious creature.

Again, ask the characters how they react. Those who approach the crossroads openly see each other coming down different paths toward the intersection. The number of paths that converge here equals the number of characters.

First Meeting. Give the characters time to meet, realize that they've all just witnessed the same thing, learn that they all received similar messages, and raise questions they have no answers for. The Mists of Ravenloft have subtly claimed them, and why they've been brought together is a mystery they might never fully understand.

One thing they are likely to realize, though, is that all of them just came from home, which is supposedly back the way they came. As characters converse, encourage them to gradually realize they're unfamiliar with the landmarks the others refer to, despite supposedly all living nearby.

What Remains. Anyone who investigates the spot the figure vanished from finds a number of sizable black feathers, one for each character. They also find a planchette—a device tied to communicating with the dead—decorated with bird skulls. This item has no magical properties or immediate use but might prove useful as the adventure proceeds.

The Mists. The day's drizzle has grown into a rainstorm, and anyone who looks back down the trails sees their path shrouded in haze. Eventually, characters will proceed along one of the paths and into this fog. Regardless of which trail they choose, those who enter the fog vanish for a moment, only to walk out of the haze a few steps from where they entered. Even if the whole party enters the fog, they soon reemerge back at the crossroads. Alternatively, you might use the Wandering the Mists table in chapter 3 to inspire other events. No matter what the characters do, the Mists lead the characters back to the crossroads.

Development. As the realization that they're trapped dawns on the characters, the gray light in the cloudy sky begins to dim. As it does, though, a faint light becomes visible through the haze, leading up a wooded hillside. If the characters approach, they'll soon find the light emanates from a most unusual structure.

Guests of the House

The characters are about to discover the haunted house known as the House of Lament. They aren't the first to arrive, though. Two investigators are already there, having come for their own reasons unrelated to the characters' strange experience. Prior the party's arrival at the house, choose which pair of investigators meets them. Unless otherwise noted, these characters are described in the "Mist Wanderers" section of chapter 3:

Alanik Ray and Arthur Sedgwick. A mysterious third party hired these detectives to recover documents related to Loren Halvhrest's business and discover the state of his missing heirs.

Gennifer and Laurie Weathermay-Foxgrove. The renowned monster hunters were hired by a family in Borca to put an end to the house's haunting.

Ireena Kolyana and Ez d'Avenir. These adventurers want to learn what made the House of Lament what it is and free the spirits that haunt it. Ireena Kolyana is a reincarnation of the fateful spirit named Tatyana detailed in the "Barovia" section of chapter 3. If you wish, she might be replaced with any other reincarnation of Tatyana detailed in that domain.

Rudolph (and Erasmus) van Richten. Doctor Rudolph van Richten appears to be alone, investigating the house to test methods of freeing lingering spirits. He has no idea—and refuses all evidence—that he is accompanied by the spirit of his son, Erasmus. Mentions of an accompanying companion elsewhere in this adventure generally don't apply to van Richten, but Erasmus gradually reveals himself to those who help his father.

ARRIVING AT THE HOUSE

When the characters seek the source of the light, read or paraphrase the following description:

> Gradually the haze and brush give way, revealing a bald hilltop. There stands a grim black tower, the last defiant turret of a long-crumbled fortress. Attached to this tower is a three-story manor house, weather beaten and veined with ivy. A porch girds the house, its sagging roof sheltering a stout front door that stands open and emits a flickering light.

This is the House of Lament. Abandoned for centuries, it was disturbed only moments ago by a pair of investigators who are in the process of bringing in their equipment for what they expect to be multiple days of exploration and study. They've identified the parlor (area 3) as the base for their investigation.

If the characters don't disguise their approach, one of the investigators calls out, identifies themselves, and welcomes the company. They invite the party inside to meet with their partner. Ultimately, if the party proves cooperative, the investigators offer the following information:

- They know nothing about the messages the characters received.

ADVENTURE FLOWCHART

ARRIVING AT THE HOUSE
The adventurers meet amid the Mists and find themselves drawn to the House of Lament. There they meet one or two determined investigators.

EXPLORING THE HOUSE
With their new allies, the characters explore the house and glimpse fleeting hauntings.

FIRST SÉANCE
The characters participate in the first of three séances, communing with Garland, Mara, or Theodora.

DEEPER INTO THE HOUSE
The adventures explore more of the house, witnessing unsettling sights and learning more of its tragic history.

SECOND SÉANCE
The spirit the characters previously communicated with provides more insights into the house and makes ominous requests.

MYSTERIES OF THE HOUSE
The characters reach the most haunted quarters of the house, potentially rousing deadly spirits.

FINAL SÉANCE
A spirit makes a desperate demand, and the full fury of the house is unleashed.

THE HOUSE AWAKES
If the house's hauntings have not fully revealed themselves, they do so now.

- They have heard of mysterious occurrences wherein strangers become "lost in the Mists" and arrive in unexpected places.
- They likely don't know where the characters hail from, but offer to lead the characters to the city of Sturben in Borca after their work is complete.
- If asked, they'll share that the house was last owned by the Halvhrest family, it's abandoned, and it has a reputation for attracting the dead.
- They offer each party member 20 gp per day to help them explore the house and document strange phenomena.

If the party accepts the investigators' offer, they acquire reliable allies. One of the investigators offers to join the party in their exploration the house. The other stays in the parlor to prepare to contact the house's spirits (see the "Séances" section). In the case of Rudolph van Richten, he remains in the parlor while the characters explore the house.

If the party rejects the investigators' offer, they stay out of the characters' way. They'll still invite the characters to participate in their séances and are amenable to collaborating if characters have a change of heart. Anyone who tries to leave the grounds surrounding the House of Lament find their way barred by the Mists. Whenever they enter the haze, the Mists lead them back to the house, just as they did at the crossroads.

THE HOUSE OF LAMENT

Once the characters meet the investigators and shift their attention to the house, their exploration begins.

HOUSE OF LAMENT FEATURES

The House of Lament appears to be an ordinary structure. It's in ill repair and the floorboards are exceptionally creaky, but the construction overall seems sturdy. The house is unlit, but abundant half-burned candles and empty lanterns appear throughout the rooms. Unless otherwise noted, ceilings inside the house are about 10 feet high, and the doors are made of stout mahogany. Any of the doors might be swollen shut, requiring a successful DC 10 Strength (Athletics) check to open.

Less obviously, the structure supernaturally resists damage. While dormant, the house appears to take damage normally, though soggy woods prevent fire from spreading. After 24 hours, though, any damage to the house repairs itself. After the house wakes, damage to the structure heals immediately, accompanied by bleeding boards or glimpses of horrifying spaces beyond the woodwork.

Discourage characters from trying to destroy the house while it's dormant (the investigators oppose demolition attempts). Should the party obsessively persist in their destructiveness, the house eventually wakes to defend itself.

HOUSE OF LAMENT LOCATIONS

Locations in the House of Lament are keyed to map 4.1. The descriptions of these areas detail the house in its dormant state. Phantasmal activity that occurs in an area regardless of the house's state is detailed in a section called "Ambient Haunt." If the area changes when the house wakes, alterations are noted in a section called "Awakened Haunt."

1. PORCH

The porch is creaky, covered in dead vines, and infested with earwigs, but otherwise unremarkable. An unlocked double door opens from the front of the house into area 2. An unlocked door on the east side of the house leads to area 10. Characters who succeed on a DC 12 Strength (Athletics) check can climb the porch's supports to area 19 above.

Crawl Space. Destroying part of the porch reveals a 3-foot-high crawl space below. Any 5-foot-square space of the porch has AC 13, 10 hit points, and immunity to poison and psychic damage. Medium creatures must squeeze to enter the crawl space, but Small or smaller creatures can enter unimpeded. Those who wriggle into the crawl space upset a swarm of unnaturally aggressive earwigs (use the **swam of maggots** stat block in chapter 5).

Treasure. In the crawl space, just in front of the house's front door, is a grave-sized rectangle of gray dust and dead bugs. Anyone who spends 5 minutes digging in this spot finds Dalk Dranzorg's cursed battleaxe Bilestongue, a *berserker axe* (detailed in the *Dungeon Master's Guide*) embossed with excessively salivating demonic toads. Characters are unlikely to find it unless Dranzorg's spirit directs them here during a séance.

2. FOYER

> Peeling wallpaper and a musty scent cling to the walls of this spacious foyer. A curving staircase rises from the cracked tile floor to a balcony above, keeping its distance from a darkened chandelier. Doors lead in every direction. At the room's center, a bronze sculpture of an antlered eagle perches atop a marble pedestal.

This once-impressive entryway is dusty and choked with cobwebs. The stairs climb to the balcony above (area 13). The ceiling here rises 20 feet from the floor. The statue is attached to the pedestal, which together weigh 800 pounds.

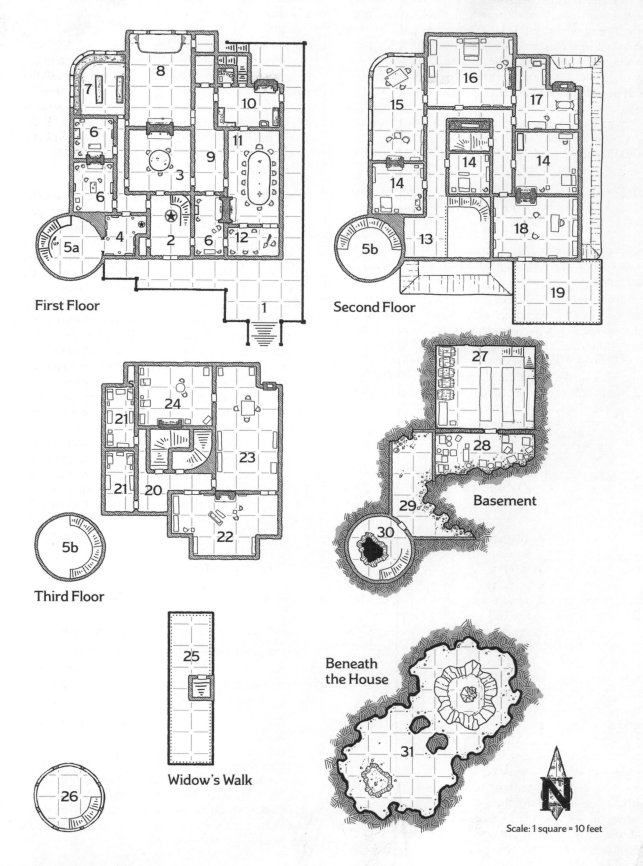

First Floor

7
8
10
6
11
3
9
6
5a
4
2
6
12
1

Second Floor

15
16
17
14
14
14
5b
13
18
19

Third Floor

21
24
21
23
20
22
5b

Widow's Walk

25
26

Basement

27
28
29
30

Beneath the House

31

Scale: 1 square = 10 feet

MAP 4.1: THE HOUSE OF LAMENT

DYSON LOGOS

Closet. A closet to the west holds several moth-eaten black cloaks and, on a high shelf, a heavy but empty leather hat box.

Awakened Haunt. When a creature enters this room, the eagle statue shudders and cracks. A round later, a wet, red **peryton** hatches from the sculpture and attacks.

3. Parlor

> Dozens of faded portraits cover this parlor's walls, the subjects' eyes fixed on a circular table that bears an ornate spirit board. A wide mirror hangs over a tall fireplace set in the north wall.

Theodora Halvhrest used this room to tastefully indulge her interest in spiritualism. Wards and images here deter the house's spirits from entering the room unless summoned via magic or an implement such as the spirit board.

DALK DRANZORG

At present, the investigators stashed their equipment here and plan to "make camp" in this room.

Séances. One of the investigators spends their time here, getting a feel for the place and poring through notes. When the party first arrives, they note that the spirit board here would be the perfect tool to contact the house's spirits, but they don't see anything suitable for use as a planchette. Encourage the characters to offer up the planchette they found. If they don't, the investigator soon finds one in the room and begins preparing to conduct the first of several séances. How and when these séances unfold are detailed in the "Séances" section.

Portraits. Portraits on the walls depict members of the Halvhrest family as well as members of the Keepers of the Feather (detailed in chapter 3), many of whom wear the Mark of the Raven. Any character who succeeds on a DC 16 Wisdom (Perception) check notices a cloaked figure like the one at the crossroads standing in the background of a portrait.

Reference Material. The investigators possess a variety of books detailing haunts and occult lore. Any character who spends an hour consulting these books gains advantage on their next Intelligence (Arcana or Religion) check related to the undead or the history of the House of Lament. These books can also be used to identify the Mark of the Raven, the symbol of the god Ezra, and the symbol of the priests of Osybus (see chapter 3).

4. Gallery

> Moody landscapes and dour busts atop marble pedestals collect dust in this modest gallery. In an alcove to the east stands a larger-than-life onyx statue of an athlete wrestling monstrous, disembodied tentacles. To the west, a wall made of black stone curves into this room, an arch opening into a darkened space beyond.

This room displays the Halvhrest family's art collection. The subject matters vary, and the works have suffered years of neglect. The ancient tower attached to the house abuts the room.

Statue. Those who investigate the statue realize it is hollow and the figure's eyes open into the cavity inside. The statue has AC 14, 10 hit points, and immunity to poison and psychic damage. If it is destroyed, characters discover a crumbling scrap of parchment inside. It bears a short message from the statue's tormented sculptor: "Shadowed fingers. Eyes like glass. Beware the below. —L. Dolan."

Awakened Haunt. When a character enters this room, the four busts here explode, unleashing four **death's heads** of the gnashing variety (see chapter 5). If the busts have been removed from this room, choose a dramatic moment after the house wakes for them to "hatch."

Treasure. The four busts and six paintings in this room are well made, and each fetches 50 gp from a collector. They are bulky, though: the busts each weigh 30 pounds, and the framed paintings weigh 15 pounds each.

5A. Tower Base

> Wind moans through the open interior of the ancient tower attached to the manor. Stairs curve from the floor to circle the dark granite walls and vanish into a chamber high above.

This tower is all that remains of Castle Laventz. Here, Dalk Dranzorg threatened to imprison Mara Silvra within the castle's walls. A bricked-over alcove remains, but while the house is dormant it's impossible to notice or access. Both the tower and the floor are protected by the structure's resistance to damage until after the house wakes.

The stairs here climb 10 feet to area 5b.

Awakened Haunt. Blood runs down the northwestern wall, outlining the hidden alcove. This part of the wall has AC 16, 20 hit points, and immunity to poison and psychic damage. Opening the alcove reveals a cramped space packed with those Mara buried in her castle's walls, specifically two **boneless** (see chapter 5) and the corpse of Dalk Dranzorg.

Dranzorg has the statistics of a **revenant** with one exception: his Rejuvenation trait restores him and the boneless after 1 minute, returning them to the alcove in this area. He wears the sinister armor and demon skull helmet he wore in life, but centuries of rust ensure they don't affect his statistics. Dranzorg can be permanently destroyed only if he's slain by Mara or a creature possessed by Mara. Consult "Tyrant's Escape" at the end of the adventure for details.

5B. Tower Heights

The stairs along the tower's interior lack railings and climb 40 feet into area 26. Creatures can climb the tower's interior or exterior walls with a successful DC 14 Strength (Athletics) check.

The Leaper. Any creature that climbs the tower hears a horrified scream. The sound of the scream originates from above, passes any climbers, moves to the tower's floor, and then repeats. The effect sounds like someone repeatedly falling through the tower. This scream is an effect created by a malicious spirit called the Leaper.

While the house is dormant, the Leaper manifests as a sound and a powerful wind issuing from above. Any creature that climbs more than 30 feet up the tower, using the stairs or otherwise, must make a DC 15 Strength saving throw. On a successful save, the creature is halted in its movement and can't climb higher due to the strong wind. On a failed save, it is thrown from the stairs and takes 10 (3d6) bludgeoning damage upon landing in area 5a. The wind supernaturally prevents flying creatures from rising more than 30 feet.

Awakened Haunt. If the house is awakened or the characters seek the Leaper as directed to during a séance, the wind is replaced by a vindictive poltergeist (a variant **specter**) that tries to use its Telekinetic Thrust to throw characters from the stairs.

6. Sitting Room

The first floor contains three sitting rooms, where Loren Halvhrest expressed his dubious taste in curio collecting. You are free to determine the contents of these themed rooms and any ambient haunts that occur within, perhaps using characters' fears or interests as inspiration.

7. Conservatory

> Desiccated vines sprawl across the tables and foggy glass walls of this conservatory. Rusted gardening tools and pots of barren soil lie scattered across sturdy wooden tables.

This indoor greenhouse was Theodora Halvhrest's pride and joy.

Ambient Haunt. The first time any character enters this room (whether the house is dormant or awakened), a vision plays out:

> Between eyeblinks, the conservatory is alive and filled with flowers. A transparent woman with a veiled hat and parasol strolls through the room. She pauses here and there to admire a bloom or adjust a pot, and then looks toward you. As suddenly as she appeared, she vanishes, and the room lies in ruin once more.

This illusory vision provides a glimpse of Theodora Halvhrest. Characters might recognize her if they've seen the portraits in areas 18 or 22. The illusion is harmless, and the characters can't disrupt it.

Haunted Trap. When the scene ends, a haunted trap with a +2 Haunt Bonus activates (see "Haunted Traps" earlier in this chapter). Any creature in the room with a passive Perception score of 12 or higher notices rusty gardening tools levitating from the tables and floors. Those who notice can take an action. After this, the haunted trap activates. Numerous troughs and gardening implements lance through the room. Every creature in the room is targeted by a ranged attack with a +2 bonus. A target that is hit takes 2 (1d4) piercing damage and must make a DC 14 Strength saving throw. Those who fail are restrained and begin suffocating as black vines erupt from their clothes and mouths then tighten around their bodies. Any creature adjacent to an affected creature can remove the vines by spending an action and succeeding on a DC 14 Strength check.

After the trap activates, cracks run through the conservatory's windows. The fractures form the word "Uninvited."

Belladonna. Inexplicably, one plant is still alive and flourishing in the room: a belladonna plant with fat, black berries. It can be useful in completing the symbol of Ezra that appears on the door to area 24.

8. BALLROOM

> Broken boards mar the weblike design worked into this ballroom's wooden floor. A short stage for long-departed musicians stands at the room's far end, overlooked by cracked stained-glass windows.

The Halvhrests held delightful gatherings here, never knowing that Warlord Dranzorg's audience hall previously occupied the same space.

Ambient Haunt. This haunting captures one side of an exchange between Dalk Dranzorg and his captives after he took Mara Silvra and her knights prisoner. The haunting occurs only once during the adventure. When two or more characters enter the room for the first time, read the following text:

> A hollow, mocking voice reaches you, echoing as if from far away. "I'll give you a simple choice, my misguided knights. You can join Lady Silvra, and I'll entomb you all within my fortress's walls. Or forsake your commander, bear witness to her execution, and then walk free to tell all of Dranzorg's justice. My mercy knows but a moment, friends. Choose!"

Ask each player how or if their character responds, as if they were the knights in question. Following this, an ear-splitting shriek fills the room, affecting each character in the area in one of the following ways corresponding to their reaction:

Join Lady Silvra or Belligerence. Characters who say they'll join Lady Silvra or who taunt the voice hear the scream but aren't affected by it. Instead, one of the stained-glass windows on the stage cracks. The fractures look like the character as if they were trapped within the glass.

Forsake Lady Silvra or Silence. Those who say they'll abandon Lady Silvra or who stay silent must make a DC 14 Wisdom saving throw, taking 10 (3d6) psychic damage on a failed save, or half as much damage on a successful one. In either case, the character's ears bleed until the end of their next turn.

Channel Divinity. If a character uses the Channel Divinity class feature, treat this manifestation as a haunted trap with a +4 Haunt Bonus. If the character's Channel Divinity disables the haunted trap, the scream that follows sounds distant and weak. The sound is harmless and thereafter the room is normal. If the haunted trap wouldn't be disabled, treat this as belligerence.

Closet. At the rear of the room is a closet filled with withered decorations from past celebrations. A faded banner depicts numerous winged seahorses and the words "Happy Birthday Regan and Vastion!"

9. FIRST FLOOR HALL

The hall is lined with broken picture frames. A rug with a dizzying geometric pattern covers the floor.

Closet. The closet is dark and conspicuously empty.

10. KITCHEN

> A rack previously suspended from this kitchen's ceiling has crashed, crushing a table and scattering rusted pots and cooking implements. A sizable iron stove is built into the north wall. Several doors lead from the room.

The kitchen of the Halvhrest home now lies in shambles. The debris and broken furnishings make the entire area difficult terrain.

Oven. This simple oven is little more than a fireplace with metal racks arranged behind an iron door. The racks can be removed, creating enough space to admit a Medium or smaller creature, but the chimney is too narrow to climb. Anyone who opens the oven finds a warm caramel chip muffin sitting inside, a gift from the Chimney Witch.

Chimney Witch. An aloof, invisible spirit dwells in this chimney. The Chimney Witch is a chaotic being that hungers equally for the house's destruction and living creatures—particularly Small or smaller creatures. The witch makes its influence known through the hearths connected to the chimney, which include the oven in this area, the bathroom (area 17) and nursery (area 23) fireplaces, and the chimney's top near the widow's walk (area 25). The witch acts subtly while the house is dormant but becomes aggressive after it's awakened. The Chimney Witch can perform the following actions:

Baleful Baker. The Chimney Witch can manifest a single baked good once per hour. Icing on the pastry might form one letter or a similar design. The witch's baked goods are delicious but sometimes have tiny, harmless surprises hidden within—perhaps a key the party overlooked, a fingertip, or a twitching lizard tail.

Witch Fingers. The Chimney Witch can manifest a claw that reaches from the chimney on a gaunt, too-many-elbowed arm once per hour. As an action, the witch can make a melee attack with a +3 bonus against a target it can see within 10 feet of one of the hearths. If hit, a target takes 2 (1d4) piercing damage and is pulled into the nearest hearth.

Witch Fire. The Chimney Witch can use an action to cause a roaring fire to blaze in one of its hearths once per hour. Any creature that starts its turn inside a blazing hearth or that enters an ignited oven or fireplace for the first time on a turn takes 7 (2d6) fire damage. The flames vanish after 1 minute.

Manifestation. After the house is awakened, the Chimney Witch can spend an action to summon a **specter** in one of its hearths once per day. The specter looks like a burned hag with flailing, overly long arms. If the specter is defeated, the Chimney Witch cannot perform any actions and remains silent for 24 hours.

The Chimney Witch wants to see the House of Lament destroyed, hoping that will free it from the chimney. It might aid the party in defeating the house's other powerful spirits but grows agitated if ignored. Use the spirit to provide subtle hints to the party as necessary and to make Small creatures wary of the house's fireplaces.

If, during a séance, Mara sends the characters to "evict" the Chimney Witch, the witch summons a **specter.** Defeating it satisfies Mara's request.

Pantry. The foodstuffs in this pantry have decayed to dust and rotten smears inside sealed glass jars.

Treasure. Searching the pantry reveals a vial with a rat skull on the label. Inside is one dose of assassin's blood poison (see the *Dungeon Master's Guide*).

11. Dining Room

> Chairs and candelabras covered in dusty sheets attend this hall's broad dining room table. Still life paintings depicting multiple grand feasts hang on the walls, their faded oils making the food look rotten.

Several doors open into the dining room, including a sliding door that connects this space and the music room (area 12). A sideboard is filled with cracked dishware and sixty-six bent spoons. The art on the walls is worthless.

Dinner Guest. A conspicuous, child-sized form is seated under a sheet covering one of the chairs. Beneath sits a ragged doll in a frilly red dress. A white patch covers a missing button eye.

12. Music Room

> Overstuffed furniture faces a handsome concert harp dramatically sculpted with a flock of flying doves.

The dusty music room holds saggy, damp, no-longer-plush furnishings.

Evensong Harp. This haunted harp stands 6 feet tall and weighs nearly 300 pounds. It's in fine condition and looks as if it's been oiled regularly.

Any character who touches the harp must succeed on a DC 14 Wisdom saving throw or be compelled to play it. A character compelled to play must make a DC 16 Charisma (Performance) check. If the character succeeds, they spend the next minute flawlessly playing a fast-paced, glass-sharp tune they've never heard before. If the character fails, they play the song brilliantly, but cut themselves messily on the harp strings, taking 1d2 slashing damage at the start of each of their turns for 1 minute. The character can't stop playing, but another creature can yank them away from the harp by succeeding on a DC 12 Strength check. After this, the harp ceases to compel characters to play it.

Anyone compelled to play the harp learns the song *Blood-Tears of Claveria*, knows it was written by the composer Lyron Evensong, and has advantage on subsequent Charisma (Performance) checks made to play the chilling tune on any instrument.

13. Second-Floor Hall

This hall starts at a balcony overlooking the foyer (area 2), the floor of which is 10 feet below. One of the doors in the hall opens to a stairway that ascends to area 20.

Awakened Haunt. The coughing from area 16 is audible in this hall.

Séance One. When the party finishes exploring the floors below, the investigators invite them to participate in the first séance (see the "Séances" section earlier in the adventure). If the party goes directly to this area, the investigators invite them to the séance after they explore two or three rooms.

14. Guest Bedrooms

Extra bedrooms on the second floor each hold a sagging bed, a wardrobe, and a writing desk.

Ambient Haunt. At your discretion, ambient haunts in these rooms employ bedsheets and dark places under the furnishings. Other possible haunts include animalistic forms stitched into the bedding; pillows contorting to form sizable, fanged maws; or a room looking exactly like a character's childhood bedroom.

15. MORNING ROOM

Wicker chairs and a small table set for tea occupy this airy morning room. Pale drapes fall away from wide windows overlooking the manor's grounds. A plump, tasseled pillow embroidered with the name "Newes" rests near a fireplace.

This room is prepared for a breakfast that never arrived.

Pet Bed. The Halvhrest's pet, Newes, slept here. A toy or evidence of its nature, whatever you decide that is, remains here.

Awakened Haunt. The first character to enter the room sees a gigantic eye staring through the window. The character must succeed on a DC 12 Constitution throw or be frightened for 1 minute.

Treasure. The tea set includes four cups and a teapot with a delicate pattern of flowering foxglove. The fragile set is worth 200 gp. One cup has tea leaves dried at its bottom, the debris forming the shape of a screaming face missing an eye.

16. MASTER BEDROOM

A grand, canopied bed occupies this room, its headboard engraved with the phases of the moon. A wardrobe, writing desk, and torn leather chair fill out the space, all bearing rampant mildew. A chemical smell, like ammonia or medication, lingers here.

Loren Halvhrest died here, succumbing to an inexplicable disease after months of illness. With the exception of the bed, the room's furnishings are rotted and fragile. They fall apart if touched.

Ambient Haunt. The smell in the room has no source, a subtle haunt that recalls the medicines that filled Loren Halvhrest's last days of life.

Awakened Haunt. Anyone in this room or an adjacent area hears wracking coughing fits. Those who enters the bedroom see a wheezing form huddled under the bed's heavy comforter. If the bed's sheets are pulled back or attacked, a **zombie plague spreader** (see chapter 5) emerges and attacks.

17. MASTER BATH

Remains of opulent fixtures fill this moldy bathroom. Wardrobes, dressing screens, and a vanity with a cracked mirror line fractured tile walls. A raised marble tub next to a built-in fireplace asserts a commitment to decadence.

The bathroom is humid and moldy, its walls stained with colorful but harmless growths.

Chimney Witch. The fireplace connects to the haunted chimney detailed in area 10.

Treasure. A perfume bottle with an ornate bulb atomizer sits on the vanity, its label bearing the name "Boritsi" in intricate cursive. The bottle and the vanilla-scented perfume within is worth 50 gp, or ten times that if sold in the domain of Borca.

18. OFFICE

This office is decorated with sturdy shelves and a desk carved with reclining satyrs. The desk's high-backed chair is turned away, obscuring any occupant.

Loren Halvhrest managed his small trading company from this office. A merchant's scale, blunt writing implements, and a tiny, framed portrait of Theodora Halvhrest sit on the desk.

A glass door leads to the exterior balcony (area 19). The bolted door is easy to open from this side.

Documents. The books and papers in the room include copious documents, Loren's business files interspersed with personal papers. Most are ruined by age, but any character who success on a DC 14 Wisdom (Perception) check finds the room's treasure and one of the following documents:

Loren's Will. Loren's will and death certificate names the four members of the Halvhrest family—Loren, his wife Theodora, their daughter Regan, and their son Vastion. An addendum notes that Loren died of "tenacious deviltry of the leftmost lung."

Deed to the House. A sheaf of dry legal documents includes the deed to the house and rights to the surrounding land. These documents enumerate the land's features, including "Ruins of Castle Laventz; prior owners: Lady Mara Silvra, Dalk Dranzorg, Lord Cordon Silvra; dates unknown."

Treasure. In addition to dull business records, the desk holds a key to the lockbox in area 22, a 4-foot-long silver chain necklace worth 40 gp, and your choice of a *wand of magic missiles* or a pistol alongside a box containing 49 bullets (see the *Dungeon Master's Guide*).

19. EXTERIOR BALCONY

This sturdy, ivy entangled balcony stands 15 feet over the porch (area 1). A glass door leads from the balcony into area 18, but it's bolted closed from the other side. The door has AC 14, 8 hit points, and immunity to poison and psychic damage.

20. THIRD-FLOOR HALL

This hall is especially creaky. It features a threadbare rug covered in geometric patterns, the lines of which are impossible to follow.

Séance Two. The second séance should occur soon after characters reach this floor. If the séance hasn't occurred yet, the clock in area 22 inexplicably chimes thirteen or a dead raven topples from a door frame. If one of the investigators accompanies the party, they are startled and encourage the party to return to the parlor to relax and renew their exploration later—ultimately, after the next séance.

21. SERVANTS' QUARTERS

These modest rooms belonged to the Halvhrests' servants. Each holds a bed, footlocker, writing desk, and chair. They're identical except as noted below.

Agatha's Room. This room is locked, and the only key is inside. A character using thieves' tools can try to pick the lock, which requires 1 minute and a successful DC 14 Dexterity check.

This room belonged to Agatha Kavenza, the nursemaid of Regan and Vastion Halvhrest. A devotee of the god Ezra, Agatha decorated her room with a plaque of her god's symbol, a shield crossed with a spring of belladonna. This displays the missing part of the symbol that appears in area 23. Agatha hid herself here when spirits overwhelmed the house. Her fate is unknown, but a series of long scratches and broken fingernails end at a conspicuous bag on the floor. This is a *bag of holding*. A superstitious character of your choice might consider this scene evidence of the Bagman (detailed in "Horror Monsters" in chapter 5).

Victro's Room. Victro's bed is unusually long, built to accommodate his 7-foot-tall frame. The key to his locked footlocker is in area 27. A character using thieves' tools can try to pick the lock, which requires 1 minute and a successful DC 12 Dexterity check. Inside the footlocker are suits custom-made for a very tall man, a pouch containing 13 sp, and an amulet bearing the symbol of a skull surrounded by a skeletal ouroboros—the icon of the priests of Osybus (see chapter 5).

22. FAMILY ROOM

Rich furniture clusters around a tall fireplace, its mantle lined with dusty knickknacks. Above it hangs a portrait of a stiff but handsome family.

The furniture here is musty and greasy with dust.

Portrait. This oil painting depicts the four members of the Halvhrest family, Loren, Theodora, Regan, and Vastion. Any character who examines the painting and succeeds on a DC 12 Wisdom (Perception) check notices a hinge that allows the frame to swing open. Doing so reveals a hidden shelf with a lockbox inside. The key from area 18 opens the lockbox. A character using thieves' tools can try to pick the lock, which requires 1 minute and a successful DC 14 Dexterity check. The "Treasure" section below details the box's contents.

Awakened Haunt. A malicious spirit animates the family portrait. The spirit isn't one of the Halvhrests, despite its claims. The Halvhrests' painted bodies perpetually melt and recongeal as the spirit speaks through each of them. It demands to know who the characters are, why they're in its house, and how they'll make amends for their trespasses. Whether the spirit can be placated and how is up to you—encourage the players to suggest ways to satisfy it. If the spirit grows displeased, the Halvhrest images push through the painting, toppling out one per round until four **ghouls** emerge. Each oil-paint-smeared ghoul attacks as soon as it appears from the painting.

The portrait has AC 12, 20 hit points, and immunity to poison and psychic damage. It can also be exorcised as a haunted trap with a +2 Haunt Bonus. If destroyed or exorcised, the painting returns to normal, the spirit no longer speaks through it, and no further ghouls emerge.

Treasure. Those who open the lockbox hidden behind the portrait find a 1-foot-long black feather and velvet pouch containing nine pieces of silver jewelry worth 10 gp each. A tenth piece is an amulet bearing the Mark of the Raven, a symbol used by the Keepers of the Feather (see chapter 3). The Mark of the Raven is not magical, but some fell forces recoil from the righteous powers it suggests (as in area 31). The amulet is worth 25 gp.

AGATHA KAVENZA'S FATE
REMAINS A MYSTERY.

23. Nursery

> This nursery lies in disarray. Toy chests, bookshelves, and chairs sized for children lie in splinters of colorful wood. Misshapen characters and bizarre animals smile from hand-painted murals covering the walls.

The remains of toys, dolls, and furnishings sized for children lie shattered about the room. The murals are creepy in the style of children's art.

Sanctuary Door. The door to area 24 is under divine protection that manifests as an *arcane lock* spell. The first time a creature touches the door, an incomplete symbol of the god Ezra appears amid the woodwork for an instant, then vanishes. This shield symbol doesn't bear the belladonna sprig that traditionally crosses it. If a character presents a belladonna sprig, such as from the plant in area 7, the *arcane lock* is suppressed for 10 minutes.

Each time the door is damaged, a blast of energy erupts from it, dealing 7 (2d6) radiant damage to all creatures within 10 feet of the door. The door takes no damage.

Awakened Haunt. The room's shattered toys animate, clattering together into three spindly forms with the statistics of two **carrionettes** (see chapter 5) and a **scarecrow**. In a hollow voice, the largest creature howls, "Halvhrests! We smell Halvhrests!"

Chimney Witch. The fireplace here connects to the haunted chimney detailed in area 10.

24. Children's Bedroom

> The room smells fresh, as if it's been recently cleaned and aired. Not a spot of dust sullies the pair of child-sized beds and other furnishings. A skeleton wearing a lady's dress with a veiled hat stares at you from where it sways in a wooden rocking chair.

The skeleton is all that remains of Theodora Halvhrest. It is not undead, but a blessing laid upon this room causes the chair to sway. If the skeleton or the chair is touched, the chair stops rocking.

After the characters first enter the room (whether the house is dormant or awakened) and react to the skeleton, read the following:

> A boy's voice issues from a stuffed purple dragon on one of the beds. "They're not like the others. Should we hide from them too, Regan?"
>
> "Well, it doesn't matter now, donkey!" a girl's voice replies from a figure of a tin knight on the other bed. "They got in, so maybe they're not hungry things yet."

The two spirits are Regan and Vastion Halvhrest. Their mother's occult knowledge and prayers to Ezra protected this room, but also trapped Regan's and Vastion's spirits here. The ghosts don't visually manifest, but they speak through their favorite toys. They eagerly converse with characters and fall silent if threatened. The spirits know the following information and share it with friendly characters:

- The skeleton is their mother, Theodora. She prayed to Ezra to protect the room and keep out the "hungry things."
- The hungry things are bad spirits that took over. They "stole" the children's parents. The children don't know any named spirits.
- They would like to leave but don't know how.

If the characters tell the spirits that Theodora sent them, they eagerly cooperate. See Theodora's parts of the "Séances" and "Escaping the House" sections for details on helping the children.

Ezra's Blessing. Thanks to the fervent prayers of Theodora Halvhrest, the god Ezra warded this room with a *hallow* spell that affects only this room and prevents all Undead (besides Regan and Vastion) from entering or seeing inside.

Development. The effects of Ezra's blessing end when anyone enters and then leaves the room. This reveals Regan and Vastion's spirits to the other apparitions in the house, causing the house to awaken. See "Waking the House" earlier in the adventure for details.

25. Widow's Walk

This walkway along the roof of the house provides either a commanding view of the lands surrounding the House of Lament or, if the Mists have risen, a foggy netherworld.

Roof. The roof beyond the Widow's Walk is treacherously angled, covered in loose shingles, and slick with moss. A character moving across the roof without the aid of magic or gear to steady themselves must succeed on a DC 15 Strength (Athletics) check or slide off the roof to the ground, taking 14 (4d6) bludgeoning damage.

Witch Stone. A ledge juts from a chimney about 30 feet east of the northeast corner of the widow's walk. This is a witch stone, a mundane architectural superstition said to provide a place for witches to rest during their nightly travels. The chimney bearing the witch stone connects to the haunted chimney detailed in area 10. Any character who succeeds on a DC 14 Intelligence (History) check knows this fact, which might help them understand a request Theodora makes during a séance. Characters with the Stonecunning trait may apply it to this check. This stone has no special properties, but a character who lights a candle here satisfies Theodora's request.

26. Tower Chamber

The tower chamber is empty except for a suit of crimson ring mail strewn across the floor. It lies in the middle of a faded chalk drawing of the Mark of the Raven. Theodora Halvhrest made this mark to stifle the evil she felt in the tower and, particularly, around the armor.

Armor. This ring mail belonged to the knight Mara Silvra. The blood red suit is of an ancient style and bears the marks of repeated repairs. It has no magical properties unless employed to do battle with Dalk Dranzorg, as detailed in the "Tyrant's Escape" section at the end of the adventure.

27. Wine Cellar

> Creaking stairs lead into a damp, cobweb-draped cellar containing dusty racks and eight-foot-tall wine tuns. One of the casks has burst, covering the stone floor in crimson stains.

All three wine tuns are empty, though the one farthest from the stairs looks as though something burst from within. The racks are packed with bottles bearing obscure names, such as "Purple Grapemash No. 3" and "Ludendorf Arsenic Wine." All the wine either leaked or spoiled long ago.

Creatures. The cellar is infested with five **gremishkas** (see chapter 5). Soon after any character enters the room, a gremishka makes a comically bad cat noise, trying to lure them closer.

Treasure. Anyone who investigates the wine racks and succeeds on a DC 8 Wisdom (Perception) check finds an especially long apron. In its pocket is a silver tastevin worth 10 gp and the key to the footlocker in area 21.

28. Storage

> Old furnishings, rotten pantry staples, and boxes of mundane junk fills this musty storage space.

Any character who sifts through the room's contents and succeeds on a DC 14 Wisdom (Perception) check finds nothing special but notes the room's west wall is distinct from the other walls. A character can make a DC 14 Intelligence (History) check to discern the wall's nature. (A dwarf's Stonecunning trait proves useful here.) On a successful check, the character realizes that this wall is part of a buried fortification. If the character has been in area 4 or 5, they note the similarity to the tower above.

Ancient Wall. The ancient wall here hides the buried ruins of Castle Laventz. While the house is dormant, this wall is impervious to harm. However, after the house wakes, the junk in the room moves into stacks against the east wall and an archway appears in the west wall, leading to area 29.

29. Buried Ruins

This hollow isn't part of a larger construction, but rather a space between buried ruins. A rusted iron door is set into the wall of what used to be the ground floor of the tower. The iron door looks thoroughly rusted. As any character tries to open it, the door slams open.

30. Buried Tower

> Stairs curve along the wall of this buried tower chamber, rising then halting abruptly at the ceiling. Much of the floor has fallen away, collapsing into darkness.

Centuries ago, this level of the tower was bricked over. The pit descends 30 feet to area 31 below.

Echoes from the Pit. As characters approach the pit, they hear their voices echo down the hole. Randomly determine one character whose voice doesn't echo. Instead, a pale amber light ignites in the dark below and something whispers the character's name from the pit.

31. Amber Cavity

> Nothing is natural about this buried cavity or the amber light flooding the space. Petrified figures lie trapped among the pale stone walls, their faces contorted in terror. Deeper, the floor forms a craterlike depression filled with inky muck. From the center of the pit rises a jagged amber monolith. A faint glow issues from within, backlighting a vague, elusive shape.

The cavern's walls are contorted in the shapes of the hundreds of souls trapped within the house. This is the heart of the House of Lament, a tortured space formed around the amber monolith that contains the Entity.

A 30-foot-diameter depression surrounds the amber monolith. The sloped sides and the 2-foot-deep, polluted water at the bottom make the entirety of the crater difficult terrain. The water isn't harmful, but it is bitter, viscous, and stains like ink.

Mara Silvra. If the characters approach the monolith, the air around them grows colder. The spirit of Mara Silvra (use the **banshee** stat block) fades into view above the crater, a spectral knight with distorted, screaming features. Mara shouts before attacking, attempting to bargain with the force in the amber monolith: "You foul thing! Take these lives and release me!"

Amber Monolith. The amber monolith is a rough block of solid amber 8 feet tall, 5 feet wide, and 5 feet thick. Within drifts a smoky wisp, the last lingering vestige of a dead, hateful deity of any origin you choose. This vestige can't be harmed or controlled, and it is immune to all conditions. Any creature that touches the amber monolith forms a telepathic link with the vestige inside. The vestige tries to coax the creature into its service by offering it a Dark Gift (see chapter 1).

The amber monolith has AC 16, 80 hit points, and immunity to poison and psychic damage. If the monolith is damaged or if a character openly bears Theodora's Mark of the Raven, inky tendrils rise from the dark water and attack. These limbs use the statistics for five **shadows** and don't leave area 31. Destroying the monolith causes the limbs and the vestige within to vanish without a trace. Whether the vestige is destroyed or released is for you to decide.

Mark of the Raven. The amulet from area 22 begins glowing when it's brought into this area. If a character uses an action to present the Mark of the Raven, Mara does not attack on the next turn, the light from the amber monolith dwindles, and the shadowy limbs have disadvantage on attack rolls, ability checks, and saving throws. A character can use the amulet multiple times, but doing so causes the shadowy limbs to focus their attacks on its bearer.

Treasure. The opaque water hides the skeletal remains of dozens of the house's past victims. Any character who uses an action to sift through the water and succeeds on a DC 10 Wisdom (Perception) check finds one of the following six treasures: one of four *potions of healing*, a *deck of illusions* in a watertight lacquered box, or Mara's crimson sword, Oathmaker—a *sword of vengeance* haunted by Mara Silvra (these magic items are detailed in the *Dungeon Master's Guide*). All of these treasures become obvious if the liquid is drained, as do 220 sp, 30 gp, and twelve amulets bearing the Mark of the Raven (each worth 5 gp).

Development. If Mara is destroyed, the cavern releases a mighty sigh. The house remains awakened, but the domain's borders open. Mara re-forms after one week, returning the house to its full power.

If the amber monolith is destroyed, the house responds as described above and the inky water drains away, revealing the treasure within. Mara's spirit fades, whispering, "Your slights are forgiven. Leave and never return to my home." Despite the monolith's destruction, the house regains its power after a week.

Escaping the House

After the house is awakened, the domain's borders close and the house's spirits set their full attention on the party. Escaping the house requires disrupting the house's spirits in one of three ways, each encouraged by the spirit the characters communed with during their séances.

Guardian Spirit

If the party communed with Theodora during the séances, the adventure's climax unfolds as follows.

Hidden Halvhrests. After the characters explore and leave area 24, the house detects the hidden Halvhrest children and wakes.

Escape the House. If the characters attempt to leave the house with the children's toys, the spirits of the house physically manifest as a **shadow demon** and two **specters** at opposite sides of the front porch (area 1). Once characters leave the house, a new specter emerges from the house every other round on the specters' initiative count. The spirits shriek things like "part of the house" and "feed us forever" as the characters try to escape. If the characters reach the Mists, the spirit of Theodora Halvhrest parts the fog, allowing them to leave the domain.

Reunion. Eventually the party emerges from the Mists, but Regan and Vastion don't follow. Looking back, the characters see the spirits of the two youngsters along with their parents as they fade into the Mists. At your discretion, the Halvhrests might grant the characters an eerie boon, potentially in the form of Dark Gifts (see chapter 1).

Mara's Bargain

If the party conversed with Mara during the séances, the adventure's climax unfolds as follows.

The Darkness Below. Mara urges the party to find area 31. This isn't to help her escape as her messages suggest, though. Rather, it's to attempt to sacrifice the characters as a way to bargain with the Entity for her freedom.

Tyrant's Escape

If the party communicated with Dalk Dranzorg during the séances, the adventure's climax unfolds as follows.

Dranzorg Released. After the house wakes, Dalk Dranzorg can be released as described in area 5a. If the party doesn't release him, he breaks free himself after an hour. Dranzorg torments the party and rampages through the house, calling for Mara to face him. Once freed, he won't enter the parlor (area 3), wandering off if the characters take refuge there.

THE EVIL BENEATH THE HOUSE OF LAMENT
ADDS TO ITS PRISON OF SOULS.

Enemy of My Enemy. Dranzorg can be permanently defeated only by Mara. If it doesn't occur to the characters, one of the investigators suggests reaching out to her spirit for help. Whether characters use the spirit board or another method to contact Mara, her furious spirit appears and demands the characters aid her in destroying Dranzorg. If they do, she'll let them leave the house. Mara demands the characters retrieve her armor from the tower chamber (area 26). If they use it in combat as described below, she can help them defeat Dranzorg.

Eternal Rivals. Dranzorg focuses his attacks on the character wearing Mara's armor. If a character wearing Mara's armor is reduced to fewer than half their hit points, Mara's spirit possesses the character. From then on, the character has advantage on attacks against Dranzorg, and their attacks deal an extra 1d6 thunder damage against him, as Mara screams through the character with every attack.

Evicted. After Dranzorg is defeated, Mara relinquishes control of the character and allows the party to leave the house. At your discretion, a character who was possessed by Mara might carry a piece of her spirit with them, potentially in the form of a Dark Gift (see chapter 1).

SAM KEISER

BEYOND THE HOUSE

From here, where the party's adventures lead is up to you. Perhaps the Mists deposit them back in their home worlds, concluding their shared nightmare. Or perhaps their fates are now inexorably bound to the Mists. In the latter case, the Dread Possibilities table suggests what might be in store for them.

DREAD POSSIBILITIES

d4	Further Adventures
1	The characters glimpse the winged figure they saw at the start of the adventure through the Mists. It leads them to a random domain.
2	The investigators invite the characters to join them in Mordentshire. The characters gain a reputation as phantom liberators, a talent the spirits of Mordent desperately need (see chapter 3).
3	The party travels from the house to Borca (see chapter 3), where they're contacted by either Ivana Boritsi or Ivan Dilisnya, who is eager to hear all about their exploits.
4	Firan Zal'honan (see chapter 3) seeks out the characters and is interested in learning about their experience at the house. He's eager to patronize their search for "amber sarcophagi."

DARKLORD MALIGNO AND HIS CARRIONETTE SERVANTS AMBUSH
THE DETECTIVES ALANIK RAY AND ARTHUR SEDGWICK.

UNTOLD TERRORS HAUNT THE DOMAINS OF Dread. Among them skulk nightmares known on countless worlds, but even familiar monsters can take on twisted forms or demonstrate unexpected abilities. This chapter explores ways to help you, the DM, make even the most commonplace monsters more frightening, as well as providing a host of horrors to add to your adventures in the Mists.

HORROR MONSTERS

For adventurers who regularly face terrifying monsters, it's easy for familiarity to sap the frightfulness from terrible foes. Restoring mystery and menace to even the most ordinary monsters can be a simple matter, though, and enhances the atmosphere of horror adventures. Six simple techniques can transform a stat block straight out of the *Monster Manual* (or other source) into a horror to haunt your characters' dreams:

Monstrous Origins. Monsters in Ravenloft can be every bit as unique as player characters.

Notorious Monsters. A monster is more frightening when its reputation precedes it.

Describing Monsters. Give yourself permission to dwell on a monster's description.

Monstrous Tactics. Monsters that fight dirty—or in a particularly fearsome way—have more impact.

Monstrous Traits. Simple tweaks to a monster's stat block can enhance its horror.

Monstrous Minions. Simple traits can reflect a monster's relationship to the evil master it serves.

MONSTROUS ORIGINS

A variety of explanations, from transformative curses to magical experiments, can justify the appearance of a unique individual with unusual traits. In the same way, monsters in Ravenloft don't need to be members of a species or society. You can have a vicious merrow living under a bridge or a yuan-ti abomination Darklord without having to explain merrows as a species or the nature of all yuan-ti in the setting. Monsters can be one-off flukes of nature or the products of insidious magic.

For significant adversaries, use the tables in the "Genres of Horror" section of chapter 2 to inspire you as you craft a monster's unique details. When it comes time for the final confrontation, it might not matter whether the bridge-haunting merrow was the product of an amoral experiment to infuse piscine traits into a soldier or the result of someone drinking from a spring tainted by demon's blood; the merrow's stat block remains the same. But those different origin stories suggest completely different paths for adventurers to follow when investigating the creature and ensuring nothing like it ever returns to be a menace again.

NOTORIOUS MONSTERS

Every monster tells a story. The more you treat monsters as unique individuals and foreshadow their threat, the larger they'll loom in characters' minds. Build dread by giving monsters reputations that suggests their form, deeds, or peculiarities while letting players' imaginations embellish details.

For example, tales describe a horrifying skeletal figure that corrupts the land wherever it walks. Its habit of whistling cheerfully while committing brutal acts is the source of its epithet: the Whistling Fiend. Characters might hear rumors of its merry tunes becoming fearful earworms for those who survive its passing. A party seeking the monster might also hear the whistling long before they confront the fiend. All that time, they can at guess at their enemy's nature, but ultimately the Whistling Fiend might be any demon or other threat you choose.

The Whistling Fiend's notoriety has little to do with its stat block. It's famous because of its habit of whistling amid acts of terrible carnage. Use the tables in chapter 4 of the *Dungeon Master's Guide* to help inspire similar characteristics to color a monster's notorious reputation.

DESCRIBING MONSTERS

When adventurers encounter a monster for the first time, especially if its reputation precedes it, dwell on its description. You could tell the players that they see a merrow or hold up the creature's picture from the *Monster Manual*. But that first moment of revelation is the best time to paint a horrifying picture of the monster in the players' imaginations. In addition to the techniques described in the "Running Horror Games" section of chapter 4, consider these concepts as you describe a monster:

ZOLTAN BOROS

Emphasize Wrongness. Focus on the features that make the creature alien, inhuman, and out of place. The Whistling Fiend looks like a humanoid skeleton dripping its own gelatinous musculature. Its skull curves to a point suggestive of a sickle.

Engage All the Senses. Describe elements of the creature that are likely to provoke a visceral response, such as the smell of rot that its oily flesh exudes, the whistled tune of a well-known nursery rhyme issuing from its lipless mouth, and the unnatural heat that forms ripples in the air around it. These details don't need to rely on grotesque descriptions. Sometimes it's a contrast between mundane and terrifying details that stands out, like a monster's soulful eyes or pearly teeth set amid vicious features.

Make it Personal. There's a fine line here: Don't dictate a character's actions in response to what they see. But you can touch on the feelings that the creature provokes, leaving it up to the players to describe how they respond to those feelings. Your gut twists in revulsion. The acrid air stings your nostrils. You're suddenly aware of how small and hollow your dreams are in a world that can spawn beings of pure evil.

Monstrous Tactics

Monsters, just like player characters, can try anything you can imagine in combat, including the full range of combat options described in the *Player's Handbook*. Monsters can use the Help action to aid each other, they can grapple or shove their enemies, and so on. Some monsters use these options to maximize their advantages in battle; others use them to sow fear among their enemies, even if they're not strategically optimal choices.

For example, creatures known as "goblyns" in Kartakass and other domains are ordinary hobgoblins in terms of their game statistics, but they're known for a tactic they call "feasting": they grapple their enemies and then make unarmed attacks to bite their faces. These attacks aren't terribly dangerous (a hobgoblin's unarmed strike deals only 2 damage, compared to the average of 5 it deals with a longsword), but the face-biting is much more shocking to the victim and onlookers.

Monsters become more fearsome if they use tactics like ganging up on the least-armored characters in a party, taking the time to take bites from unconscious foes, separating party members from each other, and attacking from hiding. Use these tactics judiciously; the goal is to surprise and scare the players, not to convince them that you're trying to make them fail.

THE WHISTLING FIEND IS NOTORIOUS FOR BEING HEARD LONG BEFORE IT'S SEEN.

Monstrous Traits

Consider undermining players' expectations about what a creature is or can do by making tweaks to the traits in its stat block. Adding a sahuagin's Blood Frenzy trait to a different monster can help it feel like a bloodthirsty horror, for example. Traits such as a troglodyte's Chameleon Skin or a doppelganger's Ambusher can help make a monster feel more sinister as it lurks in hiding and ambushes its foes. Some traits, such as a night hag's Etherealness or an imp's Invisibility, can help a monster escape from an encounter so it can return to haunt the adventurers another day. Traits such as a banshee's Horrifying Visage or a black dragon's Frightful Presence can heighten the inherent fearsomeness of truly terrifying creatures.

Of course, you're not limited to the traits that appear in existing monster stat blocks, but those are a good starting point. Feel free to invent your own.

SCOTT MURPHY

Monstrous Minions

In the Land of the Mists, many monsters serve as minions or manifestations of more powerful villains. To reflect a minion's relationship to its Darklord master or other sinister forces, add one or more of these traits to a monster's stat block.

Alien Mind. If a creature tries to read the minion's thoughts, that creature must succeed on a Intelligence saving throw with a DC equal to 10 + the minion's Intelligence modifier or be stunned for 1 minute. The stunned creature can repeat the saving throw at the end of each of its turns, ending the effect on itself on a success.

Minion's Mind. The minion can't be compelled to act in a way contrary to its master's instructions.

Sacrificial Minion. When the minion dies, its master regains hit points equal to four times the minion's challenge rating, as long as the master is within 100 feet of it.

Selfless Bodyguard. When an attack hits its master and the minion is within 5 feet of its master, the minion can use its reaction to make the attack hit itself instead.

Telepathic Minion. The minion and its master can communicate telepathically with each other, as long as they are on the same plane of existence.

Creating Unique Nightmares

Once you've considered the techniques in this section, put them all together to create your own unique terror. If you have ideas about what you want your monster to do, write them down. Then think of what stories connect the pieces you want to use or fill in gaps you don't know about yet.

For example, perhaps you've got an idea for a troll that ambushes adventurers while they rest. Considering its origins and appearance, the troll literally being a troll isn't important to you; you're more interested in that general challenge and look for the creature. To make your troll feel notorious, you think of what would scare adventurers—where they're vulnerable and what they're sensitive about. You come up with an idea for a creature that can come from anywhere, maybe even within the adventurers' own gear. With tactics and traits in mind, you think of your troll as an abductor and give it the Grappler trait of a mimic and the Amorphous trait of a black pudding so it can sneak in anywhere. Finally, you don't think of the troll as a minion, but you give it the Alien Mind trait to reflect its tormented psyche. Then you flesh out its story and give it a name: the Bagman.

Beware the Bagman

The Bagman is an urban legend about an adventurer who sought to escape doom by abandoning his party and hiding inside a *bag of holding*. When he tried to leave, though, he became lost amid a constantly increasing number of extradimensional storage spaces. Over time, the strange forces of this magical in-between place transformed the adventurer into a monstrous creature. Now, every night, the Bagman slips out from a random *bag of holding*. If he doesn't find his home, he drags someone back into the bag with him and leaves behind some trinket from his hidden kingdom of lost junk. Some say that if you speak too loudly over an open *bag of holding* or whisper "follow my voice" into a magical storage space three times, the Bagman will come for you.

Any character might know the story of the Bagman. What the Bagman is and how you use this urban legend is up to you. Is there truly a Bagman, or is he just a story? If an object vanishes overnight or if someone finds something that isn't theirs in a *bag of holding*, is the Bagman to blame? Is the Bagman just a monster that preys on adventurers, or is he the Darklord of his own hidden domain? The possibilities for horror adventures are endless, and nowhere—especially not adventurers' gear—is safe.

THE BAGMAN EMERGES FROM A BAG OF HOLDING TO COLLECT ITS NEXT VICTIM.

Bestiary

Many terrors lurk in the shadows—some in the corner of perception, and others beyond the Material Plane. This chapter presents stat blocks for a host of threats that can play a role in horror-based campaigns.

The creatures in this chapter are organized by their challenge rating in the Creatures by Challenge Rating table.

Creatures by Challenge Rating

CR	Creature
1/8	Gremishka
1/2	Death's head
1/2	Podling
1	Boneless
1	Carrionette
1	Swarm of zombie limbs
2	Swarm of gremishkas
2	Swarm of maggots
2	Wereraven
3	Brain in a jar
3	Carrion stalker
3	Swarm of scarabs
4	Strigoi
4	Zombie plague spreader
5	Vampiric mind flayer
6	Gallows speaker
6	Priest of Osybus
6	Zombie clot
7	Bodytaker plant
7	Necrichor
8	Inquisitor of the Mind Fire
8	Inquisitor of the Sword
8	Inquisitor of the Tome
8	Nosferatu
8	Relentless slasher
8	Unspeakable horror
9	Jiangshi
10	Dullahan
12	Relentless juggernaut
13	Loup garou
19	Lesser star spawn emissary
21	Greater star spawn emissary

Bodytaker Plant

Whether hailing from the stars or sprouting from hidden depths, the malicious vegetation known as bodytaker plants seek to become the dominant form of life wherever they appear. These invasive organisms subvert whole societies by consuming individuals and replacing them with duplicates called podlings. Bodytaker plants view themselves as perfect organisms and seek to dominate the lands where they grow. To their minds, a world would be healthier and more efficient were they in control. Anyone who disagrees either lacks perspective or is fit to serve only as fertilizer.

A bodytaker plant roots deep, spreading near-invisible filaments through the soil. Should any of these fibers survive the plant's destruction, the bodytaker plant regrows after a matter of months. Salting or poisoning the soil where it grew destroys these filaments and prevents the plant from reappearing.

PODLINGS

Bodytaker plants either capture unsuspecting victims with their vines or accept captives brought to them by their podling servants. In either case, they drag creatures into their central pod, where potent chemicals render the captive comatose. Over the course of hours, the creature is dissolved and its body repurposed into a podling duplicate.

BODYTAKER PLANT
Huge Plant

Armor Class 16 (natural armor)
Hit Points 92 (8d12 + 40)
Speed 10 ft., climb 10 ft., swim 10 ft.

STR	DEX	CON	INT	WIS	CHA
18 (+4)	8 (−1)	20 (+5)	14 (+2)	14 (+2)	18 (+4)

Damage Vulnerabilities poison
Condition Immunities blinded, charmed, frightened, prone
Senses blindsight 120 ft. (blind beyond this radius), passive Perception 12
Languages Deep Speech, telepathy 120 ft.
Challenge 7 (2,900 XP)   **Proficiency Bonus** +3

Podling Link. The plant can see through and communicate telepathically with any of its podlings within 10 miles of it.

Rejuvenation. When the plant dies, it returns to life in the place where it died 1d12 months later, unless the ground where it took root is sown with salt or soaked with poison.

Unusual Nature. The plant doesn't require sleep.

ACTIONS

Multiattack. The plant makes three Vine Lash attacks.

Vine Lash. *Melee Weapon Attack:* +7 to hit, reach 20 ft., one target. *Hit:* 11 (2d6 + 4) slashing damage. If the target is a creature, it is grappled (escape DC 15). Until the grapple ends, the target is restrained. The plant has four vines, each of which can grapple one target.

Entrapping Pod. *Melee Weapon Attack:* +7 to hit, reach 5 ft., one Medium or smaller creature grappled by the plant. *Hit:* 22 (4d8 + 4) acid damage, and the target is pulled into the plant's space and enveloped by the pod, and the grapple ends. While enveloped, the target is restrained, and it has total cover against attacks and effects originating outside the pod. The enveloped target must also immediately succeed on a DC 16 Constitution saving throw or be stunned by the plant's sapping enzymes until it is removed from the pod or the plant dies. The enveloped target doesn't require air and gains 1 level of exhaustion for each hour it spends in the pod. If the target dies while enveloped, it immediately emerges from the pod as a living podling, wearing or carrying all of the original creature's equipment.

As an action, a creature within 5 feet of the bodytaker plant that is outside the pod can open the pod and pull the target free with a successful DC 15 Strength check. If the plant dies, the target is no longer restrained and can escape from the pod by spending 10 feet of movement, exiting prone. The plant has one pod, which can envelop one creature at a time.

Podlings are near-perfect mimics of the creatures they replace. Despite having the knowledge of those they mimic, podlings frequently miss the nuances of interactions between sapient beings. These duplicates make excuses about their odd behavior, but those familiar with an individual replaced by a podling can often tell something's amiss. Roll on the Podling Behavior table to see what unusual habits a podling might demonstrate.

PODLING BEHAVIOR

d6	Behavior
1	The podling abandons the habits and hobbies of the creature it's mimicking.
2	The podling lavishes affection on plants and views houseplants with excessive sympathy.
3	The podling relishes exposing its skin to the sun. It resents clothing and hair.
4	The podling often reacts as if some unseen force is speaking to it, staring into the distance or nodding.
5	The podling often communicates to other podlings using Deep Speech.
6	The podling no longer understands the nuances of a relationship, system, or instrument.

PODLING
Medium Plant

Armor Class 10
Hit Points 26 (4d8 + 8)
Speed 20 ft.

STR	DEX	CON	INT	WIS	CHA
15 (+2)	11 (+0)	14 (+2)	10 (+0)	10 (+0)	10 (+0)

Condition Immunities charmed, frightened
Senses blindsight 30 ft., passive Perception 10
Languages Deep Speech, the languages the creature knew in life
Challenge 1/2 (100 XP)   **Proficiency Bonus** +2

Semblance of Life. The podling is a physical copy of a creature digested by a bodytaker plant. The podling has the digested creature's memories and behaves like that creature, but with occasional lapses. An observer familiar with the digested creature can recognize the discrepancies with a successful DC 20 Wisdom (Insight) check, or automatically if the podling does something in direct contradiction to the digested creature's established beliefs or behavior. The podling melts into a slurry when it dies, when the bodytaker plant that created it dies, or when the bodytaker plant dismisses it (no action required).

Unusual Nature. The podling doesn't require sleep.

ACTIONS

Slam. *Melee Weapon Attack:* +4 to hit, reach 5 ft., one target. *Hit:* 5 (1d6 + 2) bludgeoning damage.

IRINA NORDSOL

Boneless

Not all animate corpses shamble from their graves. Boneless are undead remains devoid of skeletons. Most rise from the bodies of those who've suffered brutal ends, such as deliberate skinning or crushing. Deathless malice infuses what remains, their husks flopping and slithering in pursuit of vengeance or at the whims of sinister masters. Slipping through cracks and under doors, these stealthy undead seek to adorn living frames once more, wrapping themselves around their victims and wringing them to death in their full-body grip.

Boneless arise in a variety of forms. While the animate skins of specific creatures are the most common, foul spellcasters might create these horrors from the scraps of failed experiments, necromantic slurries, heaps of discarded hair, abattoirs, and charnel concoctions. These origins don't affect a boneless's statistics but lend it distinct forms.

Whether through accident or depraved genius, some villains use one corpse to create two separate undead. Boneless might adorn the frames of other undead, like skeletons or zombies. The sight of a boneless peeling itself from its independently undead frame haunts the nightmares of many seasoned monster hunters.

Boneless
Medium Undead

Armor Class 12
Hit Points 26 (4d8 + 8)
Speed 30 ft.

STR	DEX	CON	INT	WIS	CHA
16 (+3)	14 (+2)	15 (+2)	1 (−5)	10 (+0)	1 (−5)

Skills Stealth +4
Damage Resistances bludgeoning, poison
Condition Immunities charmed, exhaustion, frightened
Senses darkvision 60 ft., passive Perception 10
Languages understands the languages it knew in life but can't speak
Challenge 1 (200 XP)   **Proficiency Bonus** +2

Compression. The boneless can move through any opening at least 1 inch wide without squeezing. It can also squeeze to fit into a space that a Tiny creature could fit in.

Unusual Nature. The boneless doesn't require air, food, drink, or sleep.

Actions

Multiattack. The boneless makes two Slam attacks. If both attacks hit a Large or smaller creature, the creature is grappled (escape DC 13), and the boneless can use Crushing Embrace.

Slam. *Melee Weapon Attack:* +5 to hit, reach 5 ft., one target. *Hit:* 5 (1d4 + 3) bludgeoning damage.

Crushing Embrace. The boneless wraps its body around a Large or smaller creature grappled by it. While the boneless is attached, the target is blinded and is unable to breathe. The target must succeed on a DC 13 Strength saving throw at the start of each of the boneless' turns or take 5 (1d4 + 3) bludgeoning damage. If something moves the target, the boneless moves with it. The boneless can detach itself by spending 5 feet of its movement. A creature, including the target, can use its action to try to detach the boneless and force it to move into the nearest unoccupied space, doing so with a successful DC 13 Strength check. When the boneless dies, it detaches from any creature it is attached to.

Brain in a Jar

Through rituals combining alchemy, necromancy, and grim surgical precision, the brain of a mortal being is encased in a glass jar filled with preserving fluids and the liquefied goop of their body's flesh. The transformation renders the brain ageless and imbues it with psionic power, so that it can spend eternity plotting and executing its desires.

A brain in a jar can speak without vocal cords, psionically projecting its disembodied voice outward for all to hear. It enjoys conversation so much that it is prone to talking for hours on end, sometimes to itself if there are no others with whom it can speak. It also likes to think out loud and reflect on the events and decisions that led to its great transformation.

Brain Vessels

The brain floats in a jar of solution, pulsating as it reacts to its surroundings. Some brains have been known to thump against the walls of their containers when excited or vexed. A jar's metal casing might be rusty but serviceable, or an elegantly wrought masterwork, depending on its creator. Still other brains desire nothing more than to regain a body. This might be the brain's original body, another frame they covet, or some more elaborate design of their own diabolical creation. While disembodied, a brain in a jar weighs roughly 125 pounds.

Brain in a Jar
Small Undead

Armor Class 11 (natural armor)
Hit Points 55 (10d6 + 20)
Speed 0 ft., fly 10 ft. (hover)

STR	DEX	CON	INT	WIS	CHA
1 (−5)	3 (−4)	15 (+2)	19 (+4)	10 (+0)	15 (+2)

Saving Throws Int +6, Cha +4
Damage Immunities poison
Condition Immunities exhaustion, paralyzed, poisoned, prone
Senses blindsight 120 ft. (blind beyond this radius), passive Perception 10; see also "Detect Sentience" below
Languages the languages it knew in life
Challenge 3 (700 XP)   **Proficiency Bonus** +2

Detect Sentience. The brain can sense the presence and location of any creature within 300 feet of it that has an Intelligence of 3 or higher, regardless of interposing barriers, unless the creature is protected by a *mind blank* spell.

Magic Resistance. The brain has advantage on saving throws against spells and other magical effects.

Unusual Nature. The brain doesn't require air, food, drink, or sleep.

Actions

Chill Touch (Cantrip). *Ranged Spell Attack:* +6 to hit, range 120 ft., one creature. *Hit:* 13 (3d8) necrotic damage, and the target can't regain hit points until the start of the brain's next turn. If the target is Undead, it also has disadvantage on attack rolls against the brain until the end of the brain's next turn.

Mind Blast (Recharge 5–6). The brain magically emits psychic energy in a 60-foot cone. Each creature in that area must succeed on a DC 14 Intelligence saving throw or take 17 (3d8 + 4) psychic damage and be stunned for 1 minute. A stunned creature can repeat the saving throw at the end of each of its turns, ending the effect on itself on a success.

Innate Spellcasting (Psionics). The brain casts one of the following spells, requiring no components and using Intelligence as the spellcasting ability (spell save DC 14):

At will: *detect thoughts, mage hand, zone of truth*
3/day each: *charm person, hold person*
1/day each: *compulsion, hold monster, sleep* (3rd-level version), *Tasha's hideous laughter*

CARRION STALKER

A carrion stalker begins life as a pale larva that infests a corpse. Over the course of weeks, this grub burrows, feeds, and grows, ultimately developing into a chitinous mass of pincers and tentacles. When an adult carrion stalker detects movement, it bursts from its corpse-cradle to attack, intent on implanting its young into the living and starting its species' life cycle anew.

More than one necromancer has animated a corpse infested with carrion stalker larvae. While this can prove shocking and deadly, some depraved spellcasters cultivate carrion stalkers within zombies. The embedded carrion stalkers ride along in their freshly animated conveyances, bursting forth once they detect living creatures nearby. This destroys the zombie, but unleashes a new horror.

Carrion stalkers also enjoy symbiotic relationships with carrion crawlers. Carrion crawlers won't devour bodies infested by carrion stalkers, but they often pick up stalker larvae as they root among filth. The crawlers then spread these grubs, potentially infecting whole sewers, graveyards, or battlefields with carrion stalkers. In return, carrion stalkers avoid preying on carrion crawlers.

CARRION STALKER

Tiny Monstrosity

Armor Class 14 (natural armor)
Hit Points 35 (10d4 + 10)
Speed 30 ft., burrow 30 ft.

STR	DEX	CON	INT	WIS	CHA
6 (−2)	16 (+3)	12 (+1)	2 (−4)	13 (+1)	6 (−2)

Skills Stealth +7
Condition Immunities blinded
Senses tremorsense 60 ft., passive Perception 11
Languages —
Challenge 3 (700 XP)   **Proficiency Bonus** +2

ACTIONS

Multiattack. The carrion stalker makes three Tentacle attacks. If it is attached to a creature, it can replace one Tentacle attack with Larval Burst, if available.

Tentacle. *Melee Weapon Attack:* +5 to hit, reach 5 ft., one creature. *Hit:* 5 (1d4 + 3) piercing damage, and the carrion stalker attaches to the target and pulls itself into the target's space.

While attached, the carrion stalker moves with the target and has advantage on attack rolls against it.

A creature can use its action to try to detach the carrion stalker and force it to move into the nearest unoccupied space, doing so with a successful DC 11 Strength check. On its turn, the carrion stalker can detach itself from the target by using 5 feet of movement. When it dies, the carrion stalker detaches from any creature it is attached to.

Larval Burst (1/Day). The carrion stalker releases a burst of larvae in a 10-foot-radius sphere centered on itself. Each creature in that area must succeed on a DC 13 Constitution saving throw or be poisoned. A creature poisoned in this way takes 7 (2d6) poison damage at the start of each of its turns as larvae infest its body. The creature can repeat the saving throw at the end of each of its turns, ending the effect on itself on a success. Any effect that cures disease or removes the poisoned condition instantly kills the larvae in the creature, ending the effect on it.

If a creature is reduced to 0 hit points by the infestation, it dies. The larvae remain in the corpse, and one survives to become a fully grown carrion stalker in 1d4 weeks. Any effect that cures diseases or removes the poisoned condition that targets the corpse instantly kills the larvae.

CARRIONETTE

Carrionettes arise from innocent intentions. Heart-felt wishes breathe life into a beloved toy and, for a time, a creator might feel blessed by their new companion. But carrionettes aren't content to live as toys and seek to escape the confines of their diminutive bodies.

Every carrionette possesses a silver needle that pins its soul to its body. By posing as simple toys or hiding their desires, a carrionette gets close to an unsuspecting victim. It then uses its needle to swap souls with the victim, stealing the victim's body while trapping the victim's soul in its own doll-like frame. The carrionette then imprisons its old body, keeping the animate doll hidden while it explores the world in its stolen guise—often that of the very person who wished the carrionette into being.

Carrionettes might appear as any type of toy or piece of art. While marionettes and porcelain dolls are the most common, all manner of deadly stuffed animals, crawling jack-in-the-boxes, bloodthirsty poppets, murderous jewelry box ballerinas, and so forth might be carrionettes. These malicious toys are skilled deceivers and, despite some having existed for generations, often affect unsettlingly childlike personalities. Among the most notorious of these terrors is the carrionette Maligno, Darklord of the domain of Odaire (detailed in chapter 3).

IRINA NORDSOL

CARRIONETTE
Small Construct

Armor Class 15 (natural armor)
Hit Points 27 (6d6 + 6)
Speed 25 ft.

STR	DEX	CON	INT	WIS	CHA
10 (+0)	15 (+2)	12 (+1)	8 (−1)	14 (+2)	14 (+2)

Damage Resistance poison, psychic
Condition Immunities charmed, frightened, poisoned
Senses passive Perception 12
Languages understands the languages of its creator
Challenge 1 (200 XP)   **Proficiency Bonus** +2

False Object. If the carrionette is motionless at the start of combat, it has advantage on its initiative roll. Moreover, if a creature hasn't observed the carrionette move or act, that creature must succeed on a DC 15 Wisdom (Perception) check to discern that the carrionette is animate.

Unusual Nature. The carrionette doesn't require air, food, drink, or sleep.

ACTIONS

Silver Needle. *Melee Weapon Attack:* +4 to hit, reach 5 ft., one creature. *Hit:* 1 piercing damage plus 3 (1d6) necrotic damage, and the target must succeed on a DC 12 Charisma saving throw or become cursed for 1 minute. While cursed in this way, the target's speed is reduced by 10 feet, and it must roll a d4 and subtract the number rolled from each ability check or attack roll it makes.

Soul Swap. The carrionette targets a creature it can see within 15 feet of it that is cursed by its Silver Needle. Unless the target is protected by a *protection from evil and good* spell, it must succeed on a DC 12 Charisma saving throw or have its consciousness swapped with the carrionette. The carrionette gains control of the target's body, and the target is unconscious for 1 hour, after which it gains control of the carrionette's body. While controlling the target's body, the carrionette retains its Intelligence, Wisdom, and Charisma scores. It otherwise uses the controlled body's statistics, but doesn't gain access to the target's knowledge, class features, or proficiencies.

If the carrionette's body is destroyed, both the carrionette and the target die. A *protection from evil and good* spell cast on the controlled body drives the carrionette out and returns the consciousness of both creatures to their original bodies. The swap is also undone if the controlled body takes damage from the carrionette's Silver Needle.

DEATH'S HEAD

A death's head is a disembodied, flying head. The type of creature one of these grotesque undead originated from determines how it terrorizes it prey. A death's head that arises from a person or animal swoops down to rip apart victims with its gnashing teeth. One with the head of monster like a nothic or medusa, though, retains a measure of the power it had in life and can befuddle the minds or petrify the bodies of its victims.

DEATH'S HEAD TREE

In cursed wilds grow death's head trees, **awakened trees** from which 2d6 death's heads dangle like foul fruit. The heads detach to protect the tree if it's threatened. Should the tree be destroyed, the heads scatter and plant themselves in unholy ground. A new death's head tree emerges from each planted head 1d12 months later.

DEATH'S HEAD
Tiny Undead

Armor Class 16 (natural armor)
Hit Points 17 (5d4 + 5)
Speed 0 ft., fly 30 ft. (hover)

STR	DEX	CON	INT	WIS	CHA
8 (−1)	13 (+1)	12 (+1)	5 (−3)	14 (+2)	3 (−4)

Damage Resistance necrotic
Senses passive Perception 12
Languages —
Challenge 1/2 (100 XP)   **Proficiency Bonus** +2

Beheaded Form. When created, a death's head takes one of three forms: Aberrant Head, Gnashing Head, or Petrifying Head. This form determines the creature's attack.

Unusual Nature. The death's head doesn't require air, food, drink, or sleep.

ACTIONS

Gnashing Bite (Gnashing Head Only). *Melee Weapon Attack:* +3 to hit, reach 5 ft., one target. *Hit:* 4 (1d6 + 1) piercing damage plus 7 (2d6) necrotic damage.

Mind-Bending Bite (Aberrant Head Only). *Melee Weapon Attack:* +3 to hit, reach 5 ft., one target. *Hit:* 4 (1d6 + 1) piercing damage plus 5 (1d10) necrotic damage, and the target must succeed on a DC 10 Intelligence saving throw or it can't take a reaction until the end of its next turn. Moreover, on its next turn, the target must choose whether it gets a move, an action, or a bonus action; it gets only one of the three.

Petrifying Bite (Petrifying Head Only). *Melee Weapon Attack:* +3 to hit, reach 5 ft., one target. *Hit:* 3 (1d4 + 1) piercing damage, and the target must succeed on a DC 10 Constitution saving throw or be restrained as it begins to turn to stone. The target must repeat the saving throw at the end of its next turn. On a success, the effect ends. On a failure, the target is petrified for 10 minutes.

Dullahan

Dullahans are headless undead warriors—the remains of villains who let vengeance consume them. These decapitated hunters haunt the areas where they were slain, butchering innocents in search of their severed heads or to quench their thirst for revenge.

Wicked knights or commanders in life, dullahans adhere to twisted codes of chivalry or soldiership. These fallen champions consider a specific location their battlefield. This gives rise to stories of haunted battlegrounds, ruins, roads, river crossings and other strategic locations where a dullahan continues a terrifying campaign against the living. In death, dullahans are often rejoined by those who followed them in life, either in the form of lesser undead, like skeletons or wights, or terrifying mounts, like warhorse skeletons or nightmares.

Headless Hunts

Dullahans are known for seeking their lost heads, giving rise to regional legends of headless hunters and endless searches. The Dullahan Legends table suggests dullahan hauntings that might be the stuff of local legends.

Dullahan Legends

d4	Haunting
1	A dullahan pursues anyone who has one of the shards of its shattered skull.
2	A vain dullahan pursues it own relatives, seeking to claim a head with its family resemblance.
3	A greedy dullahan seeks to recover its bejeweled helmet, caring nothing for the head that wears it.
4	Two dullahans seek the same head, both believing they're the actual owner.

Dullahan
Medium Undead

Armor Class 16 (breastplate)
Hit Points 135 (18d8 + 54)
Speed 30 ft.

STR	DEX	CON	INT	WIS	CHA
18 (+4)	14 (+2)	16 (+3)	11 (+0)	15 (+2)	16 (+3)

Saving Throws Con +7
Skills Perception +6
Damage Resistance cold, lightning, poison
Condition Immunities charmed, frightened, poisoned
Senses truesight 120 ft., passive Perception 16
Languages understands the languages it knew in life but can't speak
Challenge 10 (5,900 XP)　　　　**Proficiency Bonus** +4

Headless Summoning (Recharges after a Short or Long Rest). If the dullahan is reduced to 0 hit points, it doesn't die or fall unconscious. Instead, it regains 97 hit points. In addition, it summons three death's heads, one of each type, in unoccupied spaces within 5 feet of it. The death's heads are under the dullahan's control and act immediately after the dullahan in the initiative order. Additionally, the dullahan can now use the options in the "Mythic Actions" section. Award a party an additional 5,900 XP (11,800 XP total) for defeating the dullahan after it uses Headless Summoning.

Legendary Resistance (2/Day). If the dullahan fails a saving throw, it can choose to succeed instead.

Unusual Nature. The dullahan doesn't require air, food, drink, or sleep.

Actions

Multiattack. The dullahan makes two attacks.

Battleaxe. *Melee Weapon Attack:* +8 to hit, reach 5 ft., one target. *Hit:* 8 (1d8 + 4) slashing damage, or 9 (1d10 + 4) slashing damage if used with two hands, plus 11 (2d10) necrotic damage. If the dullahan scores a critical hit against a creature, the target must succeed on a DC 15 Constitution saving throw or the dullahan cuts off the target's head. The target dies if it can't survive without the lost head. A creature that doesn't have or need a head, or has legendary actions, instead takes an extra 27 (6d8) slashing damage.

Fiery Skull. *Ranged Spell Attack:* +7 to hit, range 120 ft., one target. *Hit:* 14 (2d10 + 3) fire damage.

Legendary Actions

The dullahan can take 3 legendary actions, choosing from the options below. Only one legendary action can be used at a time and only at the end of another creature's turn. The dullahan regains spent legendary actions at the start of its turn.

Attack. The dullahan makes one attack.
Frightful Presence (Costs 2 Actions). Each creature of the dullahan's choice within 30 feet of it must succeed on a DC 15 Wisdom saving throw or become frightened of the dullahan until the end of its next turn.
Head Hunt (Costs 3 Actions). The dullahan moves up to its speed without provoking opportunity attacks and makes one Battleaxe attack with advantage. If the attack hits, but is not a critical hit, the attack deals an extra 27 (6d8) necrotic damage.

Mythic Actions

If the dullahan's Headless Summoning trait is active, it can use the options below as legendary actions.

Coordinated Assault. The dullahan makes a Battleaxe attack, and then one death's head the dullahan can see within 30 feet of it can use its reaction to make a melee attack.
Headless Wail (Costs 2 Actions). An echoing shriek issues from the dullahan's headless stump. Each creature of the dullahan's choice within 10 feet of it must make a DC 15 Wisdom saving throw. Each creature takes 16 (3d10) psychic damage on a failed save, or half as much damage on a successful one. If one or more creatures fail the saving throw, the dullahan gains 10 temporary hit points.

Gallows Speaker

Gallows speakers arise from places of mass death or sites where creatures regularly meet their doom. Over time, pain-wracked phantoms and lingering souls combine into an entity that knows death in myriad forms. Such amalgamated spirits are tormented by their collective pain, endlessly moaning disjointed final thoughts as they lash out at the living. Having known untold deaths, gallows speakers can predict suffering, foreseeing dooms leveled against them and overwhelming their foes with visions of innumerable violent deaths.

Gallows speakers rarely speak coherently or communicate with the living, instead being entirely obsessed with their memories of death. These undead endlessly mutter to themselves, giving voice to final curses, regrets, pleas, and apologies. Those who linger and listen to a gallows speaker might gain insight into any of its many deaths.

GALLOWS SPEAKER
Medium Undead

Armor Class 12
Hit Points 85 (19d8)
Speed 0 ft., fly 40 ft. (hover)

STR	DEX	CON	INT	WIS	CHA
8 (−1)	14 (+2)	10 (+0)	10 (+0)	12 (+1)	18 (+4)

Saving Throws Wis +4
Skills Perception +7
Damage Resistances bludgeoning, piercing, and slashing from nonmagical attacks
Damage Immunities necrotic, poison
Condition Immunities charmed, exhaustion, frightened, grappled, paralyzed, petrified, poisoned, prone, restrained
Senses truesight 60 ft., passive Perception 17
Languages any languages its component spirits knew in life
Challenge 6 (2,300 XP)   **Proficiency Bonus** +3

Divination Senses. The gallows speaker can see 60 feet into the Ethereal Plane when it is on the Material Plane and vice versa.

Incorporeal Movement. The gallows speaker can move through other creatures and objects as if they were difficult terrain. It takes 5 (1d10) force damage if it ends it turn inside an object.

Unusual Nature. The gallows speaker doesn't require air, food, drink, or sleep.

ACTIONS

Foretelling Touch. *Melee Spell Attack:* +7 to hit, reach 5 ft., one creature. *Hit:* 15 (2d10 + 4) psychic damage, and the target must roll a d4 and subtract the number rolled from the next attack roll or saving throw it makes before the start of the gallows speaker's next turn.

Suffering Echoes. The gallows speaker targets a creature it can see within 30 feet of it. The target must make a DC 15 Wisdom saving throw. On a failed save, the target takes 19 (3d12) psychic damage, and waves of painful memories leap from the target to up to three other creatures of the gallows speaker's choice that are within 30 feet of the target, each of which takes 13 (3d8) psychic damage.

Gremishka

Gremishkas are the vicious products of mistakes made by novice spellcasters seeking to create life. The results are cat-sized, magically unstable creatures with a taste for the trappings of magic—particularly spellbooks, spell components, familiars, and the like. Gremishkas delight in tormenting magic-users, holding vicious grudges against those who gave them life as they infest the walls of spell-casters' homes or the surrounding lands.

Despite their feral appearances, gremishkas are cunning creatures. They might imitate the sounds of whimpering children or wounded animals to coax victims into tight quarters. While they favor attacking spellcasters, gremishkas are opportunistic hunters and lash out at anything they think they can overwhelm—or just get a bite of.

Gremishkas have an unstable relationship with magic. Spells cast near a gremishka might rebound onto those nearby or cause the monster to explode, its scaly chunks rapidly reforming into duplicate gremishkas. These spontaneously created swarms can rapidly turn a single annoying gremishka into a chittering, magic-reflecting wave of teeth and claws.

Gremishka

Tiny Monstrosity

Armor Class 12
Hit Points 10 (4d4)
Speed 30 ft.

STR	DEX	CON	INT	WIS	CHA
6 (−2)	14 (+2)	10 (+0)	12 (+1)	11 (+0)	4 (−3)

Senses darkvision 30 ft., passive Perception 10
Languages understands Common but can't speak
Challenge 1/8 (25 XP)   **Proficiency Bonus** +2

Actions

Bite. *Melee Weapon Attack:* +4 to hit, reach 5 ft., one target. *Hit:* 3 (1d4 + 2) piercing damage plus 3 (1d6) force damage.

Reactions

Magic Allergy (1/Day). Immediately after a creature within 30 feet of the gremishka casts a spell, the gremishka can spontaneously react to the magic. Roll a d6 to determine the effect:

1–2. The gremishka emanates magical energy. Each creature within 30 feet of the gremishka must succeed on a DC 10 Constitution saving throw or take 3 (1d6) force damage.

3–4. The gremishka surges with magical energy and regains 3 (1d6) hit points.

5–6. The gremishka explodes and dies, and one swarm of gremishkas instantly appears in the space where this gremishka died. The swarm uses the gremishka's initiative.

Swarm of Gremishkas

Medium Swarm of Tiny Monstrosities

Armor Class 12
Hit Points 24 (7d6)
Speed 25 ft.

STR	DEX	CON	INT	WIS	CHA
12 (+1)	14 (+2)	10 (+0)	12 (+1)	14 (+2)	4 (−3)

Skills Perception +4
Damage Resistance bludgeoning, piercing, slashing
Condition Immunities charmed, frightened, grappled, paralyzed, petrified, prone, restrained, stunned
Senses darkvision 30 ft., passive Perception 14
Languages understands Common but can't speak
Challenge 2 (450 XP)   **Proficiency Bonus** +2

Limited Spell Immunity. The swarm automatically succeeds on saving throws against spells of 3rd level or lower, and the attack rolls of such spells always miss it.

Swarm. The swarm can occupy another creature's space and vice versa, and the swarm can move through any opening large enough for a Tiny gremishka. The swarm can't regain hit points or gain temporary hit points.

Actions

Bites. *Melee Weapon Attack:* +4 to hit, reach 0 ft., one target in the swarm's space. *Hit:* 12 (3d6 + 2) piercing damage, or 5 (1d6 + 2) piercing damage if the swarm has half of its hit points or fewer, plus 7 (2d6) force damage.

Reactions

Spell Redirection. In response to a spell attack roll missing the swarm, the swarm causes that spell to hit another creature of its choice within 30 feet of it that it can see.

Jiangshi

When a soul becomes trapped within its corpse, its bitterness can reanimate its body, creating a jiangshi. These vengeful dead stalk their descendants and the communities they knew in life, sowing terror and taking retribution for the slights or neglected burial rites that led to their cursed resurrections. Rigor mortis notoriously afflicts the limbs of jiangshi, causing them to hold their arms rigidly and to walk with a stiff gait. This, along with their flight, lead many to call them hopping vampires.

By day, jiangshi lurk within their tombs and hidden ruins to avoid the attention of the living. At night, they emerge to drain life from other creatures, these vital energies sustaining their unnatural existences and granting them greater powers. Humanoids killed by a jiangshi rise as life-hungry corpses and might turn into jiangshi themselves if they feed upon the living.

Jiangshi
Medium Undead

Armor Class 16 (natural armor)
Hit Points 119 (14d8 + 56)
Speed 20 ft.

STR	DEX	CON	INT	WIS	CHA
18 (+4)	3 (−4)	18 (+4)	17 (+3)	14 (+2)	12 (+1)

Saving Throws Con +8, Int +7, Wis +6, Cha +5
Condition Immunities charmed, exhaustion, frightened, paralyzed, poisoned
Senses darkvision 120 ft., passive Perception 12
Languages any languages it knew in life
Challenge 9 (5,000 XP)   **Proficiency Bonus** +4

Jiangshi Weaknesses. The jiangshi has the following flaws:

Fear of Its Own Reflection. If the jiangshi sees its own reflection, it immediately uses its reaction, if available, to move as far away from the reflection as possible.

Susceptible to Holy Symbols. While the jiangshi is wearing or touching a holy symbol, it automatically fails saving throws against effects that turn Undead.

Unusual Nature. The jiangshi doesn't require air.

Actions

Multiattack. The jiangshi makes three Slam attacks and uses Consume Energy.

Slam. *Melee Weapon Attack:* +8 to hit, reach 5 ft., one target. *Hit:* 13 (2d8 + 4) bludgeoning damage.

Consume Energy. The jiangshi draws energy from a creature it can see within 30 feet of it. The target makes a DC 16 Constitution saving throw, taking 18 (4d8) necrotic damage on a failed save, or half as much damage on a successful one. The jiangshi regains hit points equal to the amount of necrotic damage dealt. After regaining hit points from this action, the jiangshi gains the following benefits for 7 days: its walking speed increases to 40 feet, and it gains a flying speed equal to its walking speed and can hover.

A Humanoid slain by this necrotic damage rises as a wight (see its entry in the *Monster Manual*) at the end of the jiangshi's turn. The wight acts immediately after the jiangshi in the initiative order. If this wight slays a Humanoid with its Life Drain, the wight transforms into a jiangshi 5 days later.

Change Shape. The jiangshi polymorphs into a Beast, a Humanoid, or an Undead that is Medium or Small or back into its true form. Its statistics, other than its size, are the same in each form. Any equipment it is wearing or carrying is absorbed or borne by the new form (the jiangshi's choice). It reverts to its true form if it dies.

LOUP GAROU

Loup garou possess a strain of lycanthropy more virulent than that carried by common werewolves. Aside from being deadlier than their werewolf cousins, loup garou aggressively spread the plague of lycanthropy. Only through the death of a loup garou might those afflicted by it escape their curse.

LOUP GAROU LYCANTHROPY

A Humanoid who succumbs to a loup garou's lycanthropy becomes a werewolf. This form of lycanthropy can't be removed while the loup garou that inflicted the curse lives. See the *Monster Manual* for details on lycanthropy.

Once a loup garou is slain, a *remove curse* spell cast during the night of a full moon on any afflicted werewolf it created forces the target to make a DC 17 Constitution saving throw. On a success, the curse is broken, and the target returns to its normal form and gains 3 levels of exhaustion. On a failure, the curse remains, and the target automatically fails any saving throw made to break this curse for 1 month.

LOUP GAROU

Medium Monstrosity (Shapechanger)

Armor Class 16 (natural armor)
Hit Points 170 (20d8 + 80)
Speed 30 ft., 40 ft. in hybrid form, 50 ft. in dire wolf form

STR	DEX	CON	INT	WIS	CHA
18 (+4)	18 (+4)	18 (+4)	14 (+2)	16 (+3)	16 (+3)

Saving Throws Dex +9, Con +9, Cha +8
Skills Perception +13, Stealth +9
Condition Immunities charmed, frightened
Senses darkvision 120 ft., passive Perception 23
Languages Common (can't speak in wolf form)
Challenge 13 (10,000 XP)   **Proficiency Bonus** +5

Blood Frenzy. The loup garou has advantage on attack rolls against a creature that doesn't have all its hit points.

Legendary Resistance (2/Day). When the loup garou fails a saving throw, it can choose to succeed instead.

Regeneration. The loup garou regains 10 hit points at the start of each of its turns. If the loup garou takes damage from a silver weapon, this trait doesn't function at the start of the loup garou's next turn. The loup garou dies only if it starts its turn with 0 hit points and doesn't regenerate.

ACTIONS

Multiattack. The loup garou makes two attacks: two with its Longsword (humanoid form) or one with its Bite and one with its Claws (dire wolf or hybrid form).

Bite (Dire Wolf or Hybrid Form Only). *Melee Weapon Attack:* +9 to hit, reach 5 ft., one target. *Hit:* 13 (2d8 + 4) piercing damage plus 14 (4d6) necrotic damage. If the target is a Humanoid, it must succeed on a DC 17 Constitution saving throw or be cursed with loup garou lycanthropy.

Claws (Dire Wolf or Hybrid Form Only). *Melee Weapon Attack:* +9 to hit, reach 5 ft., one target. *Hit:* 11 (2d6 + 4) slashing damage. If the target is a creature, it must succeed on a DC 17 Strength saving throw or be knocked prone.

Longsword (Humanoid Form Only). *Melee Weapon Attack:* +9 to hit, reach 5 ft., one target. *Hit:* 13 (2d8 + 4) slashing damage, or 15 (2d10 + 4) slashing damage if used with two hands.

BONUS ACTIONS

Change Shape. The loup garou polymorphs into a Large wolf-humanoid hybrid or into a Large dire wolf, or back into its true form, which appears humanoid. Its statistics, other than its size and speed, are the same in each form. Any equipment it is wearing or carrying isn't transformed. It reverts to its true form if it dies.

LEGENDARY ACTIONS

The loup garou can take 3 legendary actions, choosing from the options below. Only one legendary action option can be used at a time, and only at the end of another creature's turn. The loup garou regains spent legendary actions at the start of its turn.

Swipe. The loup garou makes one Claws attack (dire wolf or hybrid form only) or one Longsword attack (humanoid form only).

Mauling Pounce (Costs 2 Actions). The loup garou moves up to its speed without provoking opportunity attacks, and it can make one Claws attack (dire wolf or hybrid form only) or one Longsword attack (humanoid form only) against each creature it moves past.

Bite (Costs 3 Actions). The loup garou changes into hybrid or dire wolf form and then makes one Bite attack.

NECRICHOR

A necrichor is a being of living blood, formed from the ichor of evil gods or the sludge in the crypts of failed liches. Despite the loss of a solid physical form, these foul creatures retain their terrible intellects and aspire to megalomaniacal goals—the first of which involves regaining a body. To do this, they seek servants to exact their will, coercing even the most stubborn potential minions by turning their own blood against them.

Necrichors prove exceptionally difficult to destroy, since they leave a trace of their essence within the veins of every creature they've controlled and can regenerate themselves from those creatures' blood. Unable to extinguish their horrific unlife, virtuous faiths and vigilant organizations (like the Order of the Guardians detailed in chapter 3) seal these viscous horrors in magically warded prisons. As ages pass, though, the knowledge of what these prisons contain and where some lie have been lost. And every imprisoned necrichor understands that its captivity might be lengthy, but time is of little consequence to the ageless. Necrichors that escape their imprisonment have the statistics presented here.

NECRICHOR
Medium Undead

Armor Class 12
Hit Points 67 (9d8 + 27)
Speed 20 ft., climb 20 ft.

STR	DEX	CON	INT	WIS	CHA
8 (−1)	15 (+2)	17 (+3)	17 (+3)	13 (+1)	10 (+0)

Saving Throws Con +6, Int +6, Wis +4
Skills Arcana +9
Damage Resistances acid, necrotic
Condition Immunities blinded, charmed, deafened, exhaustion, frightened, grappled, paralyzed, poisoned, prone, restrained
Senses blindsight 120 ft. (blind beyond this radius), passive Perception 11
Languages any three languages, telepathy 120 ft.
Challenge 7 (3,900 XP)   **Proficiency Bonus** +3

Legendary Resistance (2/Day). If the necrichor fails a saving throw, it can choose to succeed instead.

Rejuvenation. Unless its lifeless remains are splashed with holy water or placed in a vessel under the effects of the *hallow* spell, the destroyed necrichor re-forms in 1d10 days, regaining all its hits points and appearing in the place it died or in the nearest unoccupied space.

Spider Climb. The necrichor can climb difficult surfaces, including upside down on ceilings, without needing to make an ability check.

Unusual Nature. The necrichor doesn't require air, food, drink, or sleep.

ACTIONS

Multiattack. The necrichor makes two attacks.

Pseudopod. *Melee Weapon Attack:* +5 to hit, reach 10 ft., one target. *Hit:* 5 (1d6 + 2) necrotic damage, and the target must succeed on a DC 14 Constitution saving throw or be paralyzed until the start of the necrichor's next turn.

Necrotic Bolt. *Ranged Spell Attack:* +6 to hit, range 120 ft., one creature. *Hit:* 12 (2d8 + 3) necrotic damage, and the target can't regain hit points until the start of the necrichor's next turn.

Blood Puppeteering (Recharge 6). The necrichor targets a creature it can see within 5 feet of it that is missing any of its hit points. If the target isn't a Construct or an Undead, it must succeed on a DC 14 Constitution saving throw or the necrichor enters the target's space and attaches itself to the target for 1 minute. While attached, the necrichor takes only half damage dealt to it (round down), and the target takes the remaining damage. The necrichor can attach to only one creature at a time.

The attached necrichor can telepathically control the target's move, action, or both. When controlled this way, the target can take only the Attack action (necrichor chooses the target) or the Dash action. The attached target can repeat the saving throw at the end of each of its turns, detaching from the necrichor and forcing it to move into the nearest unoccupied space on a success.

STEPHEN OAKLEY

Nosferatu

Vicious, undead hunters, nosferatu possess the endless thirst of vampires but none of their grace. For them, existence is nothing more than an everlasting string of cold, desperate nights punctuated by crimson splashes of momentary warmth and lucidity. These joys are fleeting, as their blood addiction can never be quelled.

Nosferatu feed on anything with blood. Heaps of mutilated rats and stables turned into slaughterhouses are typical first signs of a nosferatu's predation. When the sun interrupts their hunts, nosferatu retreat to favored ruins, sewers, or caves, caring nothing for their lair's comfort. Rather than retiring to crypts, they seek filthy or inaccessible fissures, places any living soul would avoid.

For a few moments after feeding, nosferatu are lucid and capable of considering more than their next meal. In these instants, nosferatu recollect glimpses of what they once were, beings who knew pride, intention, and a world beyond the shadows. They might even momentarily be convinced to converse with other creatures. However, those who talk with nosferatu typically find them selfish, duplicitous creatures whose memories are faded and whose basic respect for life is long dead.

Nosferatu
Medium Undead

Armor Class 17 (natural armor)
Hit Points 85 (9d8 + 45)
Speed 40 ft.

STR	DEX	CON	INT	WIS	CHA
20 (+5)	18 (+4)	21 (+5)	6 (−2)	17 (+3)	14 (+2)

Saving Throws Dex +7, Con +8, Wis +6
Skills Perception +6, Stealth +10
Damage Resistance necrotic
Condition Immunities charmed, frightened
Senses darkvision 120 ft., passive Perception 16
Languages the languages it knew in life
Challenge 8 (3,900 XP)   **Proficiency Bonus** +3

Regeneration. The nosferatu regains 10 hit points at the start of each of its turns if it has at least 1 hit point and isn't in sunlight. If the nosferatu takes radiant damage, this trait doesn't function until the start of the nosferatu's next turn.

Spider Climb. The nosferatu can climb difficult surfaces, including upside down on ceilings, without needing to make an ability check.

Sunlight Hypersensitivity. The nosferatu takes 20 radiant damage when it starts its turn in sunlight. While in sunlight, it has disadvantage on attack rolls and ability checks.

Unusual Nature. The nosferatu doesn't require air.

Actions

Multiattack. The nosferatu makes two Claw attacks followed by one Bite attack. If both Claw attacks hit the same creature, the Bite attack is made with advantage.

Claw. *Melee Weapon Attack:* +8 to hit, reach 5 ft., one target. *Hit:* 9 (1d8 + 5) slashing damage.

Bite. *Melee Weapon Attack:* +8 to hit, reach 5 ft., one creature. *Hit:* 9 (1d8 + 5) piercing damage plus 7 (2d6) necrotic damage. If the target is missing any of its hit points, it instead takes 11 (2d10) necrotic damage.

The target's hit point maximum is reduced by an amount equal to the necrotic damage taken, and the nosferatu regains hit points equal to that amount. The reduction lasts until the target finishes a long rest. The target dies if its hit point maximum is reduced to 0. A Humanoid slain in this way and then buried in the ground rises as a nosferatu after 1d10 days.

Blood Disgorge (Recharge 5–6). The nosferatu vomits blood in a 15-foot cone. Each creature in that area must make a DC 16 Constitution saving throw. On a failed save, a creature takes 18 (4d8) necrotic damage, and it can't regain hit points for 1 minute. On a successful save, the creature takes half as much damage with no additional effects.

PRIESTS OF OSYBUS USE SOUL TATTOOS TO CONJURE
UNDEAD SERVANTS AND ESCAPE DEATH'S GRIP.

PRIESTS OF OSYBUS

Necromancers of deep evil, the priests of Osybus
steal the souls of others to fuel the priests' malevolent magic. Using this soul power, each priest can
defy death and become an undead creature, potentially cheating the grave over and over.

This unholy order of priests was founded centuries ago by Osybus, a mysterious figure of unfathomable ambition and evil. Osybus sought to use others'
souls as springboards to his own immortality. He
forged pacts with any entity that would give him
more power and delved into any eldritch secret that
would prolong his life. He became a devotee of the
Dark Powers and tapped into their immortal malice
to fuel his apotheosis.

As his power grew, he attracted disciples who also
wished to defy life and death. He shared his dread
secrets with them and demanded their worship.
In time, his goal was achieved: he became a lich of
almost godly power. Acknowledging the role that
his disciples played in his ascension, Osybus gifted
them with a trace of his power. Taking the form of a
shadowy tattoo, this boon allows the priests to steal
souls as their master did and to cheat death and become undead horrors.

The threat posed by Osybus and his disciples
raised alarms far and wide. In response, the Ulmist Inquisition and the then-mortal Count Strahd
von Zarovich faced the lich in battle. Their bravery
would have been for naught if Osybus's disciples
hadn't betrayed him. Fearing that their master
would eventually consume their souls, the disciples aided Osybus's foes and destroyed his physical form. As he perished, he uttered a curse upon
them—that their immortality would fail them when
they least expected it and that he himself would
become one of the Dark Powers. As a result of that
curse, a priest of Osybus can't be certain that they
will be reborn when they perish.

In an effort to rid themselves of this curse, they
devoted themselves to the same Dark Powers with
whom their master had communed. They were
given a mission: provide a person of nobility and
might to serve as an earthly vessel for these powers
to enter the world and conquer it. If they succeeded,
their immortality would be assured. A suitable vessel they did then find: Strahd von Zarovich. Working
in shadows and through intermediaries, the priests
whispered hatred to the count, and when his noble
heart was corrupted, they were the ones who laid
the path before him that led to the Amber Temple
and his fall into vampirism.

But they were then betrayed. Osybus had not lied;
he had himself become one of the Dark Powers, and
he and the other Dark Powers had conjured up a
misty prison to contain the newly immortal Strahd,
thereby preventing the count from serving as the

OLLY LAWSON

conquering force that the priests sought to loose upon the world; thus they were denied their reward of immortality.

To this day, the priests of Osybus seek to unleash Strahd from the mists, often using adventurers as their pawns. They also ironically bear their hated founder's name, for they know it is his original deathly gift that gives them their horrific powers.

PRIEST OF OSYBUS
Medium Humanoid

Armor Class 14 (natural armor)
Hit Points 60 (8d8 + 24)
Speed 30 ft.

STR	DEX	CON	INT	WIS	CHA
10 (+0)	14 (+2)	16 (+3)	18 (+4)	17 (+3)	11 (+0)

Saving Throws Int +7, Wis +6, Cha +3
Condition Immunities frightened
Senses darkvision 120 ft., passive Perception 13
Languages any three languages
Challenge 6 (2,300 XP)　　　　**Proficiency Bonus** +3

Tattoo of Osybus. If the priest drops to 0 hit points, roll on the Boons of Undeath table for the boon the priest receives. The priest dies if it receives a boon it already has. If it receives a new boon, it revives at the start of its next turn with half its hit points restored, and its creature type is now Undead.

To prevent this revival, the Tattoo of Osybus on the priest's body must be destroyed. The tattoo is invulnerable while the priest has at least 1 hit point. The tattoo is otherwise an object with AC 15, and it is immune to poison and psychic damage. It has 15 hit points, but it regains all its hit points at the end of every combatant's turn.

ACTIONS

Multiattack. The priest attacks twice.

Soul Blade. *Melee Weapon Attack:* +5 to hit, reach 5 ft., one target. *Hit:* 7 (2d4 + 2) piercing damage, and if the target is a creature, it is paralyzed until the start of the priest's next turn. If this damage reduces a Medium or smaller creature to 0 hit points, the creature dies, and its soul is trapped in the priest's body, manifesting as a shadowy Soul Tattoo on the priest. The soul is freed if the priest dies.

Necrotic Bolt. *Ranged Spell Attack:* +7 to hit, range 120 ft., one target. *Hit:* 17 (3d8 + 4) necrotic damage, and the target can't regain hit points until the start of the priest's next turn.

BONUS ACTIONS

Soul Tattoo (Recharge 5–6). The priest touches one of the Soul Tattoos on its body. The tattoo vanishes as the trapped soul manifests as a shadowy creature that appears in an unoccupied space the priest can see within 30 feet of it. The creature has the size and silhouette of its original body, but it otherwise uses the stat block of a shadow.

The shadow obeys the priest's mental commands (no action required) and takes its turn immediately after the priest. If the creature is within 5 feet of the priest, it can turn back into a tattoo as an action, reappearing on the priest's flesh and regaining all its hit points.

BOONS OF UNDEATH

When a priest of Osybus drops to 0 hit points, the priest might revive with a benefit from the Boons of Undeath table, as explained in the stat block. You can give a priest one or more of these boons of your choice before the priest faces adventurers. If you do so, the priest is Undead, rather than Humanoid, and a priest can receive each boon only once.

BOONS OF UNDEATH

d6	Boon
1	**Dread.** Eerie whispers can now be heard around the priest. Any non-Undead creature that starts its turn within 30 feet of the priest must succeed on a DC 15 Wisdom saving throw or be frightened of the priest until the start of the creature's next turn.
2	**Ectoplasmic.** An otherworldly slime drips off the priest and fades away moments later, leaving a greenish stain. When any creature starts its turn within 10 feet of the priest, the priest can reduce that creature's speed by 10 feet until the start of the creature's next turn, until which the creature is covered by ectoplasm. In addition, as an action, the priest can use the slime to make itself look and feel like any creature that is Medium or Small, while retaining its game statistics. This transformation lasts for 8 hours or until the priest drops to 0 hit points.
3	**Vampiric.** When the priest deals necrotic damage to any creature, the priest gains a number of temporary hit points equal to half that necrotic damage. The priest's speed also increases by 10 feet.
4	**Blazing.** The priest sloughs off its flesh, and its skeleton crumbles away, leaving only its skull. Its stat block is replaced by that of a **flameskull**, but it retains its Tattoo of Osybus trait, and all fire damage it deals becomes necrotic damage. The Tattoo of Osybus now appears carved into the skull's forehead.
5	**Spectral.** The priest now appears wraithlike, and its challenge rating increases by 1. It gains resistance to all damage but force, radiant, and psychic, and it is vulnerable to radiant damage. It can also move through creatures and objects as if they were difficult terrain, but it takes 5 (1d10) force damage if it ends its turn inside a creature or an object.
6	**Deathly.** The priest's visage becomes bone white, and its challenge rating increases by 1. It can cast *animate dead* and *create undead* once per day each, using Intelligence as the spellcasting ability, and it gains the following action: ***Circle of Death (Spell; Recharge 5–6).*** Each creature in a 60-foot-radius sphere centered on a point the priest can see within 150 feet of it must make a DC 15 Constitution saving throw, taking 28 (8d6) necrotic damage on a failed save, or half as much damage on a successful one.

RELENTLESS JUGGERNAUT

RELENTLESS KILLER

Relentless killers are hateful, revenge-obsessed creatures that enter into pacts with fiends or other nefarious entities. Their bargains transform them into vicious butchers that exist only to indulge their endless bloodlust. While some who become relentless killers began life as innocents, any semblance of who they were is washed away in a tide of gore and rage. These killers' grisly work swiftly becomes the stuff of legends, striking fear into innocents across lands and over ages.

RELENTLESS SLASHER

A relentless slasher conducts its bloody work in silence then vanishes into shadow and infamy. Fixated on a specific individual or type of victim, it pursues its target with single-minded obsession.

RELENTLESS JUGGERNAUT

Relentless juggernauts are massive brutes that thirst for carnage. Their presence twists the world around them, allowing them to create weapons with which they can slaughter prey. Sharp iron fences, crushing stalagmites and blades of glass all conveniently appear in order to aid a juggernaut's brutality. Every juggernaut considers a certain area its territory and visits destruction upon all trespassers.

RELENTLESS SLASHER

Medium Fiend

Armor Class 15 (natural armor)
Hit Points 84 (13d8 + 26)
Speed 40 ft.

STR	DEX	CON	INT	WIS	CHA
12 (+1)	18 (+4)	14 (+2)	14 (+2)	15 (+2)	16 (+3)

Saving Throws Str +4, Dex +7, Con +5, Wis +5
Skills Athletics +7, Perception +5, Survival +5
Condition Immunities charmed, frightened
Senses darkvision 120 ft., passive Perception 15
Languages understands all languages but can't speak
Challenge 8 (3,900 XP)   **Proficiency Bonus** +3

Legendary Resistance (1/Day). If the slasher fails a saving throw, it can choose to succeed instead.

Shrouded Presence. The slasher is immune to any effect that would sense its emotions or read its thoughts, and it can't be detected by abilities that sense Fiends.

ACTIONS

Multiattack. The slasher makes two Slasher's Knife attacks.

Slasher's Knife. *Melee or Ranged Weapon Attack:* +7 to hit, reach 5 ft. or range 30/60 ft., one target. *Hit:* 6 (1d4 + 4) slashing damage plus 21 (6d6) necrotic damage. If the target is a creature, it suffers a lingering wound that causes it to take 7 (2d6) necrotic damage at the start of each of its turns. Each time the slasher hits the wounded target with this attack, the damage dealt by the wound increases by 3 (1d6). The wound ends if the target regains hit points or if a creature uses an action to stanch the wound, which requires a successful DC 15 Wisdom (Medicine) check.

LEGENDARY ACTIONS

The slasher can take 3 legendary actions, choosing from the options below. Only one legendary action option can be used at a time and only at the end of another creature's turn. The slasher regains spent legendary actions at the start of its turn.

Slice. *Melee or Ranged Weapon Attack:* +7 to hit, reach 5 ft. or range 30/60 ft., one target. *Hit:* 7 (1d6 + 4) slashing damage.
Vanishing Strike (Costs 3 Actions). The slasher makes one Slasher's Knife attack. After the attack hits or misses, the slasher can teleport up to 30 feet to an unoccupied space it can see.

CREATING A RELENTLESS KILLER

Relentless killers come into being and undertake their terrifying sprees for a spectrum of reasons. When creating a relentless killer, consider what circumstances led to their transformation and signature methods. Roll or choose options from the Relentless Origins and Relentless Methods tables when creating your own, unique monstrous slayers.

RELENTLESS ORIGINS

d6	Origin
1	It was left for dead and granted new life to seek revenge.
2	It was turned into a weapon of vengeance by a family member's bargain with sinister forces.
3	It was marked by a fiend before its birth, and its wicked nature emerged over time.
4	A wicked place or magic relic seeped into its being, turning it into a monster.
5	The killer used its body to contain an evil entity.
6	The killer appears to be an ordinary person who doesn't realize it turns into a killer when enraged.

RELENTLESS METHODS

d8	Method
1	**Artist.** The killer turns its victims into works of art, perhaps creating grisly tableaus or using their blood in the forging of new weapons.
2	**Author.** The killer leaves messages, poems, song lyrics, or parts of its creative masterpiece at the scenes of its crimes.
3	**Avatar.** The killer sacrifices its victims, believing it's a manifestation of a deity or force beyond morality.
4	**Doctor.** The killer dissects victims or harvests their organs for the sake of medical understanding.
5	**Mask.** The killer wears a distinctive disguise, its visage becoming a symbol of its crimes.
6	**Penitent.** The killer can't help itself from committing crimes and seeks help to thwart its own continuing violence.
7	**Ritualist.** The killer always attacks the same type of person in the same type of place in the same way.
8	**Trophy Taker.** The killer reliably collects something from its victims, hoarding them as trophies.

RELENTLESS JUGGERNAUT

Large Fiend

Armor Class 17 (natural armor)
Hit Points 161 (14d10 + 84)
Speed 30 ft.

STR	DEX	CON	INT	WIS	CHA
22 (+6)	12 (+1)	22 (+6)	8 (−1)	15 (+2)	16 (+3)

Saving Throws Dex +5, Wis +6, Cha +7
Skills Perception +6, Survival +6
Condition Immunities charmed, exhaustion, frightened
Senses darkvision 120 ft., passive Perception 16
Languages understands all languages but can't speak
Challenge 12 (8,400 XP)   **Proficiency Bonus** +4

Legendary Resistance (3/Day). If the juggernaut fails a saving throw, it can choose to succeed instead.

Regeneration. The juggernaut regains 20 hit points at the start of its turn. If the juggernaut takes radiant damage, this trait doesn't function at the start of its next turn. The juggernaut dies only if it starts its turn with 0 hit points and doesn't regenerate.

Unusual Nature. The juggernaut doesn't require air, food, drink, or sleep.

ACTIONS

Multiattack. The juggernaut makes two attacks. It can replace one attack with Deadly Shaping if it is ready.

Executioner's Pick. *Melee Weapon Attack:* +10 to hit, reach 5 ft., one target. *Hit:* 17 (2d10 + 6) piercing damage, and if the target is a creature, its speed is reduced by 10 feet until the start of the juggernaut's next turn.

Fist. *Melee Weapon Attack:* +10 to hit, reach 5 ft., one target. *Hit:* 11 (1d10 + 6) bludgeoning damage, and if the target is a Large or smaller creature, it must succeed on a DC 18 Strength saving throw or be knocked prone.

Deadly Shaping (Recharge 5–6). The juggernaut magically shapes a feature of its surroundings into a deadly implement. A creature the juggernaut can see within 60 feet of it must make a DC 18 Dexterity saving throw. If the saving throw fails, the targeted creature is struck by one of the following (juggernaut's choice):

Flying Stone. The target takes 22 (5d8) bludgeoning damage and is incapacitated until the start of the juggernaut's next turn, and the implement vanishes.

Scything Shrapnel. The target takes 14 (4d6) slashing damage, and the implement vanishes. At the start of each of its turns, the target takes 10 (3d6) necrotic damage from the wound left by the shrapnel. The wound ends if the target regains any hit points or if a creature uses an action to stanch the wound, which requires a successful DC 15 Wisdom (Medicine) check.

LEGENDARY ACTIONS

The juggernaut can take 3 legendary actions, choosing from the options below. Only one legendary action option can be used at a time and only at the end of another creature's turn. The juggernaut regains spent legendary actions at the start of its turn.

Implacable Advance. The juggernaut moves up to its speed, ignoring difficult terrain. Any object in its path takes 55 (10d10) bludgeoning damage if it isn't being worn or carried.
Rapid Shaping (Costs 3 Actions). The juggernaut recharges Deadly Shaping and uses it.

GREATER STAR SPAWN EMISSARY

STAR SPAWN EMISSARY

Few understand the full hungry hostility of the multiverse. Star spawn emissaries are the fingers of alien realms, digits that tip the scales of reality toward terror. Heralded by ominous astrological events, these ravenous invaders make worlds ready for unimaginable masters or distant, greater manifestations of themselves. Employing their malleable forms, emissaries work to undermine perceptions of order, trust, and reality on global scales, readying worlds for sanity-shattering revelations and cascading apocalypses. Only when truly threatened, or when their foes have lost all hope, do emissaries reveal their actual, impossible forms.

FORMS OF THE EMISSARY

Star spawn emissaries can assume two forms: a lesser form suited to infiltration and a greater, physically overwhelming form. To destroy an emissary, characters must reduce each of its forms to 0 hit points one after another. Typically, a star spawn emissary is initially encountered in its lesser form. When this form is destroyed, the emissary's body collapses into a gory slurry. It then instantly returns in its greater form. Only if the emissary is defeated in its greater form does the star spawn die.

After finishing a long rest, a greater star spawn emissary regains its lesser form if it was destroyed. When an emissary transitions from one form to another, it loses all the traits and actions of the previous form and gains those of the new form. The accompanying stat blocks detail both of the emissary's forms.

LESSER FORM

A star spawn emissary's lesser form allows it to appear as any creature. Emissaries have no misplaced pride and just as readily appear as people, animals, or other creatures—the more unassuming, the better. Should it reveal its true form, an emissary appears as a roughly bipedal mass of agitated organs, self-cannibalizing alien orifices, and appendages suggestive of forms it has previously assumed.

GREATER FORM

An emissary's greater form sheds all pretense of being part of a plane's reality and openly mocks it. A destructive titan, this form rises in a 25-foot-tall pillar of violent flesh amalgamating the meat and voices of every form the emissary has ever mimicked. Manifestations of alien hunger erupt from this horror in waves of ravenous organs and mind-breaking psychic assaults.

LESSER STAR SPAWN EMISSARY

Medium Aberration

Armor Class 19 (natural armor)
Hit Points 241 (21d8 + 147)
Speed 40 ft., fly 40 ft. (hover)

STR	DEX	CON	INT	WIS	CHA
21 (+5)	18 (+4)	24 (+7)	25 (+7)	20 (+5)	23 (+6)

Saving Throws Int +13, Wis +11, Cha +12
Skills Arcana +19, Deception +18, Perception +11
Damage Resistances acid, force, necrotic, psychic
Condition Immunities charmed, frightened
Senses truesight 120 ft., passive Perception 21
Languages all, telepathy 1,000 ft.
Challenge 19 (22,000 XP)   **Proficiency Bonus** +6

Aberrant Rejuvenation. When the emissary drops to 0 hit points, its body melts away. A greater star spawn emissary instantly appears in an unoccupied space within 60 feet of where the lesser emissary disappeared. The greater emissary uses the lesser emissary's initiative count.

Legendary Resistance (3/Day). If the emissary fails a saving throw, it can choose to succeed instead.

Unusual Nature. The emissary doesn't require air, food, drink, or sleep.

ACTIONS

Multiattack. The emissary makes three attacks.

Lashing Maw. *Melee Weapon Attack:* +11 to hit, reach 15 ft., one target. *Hit:* 16 (2d10 + 5) piercing damage plus 13 (3d8) acid damage.

Psychic Orb. *Ranged Spell Attack:* +13 to hit, range 120 ft., one creature. *Hit:* 18 (2d10 + 7) psychic damage.

Change Shape. The emissary polymorphs into a Small or Medium creature of its choice or back into its true form. Its statistics, other than its size, are the same in each form. Any equipment it is wearing or carrying isn't transformed.

LEGENDARY ACTIONS

The emissary can take 3 legendary actions, choosing from the options below. Only one legendary action can be used at a time and only at the end of another creature's turn. The emissary regains spent legendary actions at the start of its turn.

Psychic Orb. The emissary makes a Psychic Orb attack.
Teleportation Maw (Costs 2 Actions). The emissary teleports to an unoccupied space it can see within 30 feet of it and can make a Lashing Maw attack.
Psychic Lash (Costs 3 Actions). The emissary targets a creature it can see within 30 feet of it and psychically lashes at that creature's mind. The target must succeed on a DC 21 Wisdom saving throw or take 36 (8d8) psychic damage and be stunned until the start of its next turn.

GREATER STAR SPAWN EMISSARY

Huge Aberration

Armor Class 15 (natural armor)
Hit Points 290 (20d12 + 160)
Speed 40 ft., fly 40 ft. (hover)

STR	DEX	CON	INT	WIS	CHA
24 (+7)	13 (+1)	26 (+8)	27 (+8)	22 (+6)	25 (+7)

Saving Throws Con +15, Int +15, Wis +13, Cha +14
Skills Arcana +22, Perception +13
Damage Resistances acid, force, necrotic, psychic
Condition Immunities charmed, frightened
Senses truesight 120 ft., passive Perception 23
Languages all, telepathy 1,000 ft.
Challenge 21 (33,000 XP)   **Proficiency Bonus** +7

Legendary Resistance (4/Day). If the emissary fails a saving throw, it can choose to succeed instead.

Unusual Nature. The emissary doesn't require air, food, drink, or sleep.

ACTIONS

Multiattack. The emissary makes three attacks.

Lashing Maw. *Melee Weapon Attack:* +14 to hit, reach 15 ft., one target. *Hit:* 20 (2d12 + 7) piercing damage plus 13 (3d8) acid damage.

Psychic Orb. *Ranged Spell Attack:* +15 to hit, range 120 ft., one creature. *Hit:* 27 (3d12 + 8) psychic damage.

Unearthly Bile (Recharge 5–6). The emissary expels bile that splashes all creatures in a 30-foot-radius sphere centered on a point within 120 feet of the emissary. Each creature in that area must make a DC 23 Dexterity saving throw, taking 55 (10d10) acid damage on a failed save, or half as much damage on a successful one. For each creature that fails the saving throw, a gibbering mouther (see its entry in the *Monster Manual*) appears in an unoccupied space on a surface that can support it within 30 feet of that creature. The gibbering mouthers act right after the emissary on the same initiative count, gaining a +7 bonus to their attack and damage rolls, and fighting until they are destroyed. They disappear when the emissary dies.

LEGENDARY ACTIONS

The emissary can take 3 legendary actions, choosing from the options below. Only one legendary action can be used at a time and only at the end of another creature's turn. The emissary regains spent legendary actions at the start of its turn.

Attack. The emissary teleports up to 30 feet to an unoccupied space it can see and makes one attack.
Warp Space (Costs 2 Actions). The emissary causes the ground in a 20-foot square that it can see within 90 feet of it to turn into teeth and maws until the start of its next turn. The area becomes difficult terrain for the duration. Any creature takes 10 (3d6) piercing damage for each 5 feet it moves on this terrain.
Mind Cloud (Costs 3 Actions). The emissary unleashes a psychic wave. Each creature within 30 feet of the emissary must succeed on a DC 23 Wisdom saving throw or take 32 (5d12) psychic damage. In addition, every spell ends on creatures and objects of the emissary's choice in that area.

STRIGOI

The first strigoi were created by spellcasters who subjected swarms of stirges to transmutation spells. Other strigoi have emerged as the results of similar spellcraft, as the byproducts of outlandish scientific experiments, and from stirges draining well-fed vampires. When a strigoi arises, the unnatural creature is overwhelmed by instinctual hunger that drives it to undertake bloodthirsty rampages along with swarms of emboldened, bloodsucking pests.

Strigoi drain the blood, marrow, and soft tissues from their victims, leaving behind nothing but empty husks. Due to the horrifying nature of their deaths, those slain by strigoi occasionally reanimate as boneless (detailed earlier in this chapter).

Many strigoi seek ways to return to their former existence while being compelled to drain living victims. Others, though, embrace their new forms and mimic vampires. These would-be bloodsucker aristocrats create stirge courts amid scabrous husk-decorated villas and drain the life from any who balk at their grotesque gentility.

STRIGOI
Medium Monstrosity

Armor Class 16 (natural armor)
Hit Points 52 (7d8 + 21)
Speed 30 ft., fly 40 ft.

STR	DEX	CON	INT	WIS	CHA
17 (+3)	14 (+2)	16 (+3)	11 (+0)	17 (+3)	10 (+0)

Saving Throws Str +5, Dex +4, Wis +5
Skills Perception +5, Stealth +6
Damage Resistances necrotic
Condition Immunities charmed, frightened
Senses darkvision 120 ft., passive Perception 15
Languages Common
Challenge 4 (1,100 XP)   **Proficiency Bonus** +2

Stirge Telepathy. The strigoi can magically command any stirge within 120 feet of it, using a limited form of telepathy.

ACTIONS

Multiattack. The strigoi makes one Claw attack and makes one Proboscis attack.

Claw. *Melee Weapon Attack:* +5 to hit, reach 5 ft., one target. *Hit:* 7 (1d8 + 3) slashing damage plus 6 (1d12) acid damage.

Proboscis. *Melee Weapon Attack:* +5 to hit, reach 5 ft., one creature. *Hit:* 8 (1d10 + 3) piercing damage plus 10 (3d6) necrotic damage, and the strigoi regains hit points equal to the amount of necrotic damage dealt. A creature reduced to 0 hit points from this attack dies and leaves nothing behind except its skin and its equipment.

Ravenous Children (1/Day). The strigoi magically summons 1d4 + 2 stirges (see their entry in the *Monster Manual*) in unoccupied spaces it can see within 30 feet of it. The stirges are under the strigoi's control and act immediately after the strigoi in the initiative order. The stirges disappear after 1 hour, when the strigoi dies, or when the strigoi dismisses them (no action required).

SWARMS

Base creatures are among the first to respond to sinister forces at work in a land. As nefarious powers grip an area, populations of maggots, scarabs, and similar scavenging insects explode and become aggressive predators. Roll on the Swarm Behavior table to see how such swarms might manifest.

SWARM BEHAVIOR

d4	Behavior
1	Crawls on walls in a vaguely bipedal shape
2	Makes skittering noises that sound like whispered chanting
3	Skeletal visages, giant eyes, or the faces of nearby creatures appear in relief amid its mass
4	Occupies and animates a corpse or other debris as if it were alive

SWARM OF MAGGOTS
Medium Swarm of Tiny Beasts

Armor Class 11
Hit Points 22 (5d8)
Speed 20 ft., swim 20 ft.

STR	DEX	CON	INT	WIS	CHA
3 (−4)	12 (+1)	10 (+0)	1 (−5)	7 (−2)	1 (−5)

Damage Resistances bludgeoning, piercing, slashing
Condition Immunities charmed, frightened, grappled, paralyzed, petrified, prone, restrained, stunned
Senses blindsight 10 ft., passive Perception 8
Languages —
Challenge 2 (450 XP)   **Proficiency Bonus** +2

Swarm. The swarm can occupy another creature's space and vice versa, and the swarm can move through any opening large enough for a Tiny maggot. The swarm can't regain hit points or gain temporary hit points.

ACTIONS

Infestation. *Melee Weapon Attack:* +3 to hit, reach 0 ft., one target in the swarm's space. *Hit:* 10 (4d4) piercing damage, or 5 (2d4) piercing damage if the swarm has half of its hit points or fewer. A creature damaged by the swarm must succeed on a DC 12 Constitution saving throw or contract a disease.

Each time the diseased creature finishes a long rest, roll a d6 to determine the disease's effect:

1–2. The creature is blinded until it finishes a long rest.
3–4. The creature's hit point maximum decreases by 5 (2d4), and the reduction can't be removed until the disease ends. The creature dies if its hit point maximum drops to 0.
5–6. The creature has disadvantage on ability checks and attack rolls until it finishes its next long rest.

The disease lasts until it's removed by magic or until the creature rolls the same random effect for the disease two long rests in a row.

SWARM OF SCARABS
Medium Swarm of Tiny Beasts

Armor Class 13 (natural armor)
Hit Points 27 (5d8 + 5)
Speed 30 ft., burrow 30 ft., climb 30 ft.

STR	DEX	CON	INT	WIS	CHA
3 (−4)	14 (+2)	13 (+1)	1 (−5)	12 (+1)	1 (−5)

Damage Resistances bludgeoning, piercing, slashing
Condition Immunities charmed, frightened, grappled, paralyzed, petrified, prone, restrained, stunned
Senses tremorsense 60 ft., passive Perception 11
Languages —
Challenge 3 (700 XP)   **Proficiency Bonus** +2

Swarm. The swarm can occupy another creature's space and vice versa, and the swarm can move through any opening large enough for a Tiny scarab. The swarm can't regain hit points or gain temporary hit points.

Skeletonize. If the swarm starts its turn in the same space as a dead creature that is Large or smaller, the corpse is destroyed, leaving behind only equipment and bones (or exoskeleton).

Spider Climb. The swarm can climb difficult surfaces, including upside down on ceilings, without needing to make an ability check.

ACTIONS

Ravenous Bites. *Melee Weapon Attack:* +4 to hit, reach 0 ft., one target in the swarm's space. *Hit:* 14 (4d6) piercing damage, or 7 (2d6) piercing damage if the swarm has half of its hit points or fewer. If the target is a creature, scarabs burrow into its body, and the creature takes 3 (1d6) piercing damage at the start of each of its turns. Any creature can use an action to kill or remove the scarabs with fire or a weapon that deals piercing damage, causing 1 damage of the appropriate type to the target. A creature reduced to 0 hit points by the swarm's piercing damage dies.

NIKKI DAWES

ULMIST INQUISITORS

"Evil lurks everywhere. With our minds, we will unearth it, we will plumb its depths, and we will annihilate it." With those words, the psychically gifted priest Ulmed founded the Ulmist Inquisition, an order of psionic inquisitors that seeks to discover the wickedness hiding in people's souls.

In the days before Count Strahd von Zarovich became the first vampire, Strahd thundered across the lands with Ulmed. Their mission was clear: to destroy the infernal powers that had corrupted the world and to ensure that those powers never rose again. Strahd, Ulmed, and their companions hunted Fiends, Undead, Aberrations, and other supernatural threats and were tireless foes of cults like the priests of Osybus. When Strahd fell into darkness, Ulmed was heartbroken at his friend's transformation and changed the inquisition's mission. Instead of focusing on hunting monsters, it would also hunt the seeds of evil that can corrupt a person.

Ulmed and his friends Cosima, Ansel, and Tristian organized the inquisition into three orders, with each one specializing in a type of psionic power. The Order of Cosima harnessed the Mind Fire—their name for the fire of thought that blazes within each person's mind. They used that power to read thoughts, reshape memories, and dominate the recalcitrant. The inquisitors in the Order of Ansel

subjected themselves to harsh asceticism in an effort to use psionic energy to empower their own bodies. They succeeded and became the martial arm of the inquisition, represented by a sword. Finally, the Order of Tristian endeavored to use intellect to alter the environment through telekinetic force, and the order's members became the inquisition's scholars, represented by a tome.

Today the inquisition rules the city of Malitain, a vast city-state to the north of Barovia's original site, and the inquisition sends its members throughout the multiverse, seeking to thwart the work of malevolent cults, otherworldly horrors, and the malice of mortals. The zeal of the inquisitors in this work has caused them to be a source of terror in many communities, where folk fear that an overzealous inquisitor might be as great a monster as the fiends the inquisitors originally hunted.

INQUISITOR OF THE MIND FIRE
Medium Humanoid

Armor Class 16 (breastplate)
Hit Points 77 (14d8 + 14)
Speed 30 ft.

STR	DEX	CON	INT	WIS	CHA
10 (+0)	14 (+2)	12 (+1)	17 (+3)	16 (+3)	19 (+4)

Saving Throws Int +6, Wis +6, Cha +7
Skills Insight +6, Perception +6
Condition Immunities charmed, frightened
Senses truesight 30 ft., passive Perception 16
Languages any three languages, telepathy 120 ft.
Challenge 8 (3,900 XP)　　　　**Proficiency Bonus** +3

ACTIONS

Multiattack. The inquisitor attacks twice with its Silver Longsword or uses Mind Fire twice.

Silver Longsword. *Melee Weapon Attack:* +7 to hit, reach 5 ft., one target. *Hit:* 8 (1d8 + 4) slashing damage, or 9 (1d10 + 4) if used with two hands, plus 18 (4d8) force damage.

Mind Fire. The inquisitor targets one creature it can see within 120 feet of it. The target must succeed on a DC 15 Intelligence saving throw or take 17 (3d8 + 4) psychic damage and be stunned until the start of the inquisitor's next turn.

Innate Spellcasting (Psionics). The inquisitor casts one of the following spells, requiring no components and using Charisma as the spellcasting ability (spell save DC 15):

At will: *arcane eye, calm emotions, detect magic, detect thoughts, dispel magic, sending, suggestion*
1/day each: *mass suggestion, modify memory*

Inquisitor's Command (Recharge 5–6). Each creature of the inquisitor's choice that it can see within 60 feet of it must succeed on a DC 15 Wisdom saving throw or be charmed until the start of the inquisitor's next turn. On the charmed target's turn, the inquisitor can telepathically control the target's move, action, or both. When controlled in this way, the target can take only the Attack (inquisitor chooses the target) or Dash action.

INQUISITOR OF THE TOME
Medium Humanoid

Armor Class 11 (14 with *mage armor*)
Hit Points 77 (14d8 + 14)
Speed 30 ft.

STR	DEX	CON	INT	WIS	CHA
10 (+0)	12 (+1)	12 (+1)	19 (+4)	16 (+3)	15 (+2)

Saving Throws Int +7, Wis +6, Cha +5
Skills Arcana +10, History +7, Nature +7, Religion +10
Condition Immunities charmed, frightened
Senses truesight 30 ft., passive Perception 13
Languages any four languages, telepathy 120 ft.
Challenge 8 (3,900 XP)   **Proficiency Bonus** +3

ACTIONS

Multiattack. The inquisitor attacks twice.

Force Bolt. *Ranged Spell Attack*: +7 to hit, range 120 ft., one target. *Hit*: 22 (4d8 + 4) force damage, and if the target is a Large or smaller creature, the inquisitor can push it up to 10 feet away.

Silver Longsword. *Melee Weapon Attack*: +7 to hit, reach 5 ft., one target. *Hit*: 8 (1d8 + 4) slashing damage, or 9 (1d10 + 4) if used with two hands, plus 18 (4d8) force damage.

Innate Spellcasting (Psionics). The inquisitor casts one of the following spells, requiring no components and using Intelligence as the spellcasting ability (spell save DC 15):

At will: *detect magic, dispel magic, levitate, mage armor, mage hand, sending*
1/day each: *Otiluke's resilient sphere, telekinesis*

Implode (Recharge 4–6). Each creature in a 20-foot-radius sphere centered on a point the inquisitor can see within 120 feet of it must succeed on a DC 15 Constitution saving throw or take 31 (6d8 + 4) force damage and be knocked prone and moved to the unoccupied space closest to the sphere's center. Large and smaller objects that aren't being worn or carried in the sphere automatically take the damage and are similarly moved.

REACTIONS

Telekinetic Deflection. In response to being hit by an attack roll, the inquisitor increases its AC by 4 against the attack. If this causes the attack to miss, the attacker is hit by the attack instead.

INQUISITOR OF THE SWORD
Medium Humanoid

Armor Class 16 (breastplate)
Hit Points 91 (14d8 + 28)
Speed 30 ft.

STR	DEX	CON	INT	WIS	CHA
12 (+1)	14 (+2)	14 (+2)	15 (+2)	18 (+4)	16 (+3)

Saving Throws Int +5, Wis +7, Cha +6
Skills Acrobatics +5, Athletics +4, Insight +7, Perception +7
Condition Immunities charmed, frightened
Senses truesight 30 ft., passive Perception 17
Languages any two languages, telepathy 120 ft.
Challenge 8 (3,900 XP)   **Proficiency Bonus** +3

Metabolic Control. At the start of each of its turns, the inquisitor regains 10 hit points and can end one condition on itself, provided the inquisitor has at least 1 hit point.

ACTIONS

Multiattack. The inquisitor attacks twice with its Silver Longsword. After it hits or misses with an attack, the inquisitor can teleport up to 30 feet to an unoccupied space it can see.

Silver Longsword. *Melee Weapon Attack*: +7 to hit, reach 5 ft., one target. *Hit*: 8 (1d8 + 4) slashing damage, or 9 (1d10 + 4) if used with two hands, plus 18 (4d8) force damage.

Innate Spellcasting (Psionics). The inquisitor casts one of the following spells, requiring no components and using Wisdom as the spellcasting ability (spell save DC 15):

At will: *detect magic, detect thoughts, dispel magic, sending*
1/day each: *dimension door, fly, greater invisibility*

BONUS ACTIONS

Blink Step. The inquisitor teleports up to 60 feet to an unoccupied space it can see.

UNSPEAKABLE HORRORS

Untold, half-formed evils lurk amid the Mists, the yet-to-be-realized imaginings of the Dark Powers and the remnants of ruined domains. While such nightmares typically manifest as nothing more than impressions, whispers, or vaporous visions amid the fog, mysterious eddies in the Mists sometimes gather such evils, forcing them into unique, misshapen bodies untethered from the laws of reason or reality. Such unspeakable horrors might continue to haunt the misty netherworld between the Domains of Dread, or they might slink forth into other realms to slake unnameable hungers.

CUSTOMIZING A HORROR

An unspeakable horror has one of four body compositions, determined by rolling on the Body Composition table. You can roll on the Limbs to customize it further, while results from the Hex Blast table replace that action in the stat block. If the results of multiple tables conflict, chose your preferred result.

The results of these tables are meant to be broad, so feel free to describe the details of an unspeakable horror's form and the interplay between its parts however you desire. The more discordant and unexpected a horror's parts, the more unsettling it might be.

MIST HORRORS

Some who wander into the Land of the Mists seek to stay hidden in the haze. They might even wish to dwell amid the endless fog, finding it preferable to horrors elsewhere. But the Mists drifting between the Domains of Dread are far from safe—or empty.

Mist horrors are bodiless spirits of dread, entities given form by the fears of those they encounter. Mist horrors use the unspeakable horror stat block with the Malleable Mass body option, which makes them appear to be composed of living mist. Further details of a mist horror's appearance are drawn from the fears of those within 100 feet of it. This might cause a mist horror to take on a form that combines multiple fears when it encounters a group, like a wolf with snakes for eyes or a drowned giant that resembles an estranged parent. Mist horrors can't persist for long outside the Mists: after 1d4 rounds outside the Mists, they lose cohesion and collapse back into harmless vapor.

BODY COMPOSITION

d4	Body
1	***Aberrant Armor.*** The horror's body is armored in petrified wood, alien crystal, rusted mechanisms, sculpted stone, or an exoskeleton.
2	***Loathsome Limbs.*** The horror's body boasts spiderlike legs, many-jointed appendages, or thrashing tentacles.
3	***Malleable Mass.*** The horror's body is composed of a clot of boneless flesh, shadowy tendrils, or mist.
4	***Oozing Organs.*** The horror's body boasts exposed entrails, bloated parasites, or a gelatinous shroud, perhaps because it is inside out.

UNSPEAKABLE HORROR
Huge Monstrosity

Armor Class 15 (natural armor), 17 (Aberrant Armor only)
Hit Points 95 (10d10 + 40)
Speed 40 ft.

STR	DEX	CON	INT	WIS	CHA
21 (+5)	13 (+1)	19 (+4)	3 (−4)	14 (+2)	17 (+3)

Saving Throws Con +7, Wis +5
Skills Perception +5
Condition Immunities petrified (Aberrant Armor only)
Senses darkvision 60 ft., passive Perception 15
Languages —
Challenge 8 (3,900 XP)   **Proficiency Bonus** +3

Formed by the Mists. When created, the horror's body composition takes one of four forms: Aberrant Armor, Loathsome Limbs, Malleable Mass, or Oozing Organs. This form determines certain traits in this stat block.

Amorphous (Malleable Mass Only). The horror can move through any opening at least 1 inch wide without squeezing.

Bile Body (Oozing Organs Only). Any creature that touches the horror or hits it with a melee attack takes 5 (1d10) acid damage.

Relentless Stride (Loathsome Limbs Only). The horror can move through the space of another creature. The first time on a turn that the horror enters a creature's space during this move, the creature must succeed on a DC 16 Strength saving throw or be knocked prone.

ACTIONS

Multiattack. The horror makes two Limbs attacks.

Limbs. *Melee Weapon Attack:* +8 to hit, reach 5 ft., one target. *Hit:* 21 (3d10 + 5) bludgeoning damage.

Hex Blast (Recharge 5–6). The horror expels necrotic energy in a 30-foot cone. Each creature in that area must make a DC 15 Constitution saving throw, taking 45 (7d12) necrotic damage on a failed save, or half as much damage on a successful one.

Hex Blast

d4	Hex
1	**Beguiling Hex (Recharge 5–6).** The horror expels a wave of mind-altering magic. Each creature within 30 feet of the horror must make a DC 15 Wisdom saving throw, taking 33 (6d10) psychic damage and being incapacitated until the end of the creature's next turn on a failed save, or taking half as much damage on a successful one.
2	**Bile Hex (Recharge 5–6).** The horror expels acidic bile in a 60-foot line that is 5 feet wide. Each creature in that line must succeed on a DC 15 Dexterity saving throw or be covered in bile. A creature covered in bile takes 31 (7d8) acid damage at the start of each of its turns until it or another creature uses its action to scrape or wash off the bile that covers it.
3	**Petrifying Hex (Recharge 5–6).** The horror expels petrifying gas in a 30-foot cone. Each creature in that area must succeed on a DC 15 Constitution saving throw or take 14 (4d6) necrotic damage and be restrained as it begins to turn to stone. A restrained creature must repeat the saving throw at the end of its next turn. On a success, the effect ends on the target. On a failure, the target is petrified until freed by the *greater restoration* spell or other magic.
4	**Reality-Stealing Hex (Recharge 5–6).** The horror expels a wave of perception-distorting energy. Each creature within 30 feet of the horror must make a DC 15 Wisdom saving throw. On a failed save, the target takes 22 (5d8) psychic damage and is deafened until the end of its next turn. If the saving throw fails by 5 or more, the target is also blinded until the end of its next turn.

Limbs

d4	Attack
1	**Bone Blade.** The horror's limb ends in a blade made of bone, which deals slashing damage instead of bludgeoning damage. In addition, it scores a critical hit on a roll of 19 or 20 and rolls the damage dice of a crit three times, instead of twice.
2	**Corrosive Pseudopod.** The horror's limb attack deals an extra 9 (2d8) acid damage.
3	**Grasping Tentacle.** The horror's limb is a grasping tentacle. When the horror hits a creature with this limb, the creature is also grappled (escape DC 16). The limb can have only one creature grappled at a time.
4	**Poisonous Limb.** The horror's limb deals piercing damage instead of bludgeoning damage. In addition, when the horror hits a creature with this limb, the creature must succeed on a DC 15 Constitution saving throw or take 7 (2d6) poison damage and be poisoned until the end of its next turn.

VAMPIRIC MIND FLAYER

When the mind flayers of Bluetspur (see chapter 3) could find no cure for their overlord's affliction, their degenerating elder brain turned to radical methods to stave off dementia and death. The results were vampiric mind flayers, feral atrocities spawned from mind flayer tadpoles infected with vampirism. These specialized but flawed terrors serve a single purpose: to drain the cerebral fluids from sapient minds. After doing so, they return to the Elder Brain of Bluetspur, which liquefies them into its pool and releases their stolen essences amid a hormone brine. This grotesque balm stalls the elder brain's degeneration but is far from a cure.

Vampiric mind flayers are physically and mentally unstable beings. Ghoulish creatures, they let nothing stand between them and their existential imperatives. Although they possess the telepathic abilities of mind flayers, their brains aren't equipped to employ them. Instead, they bombard nearby creatures with a mental static of visceral visions. While these ravenous creatures are horrifying to behold, they unsettle none more than other mind flayers, which consider them abominations.

VAMPIRIC MIND FLAYER
Medium Undead

Armor Class 15 (natural armor)
Hit Points 85 (10d8 + 40)
Speed 30 ft., climb 30 ft.

STR	DEX	CON	INT	WIS	CHA
18 (+4)	18 (+4)	18 (+4)	5 (−3)	15 (+2)	18 (+4)

Saving Throws Dex +7, Int +0, Wis +5, Cha +7
Skills Perception +5, Stealth +7
Damage Resistances necrotic, psychic
Condition Immunities charmed, exhaustion, frightened
Senses darkvision 120 ft., passive Perception 15
Languages telepathy 120 ft. but can only project emotions
Challenge 5 (1,800 XP)   **Proficiency Bonus** +3

Spider Climb. The mind flayer can climb difficult surfaces, including upside down on ceilings, without needing to make an ability check.

Sunlight Sensitivity. While in sunlight, the mind flayer has disadvantage on attack rolls, as well as on Wisdom (Perception) checks that rely on sight.

Unusual Nature. The mind flayer doesn't require air, food, or sleep.

ACTIONS

Multiattack. The mind flayer makes two Claw attacks or one Claw attack and one Tentacles attack.

Claw. *Melee Weapon Attack:* +7 to hit, reach 5 ft., one target. *Hit:* 8 (1d8 + 4) slashing damage plus 10 (3d6) necrotic damage.

Tentacles. *Melee Weapon Attack:* +7 to hit, reach 5 ft., one creature. *Hit:* 11 (1d6 + 4) piercing damage, and if the target is a creature, it is grappled (escape DC 15).

Drink Sapience. The mind flayer targets one creature it is grappling. The target must succeed on a DC 15 Wisdom saving throw or take 14 (4d6) psychic damage and gain 1 level of exhaustion. The mind flayer regains a number of hit points equal to the psychic damage dealt. A creature reduced to 0 hit points by the psychic damage dies.

BONUS ACTIONS

Disrupt Psyche (Recharge 5–6). The mind flayer magically emits psionic energy in a 30-foot-radius sphere centered on itself. Each creature in that area must succeed on a DC 15 Intelligence saving throw or be incapacitated for 1 minute. The incapacitated creature can repeat the saving throw at the end of each of its turns, ending the effect on itself on a success.

WERERAVEN

Wereravens are secretive, cautious lycanthropes that seek to blend into society and subtly oppose evil. As avowed foes of malevolent beings, wereravens are stalked by wicked forces. Knowing this, wereravens rarely reveal their hybrid forms. Nevertheless, folktales tell of eerie, raven-winged figures who appear prior to disasters and share mysterious prophecies. Such stories are true, in a way, as where wereravens tread, evil pursues.

Wereraven employ light weapons to avoid spreading their curse to those who would abuse it.

WERERAVEN LYCANTHROPY

The lycanthropes entry in the *Monster Manual* has rules for characters afflicted with different forms of lycanthropy. The following text applies to wereraven characters specifically.

A character cursed with wereraven lycanthropy gains a Dexterity of 15 if their score isn't already higher. Attack and damage rolls for the wereraven's beak are based on whichever is higher of the character's Strength and Dexterity. The peck of a wereraven deals 1 piercing damage in raven form (no ability modifier applies to this damage), or 1d4 piercing damage in hybrid form (the character's ability modifier applies to this damage). This attack carries the curse of wereraven lycanthropy.

WERERAVEN
Medium Humanoid (Human, Shapechanger)

Armor Class 12
Hit Points 31 (7d8)
Speed 30 ft. in humanoid form; 10 ft., fly 50 ft. in raven form; 30 ft., fly 50 ft. in hybrid form

STR	DEX	CON	INT	WIS	CHA
10 (+0)	15 (+2)	11 (+0)	13 (+1)	15 (+2)	14 (+2)

Skills Insight +4, Perception +6
Senses passive Perception 16
Languages Common (can't speak in raven form)
Challenge 2 (450 XP)   **Proficiency Bonus** +2

Mimicry. The wereraven can mimic simple sounds it has heard, such as a person whispering, a baby crying, or an animal chattering. A creature that hears the sounds can tell they are imitations with a successful DC 10 Wisdom (Insight) check.

Regeneration. The wereraven regains 10 hit points at the start of its turn. If the wereraven takes damage from a silvered weapon or a spell, this trait doesn't function at the start of the

wereraven's next turn. The wereraven dies only if it starts its turn with 0 hit points and doesn't regenerate.

ACTIONS

Multiattack (Humanoid or Hybrid Form Only). The wereraven makes two weapon attacks, one of which can be with its hand crossbow.

Beak (Raven or Hybrid Form Only). *Melee Weapon Attack:* +4 to hit, reach 5 ft., one target. *Hit:* 1 piercing damage in raven form, or 4 (1d4 + 2) piercing damage in hybrid form. If the target is a humanoid, it must succeed on a DC 10 Constitution saving throw or be cursed with wereraven lycanthropy.

Shortsword (Humanoid or Hybrid Form Only). *Melee Weapon Attack:* +4 to hit, reach 5 ft., one target. *Hit:* 5 (1d6 + 2) piercing damage.

Hand Crossbow (Humanoid or Hybrid Form Only). *Ranged Weapon Attack:* +4 to hit, range 30/120 ft., one target. *Hit:* 5 (1d6 + 2) piercing damage.

Change Shape. The wereraven polymorphs into a raven–humanoid hybrid or into a Tiny raven, or back into its humanoid form. Its statistics, other than its size and speed, are the same in each form. Any equipment it is wearing or carrying isn't transformed. It reverts to its humanoid form if it dies.

ZOMBIES

Among the undead, a lone zombie ranks far from the most menacing. The horror of the shambling dead lies not in their individual menace, though, but their numbers, their persistence, and their disregard for their own well-being. A throng of zombies will douse a forest fire with their own ashes or march into a dragon's maw until the monster chokes. In the course of their relentless marches, zombies might suffer all manner of trauma, potentially reducing them to masses of crawling limbs (see the **swarm of zombie limbs** stat block), infecting them with terrible diseases (see the **zombie plague spreader** stat block), or crushing an entire horde into a single, rotting titan (see the **zombie clot** stat block).

SWARM OF ZOMBIE LIMBS
Medium Swarm of Tiny Undead

Armor Class 10
Hit Points 22 (5d8)
Speed 30 ft., climb 30 ft.

STR	DEX	CON	INT	WIS	CHA
14 (+2)	10 (+0)	10 (+0)	3 (−4)	8 (−1)	5 (−3)

Damage Resistances bludgeoning, piercing, slashing
Damage Immunities poison
Condition Immunities charmed, exhaustion, frightened, grappled, paralyzed, petrified, poisoned, prone, restrained, stunned
Senses blindsight 30 ft. (blind beyond this radius), passive Perception 9
Languages —
Challenge 1 (200 XP)   **Proficiency Bonus** +2

Swarm. The swarm can occupy another creature's space and vice versa, and the swarm can move through any opening large enough for a Tiny limb. The swarm can't regain hit points or gain temporary hit points.

Unusual Nature. The swarm doesn't require air, food, drink, or sleep.

ACTIONS

Multiattack. The swarm makes one Undead Mass attack and one Grasping Limbs attack.

Undead Mass. *Melee Weapon Attack:* +4 to hit, reach 0 ft., one target in the swarm's space. *Hit:* 5 (1d6 + 2) bludgeoning damage, or 4 (1d4 + 2) bludgeoning damage if the swarm has half of its hit points or fewer.

Grasping Limbs. *Melee Weapon Attack:* +4 to hit, reach 0 ft., one creature in the swarm's space. *Hit:* 7 (2d6) necrotic damage, and the creature must succeed on a DC 12 Strength saving throw or be restrained. The creature can repeat the saving throw at the end of each of its turns, taking 7 (2d6) necrotic damage on a failed save. The creature is freed if it succeeds on this saving throw, the swarm moves out of the creature's space, or the swarm dies.

Zombie Apocalypses

Among the types of horror adventures detailed in chapter 2, tales of uncontrolled zombie outbreaks orbit the dark fantasy and disaster horror genres. The horror of these adventures focuses not on the terror of a single zombie, but of countless individual threats overwhelming society. When creating your own undead calamities, consider the plots presented on the Zombie Apocalypses table.

Zombie Apocalypses

d4	Zombie Plot
1	A twisted wish causes those affected by healing magic and *potions of healing* to rise as zombies.
2	Overwhelming magic reanimates zombies again and again as **swarms of zombie limbs**.
3	The githyanki unleash **zombie plague spreaders** to scour mind flayers from a world.
4	The seals containing an underground zombie horde fail, releasing ancient **zombie clots**.

Zombie Clot

Huge Undead

Armor Class 12 (natural armor)
Hit Points 104 (11d12 + 33)
Speed 40 ft.

STR	DEX	CON	INT	WIS	CHA
20 (+5)	10 (+0)	16 (+3)	3 (−4)	8 (−1)	10 (+0)

Saving Throws Con +6
Damage Immunities poison
Condition Immunities charmed, exhaustion, paralyzed, petrified, poisoned, stunned
Senses darkvision 60 ft., passive Perception 9
Languages understands the languages it knew in life but can't speak
Challenge 6 (2,300 XP)   **Proficiency Bonus** +3

Deathly Stench. Any creature that starts its turn within 10 feet of the zombie must succeed on a DC 14 Constitution saving throw or take 9 (2d8) poison damage and be poisoned until the start of the creature's next turn.

Undead Fortitude. If damage reduces the zombie to 0 hit points, it must make a Constitution saving throw with a DC of 5 + the damage taken, unless the damage is radiant or from a critical hit. On a success, the zombie drops to 1 hit point instead.

Unusual Nature. The zombie doesn't require air, food, drink, or sleep.

Actions

Multiattack. The zombie makes two Slam attacks.

Slam. *Melee Weapon Attack:* +8 to hit, reach 10 ft., one target. *Hit:* 18 (3d8 + 5) bludgeoning damage.

Flesh Entomb (Recharge 5–6). The zombie flings a detached clump of corpses at a creature it can see within 30 feet of it. The target must succeed on a DC 16 Strength saving throw or take 16 (3d10) bludgeoning damage, and if the target is a Large or smaller creature, it becomes entombed in dead flesh.

A creature entombed in the dead flesh is restrained, has total cover against attacks and other effects outside the dead flesh, and takes 10 (3d6) necrotic damage at the start of each of its turns. The creature can be freed if the dead flesh is destroyed. The dead flesh is a Large object with AC 10, 25 hit points, and immunity to poison and psychic damage.

Zombie Plague Spreader

Medium Undead

Armor Class 10
Hit Points 78 (12d8 + 24)
Speed 30 ft.

STR	DEX	CON	INT	WIS	CHA
16 (+3)	10 (+0)	15 (+2)	3 (−4)	5 (−3)	5 (−3)

Damage Resistances necrotic
Damage Immunities poison
Condition Immunities charmed, exhaustion, poisoned
Senses darkvision 60 ft., passive Perception 7
Languages understands the languages it knew in life but can't speak
Challenge 4 (1,100 XP)   **Proficiency Bonus** +2

Undead Fortitude. If damage reduces the plague spreader to 0 hit points, it must make a Constitution saving throw with a DC of 5 + the damage taken, unless the damage is radiant or from a critical hit. On a success, the plague spreader drops to 1 hit point instead.

Unusual Nature. The plague spreader doesn't require air, food, drink, or sleep.

Viral Aura. Any creature that starts its turn within 10 feet of the plague spreader must make a DC 12 Constitution saving throw. On a failed save, the creature is poisoned and can't regain hit points until the end of its next turn. On a successful save, the creature is immune to this plague spreader's Viral Aura for 24 hours.

Actions

Multiattack. The plague spreader makes two Slam attacks.

Slam. *Melee Weapon Attack:* +5 to hit, reach 5 ft., one target. *Hit:* 6 (1d6 + 3) bludgeoning damage plus 9 (2d8) necrotic damage.

Virulent Miasma (1/Day). The plague spreader releases toxic gas in a 30-foot-radius sphere centered on itself. Each creature in that area must make a DC 12 Constitution saving throw, taking 14 (4d6) poison damage on a failed save, or half as much damage on a successful one. A Humanoid reduced to 0 hit points by this damage dies and rises as a zombie (see its stat block in the *Monster Manual*) 1 minute later. The zombie acts immediately after the plague spreader in the initiative count.

APPENDIX: SPIRIT BOARD

Employed by the spiritualists known as the Keepers of the Feather (see chapter 3), spirit boards are the focal points of séances and attempts to contact worlds beyond. Spirit board users rely on the collective will of those who assemble around the board and join hands upon its planchette to commune with mysterious forces.

This spirit board's matching planchette and details on how to employ it appear in chapter 4. Photocopy both the spirit board and planchette then apply them to wood or cardboard to create a mysterious prop for use in your horror adventures.